THE
STARS
ARE
OUR
WITNESS

BOOKS BY SIOBHAN CURHAM

An American in Paris
Beyond This Broken Sky
The Paris Network
The Secret Keeper
The Storyteller of Auschwitz
The Secret Photograph

The Scene Stealers
Frankie Says Relapse
Sweet FA

NON-FICTION
Something More: A Spiritual Misfit's Search for Meaning
Dare to Write a Novel
Dare to Dream
Antenatal & Postnatal Depression

SIOBHAN CURHAM

THE
STARS
ARE
OUR
WITNESS

bookouture

Published by Bookouture in 2024

An imprint of Storyfire Ltd.
Carmelite House
50 Victoria Embankment
London EC4Y 0DZ

www.bookouture.com

ISBN: 978-1-83525-177-5
eBook ISBN: 978-1-83525-176-8

How wonderful it is that nobody need wait a single moment before starting to improve the world.
Anne Frank

The credit belongs to the man who is actually in the arena, whose face is marred by dust and sweat and blood... who spends himself in a worthy cause... and who at the worst, if he fails, at least fails while daring greatly.
Theodore Roosevelt

PROLOGUE

She walked along the stubbly ground beside the barbed wire
fence, her ill-fitting shoes tearing into the backs of her heels. But
for once she hardly noticed the pain. All she could think about
was the gunpowder, hidden in a rag bundle inside her underwear. Her skin erupted in a cold sweat. If the guards found
gunpowder on her, it would mean certain death. She looked at
the chimney on the horizon, towering over the rest of the camp.
Angry flames leapt from the top, like tongues licking at the darkening sky, and a foul smell hung in the air, clinging to everything and everyone.

As the procession of prisoners drew level with a watch-
tower, she began to relax. They were almost back at the camp,
almost back to safety. She fought the nervous urge to laugh.
Previously, she never would have thought of the barracks as a
place of refuge, but that was before she'd begun working for the
Resistance. Her pulse quickened as she thought of the
gunpowder being smuggled across Auschwitz right under the
noses of the Germans. It might only be a teaspoonful at a time,
but one thing she'd learned from her time in the Warsaw ghetto

was that it was incredible what could be achieved with a little grit and a lot of patience.

Up in the sky, the stars were beginning to glimmer. *You are made from water and stardust*, she reminded herself. *You are proof that magic exists*, and her sense of elation grew. It felt so good to be doing something to fight back and to know that even in the most oppressive of places it was still possible to resist.

But then, out of nowhere, a piercing whistle cut through the gloom.

'It's a search!' one of the other prisoners gasped and it felt as if her stomach had dropped like a stone to the ground.

She peered through the lines of prisoners and, sure enough, a group of guards had gathered at the front, halting their procession. Of course, she knew that impromptu searches sometimes happened on the way back from the factory. That was why she'd made sure to walk in the middle of the group, to buy herself some time before the guards reached her. But would it be enough time to get rid of the gunpowder, and without anyone noticing? Would she be able to shake it from the bundle and tread it into the ground? What had seemed like an effective plan in theory turned out to be terrifying in practice.

Keeping her gaze fixed firmly ahead, she slipped her hand between the buttons on her dress and felt for the tiny rag bundle inside the waistband of her underwear. Her heart began to pound. The bundle must have slipped down while she'd been walking and try as she might, she couldn't reach it.

'Undress!' a guard yelled to one of the prisoners up ahead, and she felt as if she might pass out from fright.

You are made of water and stardust, she reminded herself again. *You're proof that magic exists*. But as the guards advanced, batons drawn, she felt anything but magic, just terrifyingly, helplessly alone.

PART ONE

JANUARY 1940, WARSAW

1

For as long as she could remember, Adela Rubinstein had wanted to teach. When she was a child, she spent far more time studying her teachers than the content of their lessons, making careful note of the way in which they called the names on the register, demonstrated important points on the blackboard, and brought their subject matter to life – or not. Then, back at home, she would try to replicate all she'd learned to a class of her toy animals and dolls, and, sometimes, her best friend Izabel, although Izabel was such a free spirit, it was hard keeping her pinned down for long. By the time she left school, Adela had become an expert on how to use her voice to command attention and her energy to breathe life into the driest of topics, but she'd never anticipated having to one day teach in secret. And she'd never learned how to stay calm when teaching a lesson could result in her imprisonment, or even death.

She glanced around the cellar at the circle of children all sitting on cushions, hunched over their books in the dim lamp-light. Aged between thirteen and fifteen, they were the oldest in the orphanage, and studying *Romeo and Juliet* – or trying to.

'Are you able to read in this light?' Adela asked, worried about the strain on their eyes.

They all nodded, but none of them looked up from the page. They'd reached the scene where Romeo drinks the poison, believing Juliet to be dead, and they were clearly gripped.

Adela felt a small burst of satisfaction. When the Germans had begun their occupation of Poland and forbidden Jewish people from having an education, it had felt as if her world was coming to an end. She'd been midway through a degree in literature at Warsaw University and was outraged that the Nazis had stolen her future from her. But she'd soon learned that the human spirit is an incredible thing, able to flow around obstacles like water around a rock if you're just willing to be flexible.

When she'd heard that secret schools were springing up all over Warsaw, she'd paid the local orphanage a visit and offered her services to Jaski Berman, the owner. 'I might not be a qualified teacher yet, but I have years of practice,' she'd told him, omitting to mention that the students she'd been practising on were an assortment of toys. Thankfully, Jaski loved the idea of having a clandestine school at the orphanage, so, after an interview and a trial lesson, she'd been taken on as their Secret Teacher of Literature and Other Assorted Subjects.

She smiled as she thought of her job title – it certainly had an exciting ring to it.

She was just about to ask her students to share their thoughts on Romeo's death when the sound of footsteps came pounding down the cellar steps, causing them all to jump.

'The Germans are here!' Olga, one of the orphanage nurses, called from the other side of the door.

'Thank you, Olga,' Adela called back as the students all scrambled to their feet. 'Quick, you know what to do,' she said, holding out a canvas bag for their copies of the play. She then took the bag over to a barrel of flour in the corner, and buried the plays deep inside, her heart hammering. The Germans had an annoying habit of turning up at the orphanage unannounced, so thankfully they'd practised what to do many times, but still... She dreaded to think what might happen if they were caught.

The students all hurried over to the shelves and set about cleaning the jars stored there. That way, if the soldiers decided to do a full inspection, it would look as if they were just doing chores. As Adela picked up a cloth and joined them, she glanced around anxiously to make sure they were all OK.

The sound of men's voices echoed down from the kitchen above and although she couldn't hear what they were saying, she could tell from the harsh, staccato cadence that it was the soldiers. Her skin prickled with goosebumps. What if they came down into the cellar? What if they found the books?

She heard the softer sound of Marta, the orphanage cook's voice, and held her breath. All fell silent for a moment and Adela and her students stood frozen to the spot. Then one of them let out a whimper and her heart almost stopped.

'It's OK,' she whispered. 'It's going to be OK.' If only she could believe it.

Footsteps clipped across the stone floor above and the men's voices faded.

They all exhaled with relief.

'There, see,' Adela said breezily, trying to sound calmer than she felt. 'Nothing to worry about.'

It was only when she was walking home later that evening that the impact of what had happened, or nearly happened, hit Adela like a punch to the stomach. They'd been lucky this time. But how long would their luck last? And what effect was the fear of being caught having on the students? Then she saw a sight that instantly turned her cold with dread: two German soldiers clad in their green-grey top coats and knee-high boots were marching towards her. She instinctively checked the white band with its blue Star of David on the sleeve of her coat. *It's OK, it's still there*, she reassured herself over the pounding of her heart, but, to her horror, one of the soldiers began to scowl.

'Hey you! Jew!' he yelled, pointing a leather-gloved finger at her.

'Y-yes,' she stammered.

'What are you doing walking there?'

Damn! She'd been so lost in her thoughts she'd forgotten the decree that forbade Jewish people from walking on the pavement. There'd been so many of the cursed decrees introduced since the German occupation began, it was impossible to remember all of them. 'I-I'm sorry,' she muttered.

'Get in the gutter, where you belong,' he barked.

She hurried into the gutter, head down, feeling consumed with hatred – both for the Germans and for herself, for being so helpless.

A tram rattled past, causing an icy breeze to whip at the hem of her shabby coat. Another of the new decrees banned Jewish people from riding the regular trams and they'd been relegated to their own sidecars marked 'For Jews Only'. They were also no longer allowed to visit parks or sit on benches or have more than 2,000 zlotys in their bank accounts. It was as if the Germans were trying to snuff out their very existence, law by law.

You mustn't show they're getting to you, she told herself sternly as her family's store came into view. It now bore a Star of David on a sign in the window, to signify that it was a Jewish business and should therefore be boycotted. *You have to stay strong for Mama and Papa.*

Oh, how she wished her older brother Azriel was there to help her with the burden of lifting their parents' spirits, but he'd moved away to Krakau four years before to study medicine at the university there. Then, two years ago, he'd mysteriously dropped out of university and had an awful falling out with their father. Apart from the occasional, and frustratingly unforthcoming, letter to her and their mother, they hadn't seen hide nor hair of him since. Adela swung between missing him terribly and feeling irritated by his pig-headedness. Surely whatever had happened with their father didn't warrant such an extreme response.

She took a breath to ready herself before stepping inside the store. The empty shelves lining the walls, that had once been crammed with colourful tins and packets and jars, were dull with a film of dust. The only things her parents sold now were loaves of braided challah bread and bagels, made to her great-aunt's legendary recipes. After the Germans had looted the store and the supplies in the cellar, they were the only things they could afford to still stock. The rich aroma of cheese and herbs and spices that had been the signature scent of the store, and indeed her childhood, had been replaced with the musty smell of damp. It was yet another thing the Germans had robbed them of.

'Adela! Where have you been?' her mother, Estera, cried from behind the counter. 'It's almost curfew.'

'I had to plan my lessons for tomorrow,' she replied. 'And it's only seven o'clock. There's still an hour to go.'

'I really wish you didn't work there.' Estera wrung her hands together. Her knuckles were red raw from where she'd taken to picking at the skin. 'What if you get caught?'

'Someone has to teach the children,' Adela said, joining her mother behind the counter.

In the four months since the occupation had begun, anxiety had torn through Estera like a cancer, eating away at the curves of her body and etching deep lines into her face. Adela understood that there was much for Estera to be anxious about, especially not knowing exactly where or how Azriel was, but sometimes she wished she could be calmer, like her father, Leopold.

'Where's Papa?'

'At a council meeting.'

'Have you sold much?' Adela asked, although she could tell from the tray of bagels on display that the answer would be no.

Estera shook her head. 'I don't know what we're going to do. I have barely enough money to buy flour and eggs to make a fresh batch and...'

Thankfully, her mother's spiral into gloom was interrupted by the door bursting open and Izabel strode in, a dazzling vision in her emerald-green coat, black stockings and high-heeled shoes. A matching green beret perched jauntily on top of her bobbed blonde hair.

'Good evening!' she cried cheerily.

Although Adela was always pleased to see Izabel, she couldn't help feeling a wistful pang as she looked down at her own shabby brown coat, with its fraying hem and missing buttons. Being a Catholic, Izabel and her family weren't victim to the same punitive measures as the Jewish, and with a job in an accounting office and wealthy parents, she was still able to afford luxuries like new clothes. Adela felt as if she were a fading pencil sketch of a person in comparison to her vibrant friend.

'Hello,' she replied, trying to sound as upbeat as possible.

'How are you both?' Izabel came over to the counter, bringing a sweet waft of her magnolia perfume. Her lips were painted red and the expertly applied black kohl lining her green eyes made them look even more catlike. Adela inhaled the perfume deeply, eager to smell something other than damp.

'Better for seeing you, *moj skarbe,*' she replied. She and Izabel had started calling each other 'my treasure' back when they were kids because they thought it made them sound sophisticated and grown-up. Now they used it whenever they wanted to show their love for one another.

'Surviving – just about,' her mother said, with a shrug of her thin shoulders.

Izabel glanced at the tray of bagels. 'Oh good, you've got just enough left. I'll take them all, please.'

'All twenty?' Estera asked, eyes wide.

Adela frowned. Izabel only lived with her parents and kid brother. Surely they had no need for twenty bagels.

'Yes please,' Izabel said firmly. 'My parents are having friends over for dinner.'

Now Adela knew she was lying. There was no way Izabel's mother, who always complained that bread made her stomach bloat like a balloon, would serve bagels for dinner. Her heart filled with warmth and gratitude for her friend. In these days of boycotts and persecutions, it was brave of Izabel to set foot in a Jewish store, let alone buy all their stock.

'Of course.' Estera eagerly set about bagging up the bagels and Adela's gratitude grew. Thanks to Izabel's generosity, her mother would be able to buy more ingredients and they'd live to trade another day.

Izabel fumbled in her bag and pulled out a shiny leather purse with a gold clasp. Adela felt another pang as she caught a glimpse of the zlotys inside.

'Here,' she said, putting some on the counter.

'But – that's too much,' Estera said, eying the money longingly.

'Not for your delicious bagels,' Izabel retorted. She looked at Adela and grinned. 'You will never guess what happened at work today.'

Adela smiled. Izabel had a talent for being able to spin a gripping yarn from thin air, elevating tales from her work as an accountant's clerk to the drama of a Greek tragedy or the romance of a Shakespearean sonnet. Ever since she'd been a child, Izabel had longed to be an actress, but her bank manager father insisted she pursue a career grounded in numbers rather than the 'airy-fairy' thespian world.

'What happened?' Adela asked, seamlessly falling into her customary role as Izabel's rapt audience. But before Izabel could say another word, there was a deafening smash and a brick came flying through the shop window. Splinters of glass exploded over the floor.

'Rot in hell, Jewish swine!' a man yelled from outside.

'Oh no!' Estera gasped. 'Quick, girls, go into the storeroom.'

But Izabel was already running towards the door, yelling profanities.

'Izabel!' Adela cried. 'Don't go out there, it isn't safe.' But when had the threat of danger ever deterred her fiery friend? She watched, aghast, as Izabel raced from the store.

2

As Izabel chased the man along the street, she cursed her decision to wear heels when she'd got dressed that morning. The recent fashion trends coming out of Paris, with their simple cuts designed for comfort, might have made life easier for women, but high heels did nothing to emancipate them. If only she'd worn her thick-soled pumps, she would have been able to put up more of a chase.

'Come back, you coward!' she yelled at the top of her voice, as the wretched scoundrel disappeared round the corner of a bombed-out building. When she finally reached the corner, she went crashing straight into another man.

'Whoa!' he exclaimed, grabbing her arm. He was holding a battered brown leather case in his other hand and wearing a long overcoat, with a flat cap pulled so low, she could only really see his jaw. But a very nice jaw it was too, she thought to herself, as she dusted herself down.

'I'm sorry,' she panted, 'I was trying to catch a wretched scoundrel.'

'A wretched scoundrel?' he repeated, sounding amused.

'Yes.' She adjusted her beret, which had been sent skew-

he took a step back. 'Wait, Adela's Izabel?'

She nodded. The last time she'd seen Azriel, about four years previously, she'd been sixteen, and still in that awkward gawky teenage phase, especially when she was around him. She'd had a crush on Azriel ever since she'd first met him but had been careful to keep it hidden, not wanting to upset the dynamics of her friendship with Adela. But now, completely unwittingly, she'd brazenly flirted with him.

Judging by the look on his face, he was as horrified as her by this turn of events, which didn't do anything to ease her embarrassment.

'But you look so... grown-up,' he muttered.

'I am grown-up.' She pulled her shoulders back, puffing out her chest. 'I'm almost twenty-one.'

'Of course. I'm sorry.'

'Yes, well, no need to apologise.' Then she remembered the argument that had occurred between Azriel and his father, which had led to Azriel's estrangement. Apparently, it had been over his decision to leave university, but Izabel was certain that Leopold hadn't told Adela and Estera the full story. She felt a shiver of excitement; perhaps now, finally, the mystery would be solved. 'Do your family know you're back?' she asked. She looked at his right arm. There was no sign of the cursed armband the Jewish population of Poland had been forced to wear. 'And where is your...?'

'My what?'

'Nothing.' She felt her face flush. 'Do your family know you're in Warsaw?' she asked again. 'Your mother and sister didn't say anything when I saw them just now.'

He put his cap back on. 'No. They don't. I'm on my way to surprise them now.'

Oh, how Izabel wanted to be a fly on the wall for that reunion, especially once Leopold came home and clapped eyes on his prodigal son.

'I can't believe you're back in Warsaw!'

'Shh! Keep your voice down,' he hissed, looking over her shoulder. Then, to her utter confusion, he put his case down and pulled her into an embrace. 'Pretend that we're having an intimate conversation,' he whispered urgently.

She heard the dreaded clip-clip of Nazi soldiers' boots approaching from behind and her throat tightened. If they asked to see Azriel's papers, he'd be for it, especially as he wasn't wearing an armband. She had to keep him safe.

'Oh, my darling, I have the most wonderful news!' she exclaimed, cupping his face in her hands. The sound of the boots grew louder, closer. 'Kiss me!' she hissed.

'What, but—'

She stood on tiptoe and kissed him on the lips. 'We're going to have a baby!' she declared as the soldiers drew level.

'What?' His look of surprise was so convincing, she made a mental note to praise him on his acting skills – if they managed to get away with it.

'Congratulations!' one of the soldiers commented as they walked past and the other one chuckled.

'Why did you say that?' Azriel whispered, still holding her, as the soldiers walked away.

'It worked, didn't it?' she replied, deciding to let him be the first to disengage from their embrace.

'Izabel!' She started at the sound of Adela's voice. 'What are you doing?'

Azriel dropped Izabel as if she was a hot coal and she turned to face her friend. 'Adela,' she cried. 'You'll never guess what's happened.'

But Adela wasn't looking at her; she was staring at her brother, shock and confusion written all over her face.

'Azriel? How did you get here?' she gasped before turning her gaze on Izabel. 'And why were you kissing?'

3

Azriel stared at his sister. Just like Warsaw, with its hollow, bombed-out buildings, she looked like a shell of her former self. So much thinner and paler. He felt anger stirring inside of him. It was a feeling he experienced a lot these days whenever he saw the harrowing effects of the German occupation.

'Why were you kissing?' Izabel asked again.

'We weren't, not really,' he replied hastily. He could still taste Izabel on his lips, a strange but not unpleasant blend of cigarettes and lipstick. He shot her a quick glance. Just like Adela, she was not at all how he remembered her, but in a completely different way. Rather than withering, she had burst into full bloom, with her hourglass figure and rosy cheeks.

'What do you mean, not really?' Adela said. 'I saw you.'

'I was saving him from arrest,' Izabel replied, looking to Azriel as if for corroboration.

Azriel nodded, clearing his throat. 'I, er, saw some soldiers coming and I thought that if I held her, they wouldn't notice me.' He pushed away the awkward memory of the thrill he'd felt when she had unexpectedly kissed him.

'Oh, I see.' Adela gave what looked like a relieved smile,

then she stepped closer and grabbed his arm. 'I can't believe you're here.'

'I need to get off the street as quickly as possible,' he said, remembering what was inside his case and picking it up. It wasn't just the soldiers he needed to avoid; press gangs now roamed the streets of Warsaw looking for Jews to force into unpaid labour for the Germans. 'Let's get home.'

'Shall I come too?' Izabel asked.

'No,' he replied, more curtly than he'd intended, and he saw a flicker of hurt on her face. But he couldn't afford to think of Izabel's feelings now. He'd been dreading seeing his father again; the last thing he needed was an audience.

'Come by tomorrow,' Adela said to Izabel, kissing her on the cheek. 'I'm glad you're OK. I was worried you'd been hurt.'

'Of course I'm OK,' Izabel replied brusquely, shooting a sideways glance at Azriel. 'Nice to see you again,' she muttered.

'Yes, and you.' He began walking down the street in the direction of the store, Adela running alongside him to keep up with his stride.

'We need to walk in the gutter,' she exclaimed, tugging at his arm. 'Where's your armband?'

'I had to take it off to get here,' he muttered, and once again he had to fight to contain his anger. Of all the laws the Germans had introduced to punish his people, this was the one that got to him the most. Looking at his sister scurrying along in the gutter beside him caused every sinew in his body to tense. Then he remembered why he'd come back to Warsaw and his tension turned to anger. If the rumours he'd heard were true, having to walk in the gutter would soon be the least of their worries. But the Germans were in for a shock if they thought the Jewish community would meekly comply with their latest warped plan. There was no way he was going to take it lying down and he knew he wasn't the only one.

As they reached the store, Azriel noticed a jagged hole in

the middle of the window. 'What happened?' he asked, shocked, as Adela produced a bunch of keys from her coat pocket.

As Adela explained, there was a resigned, weary tone to her voice that suggested she'd experienced far worse and again he felt anger sparking inside him. 'Izabel chased after them,' she continued, 'which was why I'd come after her. I was worried when she didn't come back.'

'The wretched scoundrel,' Azriel murmured. So Izabel hadn't been exaggerating. She really had been chasing after a thug.

'The what?' Adela asked as she unlocked the door.

'Nothing.' He glanced left and right to check the coast was clear before following her inside, holding his suitcase close.

In the dim lamplight, he saw his mother kneeling on the floor sweeping shards of glass into a dustpan. She glanced up and stared at him blankly. The sight of her caused his heart to contract. She looked so much older.

He took off his cap and smiled down at her. 'Hello, Mama.'

She dropped the dustpan, causing splinters of glass to spill onto the floor. 'Azriel! Is it really you?' she gasped, clapping her hands to her chest.

'It certainly is,' Adela said, extending her hand to help Estera up.

'But how? Oh, my goodness. Oh, my goodness. Thank you! Thank you!' As she stumbled to her feet, she raised her gaze as if talking to God. Not that Azriel believed in God anymore. After what he'd witnessed, how could he possibly believe in a benevolent creator? 'I have prayed for this moment every day,' Estera continued. 'Every day and every night.'

Azriel felt a lump forming in his throat. He coughed, trying to clear it. 'Well, it's very nice to feel welcome,' he said gruffly.

'Of course you're welcome!' she exclaimed. 'This is your home.'

He nodded, but he hadn't thought of it as home for a long time. He glanced around at the empty shelves lining the walls. It didn't even look like home anymore, or smell like it.

'Are you hungry?' Estera asked, reaching up to ruffle his hair like she always used to. 'You must be hungry.'

Azriel and Adela exchanged a knowing grin. Clearly some things never changed, and it felt strangely comforting to see that Estera hadn't lost her compulsion to feed her family at every opportunity.

'I'm famished,' he replied, placing his case down and gathering her in a hug. She felt even thinner than she looked and painfully frail. If only he could hug some strength back into her.

'Oh!' she exclaimed. 'We sold all the bagels.'

'They're still on the counter,' Adela said. 'Izabel left them there.'

'Izabel!' Estera exclaimed. 'Did you find her? Is she all right?'

Azriel followed Estera's gaze to two bags of bagels on the counter. 'She bought all those bagels?' he asked.

'She bought them to help us out.' Adela gave a sad smile.

Azriel felt a twinge of guilt that he'd been so short with Izabel. But before he could give it any further thought, the bell above the shop door jangled and he turned to see his father. His skin prickled. Now for the moment of truth.

'Leopold, look who it is!' Estera cried as Leopold shut the door behind him and rubbed his hands from the cold. He, too, looked older than Azriel remembered him, his shoulders slightly stooped and wrinkles fanning from the corners of his mouth and eyes.

Azriel watched, heart quickening, as his father did a double take and stared at him.

'Azriel?' he said incredulously.

'Hello, Papa. Happy new year.' Azriel had hoped that adopting a light-hearted approach might help to thaw things between them, but Leopold continued to stare at him without cracking the faintest of smiles.

'What are you doing here?' he asked finally, in that quiet, calm voice of his.

'He's come to see his family of course,' Estera said, taking hold of Leopold's arm. 'Let's go upstairs. Have some dinner.'

Leopold took his hat from his head and clutched it to his chest, as if it might somehow shield him from his wayward son. His dark hair was now peppered with silver. 'Why are you here?' he asked again, more forcefully this time.

Azriel wanted to tell him the truth. He was fiercely proud of the truth. But the last time he'd spoken openly to his father about his life, he'd been all but disowned.

'I've come to see my family,' he muttered, echoing his mother's words.

'Oh, this is the best thing that's happened in ages!' Estera exclaimed, scooping up the bags of bagels. 'Come. Let's go upstairs.'

Azriel glanced at Leopold, as if seeking his permission. After a beat of silence, Leopold nodded. But as Estera and Adela hurried up the stairs behind the counter leading to their apartment, Leopold stopped and turned.

'Are you lying?' he whispered. 'Are you here for *them*?'

'No,' Azriel whispered back, hating himself for lying, but hating his father more for forcing him into this position. As he stared into Leopold's dark brown eyes, he felt a pang of remorse as he remembered the way things used to be between them, back when he was a child. The chess and the card games and the fishing trips. They'd been so close back then. Leopold, with his calm, gentle manner and wry humour, had been his hero. But how could he idolise or even respect his father now?

'OK. Good.' Leopold touched him briefly on the arm. A sign that all had been forgiven perhaps, or a temporary truce at least.

Azriel followed him up the narrow flight of stairs into the apartment breathing a sigh of relief.

'I'll just put my case in my bedroom,' he said as the others headed into the kitchen. 'That's if I still have a bedroom?' He looked at his mother questioningly.

'Of course you still have a room, my son.' She kissed him on the cheek. 'You always will.' She took her apron down from the peg on the back of the door. 'Come on, Adela, let's make some soup.'

Azriel made his way down the narrow hallway to his bedroom at the end. He opened the door and stepped inside to find it exactly as he had left it. Even the medical textbook he'd been reading before he left for university remained on the nightstand. He carefully shut the door behind him and went over to the wardrobe. Then, after listening to make sure no one was coming, he opened his case and fumbled with the lining at the bottom. Finally, it came free, and he slipped his hands underneath until his fingers found the cool hard metal of the pistols.

4

'There you are!' Izabel's mother, Krysia, said crossly as Izabel walked into the living room. 'I was about to send out a search party.'

'I went to see Adela,' Izabel replied, taking off her coat and warming her hands on the fire.

'At the store?' Krysia frowned. She put her magazine down on the table beside her armchair and crossed her legs. As usual, she was dressed immaculately, in a pink dress and silky stockings, and her blonde hair was set into a helmet of perfect rolls. Krysia subscribed to the school of thought that urged wives to see their sole reason for being as playing the supporting role to their husband's star performance. She would pore over magazine articles on the subject. Articles with titles like, *How to make your husband feel like a hero*, and *Never let him see you frown*. Izabel hated these articles with a passion and she'd vowed to herself that she would never, ever marry a man weak enough to want to marry a doormat.

'Yes, at the store,' she replied. 'Where else would we meet? They're not allowed to go anywhere now.' Izabel burned with the mixture of guilt and indignation she always felt when thinking of the Germans' cruelty. It hurt her heart to see Adela's family's lives reduced to next to nothing. And she hated the fact that she was so privileged in comparison.

'I don't like you going there,' Krysia said, pursing her lips, which had been painted pink to match her dress. 'It's too dangerous.'

'Not for me!' Izabel exclaimed. 'My God, Mama, we are the lucky ones.'

'Don't blaspheme!' Her mother glanced apologetically at the picture of the Virgin Mary hanging over the mantelpiece, as if to say sorry for her daughter's insolence.

'But we are. It's terrible what they're doing to the Jewish people.' Izabel wanted to tell her about the man who threw a brick through the store window, but that would make Krysia even more determined that Izabel shouldn't go there anymore.

'Just don't go saying those kinds of things outside.' Her mother glanced around the living room anxiously, as if a German might be hiding behind the long velvet curtains.

Izabel felt her impatience rising. 'And what happens if we all say and do nothing? If we just stand by and watch.'

Her mother gave a theatrical sigh. 'The trouble with you, Izabel, is that you've always been far too impulsive. You never think before you speak, or act.'

And the trouble with you is that you've always been far too submissive, Izabel longed to reply. *You wouldn't know how to speak or act for yourself.* But she managed to bite her lip – and simultaneously prove her mother wrong.

Was it any wonder she was headstrong? She'd spent her whole life watching Krysia bend and bow to her father Lech's every wish and command, until she was no longer a person in her own right. She reminded Izabel of a paper doll she had when she was little. The doll came with a range of paper outfits for every occasion, that had to be carefully folded to fit her body. She might have looked pretty, but she was far too flimsy and dull to play with. Izabel didn't want to be flimsy and dull like her mother. She wanted to be strong and fearless like her favourite saint, Brigid – the Irish patron saint of poets and travellers, who performed miracles like turning bathwater into beer. Now that was a life well lived!

'I'll go and get ready for dinner,' she murmured.

'Dinner's going to be late,' her mother replied, picking up her glass of tonic, which Izabel knew also contained a generous slug of vodka.

'How late?'

'I'm not sure. Your father's out with Jakub.'

Izabel grimaced at the mention of her father's neanderthal policeman friend.

As she stalked up the hallway to her bedroom, her stomach growled with hunger and she wished she'd at least taken one of the bagels she'd bought from Estera. But then she instantly felt guilty again. Her hunger was nothing compared to what the Rubinsteins had to endure. She thought of how Estera's face had lit up when she had bought all the bagels and instantly her heart warmed.

She went into her room and flopped down on the bed, kicking off her useless high-heeled shoes. She wouldn't be wearing them again in a hurry – not when she might be called upon to give chase at a moment's notice. She gave a deep sigh. Azriel was back. She lay down and gazed up at the ceiling, enjoying the shivering sensation his unexpected return caused her to feel. He'd responded to their kiss, she knew. She'd felt him lean in closer, just for a second, and his lips soften against hers. But then she remembered the curt way he'd spoken to her, practically ordering her not to come back to the store, and she frowned. There was no point entertaining any romantic notions about Azriel. She'd learned that long ago. Her friendship with Adela was far too precious to risk. She was like her sister as well as a best friend, which was such a blessing given that her actual sibling could be so annoying. As if on cue, the door burst open and her younger brother, Kasper, marched in. His blonde hair was tousled and his face was streaked with dirt.

'What are you doing?' he demanded, staring at her, hands on hips. For a pipsqueak eight-year-old, he certainly took up a lot of space.

'Trying to relax,' she retorted. 'What did I tell you about knocking before you come in.'

He rolled his eyes. 'Have you got any food?'

'No, so scram!'

'Do you want any food?'

She shifted onto her elbow, surprised by this development. 'Why, do you have some?'

'Might do, depends on what you're willing to pay.'

She sat upright and stared at him.

He glanced over his shoulder before coming closer. 'I have some apples,' he whispered.

'Where from?'

'Never mind. Do you want one?'

'Yes, of course.' The thought of biting into a crisp fresh apple and feeling the tang of the juice on her tongue made her drool.

He put out a hand. 'One zloty and it's yours.'

'Are you serious?'

He nodded gravely.

'I bet you don't even have one. You're just trying to trick me.'

'Wait there.' He hurried from the room, returning a few seconds later holding a sweater.

'That's a sweater, not an apple.'

'I didn't want to get caught, stupid.' He shook the sweater and, like a magician producing a rabbit from a hat, a shiny red apple rolled from the sleeve and onto his hand.

Izabel stared at him, feeling a mixture of annoyance and awe.

'Well, do you want it or not? I've got lots of other interested parties.'

'Jesus!'

'Don't curse!'

'Don't curse?' She stared at him incredulously. 'You're the one running some kind of black-market fruit and vegetable operation.'

He nodded smugly as if this was his finest achievement. 'Fruit only – for now.'

She couldn't help laughing at this and fetched her purse from her bag.

'Two zlotys.' He held out his empty hand.

'You said it was one.'

'Yes, well. I have to cover my costs.'

'What costs?'

'For the risks I take.'

She laughed again. 'OK. I'll give you two, purely for the entertainment value.' She gave him the money and took the apple. 'Seriously though, you need to be careful. If Papa finds out about your racket, he'll have your guts for garters.'

Kasper frowned. 'At least I'm not doing deals with the Germans,' he muttered.

'What do you mean?' A feeling of dread began stirring deep inside of her.

He looked down and scuffed his toe on the carpet. 'Nothing.'

Izabel leaned closer and lowered her voice. 'Who is doing deals with the Germans?'

'Nobody,' he said, still not looking at her. 'Anyway, I have to go. Let me know if you need anything else. I might be able to get some oranges tomorrow.' And with that, he hurried from the room.

Izabel stared down at the apple in her hand, her appetite gone. There was no way Kasper would have mentioned the Germans for no reason, and clearly he was implying that their father was somehow involved with them. A memory of her father's policeman friend Jakub came back to her, deepening her sense of dread. When the Germans had begun their occupation of Poland, she'd overheard him saying to Lech that he thought it was for the best, that maybe now Poland could be returned to its 'former glory' – whatever that meant.

She put the apple down on the bed, feeling sick. What if they were both in cahoots with the Nazis? What if, while she was doing all she could to help the Rubinsteins, her own father was consorting with the very people who were making their life hell?

5

Azriel scraped the last trace of soup from his bowl and leaned back in his chair. Dinner had been a strained affair, with his mother desperately trying to compensate for his father's pointed silence, gushing and cooing about how wonderful it was to have him back home and how much they'd all missed him. At one point, Adela had gently kicked his leg under the table and given him a sympathetic grin and he'd felt a surge of relief to be reunited with her again. He'd missed her so much in the two years they'd been apart.

He shifted his chair back, about to make an excuse about being tired and go to bed, when Leopold finally looked at him.

'I need your help,' he said, 'boarding up the window downstairs.'

'Oh. OK.'

'What a great idea,' Estera trilled. 'Working together to get it fixed!'

Azriel glanced at Adela and raised his eyebrows, and she stifled a smirk. He loved the fact that they were able to slip back into their old secret sibling code so effortlessly and, again, he felt a warm burst of affection for his sister.

'Let's go.' Leopold stood up from the table and smiled at Estera. 'Thank you for the dinner, my dear.'

'You're welcome. It's so wonderful to be able to sit down and eat together as a whole family again.' Estera smiled up at Azriel as he got to his feet, and he felt a pang of guilt. He'd been so caught up in his new life in Krakau he hadn't stopped to think of how his absence might have affected her.

Leopold fetched his toolbox from the cupboard under the sink and they set off downstairs. Once in the store, he lit a calcium carbide lamp made from two small metal pots. These lamps were a common sight in Jewish homes now, due to the lack of kerosene and gas. 'Let's use some of the shelves to board the windows up,' he said, turning to Azriel.

'But won't you need them?' Azriel looked at the empty shelves lining the store.

'For what? And at least if we board all the windows, they can't be broken again.'

Leopold set about taking one of the shelves from its brackets. As Azriel watched him he was struck by the fact that this scenario perfectly summed up the chasm that had opened between them. Leopold's answer to the German oppression was to acquiesce, admit defeat, and literally shutter himself and his family away, whereas Azriel's instinct would be to chase the thug who had broken the window and deliver instant retribution. Exactly as Izabel had tried to do, he thought with a smile.

'Come on,' Leopold said, beckoning to him.

Azriel joined him and took another shelf from the wall.

'We need doctors here in Warsaw, you know,' Leopold said. 'Now that we're responsible for the Jewish Hospital.'

'What do you mean, *we're* responsible for it?'

'The *Judenrat*.'

Azriel grimaced at the mention of the Jewish council set up and controlled by the Nazis. 'Gestapo puppets,' he muttered and he noticed his father wince. 'Why did you say *we*? Are you...?' He couldn't bring himself to finish the question.

'I wanted to do something to help,' Leopold muttered.

'Help who? The Germans?' Azriel spat, unable to contain his horror.

'No, my people.' Leopold stared at him defiantly. 'And my family. Because I'm a member of the *Judenrat*, I'll be able to get you your ration card. And I can help you find a job in the hospital.'

'But I'm not a doctor.' Azriel's pulse quickened. They were straying into dangerous territory. He needed to rein in his frustrations or he'd blow it and be turfed out onto the street. But it was so hard. How could his father so willingly help the Nazis?

'No, but you had two years of a medical degree before you...' Leopold fell silent, but Azriel could imagine what he'd wanted to say. *Before you became such a shameful disgrace.* 'That has to count for something,' Leopold said instead. There was a wistful tone to his voice that set Azriel's teeth on edge. He so badly wanted to defend himself and tell Leopold what the Germans had planned for the Jews of Warsaw, but he knew it was pointless. Given that his father was a member of the *Judenrat*, he'd probably agree with their evil scheme.

'Maybe,' he muttered.

'Maybe?' Leopold peered at him through the gloom.

'Yes, maybe,' Azriel replied. He followed his father over to the broken window, feeling taut with frustration. *Remember why you're here*, he told himself. *Your father might be willing to acquiesce, but you're going to be fighting back against the Nazis and their evil plans, starting tomorrow.* As he began hammering the board over the broken glass, he felt his tension ease a little.

6

Izabel slipped into her father's study, her heart pounding. Krysia had just served him his Wednesday breakfast of naleśniki crepes with a sweet cheese filling. Her father ran his life as if it were a neatly ordered ledger, and routine was everything. Heaven forbid Krysia should go rogue and make Thursday's semolina porridge a day early.

Being a creature of routine had its advantages though, as Izabel knew she had precisely fifteen minutes in which to snoop about, before he'd take his last sip of tea, clear his throat and fold his newspaper before getting ready to leave for the bank. Making a beeline for his briefcase, which had been placed neatly beside the desk, she opened it and memorised exactly how everything was arranged before having a root about. She'd watched enough private investigator flicks to know how to have a good snoop without being detected.

The contents of her father's briefcase were disappointingly, although not surprisingly, dull: a file of papers, his leather-bound diary, wallet and pen. She took out the file and flicked through the papers inside. As far as she could tell, they were just boring memorandums from the bank where he worked. She placed the file back inside and took out his wallet. It was full of crisp banknotes and she felt a pang of sorrow as she thought of the Rubinsteins and how poor they'd become since the German campaign against Jewish businesses. What if her father had earned this money doing some kind of deal with the Germans? How would she be able to face Adela and her family again?

She was about to close the wallet when she noticed a scrap of paper tucked in between the notes. She took it out and held it up to the weak morning light filtering in through the gap in the curtains. A name and address were written on the paper in pencil. The address was for a street in Poland, but it was the name that caused her stomach to turn. Herr Schmidt. She stared at it, hoping that her eyes might be deceiving her, but no. Her father had a German man's name and address tucked inside his wallet.

As her shock faded, Izabel tucked it back inside the money and put the wallet back in the case. There was no way she could ask her father what it was doing there, so there was only one thing for it. She would have to go to the address after work to try to find out more.

Azriel hurried along in the gutter, holding his satchel tight to him and pulling up his collar against the biting cold. His first twenty-four hours in Warsaw had not gone as well as he'd hoped. It had been horrible to see his beloved home city devastated by the German bombing raids and their subsequent occupation, and heart-rending to see the people looking so defeated. He grimaced as he thought of how delighted his father had been to help him get his papers and wretched armband that morning. And it had turned his stomach when Leopold had told him he could arrange for him to have a job in the hospital. He didn't want special favours for being Leopold's son because he was a member of the traitorous *Judenrat*. How would he be able to face the other men who were forced to go and work for free in the German factories?

As he continued along the street, he glanced over his shoulder for any sign of soldiers. Thankfully, the coast was clear and he breathed a sigh of relief. When he reached the address he'd been given, a five-storey apartment building with half the windows boarded up, he checked again that there was no one lurking, before slipping inside.

The apartment he'd been summoned to was at the very top of the building. As he rounded the final flight of stairs, he thought he heard someone coming out of one of the apartments below and waited in the shadows, pressed against the wall. But there was no further sound, so he quickly continued. When he reached the door to the apartment, he gave a coded knock and waited, fearful thoughts filling his mind. *What if he isn't here? What if he didn't make it back to Warsaw safely? What if he's been arrested?*

Azriel heard footsteps from inside the apartment and the door opened a crack and a pair of familiar eyes stared out at him.

'Good day, comrade,' Azriel said quietly.

The door opened fully and Berek beamed at him. 'You made it!'

'I did indeed.'

'And do you have the goods?'

'I do.'

'Great work!' Berek exclaimed. 'Come in!'

Azriel stepped inside the darkened apartment and Berek shut and bolted the door behind him.

∾

Izabel stared at the clock on the office wall at Bolek Accountancy. It had been the longest, most tedious day she'd ever experienced, and it was starting to feel as if the clock's hands were going backwards. When they finally reached five o'clock, she had to stop herself from leaping from her chair and punching the air. She went over to the stand in the corner and put on her hat and coat.

'Are you off already?' her boss, Mr Bolek, said, peering at her over his half-moon spectacles.

'I have to leave on time tonight,' Izabel replied, adopting an expression of deep sorrow and regret. 'Sadly, my mother needs me to help her with the laundry. It's lingerie day,' she added, knowing that Mr Bolek cringed at the mention of anything of an intimately feminine nature. 'And you know how tricky it can be to wash things as delicate as silk stockings.'

'Oh, well, er, as it happens I don't,' he stammered, his cheeks turning a vibrant shade of puce. 'But, in that case, you'd better hurry along.'

'Thank you,' she replied, although she hardly felt grateful for what she was really about to do. The prospect of discovering that her father was a despicable traitor made her skin crawl.

It was about half a mile from Bolek Accountancy to the address on the piece of paper, so she set off at a brisk pace. It could all be a storm in a teacup, she told herself as she strode along the pavement. It could all be perfectly innocent. Perhaps Herr Schmidt was a Pole of German descent who'd been born in Poland and was a perfectly fine and upstanding citizen. Just because he had a German name – and title – it didn't mean he was a Nazi. But as soon as she reached the address and stared up at the plush apartment building in front of her, her heart sank. A red flag bearing a swastika had been attached to a pole outside and was blowing about in the breeze.

When the Germans had begun their occupation, they'd

requisitioned many Warsaw buildings – some for offices and some for accommodation. Judging by the grandeur of this building, with its ornate stone cornices and polished glass door, there wouldn't be just any old Nazi living or working here. No, this building had officers' quarters written all over it.

As if on cue, the door opened, and a German officer clad in the sinister black uniform of the SS came out. Izabel turned and watched as he marched down the street. She wondered if he was Herr Schmidt. Even if he wasn't, she now knew that her father's contact lived or worked in a building linked to the SS.

Her mind in turmoil, she did what she always did in times of need and headed like a homing pigeon to the welcoming warmth of the Rubinsteins' home.

Azriel followed Berek into a small living room.

'It's so good to see you,' Berek said, flinging his thin arms around him.

'And you.'

'Come, let's have a drink.' Berek led him into a small, sparsely furnished living room, lit only by a calcium carbide lamp. He took a bottle of beer from the sideboard and poured it into two tin cups. '*Na zdrowie!*' he said, handing a cup to Azriel.

Azriel raised his. '*Na zdrowie!*'

'Bernard's going to be so happy you're here.'

Azriel felt a burst of pride. Bernard Goldstein, the leader of the Jewish Labour Bund in Poland, was a legendary figure and his daring deeds campaigning for Jewish civil and cultural rights and fighting anti-Semitism were the stuff of folklore. To think that such a man would be happy that Azriel was in Warsaw as part of the Jewish Resistance movement made all the stress and disappointment with his father fade somewhat.

'So, he made it back safely?' Azriel asked, sitting on one of the shabby armchairs by the empty fireplace.

Berek took a seat opposite him. He'd grown a beard since Azriel had last seen him. It made him look older, but he still exuded the effusive, puppyish energy that made him one of the most instantly likeable people Azriel had ever met. 'Yes, but he's having to keep a very low profile, staying in his apartment, working strictly undercover.'

'I understand.' Azriel leaned forwards, trying to get a better look at Berek's face in the dim light, to read his expression. 'How have things been going?'

To his relief, Berek looked genuinely hopeful.

'Good. We've set up soup kitchens and underground trade unions, and our own Red Cross organisation. And I need your help with something else.' Berek pulled his chair closer to Azriel's, leaning in and lowering his voice. 'We're organising an underground militia. Bernard is Commandant. He only wants men who were in the pre-war militia, men who can be trusted. Men like you.'

Again, Azriel's heart swelled with pride. Berek had been a commander in the Youth Militia of the Bund before the war, self-defence units formed to protect the Jewish people, and he was someone Azriel deeply respected. To receive his praise was praise indeed.

'Of course. I was hoping you would ask. And on that note...' He opened his satchel and took out the bundled-up trousers, unravelling them to reveal the guns and some rounds of ammunition.

Berek's face lit up. 'Excellent! These will come in very useful indeed, especially if the rumours about the ghetto are true.'

Azriel nodded, a shiver of anticipation running down his spine. When he'd first heard about the Germans' plans to build a ghetto for the Jews in Warsaw, he'd felt crushed. There were hundreds of thousands of Jews in the city; forcing them all into one small section was akin to putting them in an open-air prison. But, thankfully, the Bundists weren't willing to meekly accept it. He passed Berek the guns and his resolve hardened. No, they were going to put up a fight – to the death, if necessary.

7

Adela watched as Izabel tapped her long, elegant fingers on the kitchen table, a frown deeply etched into her face. 'Are you sure you're all right?' she asked.

'Of course. Why wouldn't I be? Everything is just fine and dandy,' she replied gaily, but, for once, her acting skills seemed to have deserted her and her voice sounded strained. Ever since Izabel had turned up unexpectedly after work, Adela could tell she was upset about something. And she wasn't the only one.

Adela glanced over to Estera, who was standing by the kitchen counter, fiddling anxiously with the potato peeler.

'Where are Leopold and Azriel?' Estera asked for the third time in as many minutes.

'I'm sure they'll be back soon,' Adela replied soothingly, as she began stirring the soup on the stove.

'But Leopold's never normally back this late.' Estera's voice seemed to rise an octave. 'What if one of the press gangs got them? What if they've taken Azriel to work for the Germans?'

'I hate the Germans!' Izabel exclaimed with such fervour Adela glanced back at her over her shoulder. What on earth could have happened to make her so tense?

'Careful, Adela, you're spilling the soup!' Estera cried.

Adela looked back at the stove and saw that some had sloshed over the side.

'Let's put it back in the pot,' Estera said, fussing around her with a spoon, trying to scrape up a couple of errant potato peelings.

Adela felt frustration building inside of her – at the fact that they were now so hungry they had to eat vegetable peelings, at her mother for bustling and squawking around like an anxious hen, and at Izabel for not telling her what was wrong. But, mostly, she was angry that the Germans had reduced them to this, and that their nerves were being torn to shreds and their dignity stripped away by the day.

They both jumped at the sound of someone coming up the stairs and Adela's spirits lifted a little.

'Azriel, is that you?' Estera cried.

They all stared at the kitchen door expectantly. Adela's heart sank as Leopold walked in on his own. She'd noticed recently that he'd started walking with a stoop, as if he was literally carrying the weight of this cruel new world upon his shoulders.

'Good evening,' he said, taking off his hat.

'Where's Azriel?' Estera asked with a frown.

'Well, that's a fine welcome for your beloved husband of twenty-five years.' Leopold gave her a wry smile.

'Where's Azriel?' Estera said again, more insistently.

Adela felt a wistful pang. Her parents used to playfully banter with each other all the time, filling their home with warmth and laughter. But that was another thing the Germans had stolen.

Leopold's smile faded. 'Isn't he home already?'

'No!' Estera flung the potato peeler down on the counter. 'Why isn't he with you?'

'I had some paperwork to do.' Leopold began to frown. 'He

told me he was going straight home – but that was over two hours ago.'

'I knew it!' Estera plonked herself down in one of the kitchen chairs. 'One of the press gangs have got him. Oh, Leopold, how could you leave him on his own?'

'I'm sure he's all right,' Izabel said, placing a reassuring hand on Estera's shoulder. 'Maybe he ran into someone he knew.'

'Yes,' Adela said, turning down the heat on the soup. 'He's been away for so long; he might have gone to see an old friend.'

But Estera kept looking at Leopold accusingly. 'How could you leave him on his own when he's only just got back here? Isn't it bad enough that you drove him away for two years?'

'Drove him away?' Leopold slammed his hand on the table, causing Adela to flinch. Her father never lost his cool. Not even when the Germans had made their rabbi set fire to the synagogue and they all had to watch it burn to the ground. Leopold had wiped the tears from his eyes and simply said, 'You don't find God in bricks and mortar.' She and Izabel exchanged anxious glances. 'I didn't drive him away,' he continued, his voice tight. 'I was ashamed of him and what he'd become!'

'What are you talking about?' Estera asked, her voice rising again. 'Why won't you tell me what happened between you? I'm his mother. I have a right to know! And don't tell me that rubbish about you being disappointed about him leaving university. I know that isn't the full story. It can't be!' She folded in on herself, head bowed, as if all the air had been sucked from her.

Leopold kept his gaze fixed on Estera. 'I didn't tell you the full story because I didn't want to upset you, but if you want to know the truth about your precious son, I'll tell you.'

Adela stood, still as a statue by the stove, her heart pounding. What was he about to tell them? What had Azriel done?

'The reason he left university was to join the Bund.'

'The Jewish labour movement?' Estera looked at him quizzically.

'Yes.'

'But what's wrong with that?' Estera said.

Leopold gave a heavy sigh. 'He joined their military wing.'

Izabel let out a gasp and Adela had to lean against the stove to steady herself.

'You're lying!' Estera cried. 'I know my son; I know he would never do such a thing.'

'And that is exactly why I didn't tell you,' Leopold replied. 'I knew you'd refuse to believe me. That boy has never been able to put a foot wrong in your eyes.'

'You're lying!' Adela watched in horror as Estera flew out of her chair and began pummelling Leopold's chest with her fists. 'Lying! Lying! Lying!' she sobbed.

Leopold wrapped his arms around her and hugged her into submission. His eyes met Adela's over Estera's head. 'Could you and Izabel give us a moment alone, please?' he asked softly.

'Oh – uh – yes of course,' Adela stammered. Izabel stood up and they both made their way to the door. As she walked past Leopold, he began stroking Estera's hair.

'It's true, my dear,' he said softly. 'Why would I make such a thing up?'

'But how could he?' Estera exclaimed. 'He was going to be a doctor. He wanted to save lives, not...' She dissolved into sobs again.

Adela shivered as she silently finished her mother's sentence. *He wanted to save lives... not take them.*

'Heavens to Betsy!' Izabel exclaimed as she followed Adela down the corridor to her bedroom. 'I did not see that coming.' Never, in all her wildest speculation about why Leopold and Azriel had fallen out, had she imagined something like this. Growing up, Azriel had never been the kind of boy to get into fights. He'd inherited the same calm and easy-going temperament as his father and, more often than not, played the role of the neighbourhood peacemaker whenever childhood rivalries erupted into violence. When he'd gone to university to study medicine, it had surprised no one. She found it impossible to believe that he could have turned his back on a career as a doctor to join some kind of militia.

She thought back to when she'd bumped into him, and how swarthy and mysterious he'd appeared before she'd realised his true identity. Could he really have changed that much in just a few years? It would certainly explain why he and Leopold had stopped talking though.

'Where are we going?' she asked as Adela marched straight past her bedroom.

'To try to find out if my father is telling the truth,' Adela muttered grimly. She stopped outside Azriel's room and flung the door open.

Izabel eagerly followed her inside. This was a snooping operation she could enjoy taking part in.

'There might be something in here, some proof that he is in the militia,' Adela said, heading straight for Azriel's suitcase.

Izabel's pulse quickened. While she understood how Leopold's revelation might be upsetting to Estera and Adela, the thought of Azriel taking up arms to fight the Nazis wasn't doing anything to dampen her ardour – quite the opposite in fact. She fanned her face with her hand.

'There has to be something,' Adela said, riffling around in the suitcase. Izabel knelt on the floor beside her. Disappointingly, the contents seemed to consist solely of clothes. 'Wait a second, what's this?' Adela said, fumbling with something under the clothes.

'What?' Izabel leaned closer and eagerly peered inside.

'The bottom of the case is loose.' Adela tugged on the lining and it came away to reveal a cavity in the bottom.

'A secret compartment!' Izabel exclaimed. 'Is there anything in there?'

'No, I don't think so. Oh, hold on...'

Izabel watched, rapt, as Adela brought out her hand and opened it. 'Wowie!' she gasped. Two shiny gold bullets were lying in her palm.

Adela gazed at Izabel, her dark eyes full of worry. 'Papa must have been telling the truth. Do you think that's why he's come back to Warsaw? Do you think he's here for the Bund? Why else would he have brought bullets with him?'

Izabel's skin erupted in goosebumps. 'Maybe he plans to kill a German,' she whispered.

'Don't say that!' Adela gasped.

'Why not? Surely the world would be a better place without them.'

'I know but...' Adela shook her head. 'There's no way Azriel could kill someone. And surely he would never take such a risk.'

'Well, it sounds as if he's already taken a huge risk by bringing them here,' Izabel replied, thinking of how he'd been carrying the suitcase when they had bumped into each other on the street. The bullets must have been in there the whole time. She shivered as she thought of the German soldiers who'd passed them. No wonder Azriel had been so jumpy. What if the soldiers had searched his case? By getting her to embrace him, he'd have implicated her too. She wasn't sure what she thought of this. Part of her was angry that he would have risked her safety, but another part felt thrilled that she'd inadvertently been involved in helping him smuggle ammunition into Warsaw, especially if it was going to be used against the Germans. That was a cause she'd very much like to be a part of.

'I can't believe he'd be so reckless.' Adela stood up and began pacing the room. 'And now he's put us all at risk. What if the Germans search the apartment and find them? They're always doing random searches now.'

Izabel nodded, the thought of her beloved friend being at risk of arrest instantly dampening her excitement. 'I think you need to tell him you found them.'

Adela frowned. 'But then I'd have to admit that I was—'

They both jumped as the door burst open and Izabel turned to see Azriel standing there.

'What are you doing?' he asked, glaring down at them.

'Don't you think you should be answering that question?' Adela retorted, holding out the bullets.

8

Azriel stared at Adela and Izabel, oscillating between feelings of horror that they'd found the bullets – he'd been certain he'd taken all of them to Berek's – and outrage that they'd been snooping around in his room in the first place. This was the kind of irritating thing they'd done when they were kids. But now they were adults. Surely, they should have grown out of this. Surely, they had more important things to do. The worst thing was, Adela showed no signs of remorse, and Izabel could barely disguise her obvious glee.

'So, why do you have bullets hidden in your case?' Adela said, brandishing the ammunition.

'Shhh!' Azriel quickly shut the door behind him.

'It's all right, Papa told us your secret.'

'What secret?'

'That you're a freedom fighter,' Izabel said, her eyes wide. She stood up beside Adela.

'A what?' He stared at her, bewildered.

'A soldier of fortune,' Izabel continued. 'Willing to risk everything to defeat—'

'Shhh!' Adela interrupted before looking back at Azriel. 'Papa told us why he stopped speaking to you.'

Azriel's heart began to thud. Surely Leopold wouldn't have said anything in front of Izabel. 'Yes, because I dropped out of university.'

'No. That's what he told us before, but tonight he told us the real reason – that you'd joined the Bund militia.' Adela looked back at the bullets. 'Which explains why these were in your suitcase.'

'I don't want to talk about this right now. Not in front of...' He glanced at Izabel. He couldn't believe his father had been so indiscreet in front of someone who wasn't family.

Izabel gave a gasp of indignation. 'If you are implying that I can't be trusted, then I'm afraid I'm going to have to take umbrage at your insolence!' she exclaimed.

'What?' He stared at her and scratched his head.

'I assume that these bullets were in your case when I bumped into you on the street – when I saved your bacon with those German soldiers.'

Much to his annoyance, he found himself nodding sheepishly beneath her scorching glare and he sat down on the bed.

'Just as I suspected,' she continued. 'And I'll have you know that when I found out your secret and realised that I hadn't just saved my dear friend's brother, but a member of the Bund militia no less, I was thrilled.'

'Izabel!' Adela exclaimed.

'What?' Izabel turned her indignant stare upon her. 'I was!' She looked back at Azriel, her gaze softening slightly. 'Even though you risked my safety too by getting me to kiss you.'

'I didn't—' Azriel began, but Izabel cut him off.

'Because I hate those infernal Nazis and what they're doing,' she continued. 'And if I were Jewish, I'd be joining a militia too.'

Adela gave a weary sigh and sat down beside Azriel.

'So, can I stay?' Izabel looked at him hopefully.

He nodded and she sat down beside Adela.

'Thank you,' she said softly. 'You won't regret it. I want to help.'

Azriel felt a glimmer of hope at this. Perhaps Leopold's indiscretion wasn't as bad as he thought. Perhaps he could enlist Adela and Izabel's help. The Bund would certainly need all the assistance they could get in the coming months.

'Is it true?' Adela whispered. 'Did you really leave medical school to join the Bund militia?'

He nodded. 'But Papa has it all wrong. We aren't a bunch of bloodthirsty bandits. We have strict rules we have to adhere to. We aren't allowed to shoot anyone unless it's in self-defence and we've been ordered to.'

'But you are allowed to shoot people?' Adela said in a clearly disapproving tone.

'Only in self-defence,' he repeated, feeling increasingly impatient. 'The militia was formed to protect our people. Things have been terrible for the Jewish here in Poland for years, since way before the Germans arrived. Why should we just sit back and take it? Why shouldn't we be allowed to protect ourselves?'

'You should!' Izabel exclaimed.

'But...' Adela muttered, still looking unconvinced.

Azriel's impatience grew. 'I wouldn't expect you to understand,' he muttered.

'Why not?' Adela replied, looking taken aback.

'Because you're just like Papa, living constantly in your head, in your world of books and theories. You haven't experienced...' His voice began to waver, and he fell silent.

'I haven't experienced what?' Adela's tone softened.

'You haven't experienced the pain of seeing someone you care about killed right in front of you.' He leaned forward and cradled his head in his hands.

Adela placed a hand on his arm. 'And you have?' she whispered.

He nodded, not looking at her.

'Who?'

'Was it a woman?' Izabel asked.

'No, a man, named David. He was a friend of mine from university,' he replied.

'What... what happened to him?' Adela asked.

He swallowed hard before speaking. 'He was shot by a member of Haller's Army during an attack on a synagogue.' He shuddered as he recalled that terrible day. Haller's Army, the Polish military contingent also referred to as the Blue Army, were renowned for their anti-Semitic attacks, and, prior to the Germans arriving, they had been one of Azriel's main sources of fear. 'He was studying medicine just like me and he was one of the kindest people I ever met. All he wanted was to help people, but those thugs didn't care about that. All they cared about was killing the Jewish.'

He heard a sniff coming from Izabel's direction.

'That's so sad,' she said softly. 'I'm so sorry.'

Then, to his relief, Adela put her arm around his shoulders.

'I'm so sorry too,' she whispered. 'Did you tell Papa about him, about him being your reason for joining the Bund?'

'No, and I shouldn't have to.' He shifted slightly to look at her. 'Even if David hadn't been killed, I would have ended up joining once the Germans arrived. I don't understand how Papa can be a part of their *Judenrat*. Doesn't he see that they're just the Germans' playthings? We can't go along with them. We have to fight back.'

Izabel nodded enthusiastically.

'I understand,' Adela whispered.

He looked at her in surprise. 'You do?'

'Yes. It might shock you to discover that even though I

spend my whole life in my head and my books, I've found my own way to fight back,' she said tartly.

'You have?'

'Yes. I've been teaching children in secret, at an orphanage here in Warsaw.'

'That's fantastic! I'm so sorry, I had no idea.' He felt a wistful pang. Clearly he wasn't the only one whose life had changed irrevocably since he'd left home. He felt awful for having become so detached from his sister. 'I'm so proud of you, little bookworm.'

She laughed. 'I was hoping you'd forgotten you used to call me that!'

'Can I ask you a question?' Izabel said.

He nodded.

'Have you killed anyone?' she whispered, eyes wide.

'No,' he replied. 'Not yet.' He cleared his throat, deciding that he may as well go for broke. 'There's something I need to tell you both.'

Adela instantly looked alarmed. 'What is it?'

'The Germans want to build a ghetto here in Warsaw. They're going to force us to live there, locked away from everyone else.'

'When you say us...' Izabel said.

'I mean the Jewish,' he replied.

'What? But they can't!' Adela exclaimed. She and Izabel looked at each other, distraught.

'We have to stop them,' Izabel said.

'That's why I came back,' Azriel whispered. He paused before continuing. 'And that's why I'd be prepared to kill if I had to. We can't let them treat us like this; we have to fight back.'

Adela nodded and she took hold of his hand and clasped it tightly. 'I'm not sure I can ever agree with taking another life, but I do want to fight back, in my own way.'

'Me too!' Izabel said, her expression deadly serious.

Azriel smiled at them both. 'Thank you,' he said, his voice cracking as relief washed through him. Since returning to Warsaw he'd been missing the companionship of his Bund comrades and friends in Krakau. It felt good to be building a new network in the capital, although he'd never expected his sister and her friend to be a part of it, and he instinctively wanted to protect them. He gave Adela's hand a grateful squeeze. 'Knowing that I've got your support means so much to me, and I'd never do anything to put either of you at risk. What you're doing at the orphanage is a wonderful way of fighting back.'

She gave him a warm smile and the gratitude in his heart grew, but it was tempered with a twinge of sorrow. Sitting there together in the bedroom, it felt like only yesterday that the three of them were kids, with nothing more important to worry about than petty squabbles over toys. How on earth had it come to this?

9

Adela watched as Marta, the orphanage cook, ladled soup into rows of tin bowls.

'So, if Marta put forty-seven carrots and twenty-three leeks and seven potatoes into the soup, how many vegetables would she have?' she called to the children sitting at the table. But the children were so hungry, they only had eyes for the food.

'She'd have more vegetables than she's had for the entire occupation,' Marta retorted. She was a stern woman who didn't suffer fools gladly, but when it came to the children, or her 'little chicks' as she called them, she had a heart of gold.

Adela smiled and stood up. 'Forty-seven carrots, plus twenty-three leeks, plus seven potatoes?' she said again, louder this time. But, again, the children ignored her, eyes wide at the sight of the soup. And how could she blame them; the rations they had to live on were so punitive. But since the most recent surprise visit from the soldiers, Jaski had asked her to teach during mealtimes instead. That way, if the Germans turned up unannounced again, nothing would look untoward.

As she gave up on her maths class and helped Marta hand

out the bowls, Adela thought back to her conversation with Azriel the night before. If only he would tell Leopold his reason for joining the Bund militia and what he'd learned about the Germans' ghetto plans. Their father wasn't made of stone; she was sure he'd understand, or have more of an understanding at least. Hearing what had happened to Azriel and how he'd lost his friend had tugged at her heart strings, especially when she tried to imagine how she would have felt if she'd seen Izabel killed. Although she felt certain she'd never be able to take someone's life, even in self-defence, she felt compassion for her brother, and proud of him too.

Catching a waft of soup, she instantly drooled. Her stomach ached with hunger, as it did almost permanently these days. There were many weapons being used in this war, she mused, not just guns and bombs but starvation and exhaustion too. And perhaps the latter were the more insidious, creeping through the population and weakening them physically and mentally by the day. She remembered Azriel's revelation about their plans to build a ghetto in Warsaw and instantly lost her appetite. Were they deliberately being weakened so they wouldn't have the energy to put up a fight?

Her thoughts were interrupted by the door opening and her heart gave a little lift as Jaski walked in. As always, he was dressed in a riot of colours, today wearing a scarlet velvet jacket and a brightly patterned cravat. His short dark beard was sculpted into its customary neat point and his round, wire-framed glasses were perched on the end of his nose. As usual, he was smiling from ear to ear, his hazel eyes twinkling.

'Well, hello, everybody!' he cried gaily. 'How are you all enjoying your magnificent feast?'

Marta looked at Adela and raised an eyebrow. She liked to remark that the orphanage had a hundred and one children – the one hundred orphans, plus forty-year-old Jaski – but Adela loved his childlike zest for life. It was all the more remarkable given that he'd lost his pregnant wife to cancer back when he was in his twenties. Rather than stewing in grief for the family he'd lost, he'd thrown all his energies into starting an orphanage. Jaski was the only person she knew these days who remained resolutely sunny, despite the dark clouds of war, and for that she was truly grateful. And she wasn't the only one.

She watched the children all chattering with enthusiasm about their soup as Jaski flitted between the tables like a butterfly, engaging with each of them in turn. When he finally reached Adela and Marta, he greeted them like long-lost friends, then he clapped his hands together, his signal that he was about to make a public address. The children instantly fell silent.

'Ladies and gentlemen, boys and girls... and Marta,' he added, winking at his long-suffering chef. Marta was frequently the butt of his jokes, but she took it all in good grace and played along, and the kids adored their pantomime-style antics.

'Why, and Marta?' she asked gruffly, wielding her soup ladle at him like a truncheon. 'Am I not a lady?'

The children began to giggle.

'You, Marta, are so much more than a lady,' Jaski replied. 'You are formidable as a dragon, fearless as an ox, and a wizard in the kitchen.'

'Hmm, and you'll be dead in the dining room if you keep this up,' she grumbled, before picking up the empty soup pot and marching back to the kitchen.

'Ladies and gentlemen, a round of applause for our wonderful Marta!' Jaski said, and the children all burst into riotous applause. 'Now I am delighted to share with you some most excellent news.'

'Are the Germans leaving?' a little boy named Georgi piped up hopefully.

'No, sadly, my news isn't quite that excellent,' Jaski replied.

There was a collective groan.

'But it is excellent none the less.' He shone his beaming smile like a spotlight around the room, finally coming to rest on Adela. 'We are putting on a play!'

A handful of the children cheered, but a large proportion looked unimpressed.

'That's wonderful news,' Adela said quickly, trying to build enthusiasm.

'It is. And it's the best kind of play,' Jaski continued.

'And why is that?' she asked, warming to her role.

'Because you children will be writing the play as well as starring in it.' He looked at them eagerly. 'So you decide what it gets to be about. With the help of the wonderful Adela,' he added. He pointed at her. 'She might look meek and mild, but, trust me, beneath the drab brown exterior beats the heart of a lioness and the imagination of a story unicorn.'

'What's a story unicorn?' a little girl called excitedly.

But Adela wasn't concentrating anymore. What did he mean by 'drab brown exterior'? She looked down at her beige blouse and mud-coloured tweed skirt. Yes, it was true that she wore a lot of brown clothes, but...

Jaski came and stood behind her and grabbed the sides of her arms, as if presenting her to the crowd. 'A story unicorn is a very rare creature with an imagination so sharp it has been known to slice through clouds.'

The children were now gazing at her with something close to awe.

Jaski spun her round so she was facing him. 'What do you say?' he asked. 'Are you prepared to help these wonderful children create the most dramatic, the most exciting, the most tantalising play that's ever been staged?'

She couldn't help but laugh. 'Yes, yes I am!' she declared,

and the children began to cheer. As Adela looked at their smiling faces, she felt her determination grow. They deserved to feel happy and safe every day, and she would do everything in her power to help make that happen – even if it meant risking her life.

10

Azriel strode along Chłodna Street, his heart pounding. A cold fog hung in the air, clinging to his skin, and icy puddle water from the gutter was leaking in through a hole in his boot. He'd been back in Warsaw for a week now and finally he'd received instructions to report to a meeting of his cell. The Bund in Warsaw had been organised into groups of five to ten men, each reporting to their own separate handler. That way, if anyone was caught and broke under German interrogation, they would only be able to inform on a small number of people and the larger organisation would remain unharmed. Not that Azriel would ever inform on anyone, he thought to himself as he reached the address he'd been given. He'd sooner die than betray one of his brothers.

He looked up at the tenement building looming in front of him, grey and uninviting in the gloom. There was a library next to it, but the windows and door had been boarded over. The Germans had shut and sealed all the Warsaw libraries months ago. Azriel felt a surge of indignation as he thought of how they'd closed the universities too. As far as he was concerned, depriving a people of their education and culture was as bad as starving them of food. After all, what was learning if not food for the mind?

He slipped inside the tenement building and headed to an apartment at the end of the ground-floor corridor. He gave the coded knock on the door and glanced around. Aside from the slow drip, drip of water coming from somewhere, the building was eerily quiet. Azriel wondered what he'd been summoned there for. Hopefully, it was to plan an act of sabotage against the Germans. Blowing up a bridge perhaps, or one of their arms factories. The urge to do something to fight back was building like a volcanic force inside of him, especially since being back in Warsaw and seeing what the German occupation had done to his loved ones.

The door opened a crack and a man with curly greying hair peered out.

'I'm Azriel; Berek sent me,' Azriel said, as instructed, and he was ushered inside.

'Welcome, I'm Mendel. Come,' the man said, leading him down the hallway and into a darkened living room. Four other men were there already, three of them bundled together on a two-seater sofa; the other, an older gentleman with a long white beard, sat in a rocking chair. He looked as thoughtful and wise as Old Father Time. 'Greetings, comrades,' Mendel said as Azriel sat down in the one remaining chair. 'You're no doubt wondering what you have been called here for.'

They all nodded.

'As I'm sure you're aware,' Mendel continued, 'the Nazis have begun pillaging Warsaw for our cultural treasures. They've already stolen the entire contents of the City Art Museum and the Jewish Art Museum and sent them to Germany, not to mention the entire stock of the Judaica Library – thousands upon thousands of our books.'

The room filled with murmurs of disapproval.

'Well, we're determined that the same fate does not befall

our Bronislaw Grosser Library next door,' Mendel said. 'A library that was built by the Jewish workers of Warsaw, with great toil and sacrifice.'

Azriel's skin prickled with goosebumps. Could it be that his first mission for the Bund in Warsaw would be to save a library?

'The Germans have sealed up the library already; it's only a matter of time before they loot our books...' He paused. 'Unless we get there before them.'

'But how can we break in and without being seen?' one of the men on the sofa asked.

'We're going to tunnel in, via the cellar,' Mendel replied. He turned and gestured to the man in the rocking chair. 'This is Moishe Suffit. He has worked in the library since it was founded in 1915. He is going to oversee our operation, and make sure we save the most valuable books first.'

Moishe nodded and smiled.

'But how will we smuggle them out without being noticed?' Azriel asked, his excitement growing.

'We'll hide them in sacks of other, less suspicious goods. Coal, potatoes, vegetables. We've bribed the tenement house watchman to look the other way.'

Azriel grinned. He never would have guessed that this would be his first mission for the Bund in Warsaw, but he couldn't think of anything he'd rather do to get one over on the Germans than steal back the books from under their noses.

Izabel looked at her watch and frowned. Its elegant gold hands informed her that only two minutes had passed since she had last checked the time. Surely that couldn't be right. It felt as if twenty minutes had gone by at least. She pressed the watch to her ear to make sure it was still ticking. It was.

She stared up at the orphanage door. Where was Adela?

She always finished work at three, but it was now almost half past. It had taken all Izabel's acting skills to be allowed to leave work early, doubling up in pretend pain over her desk, praying out loud to the Virgin Mother to save her. In the end, it had been mentioning 'women's issues' and her 'monthly bleed' that clinched it. Looking as if he were about to pass out, Mr Bolek had shooed her from the office as if she were a fly.

Izabel glanced down the street and her heart sank. A couple of German soldiers were making their way towards her. *Hurry up, Adela!*

Perhaps she should go. But going home would mean walking towards the soldiers anyway. She opened her bag and pretended to be looking for something.

'Well, hello!' one of them called as they drew nearer. He had pale blonde hair and the kind of angular jaw that looked as if it had been designed with a ruler and set square.

She tried not to shudder and summoned her acting skills once again. 'Hello!' she replied cheerily.

'Do you need help with something?' he asked in perfect Polish.

The other soldier, a stocky man with cropped pale brown hair, looked her up and down with weaselly eyes. 'I wouldn't mind helping her with something,' he muttered in German with a snigger.

Izabel, who was almost fluent in German, thanks to her aunt Gertrud, who'd grown up in Nuremburg and minded Izabel as a child, fought the urge to punch him in the face.

'No thank you, I'm just looking for my lipstick.'

'A woman as beautiful as you doesn't need lipstick,' the blonde soldier said.

Before Izabel could think of a response, the door of the orphanage slammed shut and they all turned to see Adela coming down the steps, buttoning up her coat. As always, Izabel was filled with indignation at the sight of her friend's wretched armband.

'Bloody Jew,' the weaselly-eyed soldier muttered. 'Perhaps we should pay the orphanage a visit, Gustav? Make sure their papers are in order.'

Gustav nodded.

Adela glanced over and gave a look of surprise when she saw Izabel.

'Oh, I'm sure you brave soldiers have far more important things to do than check on orphans, don't you,' Izabel said loudly so that Adela could hopefully hear. 'You must be up to all kinds of exciting things here in Poland,' she added in German.

'You speak German?' Gustav said with a smile.

She nodded. 'A little.'

The weaselly-eyed soldier stood tall and pulled his shoulders back, like a cockerel puffing up his chest. 'Well, yes, we do have a lot of important things to do here.' He looked across the street at Adela. 'Like rounding up vermin like her.'

Adela gave Izabel another glance before hurrying into the gutter.

'Hey, Jew!' the soldier called, making Izabel's skin crawl. She watched as Adela stopped and slowly turned.

'Yes?' she said quietly.

'Come here.'

'Oh, don't bother with her, I'm far more interesting company,' Izabel said quickly.

'I'm sure you are, but I want to check her papers,' he replied.

Izabel felt sick as Adela came over. She looked down at her feet, afraid to give away the fact that she knew her.

'Papers!' the soldier ordered.

Izabel continued staring at the ground as Adela fumbled in her bag.

'What were you doing in there?' Gustav asked, pointing to the orphanage.

'I help out... in the... in the kitchen,' Adela stammered.

Izabel winced. She sounded so nervous, like she had something to hide. She needed to help her, divert the soldiers' attention.

'So, what do you two handsome boys like to do for fun?' she asked.

'We torment Jews,' the weaselly-eyed soldier said with a snigger, and it took everything Izabel had not to launch herself at him. He turned his attention back to Adela. 'Papers!' he yelled.

'I'm sorry, here – here you are.' She handed him her papers.

There was a terrible silence as he checked them, broken only by the rumble of a passing tram. After what felt like forever, the soldier held the papers out to Adela, but as she reached for them, he whisked them from her grasp, as if teasing a cat with a toy mouse. But this wasn't a harmless game; this was all about humiliating her, and Izabel's heart ached with the injustice of it all.

'Try again, Jew,' he said, holding them out in front of her.

Adela reached for the papers and again he whisked them up out of her reach. Izabel had to do something. But what?

'Oh!' she gasped, clutching his arm.

'What is it? What's wrong?' he asked, turning to her.

'I'm sorry, I came over all faint.'

'It's probably being so close to a Jew,' he said. 'They're known to spread disease, you know.' To Izabel's huge relief, he turned and shoved the papers at Adela. 'Get out of here.'

Adela took the papers and hurried off along the gutter.

'Are you all right?' Gustav asked Izabel, looking genuinely concerned.

'Yes, I think so.'

'The sooner we get those vermin rounded up and away from people like you, the better,' the other soldier said.

Izabel felt consumed with dread. 'What do you mean?'

'You'll see,' he sniggered. 'Now, how about you come with us to a café and get something to drink?'

'Oh, no, it's OK, I don't want to keep you from your important work.' Izabel stared after the rapidly departing Adela helplessly.

'A brandy will make you feel a lot better.' He gripped her elbow like a vice, the implication being that she had no choice.

She looked at Gustav, but he just smiled. Then she had an idea. Perhaps if she went with them, she could question them about their plans for the ghetto and pass on anything she found out to Azriel. It could be her way of proving her loyalty to him and the Bund, not to mention fighting back against the cursed Germans.

'That would be lovely, thank you very much,' she replied with what she hoped was a winning smile, her stomach churning.

11

All the way home, Adela held in her tears, but the moment she opened the door and stepped inside the store, it was as if the dam burst and she started to sob. She'd been so happy when Jaski had made his announcement about the play, and it had been wonderful to see the children buzzing with excitement for the past few days as they started coming up with ideas. Walking out of the orphanage to see her best friend chatting away with two German soldiers felt like having a pail of icy water thrown over her. And to be humiliated by the men in front of Izabel made it a thousand times worse. Logically, she knew that if Izabel had leapt to her defence she would have got into trouble too, but there was nothing logical about the world anymore, and Adela couldn't help feeling hurt. Had it really been necessary for Izabel to flirt with them? She shuddered as she thought of the stupid girly voice Izabel always used when she was trying to wind a man around her little finger. How could she have flirted with the soldier after what he'd said to Adela? Where was her loyalty to her friend?

She wiped her eyes and looked at the rocking chair in the corner of the store. She'd been sitting on that very same chair when she had first met Izabel some twelve years before. Up until then, Adela had found her school friends and their rambunctious ways slightly irritating and concluded that she could get by just fine with the fictional friends from her favourite books for company. But that fateful day she'd been reading a disappointing book with a paper-thin plot featuring an insipid heroine named Mabel, who had an annoying habit of saying 'by golly' in nearly every paragraph. When Izabel had burst through the door with all the pizzazz of a circus performer arriving in the ring, Adela's irritation instantly gave way to curiosity. Who was this odd creature dressed in a pink frilly dress and scruffy hobnail boots, looking half princess, half street urchin?

Izabel had taken one look at Adela and exclaimed, 'There you are!' as if she'd been searching her entire life for her.

'Here I am,' Adela had replied, somewhat glumly. And so, a deep and heartfelt friendship had been formed.

Being the more melodramatic of the two, Izabel was convinced that the connection they shared was because they'd been twin sisters in a previous life, who had tragically perished in a house fire and vowed on their last dying breath to find each other again. Adela, who was far more pragmatic, thought that it was simply because the time had been right for her to find a best friend in real life.

Now she went and sat on the chair and gazed into the darkened store as the ghosts from her memory of that day began playing out in front of her.

'Would you like to help me solve a mystery?' eight-year-old Izabel had asked, instantly commanding Adela's attention. This was the kind of unexpected plot twist she'd been so longing for in her book.

'What kind of mystery?' she'd replied.

'The mystery of the missing doll,' Izabel had declared theatrically, flicking her blonde ringlets over her shoulder. 'I fear it may end in heartbreak though, so I hope you're up to it.'

Adela had stifled a smirk. 'Oh, I'm up to it.' She had closed her book and got to her feet, then turned to the shop counter where her father was slicing some cheese for a customer. 'I'm going out for a while, Papa,' she'd called.

'Where to, *ketzeleh*?' he'd called back, causing her to grimace. She privately liked it when her father called her his little kitten, but this was not the first impression she wanted to make on her new friend. And she already knew for certain that she wanted to be this odd girl's friend.

'She's helping me solve a mystery,' Izabel had called.

'Oh, well, in that case, how could I say no,' Leopold had replied with a chuckle. 'Don't go too far now,' he'd added.

'I won't.' Adela had shoved Mabel and her incessant 'by golly's under the chair and followed Izabel out of the store.

'Thank you for helping me,' Izabel had said. 'I think we should start by interviewing the main suspect.'

'OK.' Adela had fallen into step beside her as they marched along the street. 'Who is the main suspect?'

'My very own mother!' Izabel had exclaimed with a horrified shudder.

Adela sighed and got up from the chair. Right from that very first day, she'd loved Izabel like a sister. It was precisely because she loved her so much that what had happened with the soldiers hurt so much. She let herself behind the counter and began climbing the stairs to the apartment with a growing sense of foreboding.

12

Izabel watched as the weaselly-eyed soldier stood, hands on hips at the bar, ordering their drinks. Gustav had made his excuses and joined a group of soldiers at another table, which only added to her unease. But then she remembered Azriel's emotional revelation about why he'd become a member of the Bund and she thought of the name and address she'd found in her father's wallet. She was here for a very good reason – to help the Rubinsteins, to try to compensate for whatever her treacherous papa was up to. And at least she'd stopped the soldiers from harassing Adela and helped her get home safely.

As she thought of how the soldiers had tormented her friend, she clenched her hands into tight fists beneath the table. She was going to have the last laugh and play that arrogant weasel of a Nazi like a fiddle. She would model herself on Marlene Dietrich's character, Concha Perez, in *The Devil is a Woman* – the ultimate femme fatale. Hopefully she'd have him spilling the beans about the German plans for Warsaw in no time. She took her lipstick from her purse and applied a quick coat.

The soldier returned to the table holding two large glasses of brandy.

'How are you feeling now?' he asked, plonking himself down in the chair beside hers.

'I feel as dizzy as a spinning top!' she replied, fanning herself with one of the neatly folded napkins on the table.

'Perhaps you need to eat? Would you like some food?' His voice was so harsh and shrill, everything he said sounded like an order.

The truth was, Izabel would have loved something to eat. She'd forgone her lunch to convince Mr Bolek she was ill, but there was no way she was going to have dinner with a German soldier; she'd probably throw it up all over the table.

'That's really very kind of you, but I fear that food might make it worse.' She gazed at him as coquettishly as she could muster.

'Let me get some bread at least,' he said, gesturing at a waiter to come over.

'Oh well, if you insist.'

'I'm Dieter by the way,' he said, as soon as the waiter had gone.

'What a delightful name,' she gushed. 'I'm Izabel.'

'Very nice to meet you,' he said sharply.

'It's a thrill to meet you!' She leaned closer. 'I've always wanted to get to know a German soldier. You're so... so...' She broke off to increase the anticipation.

'What?' he asked, looking genuinely curious.

'Masterful,' she replied with a delicate sigh, certain that Marlene Dietrich herself would be proud of this performance.

He gave an arrogant smirk. 'Well, we are the master race.'

'Oh, you are!' she exclaimed.

'*We* are,' he corrected, touching the end of her bob with his stocky finger. 'With hair that blonde, you're clearly Aryan too.'

She stifled a grimace. 'But of course.' It was time to steer the conversation onto meatier matters. 'So, how are you finding Poland? I hope you're enjoying it here.'

'It's all right.'

She waited for him to say something more, but instead he took a sip of his drink. He was clearly as dull as he was vain.

She broke off a piece of bread roll and put it in her mouth, licking her lips seductively – a move she'd practised many times in the mirror. 'So, what do all of those mean?' she asked, eyes wide, pointing to the stripes on his uniform.

'They mean that I'm very important,' he replied, and she felt a brief moment of fear. But she couldn't waver now; she had to see this thing through.

'I knew it!' she exclaimed. 'The moment I clapped eyes on you, I thought to myself, that man is a somebody.' She gave him an adoring gaze. 'Some men just exude power, and I have to admit...' She leaned closer and lowered her voice. 'I find it intoxicating.'

'Is that so?' For a moment, she thought he hadn't taken the bait, but then a smile began playing on his lips.

'Oh yes. No wonder I came over all faint when I met you.' She giggled.

He sat upright and puffed out his chest. Her plan was working!

She took a breath and said a silent prayer to Saint Brigid and Adela to forgive her for what she was about to say. 'The way you spoke to that woman earlier and tried to protect me from her was wonderful. You made me feel so safe.' She cringed inside and took a large gulp of her drink.

His arrogant smirk grew. 'You'll feel even safer soon.'

Her pulse quickened. 'What do you mean?'

He glanced over his shoulder before looking back at her. 'We're going to clean up Warsaw.'

'Repair the bomb damage, you mean?' she asked, deciding to play it dumb. One thing she'd learned long ago was that men like Dieter loved a vacuous blank canvas of a woman to project their egos onto.

'Oh, yes, that too. But first we're going to stop people like that Jew from spreading their diseases to the rest of the community.'

She stared at him. Was he really so ignorant that he believed the ridiculous rumour put around by his leaders that Jewish people spread disease? Judging by the knowing look on his face, he was. She suppressed a sigh. But before she could say anything, a thin young man hurried over to their table. His coat collar was pulled up to his cheekbones and his eyes darted about the café anxiously, as if he was expecting trouble.

'Speaking of Jews,' Dieter muttered.

Izabel felt a burst of concern as she noticed the Star of David armband on the young man's coat. What was he thinking, coming into a café full of Germans like this? It was surely akin to walking into the lion's den.

'Yes?' Dieter barked at the man.

'I have what you were asking for,' the man said quietly. 'The name.' He looked around again before taking a folded piece of paper from his pocket and handing it to him.

Izabel frowned, imperceptibly leaning in so she could hear him better.

'He's back in Warsaw, but I'm not sure where he's staying,' the man gabbled. 'But I'm working on it and should find out soon.'

Dieter nodded. 'Good work.'

The man gave a relieved smile.

'OK. You can go now,' Dieter said curtly, and the man scurried off.

'Did you say he was Jewish?' Izabel asked.

Dieter nodded.

'Is he an informant?'

'Yes.' He smirked. 'He thinks that by informing on his fellow Jews we'll be more lenient on him.'

'And won't you?' She looked at him innocently.

'What do you think?' He gave her a smug smile before slipping the piece of paper into the pocket of his coat hanging on the back of his chair. 'He'll be in the ghetto soon with the rest of them.'

'The ghetto?' She tried really hard to keep her voice neutral but her blood ran cold.

'Yes. We're going to round them all up and keep them away from people like us.'

Izabel felt sick. Ever since Azriel had made his revelation about the German plans to build a ghetto, she'd been hoping he'd been misinformed. She couldn't bear the thought of being separated from him and her beloved Adela. But now she'd heard it from the wolf's mouth. 'How on earth would you manage to get all of the Jews in Warsaw into one place?' she said, trying to appear calm. Surely this plan of theirs couldn't possibly work. There were hundreds of thousands of Jews living all over the city.

'Oh, don't you worry your pretty little head about it. We know how to do it,' he said.

There was something about his smugness that sent Izabel into a cold hard fury. He might think that he was much cleverer than her, but she was going to have the last laugh, of that she was certain. If only there was some way she could read the name on the piece of paper. There might be something she could do to warn them. Then a terrible thought occurred to her. What if the name was Azriel's? He'd recently returned to Warsaw, and with weapons. Could it be that the Germans were on to him?

'I think I will have something to eat after all,' she said. 'If the offer still stands.' She gazed at Dieter adoringly. 'You're such interesting company.'

He nodded smugly. 'Of course. I'll go and fetch a menu.'

As he stood up, Izabel did a quick calculation. The menus were on the bar only a few yards away. She would have a matter of seconds to take the paper from the pocket, read the name and put it back again before he turned to come back. Not wanting to waste another second, she snuck her hand into Dieter's coat pocket, pulled out the paper and unfolded it on her lap. The name *Berek Bergson* had been scrawled on it in pencil. She was about to slip the paper back into the pocket when a man's voice caused her to jump.

'Are you feeling better now?'

She looked up to see Gustav smiling down at her, and her face began to burn. 'Yes, fine, thank you,' she stammered, cursing herself for looking so nervous. She saw Dieter start making his way back to the table and slid the paper from her lap, tucking it under her leg on the chair. What if Dieter told Gustav about the note, and Gustav asked to see it?

'Your friend is making me feel so much better,' she said, cringing inside.

'Is he indeed?'

'Yes, we're having the most interesting conversation,' she continued, hoping he'd take the hint that three was a crowd and make his excuses and leave.

'Well, I'm very pleased to hear that,' Gustav said, just as Dieter arrived back at the table.

'Very pleased to hear what?' Dieter asked.

'That you've made such a fine impression on our friend here.' He nodded at Izabel.

'Have I indeed?' Dieter gave Gustav a knowing grin.

Gustav slapped him on the shoulder and returned the grin. 'I'll leave you two in peace then.'

'Are you sure?' Dieter asked.

'Yes!' Izabel couldn't help bursting out.

Both men looked at her.

Gustav laughed. 'Clearly someone wants you all to herself.'

Izabel threw her hands up in mock surrender. 'Was it really that obvious?' She giggled.

Dieter gave yet another arrogant smirk, but, thankfully, Gustav took the hint and left. Now she just had to work out how to slip the piece of paper back into Dieter's coat pocket without him seeing.

'So, you want to have me all to yourself, do you?' Dieter said in a sleazy voice that made her feel sick. He shifted his chair closer to hers.

'Guilty as charged!' She laughed.

'And why is that?' He leaned in close.

Izabel took a breath. She had to do whatever it took to get the piece of paper back in his pocket, however awful it might make her feel. She placed one hand on his shoulder and slid the paper out from beneath her leg with the other. 'I think you're incredible,' she whispered. 'So brave and strong. Thank you for rescuing Poland.' She slipped the paper into the coat pocket and for a terrible moment she thought he'd noticed as she heard the breath catch in his throat. Then she felt his hot hand on her knee.

'I feel like it's fate that we met today,' he said breathlessly in her ear.

Hardly, she felt like replying. Unless the fates really had it in for her.

'I do too,' she lied instead. At least she'd got the paper back in the pocket; now she had to tolerate his pawing and get away as soon as possible. She only hoped that the information she'd got would be of some use to Azriel and that the name Berek Bergson would mean something to him.

13

Adela set off for work the next day determined to put what had happened with Izabel and the soldiers behind her. But trying to find a cheery thought was like trying to spy a glimmer of sun in the relentlessly grey sky that seemed to be pressing down like an iron lid upon her. Try as she might, she couldn't shake the residue of bitterness and despair. And if what Azriel had said about the German plans for a ghetto was true, things were going to get a lot worse. Her world was going to shrink even smaller, and all of her hopes and dreams were going to be snuffed out. How would she ever be able to complete her degree or get a career as a university lecturer if they were going to be trapped in a prison they weren't allowed to leave? How would she ever be able to get married and have children?

She sighed. Before the war, she hadn't given marriage much thought – her passion for books far outweighed any desire for romance. But now that it was something that could be denied to her, she felt a craving deep inside. She pictured herself in an ivory bridal gown walking down the aisle on Leopold's arm towards her husband-to-be... 'Stop it!' she muttered under her breath, and she hurried on along the gutter.

When she reached the orphanage, she marched up the steps and burst through the door – straight into Jaski, who'd been holding a folder of papers, which were sent flying all over the floor.

'Oh no! I'm so sorry!' she exclaimed.

'Goodness me, you're like a hurricane on legs!' he said and a couple of the children who'd been sticking their paintings up in the hallway started to giggle.

Adela thought back to what had happened at lunchtime the day before and she felt hot with embarrassment. Even at the orphanage, where she had tried her hardest to teach the children, she couldn't compete with a bowl of soup for their attention. Even Jaski had commented on her drab, brown exterior. Clearly, she was just as drab and colourless on the inside too. And now they would all think she was clumsy too. To her horror, she started to cry.

'I'm sorry!' she gasped, before racing down the corridor and taking refuge in a storeroom. She sank onto the floor in the corner and dropped her head onto her knees, unable to stop the torrent of tears. A few moments later, the door slowly creaked open.

'Adela?' Jaski said softly. 'Can I come in?'

'Of course you can, it's your storeroom.' She sniffed.

'That is true, but it's your sadness and I wouldn't like to intrude upon it unless invited.' He took a bucket from the shelf, turned it upside down and perched on it in front of her. As always, there was no drab brown exterior for Jaski. He was clad in a pea-green suit and matching cravat. 'Now, whilst I admit that our little accident was indeed a tragedy for my filing system' – his hazel eyes twinkled – 'my intuition tells me that your tears might be to do with something else.'

She nodded, realising that her crying wasn't really to do with the spilled files or her drab clothes at all.

'Would you like to tell me about it? God gave me these big

ears for a reason, you know.' He pulled his earlobes out from his head. 'I am a very good listener, and, sadly, not many people can say that these days. If only more people listened to each other, the world might not be in this state.'

Adela gave him a weak smile.

He took a rust-coloured silk handkerchief from his breast pocket and handed it to her. 'So, what caused these tears?'

'Something happened yesterday that really shook me up.' She wiped her eyes. 'I was stopped by a couple of German soldiers when I left here.'

Jaski instantly looked aghast.

'They wanted to see my papers,' Adela continued. 'But that's not why I'm upset. My best friend was with them. I think she must have come here to meet me after work.'

'Right.' He nodded.

'The soldiers started to insult me and she...' Adela paused; Izabel's behaviour might have hurt her, but she didn't want him thinking badly of her friend.

'Go on.' He nodded encouragingly.

'She flirted with them. I'm sure it was to try to distract them from bothering me but...' She broke off, feeling embarrassed for possibly sounding whiney or immature.

'But?'

There was something so reassuring about his tone and the attentive way in which he was looking at her that made Adela feel completely free to open up.

'But I'm so tired of the constant humiliation. And I feel really guilty because...' Again she paused, too ashamed to speak her innermost thoughts.

'Because?' Jaski gave her an encouraging nod.

'I felt jealous of her. Not for flirting with the Germans,' she added quickly.

'Of course not.'

'But of her freedom. She's Catholic. She doesn't have the same restrictions that we do. She's still free to work and to dream... and to fall in love,' she added, her face flushing.

'And you're not?' He sounded genuinely surprised.

'No! They've taken all of my dreams from me – all that's left is this drab brown exterior.' She gestured at her dreary clothes.

Jaski flinched. 'Oh, Adela, I'm so sorry. I only said that to make the children laugh. I didn't mean...' He leaned forwards and placed his hands on hers. They felt warm and comforting. 'You are a wonderful human being.'

She felt her face flush again. 'Oh, I don't know about—'

He put a finger to his lips. 'Shhh! Now it's your turn to listen, really listen, as what I'm about to say is of the utmost importance.'

'OK,' she whispered back.

'I'm grateful every day that you came to work here. And I know that you're only here because you're no longer able to attend university, but you are such a blessing to me and the children and we all love you dearly.'

She stared at him, trying to work out if he was lying to make her feel better. But Jaski was such a genuine soul, he seemed incapable of any kind of deception.

He cleared his throat. 'Even Marta loves you, and she loves no one.'

Adela couldn't help laughing at this.

'The trouble is, you've let the Germans occupy here as well as Poland.' He gently touched the side of her head. 'But that's one place you have full control over, and always will. You don't have to allow their insults to live in your mind. You have the power to shut them out.'

He made it sound so easy but she really didn't feel as if she was strong enough. 'I don't think I can. It's just too much.'

He leaned forward and looked at her conspiratorially. 'I'm going to teach you my secret technique.'

'OK.'

'Every time a German says something rude to me, I block out their words by thinking this instead.' He stood on the bucket as if it were a podium and took a deep breath. 'I am made of water and stardust,' he declared, as if addressing the nation, rather than a cramped broom cupboard. 'My very existence is proof of magic.'

She frowned up at him. 'What do you mean, you're made of water and stardust?'

'It's a scientific fact,' he said, his eyes sparking with excitement. 'Everything on planet earth was originally made from the dust of exploded stars, including you. And some people still contain starlight within them too.' He sat back down on the bucket and looked her straight in the eyes. 'I consider you to be one of those people.'

Adela felt her cheeks warm. His gaze was so intense, it was as if he could see right into her soul.

'You shine so brightly,' he continued, 'and even your love for brown clothes can't dim that.' He grinned his twinkly-eyed grin.

'Thank you.' She smiled back at him.

'You are a beautiful woman, and you are still perfectly capable of dreaming... and falling in love,' he said softly. Something in the air between them seemed to shift. All trace of his usual jovial façade slipped away and the connection she felt with him was so powerful, she could barely breathe, let alone speak. 'I—' he began but was interrupted by a knock on the door.

'Mr Jaski, are you in there?' one of the children called.

'Yes, yes, just coming,' he replied, back to his normal self. He picked up the bucket and returned it to the shelf. Then, just as he was about to open the door, he stopped and looked at

Adela. 'Your very existence is proof of magic, Adela,' he said softly, before opening the door and stepping outside.

Adela sat there for a moment unsure of what had just happened. All she did know was that the pain she'd been feeling had completely disappeared and her body was tingling. She looked down at the silk handkerchief in her hand and smiled, before stuffing it into her pocket.

14

As soon as Mr Bolek took his hat down from the stand, signalling the end of his working day, Izabel hurriedly gathered her things together. The longer the day had gone on, the more worried she'd become about Adela and what had happened with the soldiers the night before. She had to go to the store and make sure everything was all right. Hopefully she'd see Azriel too and tell him she had some intelligence for him. A shiver ran up her spine at the thought. As much as it had made her skin crawl having to fraternise with the insufferable bore, Dieter, it was wonderful to think that she might be able to help her beloved Rubinsteins and the Bund.

She arrived at the store to find Estera and Adela behind the counter.

'Izabel!' Estera cried with a welcoming smile.

'Good evening!' she called in response, studying Adela's expression for any sign of displeasure.

'Hello,' Adela said, her tone slightly flat.

'Would you like to stay for shabbat dinner?' Estera said. Clearly having Azriel home was agreeing with her; Izabel hadn't seen her look this happy in months.

'I would love to,' she replied, then frowned. 'Are you sure you have enough food, though?'

'Of course.' Estera made her way over to the stairs leading to the apartment. 'I need to take the bread out of the oven. I'll see you up there.'

As soon as she'd gone, Izabel headed over to the counter. 'Are you all right, *moj skarbe?*' She gave Adela a nervous smile. 'I've been worried about you – since yesterday and what happened with those odious soldiers.'

Adela remained grim-faced. 'You didn't seem to find them very odious.'

'What do you mean?' Izabel stared at her, horrified. 'Of course I did! I was just trying to distract them so you could get home safely.'

Adela sighed. 'Did you have to put on that voice?'

'What voice?'

Adela tilted her head to one side and fluttered her eyelashes. 'What do you boys like to do for fun?' she said in a ridiculous, breathless voice. It was nothing like the husky Hollywood siren drawl that Izabel had carefully cultivated over the years, but Adela was clearly vexed, so now was not the time to quibble.

'I didn't realise how it might have made you feel, but I've been thinking of nothing else all day and I'm really truly sorry. And I will never ever do anything like that ever again.' She paused. 'I mean, obviously I will always try to help you if you're in a fix – you're my best friend, *moj skarbe*, the person I love the most in the whole world – but I hereby solemnly swear that I will never, ever use that voice in the presence of a German soldier ever again.' She glanced at her friend hopefully.

'Arrghh, you can be so annoying,' Adela said, but with a smile, thankfully.

'Perhaps, but endearingly annoying, right?'

Adela's smile grew. 'Hmmm.'

Izabel looked at her hopefully. 'So, am I forgiven?'

Adela nodded.

'Hurrah!' Izabel went behind the counter and gave her a hug. 'I love you, *moj skarbe.*'

'I love you too.' Adela pulled back from her embrace. 'And I need to ask you something.' She looked around furtively.

Izabel's heart sank. She really hoped Adela wasn't going to ask what happened with the soldiers after she'd left. She didn't want to have to lie to her but was too scared to tell her the truth for fear of upsetting her even more. 'Of course. Anything.' She held her breath.

'How do you know if you've fallen in love?' she whispered, her face glowing pink.

'What?' Izabel stared at her, stunned and relieved. '*Moj skarbe!* Is there something you need to tell me?'

Azriel wriggled through the hole in the cellar wall, emerging like a mole into the basement of the library. He stood up and took the note Moishe Suffit, the Bronislaw Grosser librarian, had given him from his pocket. It was a list of the most prized books in the library's collection. Suffit had talked about them as if he was talking about his beloved children, reminding Azriel of his bookworm of a sister, and making the mission seem even more important.

Azriel's pulse quickened. The library basement was pitch black, so he felt along the wall until he reached the door. As he climbed the stairs leading up into the library, he tried not to think of what would happen if any passing German soldiers saw him inside. He needed some light in order to find the books, so he'd brought a candle and some matches. He only hoped that the light wouldn't be visible from the outside.

He opened the door at the top of the stairs and it gave a

deafening creak, causing his heart to skip a beat. *It's all right*, he told himself, *there's nobody here but you.* He waited for a moment, but all remained silent, so he stepped into the library. The air was thick with the scent of books.

When they were kids, he'd tease Adela about how she loved to sniff the pages of a book, telling her that food smelled far nicer. But now the smell conjured a host of happy memories. He inhaled deeply and thought of how Leopold would bring them to the library every week, come rain or shine. Once, when Azriel had complained that he'd rather be outside playing with his friends, Leopold had looked at him as if he were crazy. 'But in the library you can go anywhere,' he'd said. When Azriel had asked him what he meant, Leopold had led him through all the different sections, plucking books from the shelves. 'You can visit the polar bears in Antarctica. You can journey to the moon. You can become a cowboy, or a Viking or a king,' he'd said, passing the books to Azriel, and his enthusiasm had been infectious. Although Azriel had never become as much of a bookworm as Adela, Leopold had made him see that books weren't nearly as boring as he'd initially thought.

He sighed and pushed the memory from his mind. It hurt too much to think of how distant he and his father had become. He wondered what Leopold would think if he knew what he was doing. The books he was about to smuggle to safety were going to be taken to the house of a Bund member named Shur, who'd been a partner in a Vilna publishing house before the war and was going to set up a secret library lending circle. Azriel felt thrilled and proud to be able to help make it happen.

Following the detailed directions Suffit had given him, he made his way over to a section at the back of the cavernous space. Then, with trembling fingers, he lit the candle and held the flickering light up to the shelf.

Slowly but surely, he made his way through the list, finding all but one of the titles. Just as he was putting the books into the sack he'd brought to carry them in, he heard the sound of a car stopping outside. Quick as a trice, he blew out the candle and stood, back pressed to the wall.

Please don't be the Germans, he silently implored as all kinds of fears started filling his mind. What if someone had seen the candlelight and reported it? What if there was a traitor in his Bund cell and they'd informed on him? Whatever it was, he couldn't stand there like an idiot waiting to be caught – he had to warn the others.

Hoisting the sack over his shoulder, he started creeping back towards the basement door. Outside, he heard the low rumble of a man's voice, but he couldn't tell what he was saying. Azriel's mouth went dry and his throat tightened. He had to stay calm and get back to the others.

He opened the door, grimacing as it let out a creak. Logically, he was pretty sure it couldn't be heard from outside, but everything seemed to be magnified now, including his fear. He raced down the steps and shoved the bag of books through the hole into the tenement building cellar, wriggling through after them.

'There's someone outside the library,' he gasped to his comrades standing waiting in the dark for him.

'Shit!' Mendel exclaimed. 'Quick, cover the tunnel entrance!'

The men sprang into action, trying to place an old cabinet in front of the hole in the cellar wall as quietly as possible. The silence was broken by a pounding on the door at the top of the cellar steps and Azriel's heart plummeted. If it was the Germans, it would mean certain arrest. Could his work for the Bund in Warsaw be over before it had even begun? He thought of the pistol tucked beneath his trouser leg, inside his boot. He gave Mendel a questioning look and his handler nodded.

Azriel hid the sack of books in the corner of the cellar and stood, pistol ready, by the foot of the steps. The door at the top creaked open and he heard footsteps coming down. From what Azriel could make out, there was only one of them. That was good. If he needed to shoot them, there hopefully wouldn't be any Bund casualties. But smuggling a dead German out of the cellar would be a whole lot harder than some books. His mind raced as the footsteps grew closer.

'You have to stop,' a man hissed at them in the darkness. 'The Germans are here. They're about to unseal the library!'

'Shit! Thank you. Get yourself to a safe place and stay out of their way,' Mendel whispered and he lit the lamp.

Azriel quickly tucked his gun back in its hiding place.

A man dressed in overalls was standing at the foot of the stairs. 'You need to cement up the hole,' he said, clearly agitated. 'And remove all trace of the tunnel.'

'We will, don't worry,' Mendel reassured him and the man hurried back upstairs. 'The tenement house watchman,' Mendel said by way of explanation. 'Right, we need to get to work, make some cement.'

Thankfully, they'd been prepared for this eventuality and the men sprang into action, dragging a sack of sand over to an empty barrel where they began mixing the cement.

'Moishe, you need to leave,' Mendel said to the librarian. 'It's not safe for you to be here.'

Moishe nodded and he shook the others' hands. 'Good luck, comrades.'

'And you,' Azriel replied. His heart hurt as he thought of the elderly man, a librarian, whose life was in danger for simply saving some books. He couldn't think about it too much or he'd get too angry.

'Azriel, take the books and get out of here,' Mendel instructed. 'Use the back entrance.'

'Are you sure?' he asked, not wanting to leave his comrades in their hour of need.

'Yes,' Mendel replied. 'We need to save the books.'

Azriel nodded. 'Good luck,' he whispered to the men before hurrying from the cellar.

Thankfully, he made it back home without incident and his fingers fumbled with the keys before bursting into the darkened shop. He hid the sack of books under the counter, ready to take up to his room once his parents were asleep. Again, he was struck by the absurdity of the situation, and that so much should be at stake over a sack full of books.

He took a breath and headed upstairs, to find his parents, Adela and Izabel all seated around the table. The shabbat candles flickered beside two braided loaves covered in the decorative challah cloth.

'Azriel, where have you been?' his mother asked anxiously. 'And what's that on your trousers?'

He looked down to see flecks of dust all over the fabric. 'I was helping a friend repair some bomb damage to their building,' he replied, wondering at how effortless it had become for him to lie to his parents.

Leopold frowned at him and Azriel felt his hackles rise. Why should he feel guilty for doing something to help protect their heritage? He had half a mind to tell his father the truth, but he couldn't put his comrades at risk and he still wasn't entirely certain he could trust Izabel with Bund secrets. She might be his sister's best friend but she wasn't Jewish. Could she really understand their predicament?

'Sit down, son,' Estera said with a smile, gesturing at the empty chair. 'Unless you'd like to sing the hymn.'

Azriel shook his head and sat down.

'I'll sing it,' Leopold said, getting to his feet.

They all stood and Azriel stared at a spot on the tablecloth. How could his father still sing to a God that allowed them to be relentlessly persecuted? How could he sing about peace at a time of such discord and pain? But as Leopold's voice grew in strength, Azriel felt the ice encasing his heart begin to melt. As a child, he'd loved hearing his father sing 'Shalom Aleichem'. He could remember gazing up at him and half believing that Leopold, with his radiant smile and gentle voice, was one of the angels he sang about.

He glanced up and saw that Leopold was looking straight across the table at him as he sang. For the briefest of moments, Azriel felt a jolt of connection. Leopold must have felt it too, as his eyes filled with tears.

Damn it! Azriel looked away. He couldn't afford to waver. He had to stay strong. Until his father saw the light and left the wretched *Judenrat*, there could be no hope of a reconciliation between them.

Leopold finished singing and sat down heavily in his chair, wiping his eyes with the corner of his napkin.

15

All through the meal, Adela felt a growing impatience, desperate to resume her conversation with Izabel, who clearly felt the same, given the intense looks she kept shooting her from across the table. One by one, the others finished until Estera was the only one left eating, scraping the very last of the remains from her plate. *Hurry up!* Adela wanted to yell. And then, mercifully, her mother put down her knife and fork.

'Mama, Papa, go and rest in the living room,' Adela cried, leaping to her feet. 'Izabel and I will clean up.'

'Yes, yes, go and rest,' Izabel chimed in eagerly. 'You too, Azriel. Or maybe you'd like to go and clean your trousers?' she added with a grin.

'Maybe *you'd* like to clean them,' he retorted.

'I'll have you know that I don't do laundry for any man,' Izabel replied. 'It's one of my ten commandments.'

'Your what?' Azriel looked at Adela and raised his eyebrows.

'Please don't share them,' Leopold said with a laugh. 'I don't want Estera getting ideas.'

'I shall always do your laundry, my love,' Estera joked,

squeezing Leopold's hand. Instantly, Adela's heart warmed. It was so nice to see her parents joking with each other again. Estera smiled at Izabel. 'I'm sure when you find the right man you'll want to take care of him.'

'Hmm, I can think of other, less tedious ways to take care of him,' Izabel muttered, causing Azriel to have a coughing fit.

Laughing, Estera and Leopold stood up from the table. 'Azriel, make sure you walk Izabel home before curfew,' Estera said before leaving the room.

'That's so kind of you, thank you,' Izabel gushed to Azriel as if he was the one who'd suggested it.

'Oh, er, you're welcome,' Azriel replied, clearly bewildered. 'Call me when you're ready to go,' he muttered before leaving the kitchen.

'Alone at last!' Izabel exclaimed, picking up a dishcloth. 'So go on, spill. Who have you fallen in love with?'

'Shh!' Adela hissed, looking anxiously at the door. 'I didn't actually say that I'd fallen in love.'

As Adela began collecting the dirty dishes from the table, she felt a twinge of doubt. What if she'd imagined the magical connection she'd felt with Jaski in the storeroom? She'd been so emotional, maybe she hadn't been thinking straight. Would she seem foolish now, confiding in Izabel?

'No, but your cheeks did,' Izabel retorted. 'They flushed pinker than... than two slices of ham.'

'Eew.' Adela grimaced.

'Well?' Izabel asked.

'The truth is, I'm not sure if I have or not. That's why I wanted you to tell me how it feels. How do you know if it's love?'

'Hmm.' Izabel came and stood beside her at the sink. 'You know because your body tells you.'

Adela began filling the sink with water. 'What do you mean?'

'Well, whenever you see or think of the object of your desire, your heart starts racing and your mouth goes dry and your skin tingles and you find it really hard to swallow your food, especially if they're sitting right next to you.' Izabel clutched the dishcloth to her chest and stared dreamily into space.

As Adela contemplated what she was saying, she thought back to her time with Jaski in the storeroom. What she'd felt was more like a jolt passing right through her. A jolt of realisation and recognition.

'But that's just my experience,' Izabel continued. She clutched Adela's arm. 'Please, *moj skarbe*, put me out of my misery! What in heaven's name has happened?'

'Well, I'm not entirely sure. It all happened quite suddenly. But I think...' She lowered her voice. 'I think I might be in love with Jaski.' She held her breath, unable to look at her friend for fear she might think her ridiculous.

'Jaski? The man who owns the orphanage?'

'Yes.' Adela cringed, waiting for a deluge of criticism from Izabel, or, even worse, peals of laughter. 'Before you say anything, I know he's older than me and I know you probably think I'm crazy, but something happened today, in the storeroom.'

'In the storeroom. Oh, Mary and Joseph!' Izabel began fanning herself with the dishcloth.

'Nothing like that!' Adela exclaimed. 'He was giving me some advice about how to stay strong and then suddenly it was as if everything changed between us. Even the air. And I know he felt it too. It was like... like something magic had happened.'

'Wowie!' Izabel exclaimed.

'Do you think I'm crazy?' Adela asked anxiously.

Izabel stared at her and shook her head. 'No, *moj skarbe*. I think your suspicions are correct. I think you might have been struck by Cupid's arrow!'

Azriel lay on his bed staring up at the ceiling. As much as he didn't want to go out again after the drama at the library, walking Izabel home would give him an opportunity to see if she could be trusted *and* he could retrieve the books from under the counter on his return and sneak them up to his room.

He looked at his watch and saw that curfew was drawing close so he put on his coat and flat cap and made his way to the kitchen. He found Izabel and Adela sitting at the cleared table, huddled together in conversation.

Izabel looked up at him and beamed. 'Aha, my chivalrous escort has arrived.'

'Well, I wouldn't say that—' he muttered gruffly.

'And humble too!' Izabel cut in. She stood up and grinned at Adela. 'What a wonderful night it has been. Your news has made me so happy.'

'What news?' Azriel asked.

'Nothing!' Adela exclaimed, giving Izabel a pointed stare.

Azriel shrugged and Izabel put on her coat.

'Come on then, Sir Galahad,' she said.

'Sir what?' He frowned.

'She's teasing you.' Adela grinned.

Ordinarily, being teased by his kid sister's friend would have annoyed Azriel, but ever since Izabel had planted that kiss on his lips the night he'd arrived back in Warsaw he'd found himself feeling strangely conflicted.

'Well, are you going to stand there gawping all night or are we going?' Izabel said, marching past him to the door.

Azriel tugged on his cap in mock deference. 'Yes, m'lady.'

As they headed down the narrow stairs and into the shop, Azriel caught a waft of Izabel's perfume. Once again, it took him back to the day he'd returned to Warsaw and their unexpected kiss, and he shivered.

As soon as he'd locked the shop door behind them, she linked her arm through his, which didn't do anything to dampen his excitement.

'What are you doing?' he asked.

'I need to be close to you,' she whispered. 'I have something to tell you. Something of the utmost secrecy.'

'Oh really?' He sighed, unsure if he found her theatrical ways irritating or amusing.

'Yes.' She glanced around, then gripped his arm tighter. 'Yesterday, I had the misfortune of going for a drink with a German soldier.'

'What?' He stopped dead and stared at her.

'Don't blow your wig! I was only doing it to try to help.'

'Help who exactly?' he snapped.

'You! I wasn't lying the other day when you confessed about your heroic endeavours.'

'My what?' he whispered.

'Your secret life as a soldier of fortune.'

'I don't think you have the correct meaning of the term "soldier of fortune",' he said, stifling a smirk.

'Oh Lord, give me patience!' she exclaimed. 'Do you want to know what I learned from the odious toad or not?'

'I want to know.' He glanced up and down the street, then led her into a darkened shop doorway. 'How did you come to have a drink with him?'

'A chance encounter in the street,' she replied.

'What, and he asked you to go and have a drink?' he asked, raising his eyebrows.

'Yes.' She frowned. 'Don't look so shocked. I happen to have a talent for making men go goo-goo-eyed over me.'

'Oh really?' He smirked.

'Yes. Well, most men, anyway,' she muttered. 'And this German was no exception. All it took was a few oohs and aahs and pretending to find him the most scintillating creature ever to have walked God's green earth – which he most certainly wasn't – and I had him eating out of my hand.'

Azriel couldn't help grimacing at the thought.

'I did it for you!' she said indignantly.

'Shh!' He glanced up the street to make sure no one was coming.

'But I did.' She gave a heavy sigh. 'You were right about the ghetto. They're going to section off part of Warsaw and send all the Jews in the city to live there.' She looked at him mournfully. 'I'm so sorry, I wish it wasn't true.'

Although Azriel already knew about the ghetto, hearing it from Izabel made him shudder. Perhaps part of him had been hoping it was only a rumour. Izabel hearing it direct from a German meant that there really was no disputing it.

'I'm sorry,' she said softly. 'They make me so angry. You have to believe me. I want to help you.'

'How do I know I can trust you?' he whispered.

She fumbled in her coat pocket and pulled out a folded piece of paper. 'I thought this might be of use to you.'

'What is it?'

'It's the name of someone that was given to the soldier I was with...' She paused. 'By an informant. A *Jewish* informant.'

His stomach lurched. 'What?'

'He came into the café we were at and told the soldier that he had a name for him and he gave him a piece of paper. He said that the person on the paper was back in Warsaw. For a terrible moment, I thought it might have been you.'

Azriel's unease grew. He unfolded the paper and his heart almost stopped when he saw Berek's name written in a curly, looping script. 'What else did this informant say? Did he know where this person on the paper was?'

Izabel shook her head. 'The soldier asked him that and he said no, but he'd try to find out.'

'Who is this informant?' he asked as they resumed walking. 'Did you get their name?'

'No, but he looks about thirty and he speaks with a lisp. Oh, and I would hazard a guess that he was his parents' least favourite child. Probably the middle of three children.'

'What makes you say that?' Azriel asked, bemused.

'As he wasn't the eldest or the baby of the family, he had no clearly defined role growing up, making him desperate for approval as an adult,' Izabel replied.

'So, he becomes an informant?' Azriel fought the urge to laugh.

'Exactly!'

'You're quite the detective, aren't you?'

'I have to admit that I am a fan of the great Sherlock Holmes.' She looked at him gravely. 'But, more than that, I'm a friend. A friend who wants to see the Germans out of Warsaw. Out of Poland. So, is this information of any use to you or not?'

'It might be.' He looked at the piece of paper. 'How did you get hold of this if it was given to the soldier?'

'That's not the original note. I sent the soldier to the bar to get a menu and I snuck it from his coat pocket while he was gone. Trouble was, he came back before I had a chance to return it, so I had to whisper sweet nothings in his ear to get close enough to put it back.' She pursed her lips. 'I hope you appreciate the lengths I went to. The whole thing was quite disgusting.'

'I can imagine.' He felt a weird mixture of concern for her safety and something uncomfortably close to jealousy at the thought of her whispering in a German soldier's ear.

'Although not quite as disgusting as the informant. What a snake!' she said angrily, and her anger and obvious sense of solidarity went a little way towards easing his own disgust.

Nothing made sense in this strange new world. People like this informant and even his own father pandered to the

Germans, while his sister's melodramatic friend was proving to be an unlikely ally.

'The worst thing is, the Germans hate him,' Izabel continued. 'As soon as he'd gone, the soldier started making fun of him.' She moved closer. 'I have a proposition for you,' she whispered and something about their proximity and the breathless way in which she spoke created an unexpected jolt of desire in the pit of his stomach.

'Oh, yes?' he whispered coolly, trying to ignore the feeling.

'If you like, I can see the soldier again, to see if I can get more information from him. As I said, I do have a talent at getting men to open up to me and I'm a very accomplished actress.'

'Really?'

'Yes.' She gave a weary sigh. 'I could have been Poland's answer to Marlene Dietrich if it weren't for my numbers-obsessed father.'

Azriel wasn't sure what she meant by this but decided it would probably be simpler and a whole lot quicker not to ask.

'So, what do you say?' She looked at him hopefully. 'Could that be of any use for you?'

'Possibly.'

She frowned. 'I'm not going to whisper sweet nothings to an odious toad for "possibly". Is it a yes or a no?'

'It's a yes,' he replied. 'But are you sure you want to take the risk? It could be very dangerous.'

'I'm certain,' she replied firmly, and he felt a warm rush of gratitude. Knowing that Izabel was prepared to go to such lengths to help him and the Bund was really touching.

'Thank you.'

'You're most welcome.' She grinned up at him as they carried on walking.

They reached Izabel's building and came to a halt.

'Goodnight then,' he said.

'Goodnight. Oh, and Azriel?'

'Yes?'

'It's probably best if we don't tell Adela about this. I don't think she'd like me fraternising with enemy and I don't want to upset her.'

He considered this for a moment. He didn't want to have any secrets from Adela, but he knew from his life in the Bund that the fewer people in a chain of intelligence, the better, and more importantly, what she didn't know wouldn't hurt her.

Izabel held her hand out for him to shake. He took it, feeling slightly confused.

'It's a pleasure doing business with you,' she said.

'Oh. Yes, you too,' he muttered.

She stood up on tiptoes and kissed his cheek. 'Goodnight.'

'Goodnight.' He turned and walked away, the skin on his cheek tingling from the imprint of her lips, or perhaps it was just the cold.

Yes, he told himself firmly. *It is just the cold.*

16

I am made of water and stardust, Adela repeated to herself silently as she made her way along the street. *My very existence is proof of magic.* Ever since Jaski had shared his secret mantra with her, three months previously, it had become a part of her daily routine, as natural and as vital as breathing. And it had helped her enormously as life in Warsaw became increasingly fraught.

She heard a yell from around the corner and instinctively hurried from the gutter to hide in a nearby doorway. She didn't need to see what was happening to know the cause of the commotion. From the men yelling, 'Hey, Jew!' she knew that a press gang had pounced and were no doubt dragging their poor victim off to a long day of forced labour for the Germans. She shrank back into the shadows, her skin erupting in a cold sweat at the thought of being sent to work in one of the German factories, or, even worse, in a labour camp, where Jews were forced to do pointless and humiliating work, like breaking stones.

In the past few months, the orphanage had become like a second home for her – a place where she could escape the horrors of the outside world. Creating a play with the children had been a wonderful experience. Together they'd come up with an ambitious and swashbuckling tale of derring-do, featuring wily pirates, fearless princesses and a crocodile named Snapper, who was being played by Jaski. And now, after three months of brainstorming, writing and rehearsing, it was time for their grand performance, in front of a select audience of staff and their family members.

It had been wonderful to see the kids so animated and engrossed in something a world away from the horrors unfolding outside the orphanage. But the icing on the cake had been her daily meetings with Jaski. Officially, they'd been meeting at the end of her shift every day to discuss the play, but, in reality, they'd spent hours sharing quotes from favourite books and poems and discussing ideas about life and the future of humanity. It felt as if their minds were two vines that had become beautifully intertwined, but when Adela tried explaining this to Izabel, she was met with looks of confusion. 'But why hasn't he tried to kiss you?' she'd ask. She didn't seem able to understand that Adela's meeting of minds with Jaski felt just as intimate as any physical encounter, if not more so.

And, the truth was, Adela was glad that they hadn't crossed that line. She was worried that, with Jaski being her boss and older than her, it would only create complications, and life was already complicated enough.

The commotion around the corner faded away and Adela stepped back onto the street. *I am made of water and stardust,* she told herself firmly, as she made her way back to the gutter. *My very existence is proof of magic.*

Izabel watched Dieter marching across the park towards her, a cold streak of grey slicing through the vivid green of the grass, and she suppressed a shudder. *You're doing this for Adela and*

Azriel, she reminded herself. *You're doing this for the freedom of Poland.*

In the three months since they'd met, she and Dieter had fallen into a routine of meeting some Wednesdays for lunch and one evening a week for dinner, and in this time, she'd come to the conclusion that he was a truly vile specimen of a human being. It transpired that he had a wife and three children at home in Germany, but, according to Dieter, taking Izabel out for meals didn't constitute cheating. 'You and I are doing nothing wrong; we are just friends,' he'd told her after dinner one night, before forcefully kissing her upon the lips. She had refrained from pointing out that she couldn't imagine him kissing Gustav goodnight in this way.

Another of his failings, his chronic self-absorption, actually worked in her favour because it meant that he wasn't remotely interested in her life away from him. It was as if he saw her as a mere accoutrement to be worn on his arm a couple of times a week, then put away again until they next met. He never asked her what she'd been doing while they were apart, which was just as well, given the work she was now doing for Azriel and the Bund. She smiled at the thought.

'Well, you look very pleased to see me,' Dieter said smugly as he reached the bench. He was clutching a package in his stubby fingers.

'But of course,' she replied, feeling slightly sick. 'It always brightens my day to see you, so handsome in your uniform.'

He gave an arrogant smile and she cringed at his vanity and stupidity.

'I have a gift for you,' he said, shoving the parcel at her.

'I love presents!' she gasped, trying to smile demurely. 'What's the occasion?'

'You'll see.' He sat down on the bench beside her. 'Open it,' he said as if barking an order to a soldier.

She opened the box to see folds of blossom-pink tissue

paper. Nestled inside was a black lace and satin underwear set. In any other circumstances, she would have thought them beautiful, but coming from Dieter, with the obvious implication attached, they made her feel clammy with dread.

'I thought you could wear them to our next dinner,' he said, making anxiety swirl in the pit of her stomach.

'Wouldn't I be a little cold?' she quipped.

He frowned, causing his beady little eyes to shrink to the size of raisins. 'Under your dress, obviously,' he snipped.

God, he really is a humourless toad!

'Obviously,' she said, trying to sound as meek and compliant as possible.

He put his hand on her knee and gripped it tightly. 'I can get to see them after dinner. I was thinking we could go to a hotel.'

'What, to stay over?' she blurted out, unable to contain her horror at the mere thought.

'Obviously,' he said again, sounding even more condescending.

'But... but what about your wife?' She'd previously tried to steer clear of mentioning his family, but desperate times called for desperate measures.

He glared at her. 'My wife is miles away, in Hamburg. She will never know.' He took hold of her hand. His fingers were sweaty. 'It's about time you paid me back for all of the meals I've bought you, don't you think?'

'But I...'

'What?'

'I'm a Catholic,' she said lamely.

He gave a snort of laughter. 'Oh please.'

'I'm saving myself until I'm married.'

'Are you turning me down?' he asked, his voice tightening, and her anxiety grew.

'No, of course not. I adore you. I just wish that you weren't already taken.'

He smirked. 'Well, maybe if it goes well tomorrow night, I shall leave my wife for you.'

She didn't believe him for a minute but had no choice but to play along. 'Really?' she said in what she prayed was a hopeful voice.

'Yes.' His smirk grew. Then, to her relief, he got to his feet. 'I have to get back to the barracks, but I'll see you tomorrow. Be at the Crescent Hotel, at seven. And don't forget to wear them.' He gestured at the box.

'I will. Thank you.'

He nodded curtly and turned on his heel.

As she watched him stalk past the women and children playing in the spring sunshine, Izabel felt as if she'd just been handed a notice of execution and that her death was to be the slowest and most painful imaginable. Her chest tightened. For the first time since she'd begun her flirtation with Dieter, she felt that she'd strayed dangerously out of her depth.

As Azriel stepped inside the store, it took a moment for his eyes to adjust to the lack of light. The boarded-up windows cast an eerie gloom over the place, allowing only paper-thin shafts of light through the cracks. He heard the low murmur of men's voices coming from the room at the back and frowned, hoping it wasn't one of his father's *Judenrat* friends. Still, it might be useful to find out what they were up to, and if their German bosses had issued any new directives. He crept over to the counter, being careful to stay out of sight of the open storeroom door.

'*Todah rabah rabah*, Leopold,' he heard a man say. He didn't recognise the voice, but whoever it was clearly couldn't contain their gratitude to his father, thanking him over and over again.

'Of course,' his father replied. 'And don't worry, I will get the rest of the paperwork to you tomorrow.'

'*Todah rabah!* May God bless you.'

There was the sound of chairs scraping on the floor and Azriel quickly took a few steps back to make it look as if he was just coming in.

Leopold emerged from the storeroom accompanied by a handsome middle-aged man dressed in well-cut trousers and a crisp cotton shirt. Chunky gold cufflinks glinted at his wrists.

'Azriel!' Leopold exclaimed. 'You're back early!'

Azriel frowned. His father seemed rattled.

'Is this your boy?' the man asked, and Leopold nodded.

'Your father is a very good man,' he said, clapping Azriel on the shoulder. He smelled of expensive cologne. 'A very good man indeed.'

As Leopold ushered him over to the door, Azriel slipped behind the counter and peered into the back room. A pile of zlotys lay in the middle of the table. Azriel wasn't sure he'd ever seen so much money, not even before the war.

Leopold came up behind him. 'What are you doing?' he asked defensively.

'I was about to ask you the same thing,' Azriel replied. 'Where did you get that money?'

'That's of no concern to you.' Leopold pushed past him into the back room and began gathering up the zlotys.

'Who was that man? Why was he so thankful? What have you done for him?' Azriel felt sick as the pieces of the puzzle began falling into place in his mind. As a member of the *Judenrat*, Leopold had certain privileges. Was the money on the table some kind of bribe? Paid by the man in exchange for the mystery paperwork they'd been discussing.

'And to think that you had the nerve to call me a disgrace to

our family,' he said, remembering his father's response the day
he told him he'd joined the Bund militia.

'You don't know what you're talking about,' Leopold
muttered as he put the money in his pocket.

'I know that my father is in the pocket of the Nazis and now
he's taking bribes,' Azriel said.

'Don't talk to me like that! Show some respect!' Leopold
shouted.

'You need to earn my respect!' Azriel spat back.

'What on earth's going on?' Estera cried as she came
running down the stairs. 'Why are you shouting at each other?'

'Ask him,' Azriel said, glowering at Leopold. 'Does Mama
know what you've been doing?'

'What's he talking about?' Estera looked at Leopold
anxiously, but before he could respond, there was a knock on
the shop door.

'That'll be Izabel,' Estera said.

'Izabel?' Azriel looked at her questioningly.

'Yes. She's coming with us to see the play at the orphanage.
So I suggest you two stop your bickering and go and get ready.'
Estera hurried over to unlock the door.

Azriel internally groaned. The last thing he wanted to do
now was go to a play with his father. But Adela had begged him,
saying that the orphans didn't have any family of their own to go
and watch and they needed an audience, so there was no way
he could say no.

'Hello,' Izabel said as Estera let her in. As usual, she was
dressed to the nines, wearing a dark grey skirt and rose-pink
blouse, but her normal effervescence seemed to be missing, and
she gave the men a feeble nod. But Azriel couldn't worry about
Izabel now, not on top of everything else.

'I'll just go and get changed,' he muttered and hurried
upstairs, cursing the day he'd ever moved back to live with his
traitorous father.

17

'Children, children! Gather round!' Jaski called. He was wearing his crocodile costume minus the head and Adela couldn't help smiling at this bizarre bespectacled creature addressing them.

There were just a few minutes left before curtain up and they'd all gathered in the orphanage kitchen, which Marta had grudgingly agreed to allow them to use as the backstage area. The room was a mass of excited children, all clad in their colourful costumes. Adela had enlisted the help of Estera as wardrobe manager and she'd come up with some incredible creations, mainly crafted from dyed bed sheets and a pile of old curtains Jaski had found in the orphanage loft.

'Your audience has arrived and is filling the theatre as we speak,' Jaski continued. The children all fell silent, exchanging a few anxious glances. 'Now, it's perfectly normal to feel as if you have butterflies fluttering around inside of you on such a momentous occasion,' he said, grinning at Adela over the tops of their heads. 'And sometimes it's easy to think that those butterflies are fear, but they're not, they're excitement. And excitement is a very good thing indeed, so there's no need to worry. Now, does anyone have any questions?'

'What if I forget my lines?' a timid little girl named Emily asked.

'If anyone forgets their lines, I shall whisper them to you from the side of the stage,' Adela reassured them.

'Yes, your guardian angel, Adela, shall be looking after you from the wings,' Jaski added, and he gave her a beaming smile that made her feel warm inside. Then his smile faded and he looked back at the children. 'You have no idea how proud I am of you,' he said softly. 'The play you've created is such a wonderful achievement, and you're going to give your audience the greatest gift. Do you know what that is?'

The children shook their heads.

'Hope. That's what.' Jaski picked up his giant papier-mâché crocodile head and put it on. 'Now, get ready for the opening scene before I gobble you all up.'

The children laughed and started filing out of the room.

Adela hung back for Jaski.

'Good luck, Snapper,' she whispered.

He took her hand and gave it a gentle squeeze and she felt a wave of joy roll right through her.

For the entire hour and a half of the play, Adela wasn't sure if she blinked or even breathed. Every ounce of her energy was focused onto the stage and into the children, willing them to remember their lines and give their best performances. And, mercifully, it worked. Apart from an initial wobble, where the pirate ship constructed from old crates almost capsized, the whole thing went without hitch, and, buoyed by the enthusiasm of their audience, the children gave the performances of their lives. As she watched from the wings as they took their final bows, she couldn't have felt any prouder.

When the applause finally faded, Jaski produced a bouquet of flowers from somewhere and began to speak. 'Ladies and gentlemen, tonight would not have been possible without the talents of our director, script editor and all-round guardian angel,' he announced, beckoning her over. 'So please join me in a round of applause for Adela Rubinstein!'

Adela stepped out onto the stage, her face flushing as the applause grew. She heard a whoop from the front row and saw Izabel cheering wildly. Next to her, Azriel was grinning up at her. Her parents were both beaming too. Adela hadn't seen them look so joyful since before the war and her heart burst with gratitude.

Finally, the applause ended and they all made their way back into the kitchen, where a grinning Marta was ready with jugs of lemonade and plates of cinnamon cookies. When the children saw them, they squealed with delight and, simultaneously, Adela's eyes filled with tears.

'Are you all right?' Jaski asked.

'I think this might be one of the happiest moments of my life,' she whispered.

'Mine too,' he replied, and she was once again reminded of that day in the storeroom, when she'd felt so certain that she'd never feel happiness again – or love, for that matter. And now, here she was filled to the brim with both. 'I was wondering,' he said, looking slightly bashful.

'Yes?'

'Perhaps you'd like to join me for a late supper once we've got our theatre troupe in bed? I have something I'd like to talk about with you.'

'Of course.' She glanced at the clock on the kitchen wall. 'But what about curfew?' She felt a stab of anger at the Germans for controlling even the hours of the day.

'You are welcome to stay the night – in the guest room,' he hastily added, and she noticed that his face was flushed.

'I'd like that very much,' she replied softly.

Azriel gazed at the empty stage, wishing his sister would reappear so they could get back home. He'd enjoyed the play far more than he'd anticipated, but now they'd returned to the real world with a bump and he was itching to be away from his father. Perhaps he could walk Izabel home instead. He needed to talk to her about the latest issue of *Bulletin*, the new clandestine Bund newspaper. Izabel had offered to distribute copies – women made the best distributors as they were far less likely to be stopped by the Germans. He glanced at her. She was shifting restlessly from foot to foot, clearly as eager to leave as he was.

'Shall I walk you home?' he asked.

'Oh... yes, OK then,' she muttered. Something was clearly distracting her.

'Good boy,' Estera said, nodding approvingly.

He noticed Leopold roll his eyes and his anger grew.

'Come on,' he said to Izabel brusquely.

'But aren't we going to wait and congratulate Adela?' Izabel asked.

'We can do that later.' He took her by the arm and started steering her towards the door.

'Please tell Adela that I loved the play,' Izabel called to Estera over her shoulder. 'I'll come and give my congratulations in person tomorrow.'

'Of course. Get home safely,' Estera replied.

It was only when he was outside and able to inhale a lungful of the cool evening air that Azriel felt his indignation towards his father begin to abate.

'So, why the hurry?' Izabel asked as they fell into step, with him in the gutter and her at the edge of the pavement. 'Are you that desperate to get me on my own?'

'No!' he exclaimed. 'I'm that desperate to get away from my father.'

She stopped walking and stared at him. 'But Leopold's one of the nicest men on earth. How could you possibly be angry with him?' She ran to catch up.

Azriel glared at her. 'He's a traitor to his people,' he hissed.

She looked genuinely shocked. 'But you and your father used to be so close.'

He felt a twinge of remorse but pushed it away. '*Used* to,' he echoed for emphasis.

'But don't you think that now is the time for sticking together?' she asked. 'Haven't you got more important things to worry about?'

The frustration he'd been holding inside all evening came bubbling over. 'Tell that to my father!' he snapped, coming to a halt. 'Where's his loyalty to me?'

'But what has he done that's so wrong?'

'You wouldn't understand. It's all right for you; your people haven't been forced into a situation where they're being pitted against one another.'

'My people?' She stared at him.

He stared back at her defiantly.

She shook her head slowly. 'Unbelievable!'

'What?'

'You.' She stepped closer and glowered up at him. 'Do you have any idea what I'm doing for *your* people? The risks I'm taking? The horrible—'

'Yes of course but—' he interrupted.

'*I'm* talking!' she practically yelled.

'I'm sorry,' he mumbled, glancing anxiously to see if anyone had overheard. Thankfully, aside from a homeless man lying asleep in a doorway, the street was empty.

'I'm so sick of being patronised,' she continued, her green eyes sparking with anger. 'Yes, I know I am an attractive woman and, as such, men assume that all of God's creative powers must have gone into constructing my hourglass figure and my winning smile and my perfect hair...'

Not to mention your outrageous self-confidence, Azriel was tempted to quip but thought better of it.

'And, admittedly, I might not be as academic as you and Adela, but I do have a razor-sharp wit and the courage of a lioness.'

'Can I say something?' he asked.

'As long as it's brief and not patronising,' she retorted.

'I never meant to patronise you,' he said cautiously.

'Go on,' she said.

'In fact, I have great respect for you.'

For a moment, her face lit up, but her scowl was quick to return.

'And I do appreciate what you've been doing for us – the risks you've been taking.' He paused to look around, then leaned in closer. 'I came across my father taking a bribe today.'

Her mouth fell open in shock. 'From who?'

'I don't know, some wealthy guy he'd promised to get papers for.'

'Because he's on the *Judenrat*?' Izabel's voice softened.

He sighed. 'He's betraying his people for the Nazis and he can't even see it.'

To his relief, she nodded. 'That must be really tough.' She sighed. 'Trust me, I know all about being disappointed by your father. I mean, *my* father,' she quickly added. 'He's a huge disappointment to me.'

'Why?' He stared at her curiously.

She looked away, clearly upset, and he felt a pang of concern. 'He just is,' she muttered, before looking back at him. 'Did you mean what you said – about having a lot of respect for me?'

'Yes. Somehow I'm able to see beyond the dazzling beauty that God spent so much time and energy on,' he said drily.

'You think I'm vain and silly,' she said flatly.

'No!' he exclaimed, placing his hand on her arm. Their eyes met and he felt a moment of connection so strong, it almost floored him. 'I'm being serious,' he said softly. 'I respect you a lot. And I think you're very brave too.'

To his horror, she sniffed and let out a sob.

'Goddammit!' she exclaimed. 'I hate crying.'

'Why?' He fought the sudden urge to wrap his arms around her.

'Because it's a sign of weakness and it never achieves anything.' She wiped her eyes angrily. 'I had a horrible day too,' she said quietly, looking down at the ground. 'Dieter, the German soldier I've been fraternising with, has made it clear that he wants payment for the meals he's bought me.'

'What do you mean, payment?'

'He wants me to sleep with him tomorrow.' Her words instantly made him crackle with anger. She looked up at him imploringly. 'Oh, Azriel, I don't know what to do. I mean, I know I have the courage of a lioness, but how am I going to get out of this? I can't let him do that to me, I can't.' She lowered her voice. 'I... I've never been with a man before.' Another tear rolled down her face and Azriel reached out and gently wiped it away. 'I don't know what to do,' she said again, looking up at him.

And in that moment the only thing that Azriel could think to do, the only thing he wanted to do, was to cup her face in his hands and kiss her softly.

18

Adela looked across the desk at Jaski in the flickering candlelight. The children had finally calmed enough to be corralled into their dormitories, and peace and quiet had descended upon the orphanage. The only sounds were the occasional creaks from the rafters and the gurgle of a pipe as the building settled itself for the night. Jaski had magically produced a supper of ham and cheese and bread and one large tomato which he'd laid out on a gingham tablecloth on the desk, along with Adela's bouquet of flowers in a glass jar.

'What a magical night!' she exclaimed.

He smiled at her. 'And to think that you thought the Germans had stolen our capacity for magic.'

'Thank you for helping me find it again.'

'Oh, you are most welcome.' He cut the tomato into slices and divided them onto their plates. She couldn't help noticing that he'd given her the biggest, most juicy slices from the centre, leaving himself the smaller ends. This simple act seemed so typical of Jaski, always putting others' comfort and happiness before his own.

'So, what was it that you wanted to talk about?' she asked.

Perhaps he wanted her to work more hours in the orphanage. Or could he finally be going to address the growing closeness between them? She hardly dared hope that this might be the case.

'I have a confession to make,' he said, and her heart sank. From the gravity of his tone, it was clearly not something positive.

'Please don't tell me that you're a Nazi in disguise,' she joked lamely.

The joke fell flat and he shook his head. 'These past few months I've really enjoyed getting to know you and spending time with you.'

Adela stopped eating. Why did it sound as if a 'but' was coming?

'And in that time, I've developed certain feelings for you.'

She felt a spark of hope.

'I've fallen in love with you, Adela.' He gazed at her intently in the flickering candlelight. 'I never thought it would be possible to feel like this again – after losing my wife, I thought I'd be on my own forever.'

Adela held her breath. In her more insecure moments, she worried that she'd never measure up to his wife, never be able to compete with the history they'd shared together.

'You've made me happier than I ever dreamed possible.' He sighed. 'But I know that my feelings aren't reciprocated. How could they be? You're so much younger than I am. You have your whole life ahead of you, and obviously you will want to marry someone of your own age one day. And I'd never want to get in the way of that. I just couldn't keep my feelings to myself anymore.' He looked down into his lap. 'I totally understand if you'd like to stop working here in the light of my confession.'

'Of course I don't want to stop working here!' she exclaimed. 'And who cares that I'm younger than you? For a start, you hardly seem your age. You're the most childlike forty-year-old I've ever met!'

He let out a laugh. 'Are you saying that I'm immature?'

'No!' she exclaimed. 'I said child*like*, not childish. I love the fact that you're able to see the wonder and joy in everything, even now, during the occupation. And I also love the fact that you know so much about philosophy and art and literature. When I'm with you, it feels as if my brain and my soul expand.'

He shook his head in disbelief. 'I really make you feel like that?'

'Yes! And I never feel like that with men my own age. Not that I've had much experience with men my own age,' she added. 'But I don't want to. The only man I'm interested in – the only man I'm in love with – is you.' She sat back in her chair, hardly able to believe that she'd said the words out loud.

Jaski looked equally shocked. 'Oh, Adela.' His voice was barely more than a whisper. 'Thank you.' His eyes became glassy with tears.

'These past few months have been the happiest of my life because of you.' Her voice wavered.

He leaned across the table and gently placed his hands over hers, and it was as if she could feel the love from him surging into her, up through her arms and into her heart.

Izabel stared up at Azriel, speechless. 'Did you... did you just kiss me?' she whispered.

'It would seem so,' he said. 'I'm sorry. I don't know what happened. I just...' He broke off, looking embarrassed.

'Don't apologise,' she said softly. 'I've been dreaming of you doing that for a very long time.'

He looked back at her curiously.

She leaned forward and rested her forehead on his chest

and, to her joy, she felt his arms wrap around her and he held her tight.

Then, from further up the street came the distinctive clip-clip of a soldier's boots.

'Damn!' Azriel muttered.

'Quick, come inside,' she said, turning and opening the door to her apartment building.

'But...'

'It's OK, my family are away for the weekend.' She ushered him into the lobby and up the first flight of stairs.

'But it's almost curfew,' he said.

'God, I hate that cursed curfew!' she exclaimed. 'It's like being Cinderella every night, having to rush home before you turn into a pumpkin.' She stopped outside her apartment door and took her keys from her bag. 'Why don't you come in for a while?' She looked at him and held her breath, feeling certain he'd refuse, but, to her surprise, he nodded.

'Why not?' he said, causing her heart to pound.

She unlocked the door and led him through to the kitchen.

'It's so tidy!' he exclaimed, looking around at the highly polished table and chairs and the pristine dresser, with its shelves full of gleaming plates and bowls all perfectly arranged.

'My mother,' she said by way of explanation. 'She believes that her whole reason for living is to keep a pristine home – perhaps to cover for the fact that everything beneath the surface is broken and tarnished.' She went to the cupboard and took out Krysia's bottle of vodka from its hiding place behind the large earthenware flour jar. 'Drink?'

'Please.' He sat down at the table and took off his cap.

Catching a glimpse of his eyes with their fringes of dark lashes caused her heart to flutter once again. She couldn't believe he was here, in her apartment. She couldn't believe that he'd kissed her! If she was dreaming, she didn't ever want to wake up.

She fixed them both generous measures of vodka and sat down beside him.

'Thank you,' she said.

'What for?'

'Coming in. I really didn't want to be alone tonight. I've been going out of my mind all day.'

He took a sip of his drink, then placed his glass down and looked at her intently. 'I don't want you to see him tomorrow. I don't want you to see him ever again.'

She was so grateful, she had to fight back another onset of tears.

'There are other ways you can help us,' he continued. 'I don't want that animal laying a finger on you.'

'You sound...' She broke off.

'What?'

'Almost jealous.'

'Maybe I am.' He took another sip of his drink, and it was as if the air in the kitchen had become charged with static, like the moments just before a lightning storm.

'I was so certain you found me annoying,' she said with a laugh.

'I do,' he replied drily, and then he grinned, and she felt such an urge for him to kiss her again, she could barely breathe. 'I find you intensely annoying,' he whispered, leaning closer, and then his lips were on hers again and her mind tumbled and twirled in a kaleidoscope of colour.

19

Jaski gently set the needle of the gramophone onto the vinyl and after a few crackles, the sweetest lilting violin music filled the room.

'It sounds like a bird singing,' Adela said.

'That's exactly what it's supposed to be,' Jaski replied with a smile. 'It's by a British composer named Vaughan Williams; it's called *The Lark Ascending*.'

They both listened for a moment as the notes became higher and purer, and Adela imagined a little bird covered in musical notes instead of feathers soaring above them.

As other instruments joined in and the music built, Jaski held out his hand. 'Would you care to dance?'

'I would be delighted,' she replied in a coquettish tone she didn't know she was capable of.

She took his hand and he pulled her to him. At first, she felt a little awkward; she'd never danced with a man at such close quarters before and anxious thoughts started buzzing around her head. *What if I get the steps wrong? What if I step on his feet?* But Jaski felt surprisingly strong, and the music was so beautiful, her body felt compelled to relax and she leaned her head against his shoulder as they swayed together. It felt so wonderful to be so physically close to another human being after so many months of tension and fear. It was such a gift to be able to share this moment, with the music swirling around them like a protective cloud, and she never wanted it to end.

'I wish we could save this moment forever,' she murmured.

'We can.' He pulled back slightly to look at her.

'How?'

'Our minds are like movie cameras. They are recording it right now, for us to play over and over whenever we want.'

She smiled as she thought of a tiny film crew inside her mind, complete with miniature cameras and clapperboard.

'And hopefully we will have many more of these moments,' he said.

'Yes, I hope so.' But as she replied, an icy shiver ran through her. Would it really be possible, with the Germans becoming ever more powerful and oppressive? Her face must have betrayed her because Jaski stopped dancing and stared at her intently.

'What's wrong?'

'I'm scared the Germans won't allow us to have many more of these moments.'

He shook his head. 'We have to keep the faith that in a world where composers like Williams can create music like this...' He paused as the music reached a crescendo. 'Beauty will triumph over evil.'

He pulled her close again and Adela rested her head on his shoulder, wishing with all her might that he was right, but it didn't stop a tear from spilling onto her cheek.

Izabel wasn't sure how long her kiss with Azriel lasted. It was as if time had ceased to exist. In sharp contrast to Dieter, who kissed her like it was an act of aggression, Azriel was surprisingly tender, stroking her hair and her cheek. As a result, it felt as if she was coming undone. The tough, wise-cracking exterior she'd so carefully cultivated throughout her teenage years and into adulthood was melting away beneath his touch. It was simultaneously thrilling and terrifying.

'Are you all right?' he whispered. 'Do you want me to stop?'

Dieter had never asked her that either.

'I never want you to stop,' she replied, instantly feeling a stab of vulnerability for being so open. But instead of laughing or cringing, he held her tighter.

'I don't want to stop either,' he whispered in her ear.

She thought of him leaving to go home and it sent panic surging through her. After the dread and fear she'd been consumed with all day, it was such a blessed relief to feel safe, if only temporarily. Ever since her meeting with Dieter in the park, she'd been left with an acute sense of foreboding that things were about to spiral horribly out of control. If she asked Azriel to stay, it felt like her way of regaining control of her destiny, for a brief moment. But what if he said no, or judged her for being loose? She normally didn't give a hoot what people thought of her, but not so with Azriel. For as long as she could remember, she'd wanted to win his favour; she didn't want to blow it now.

'Azriel,' she said in between kisses.

'Yes?'

'Would you stay with me tonight? I don't mean for anything untoward,' she quickly added. 'I just want to be held by you,' she whispered, cringing at how desperate she must sound.

'I would like nothing better than to hold you,' he replied, and she was flooded with relief.

'Shall we... shall we go to my room?' she asked, feeling uncharacteristically shy.

'OK,' he murmured.

They both stood motionless for a moment and she realised from the unsure way in which he was looking at her that he was feeling nervous too. This only made her like him even more.

'Are you sure?' he asked softly.

'Yes.' She took his hand and led him from the room.

Azriel followed Izabel into her bedroom, a cocktail of nerves and excitement coursing through his veins. It had been so long since he'd felt like this, every fibre in his being crackling and sparking into life, and it was such a welcome contrast to the anger and frustration he'd felt earlier. Somewhere in the recesses of his mind, a voice of caution murmured something about Izabel being his sister's friend, and was he sure, but his mind was no longer in control now; his heart was. Over the past few months as he'd witnessed Izabel's bravery, fraternising with the German soldier to bring the Bund vital intelligence, his respect for her had grown and grown. And tonight, when she'd finally let her arrogant persona slip and shown him her vulnerability, he'd felt the strongest urge to protect her.

Izabel turned on the bedroom light and he looked around. Unlike the kitchen, which was so pristine it looked like a magazine advertisement for the perfect home, Izabel's room was a riot of colour and full of character. Framed film posters hung on the wall, clothes were draped over just about every piece of furniture, and a stack of records teetered beside one of the latest model record players on the floor.

'Excuse the mess,' Izabel muttered.

'I like it,' he said with a smile.

She looked up at him hopefully.

He stepped towards her and took her hands. 'It's like you.'

'How do you mean?'

'Surprising and full of character.'

'Thank you,' she whispered.

And then they were kissing again, and for the first time in what felt like forever, Azriel didn't think about the war, or the occupation, or his father, or the Bund. It felt as if he was teetering on the edge of a precipice, and it was so good to be this close to Izabel, he closed his eyes, and he felt himself dropping.

20

Adela set off for home the next morning feeling so light and full of joy, it was as if she was the lark that had inspired the beautiful music Jaski had played her. They'd stayed up for hours, listening to music and talking and dancing. And then, finally, after he'd prepared the spare room for her, he had kissed her goodnight. As she thought of their kiss now, she didn't care that she was having to walk in the gutter. She didn't care that a passing tram almost knocked her from her feet. She felt like skipping with glee.

She brought her fingers to her lips as if retracing his kiss. He'd been so gentle and so respectful, not pressuring her for anything more, which she was very grateful for. She'd been really worried about her lack of experience, but Jaski was so tender and caring, she knew that things would only ever happen between them when she was ready.

She turned the corner onto her street and saw a familiar figure striding ahead of her.

'Azriel?' she called in surprise.

He stopped and turned. 'Good morning, little bookworm,'

he called cheerily. Then he frowned. 'What are you doing up and about so early?'

'I was just going to ask you the same.' She ran to catch up with him.

'I, uh, I stayed out last night,' he murmured into his collar.

'Where? Mama told me you were walking Izabel home.'

'I did.' His cheeks burned red.

Adela frowned. Surely he couldn't have stayed the night at Izabel's. Her parents would never have allowed it. But then she remembered Izabel saying that her family were away for the weekend. 'Did you stay at Izabel's?'

He nodded, still not looking at her.

But instead of feeling awkward or jealous at the thought of Azriel and Izabel together, she felt strangely calm. It was as if she was so full of joy from her night at the orphanage, there wasn't room for any negative emotions.

'I really like her,' Azriel muttered.

'Good.'

He looked at her hopefully. 'So you don't mind?'

'As long as you don't do anything to hurt her.'

'I won't, trust me.' He linked his arm through hers. 'So, where have *you* been all night, sister of mine?'

But before Adela could answer, she heard what sounded like a hundred men all yelling in the distance. She looked at Azriel anxiously. 'That doesn't sound good.'

'No. We need to get home. Quick.' He took hold of her hand and they started to run.

As they raced up the street, the yelling grew louder and louder and Adela's skin erupted in goosebumps as she made out the words.

'Beat the Jews! Kill the Jews!'

After what felt like an eternity, they reached the store and she glanced over her shoulder. A baying mob was heading down the street straight towards them. Her fingers shook as she fumbled in her bag for her keys and dropped them on the floor. 'Damn!'

'It's OK.' Azriel picked them up and quickly unlocked the door. 'Get Mama and Papa and go down into the cellar,' he said as they hurried inside. He locked the door behind them, plunging them into darkness.

Adela raced upstairs to find her parents having breakfast in the kitchen. 'We have to go down into the cellar, now!' she gasped.

'Why?' Estera leapt to her feet, instantly paling.

'There's a group of thugs coming down the street. Quick!' She heard something being smashed outside and her stomach lurched.

'Oh no! Oh Leopold!' Estera cried.

'It's all right, dear.' He put his arm around her and guided her out of the room and down the stairs, with Adela close behind.

They found Azriel in the shop, taking one of the remaining shelves from the wall.

'What are you doing?' Leopold asked.

'Getting ready to defend myself and protect Mama and Adela,' he replied grimly.

'Don't be so stupid,' Leopold replied as the shouting grew louder and louder. 'There's too many of them out there. You'll be no match for them. Come and hide with us.'

'I'm not hiding from anyone,' Azriel snapped.

Leopold stood motionless, as if unsure what to do.

'Please, Azriel,' Estera exclaimed. 'Let's all go to the cellar.'

'No!' he yelled above the din outside. 'I'm staying here.'

The sound of glass smashing filled the room.

'Come, quick,' Leopold said, gesturing at Estera and Adela to go to the cellar.

Adela shook her head. 'I'm going to stay here with Azriel,' she said firmly, despite the fear growing inside her.

'Are you sure?' Azriel asked as the yelling grew ever closer.

'Yes,' she replied, her heart thudding. 'Give me one of those shelves.'

Izabel happily hummed away to herself as she got dressed. Azriel had only been gone half an hour or so, but their night together was already starting to take on a dreamlike quality. She went over to the bed and rested her hand on the pillow that was still imprinted with his head and a shiver of excitement coursed through her. He really had been there; they really had made love. She and Azriel had made love!

She sat down and hugged her arms around her, as if trying to keep the magical feeling from escaping. She'd spent hours imagining how her first time would be, many of them in this very room, lying on this very bed. And now, finally, it had happened and, even better, it had been with Azriel, the object of her heart's desire for so many years. The best thing about it was that in the past few months as she'd been passing him information she'd acquired from Dieter, her feelings had developed from a teenage crush into something far deeper. When he'd told her that he felt the same, she'd wanted to sing for joy.

She glanced at the nightstand and saw his watch lying there. He must have forgotten it. She picked it up and held it to her chest. She could drop it off to him on the way to work. Her heart raced at the thought of seeing him again.

Izabel set off for the store with a spring in her step. But she'd only got a few yards when she saw a man wearing an armband running towards her.

'Go home!' he cried to a Jewish woman who'd set up a makeshift stall on a card table, selling a set of silver cutlery. 'A pogrom has begun. They're destroying everything in their sight. It's not safe to be out on the street.'

Izabel's blood turned to ice. She'd heard Adela's parents talk about the pogrom that had happened in Poland and Ukraine in 1919, when hundreds of thousands of Jews had been massacred. Surely this couldn't be about to happen again.

As the man drew level with her, she saw him glance at her arm, as if looking for the cursed armband. She hoped that the fact she wasn't wearing one wouldn't make him think she sided with the pogromists or the Germans.

'You should go home,' the man said to her. 'It's not safe down there.' He nodded in the direction of Adela's street. 'The hooligans are on the rampage.'

She gave him a weak smile. 'Thank you, but I need to check that my friends are safe.'

'Please yourself.' He hurried off and the woman with the stall hastily gathered up her things.

Izabel continued in the direction of Adela and Azriel's street, adrenaline coursing through her veins. *Please, please, please, let them be OK*, she thought as she heard glass smashing and men yelling, 'Beat the Jews!' She felt sick as she thought of Azriel and Adela and their lovely parents.

People kept passing her, fleeing in the opposite direction, but like a fish swimming against the tide, she kept going, pausing only when she reached the corner. She peered round it cautiously and her heart almost stopped. A gang of Polish men with short, cropped hair were yanking some of the boards from the front of Leopold's shop. Another was stuffing a rag into a milk bottle, while another appeared to be about to light it with a match. Izabel leaned against the wall for a moment and took a breath. She knew that she was no match for the gang of thugs, that there was nothing she could do to stop them. But her loyalty to the Rubinsteins was like a magnetic force, pulsing away deep inside of her, compelling her to keep going.

Clenching her hands into tight fists, she began marching down the street, straight towards the men.

21

Adela crouched behind the counter, holding the wooden shelf Azriel had given her to use as a weapon. She was gripping it so tightly, she felt a splinter pierce her skin and she flinched from the prickle of pain. *That could be nothing compared to the pain you're about to feel,* she thought as the yelling outside grew ever louder. Then she heard a strange wrenching sound.

'What are they doing?' she whispered to Azriel, who was hiding in wait behind the curtain leading to the stairs.

'Taking the boards off the window,' he whispered back and suddenly the darkened store was flooded with daylight.

'There's nothing in there,' she heard one of the men outside say.

'Let's torch it then,' another replied to a chorus of cheers.

'No!' Adela gasped.

There was a moment's pause before another crash and then there was a flash of light and the smell of petroleum filled her nostrils.

'Quick!' Azriel cried, hurrying out from behind the curtain. 'Get water.'

They rushed through to the kitchen and filled a pail with

water. By the time they got back to the store, flames had begun leaping around, greedily eating at the wooden floorboards. Outside, a woman screamed and one of the men yelled, 'Get her!' and their footsteps pounded off into the distance. As Azriel threw the water on the fire, Adela went and filled a saucepan, but when she returned, the flames had grown higher.

'Get Mama and Papa!' Azriel called as he raced back into the kitchen to refill the bucket.

Adela ran down the cellar steps. She found Leopold pacing up and down and Estera crouched in a corner, head in hands.

'You have to come upstairs,' Adela said. 'They've set fire to the store.'

'No!' Estera cried.

'Is Azriel all right?' Leopold asked, his eyes wide with fear.

'He's trying to put it out, but we need your help.'

Thankfully, when they got up into the store, there was no sight or sound of the thugs. The fire was still burning though, and the air was filling with smoke.

'We need more water,' Azriel yelled as he threw another bucketful onto the blaze. They raced into the kitchen, grabbing anything they could find to fill.

Adela coughed as smoke tore at her lungs. But now all four of them were tackling the blaze, the flames started to subside, and eventually they sputtered out.

'Why are they doing this to us?' Estera wailed, sinking down to the floor. 'What have we ever done to deserve such hatred?'

'Hush, dear,' Leopold soothed. 'It's all right. We put the fire out.'

'Until next time,' Estera replied.

'There shouldn't be a next time!' Azriel hissed, grabbing his jacket from the counter.

'Where are you going?' Estera cried as he headed towards the door.

'To do something about this,' he replied.

'No, son, it's too dangerous,' Leopold said, stepping in front of him as if trying to block his way.

'Standing by and doing nothing is too dangerous,' Azriel snapped back, marching past him.

'Please don't go out there,' Estera begged.

'I'll be all right, Mama,' Azriel said, his voice softening. Then he turned to Adela and gave her a weak smile. 'I'll see you later, little bookworm. Take care of Mama and Papa.'

'Please be careful,' she implored, and he nodded grimly before slipping out of the battered door.

Azriel made his way along the deserted street, darting from doorway to doorway. About halfway along, he noticed a bright green beret lying discarded on the floor. It was like the one Izabel sometimes wore and, for a second, he felt a stab of concern. But then he remembered that Izabel had been going straight to work after he'd left her, so it couldn't possibly be hers.

As he continued on his way, he felt a great weight of despondency pressing down upon him. After everything that had just happened it was almost impossible to believe that he and Izabel had spent such a special night together. All around him, the streets echoed with yelling and the sounds of destruction. What had happened at the store was clearly not a one-off incident. It was obvious that some kind of orchestrated attack had begun.

Sure enough, as he reached the junction, he spied a couple of German soldiers with cameras, taking photographs of the Jews fleeing their homes. The soldiers were laughing and joking as if they were taking snaps on a family vacation – a sight that made him sick to his stomach. How much more of this barbarity could they be expected to take?

You have to stay strong, he urged himself as he continued on his way. If a pogrom had begun, he was certain the Bund wouldn't sit back and do nothing, which was why he had to go and see Berek and report for duty.

When he got to Berek's new apartment – after Izabel's tip-off about the informant, he changed location every week – he found him grim-faced and taut with nervous energy.

'We've got to go to Bernard's place,' he said, handing Azriel a canvas duffel bag. It weighed a ton and whatever was inside clinked as he slung it over his shoulder.

'Of course,' Azriel replied, feeling a burst of adrenaline. Surely this meant that a fightback against the thugs was imminent.

As they reached Goldstein's apartment on Novolipya, Azriel's nerves grew. He was finally going to meet the legendary Comrade Bernard, the man who had so bravely fought the communists in Russia and the fascists in Poland and had even survived a period of exile in Siberia.

Of all the stories Azriel had heard about Goldstein, and there were many, his favourite was when the Bund commander had travelled to the town of Mińsk Mazowiecki in 1930. Tensions were high in the area after a young, mentally unwell Jewish man had shot and killed a sergeant from the Polish army, sparking the right-wing nationalist party, the Endeks, to call for the blood of all the Jewish in retribution. 'Blood for blood' was their slogan. Just before the funeral of the sergeant, the Endeks set fire to a Jewish home that had been abandoned by its terrified tenants. The fire tore through the house and then began burning through the roof of the house next door, home to a non-Jewish family. Goldstein had raced through the gathered crowd and rescued some children and an elderly woman from their home. Then he'd climbed onto the roof and called out to the crowd to fetch water to fight the blaze. When the crowd saw that a Jewish man had gone to the aid of a Polish family, whose home had now been destroyed by the Endeks, they began shouting, 'Down with the Endeks! Down with the hooligans!'

The story spread through the village faster than the fire had torn through the houses, and Goldstein urged the Jews who'd been hiding to come out and take advantage of the change in mood and re-establish their friendships with their Polish neighbours. Azriel tried to imagine doing the same now, after the hooligans had tried to set fire to his family's store, and it made him wince. It took a special kind of person to suffer such provocation and not rush to retribution. He hoped he could be that level-headed, but he wasn't so sure. After David had been killed, he'd felt a need for vengeance so powerful, it had almost consumed him.

Azriel followed Berek into the apartment, where a group of men were sitting around an oval wooden table, with others standing lining the walls. A heated conversation was already in mid flow.

'But if we fight back, surely the Germans will use it as an excuse for their doctrine of collective responsibility and punish all the Jewish in Warsaw,' one man said.

'Yes,' another agreed. 'They love an excuse to hurt us. I don't want to be responsible for more pain being inflicted.'

'But they're going to keep inflicting more pain on us anyway,' Azriel couldn't help exclaiming. 'Surely we have to do something.'

'What was that?' a man sitting at the head of the table asked.

Azriel realised that it was his hero, Goldstein, and his pulse quickened. 'I'm sorry, the mob just tried to burn my father's store to the ground. I don't see why they should be able to get away with it.'

'I agree,' said Berek. 'If we don't fight back, it will only get worse.'

'But what if we accidentally kill one of the pogromists?' another man said, his brow furrowed with concern. 'Then there'll be all hell to pay.'

'Hmm.' Goldstein looked thoughtful for a moment. 'We have to choose our weapons wisely and minimise the risk of that happening. So, no knives or guns.'

'I thought you might say that, so we came prepared.' Berek gestured at the duffel bags he and Azriel had been carrying. 'Pipes and brass knuckles,' he explained.

'Good.' Goldstein nodded approvingly. 'Now we need to mobilise each of our fighting contingents – the slaughterhouse workers, the transport workers and the party members.'

'How shall we organise them?' Berek asked.

'Let's split them into three regions,' Goldstein replied. 'One by Mirovsky Market, one in the Franciskanska-Nalefky-Zamenhof district, and one in Leshno-Karmelitzka-Smotcha. Tell your men to be there early – the minute curfew ends,' he continued. 'So we can surprise the hooligans when they arrive.'

'I can't wait to wipe the smiles off their faces,' a man said, and the others all nodded and murmured their agreement.

'Of course, we are bound to suffer some casualties and we can't allow them to be taken to hospital as they'll face certain arrest,' Goldstein said. 'So, any injured parties are to be taken to a Bund safe house and treated by a member of our Red Cross.'

'Azriel here is a member of our Red Cross as well as the youth militia,' Berek said. 'He will be able to treat anyone seriously injured.'

Azriel's heart sank. Normally, he'd be only too happy to treat an injured Bund member, but surely they'd need him to fight in the first instance.

His disappointment must have shown as Goldstein looked at him quizzically. 'I'd say we need all the young men we can get to do the fighting. Only call him for medical duty if it's an emergency.'

'Thank you!' Azriel said, his pulse racing. Much as he wanted to do his bit, he wasn't the most experienced of fighters. He really hoped he wouldn't let Bernard and his other comrades down. Then he thought of his friend David and how he'd died in his arms after being shot, a crimson stain blooming like the very worst kind of flower upon his shirt. Azriel had vowed there and then to do everything he could to avenge him. Perhaps now, finally, he could.

22

Izabel stood, pressed against the wall at the end of the alleyway, stomach churning and fists clenched, as the men advanced towards her. Two of them had broken away from the pack to chase her after she'd begged them not to attack the Rubinsteins' store. They both had shallow foreheads and closely set, pale blue eyes, and she wondered if they might be brothers, although this really was the least of her concerns.

'I think you need to be taught a lesson, Jew-lover,' one of them said as he grew closer. His nose was squashed and misshapen, as if it had been broken in more than one fight.

'Yeah,' the other one sneered. 'You need to stop being a traitor to your people.'

'Those *are* my people!' she couldn't help exclaiming.

He stopped and stared at her. 'You don't look Jewish. Why aren't you wearing an armband?'

He came close enough to touch her.

'I'm not Jewish. They're my friends,' she said proudly, despite her racing pulse.

'You need to start choosing your friends more wisely,' the

other one scoffed. 'Don't you know that the Jews spread diseases?'

'Don't be so ridiculous!' she blurted out. 'Of course they don't. The only ones spreading a disease around here are thugs like you – the disease of untruths!' She felt rather proud of this line, but before she had time to feel too pleased with herself, he pulled his fist back and sent it smashing into her face.

'Don't talk to me like that, you stupid bitch!' he spat, punching her on the face again and again until she was sliding down the wall and onto the floor.

'You need to learn some respect,' the other one said, before kicking her in the stomach.

'Ow!' she cried, curling into a foetal position to try to protect herself, but the kicks kept raining down, into her head and all over her body. She tasted the metallic tang of blood on her tongue, and stars cascaded before her eyes.

Adela watched as Leopold used a crowbar to lever up a floorboard in the bottom of the kitchen cupboard and Estera shoved her jewellery boxes into the hole beneath.

'Are you sure you don't want to put anything down here?' Estera asked, staring up at her. Her dark brown eyes were haunted with fear.

Adela shook her head.

'You could always give your jewellery to Izabel for safekeeping,' Estera suggested.

'No!' she exclaimed. 'I need to go to work.'

'You can't! It isn't safe.' Estera scrambled to her feet and grabbed Adela's arm.

'The children need me.'

'The children have Jaski,' Estera replied.

'Jaski needs me.'

'Jaski is a grown man; he can take care of himself,' Leopold said.

'I want to be with him!' Adela exclaimed.

'Adela?' Estera looked at her questioningly. 'What's going on?'

Adela was so desperate to go, she felt she had no choice but to tell them the truth. 'We... we love each other.'

'Love?' Leopold blurted out, a look of utter confusion on his face.

'Yes.' She stared at him. Never in all her twenty years had she defied her father, but this felt too important. Jaski and the children were the only things that had brought her joy for months. She had to get them to understand why she needed to go to the orphanage.

'So, when you stayed there last night, it wasn't to be with the children and to help clear up?' Estera said slowly.

'Yes, it was. But then Jaski and I had supper together.'

'I don't believe it!' Leopold exclaimed. 'I can't believe he would take advantage of you, and at a time like this.' He frowned at Adela. 'You're not to go back there again.'

'He isn't taking advantage of me – the very opposite in fact; he's been nothing but respectful to me.'

'Respectful!' Leopold huffed. 'I've got half a mind to go over there and talk to him about respect.'

'No, Papa!' Adela exclaimed, horrified. 'I'm a grown woman, not a child.'

'You're twenty,' Leopold replied. 'How old is he?'

'Forty,' she muttered.

'He's a lovely man, but he's old enough to be your father,' Estera said softly.

'I don't care how old he is. I love him.' Adela felt dangerously close to tears.

'Oh, Adela,' Leopold said with a sigh, 'how could you be so naive?'

'I'm not naive,' she cried. And then, in her desperation, she said the one thing she'd vowed never to say. 'At least Jaski hasn't sold out to the Nazis.'

Leopold recoiled as if she'd slapped him.

She stormed past them and down the stairs. She arrived in the store to find Azriel coming in, grave-faced and carrying a duffel bag.

'Where are you going?' he asked.

'To the orphanage.'

'But it isn't safe out there.'

'Oh, don't you start!' she cried. 'I'm going!'

'Little bookworm, what's wrong?' He looked so concerned, it took everything she had not to fall into his arms and start to wail.

'Ask our parents,' she muttered.

But just as she was about to storm outside, the door crashed open and a figure stumbled in, doubled over and covered in blood.

23

Izabel tried to maintain her balance, but her head was spinning and her vision was blurred. She was just able to make out a couple of figures standing in front of her before she sank to her knees.

'What on earth?' she heard someone say. Was it Estera? She couldn't be sure due to the ringing in her ears.

'Izabel!' Adela exclaimed.

The sound of her friend's voice made Izabel want to weep with relief.

'What happened to you?' She heard Azriel, and then felt a pair of strong hands gripping either side of her shoulders. She winced in pain. Every inch of her body felt tender; even her bones seemed to ache.

'Who did this to you?' She heard Azriel again.

She tried to say, 'The thugs attacking your shop,' but her mouth felt as if it had been stuffed with great wads of cotton and her voice came out muffled, the words indecipherable.

'Bring her through to the back,' someone said, and she felt more hands gently propping up her arms and lifting her.

'Oh, *moj skarbe*,' Adela said from somewhere in the distance.

'Sit her down on the chair.'

'Get her some water.'

'Be gentle with her.'

The Rubinsteins' concerned voices sounded sweeter than a chorus of angels.

Izabel sniffed and the smell of smoke filled her nostrils. She had a flashback to the thug lighting the rag that had been stuffed into a bottle and her heart raced. But their plan must have failed. The shop was still standing. The Rubinsteins must have been able to put the fire out. She'd distracted the thugs away from finishing off the job.

She felt a cup being placed next to her mouth and cold water sloshed against her swollen lips.

'Careful,' Estera said.

'Oh Izabel,' Adela whispered from right beside her, and she felt someone softly stroking her hair.

'*Moj skarbe*,' Izabel rasped.

'Did *he* do this to you?' Azriel's voice came from somewhere above her. She tried to look up, but it was as if her eyes had been swollen shut.

'Who?' Adela asked and panic sliced through the fog in Izabel's brain.

'No,' she croaked.

'What are you talking about?' Adela pressed.

'It doesn't matter,' Azriel muttered. 'I need to check her injuries, see if anything's broken.'

She felt his hands on her body, tenderly touching her limbs. It was heartbreaking to think that those same hands had been caressing her body just hours before.

As he felt her ribcage, she screamed out in pain.

'I think you may have some broken ribs,' he said softly. He

was so close, she could feel his breath on her cheek. 'She needs to go to hospital,' he said, his voice further away.

'But how can we get her there?' Estera asked.

'Perhaps we should get her parents?' Leopold suggested.

'They're away,' Azriel said. 'I'll take her.'

'I'll come too,' Adela said.

'No!' Izabel tried to cry but it came out like a moan. She didn't want the Rubinsteins to have to go anywhere while the streets were crawling with thugs.

'It's all right, my dear,' Estera said. 'We're going to get you to the hospital.'

Izabel tried to get to her feet but lost her balance and went toppling to the side, her head filling with stars again.

When Izabel regained consciousness, someone was shining a dazzling light into her eyes.

'Welcome back,' a man's voice said. It was a voice she didn't recognise, and she tried to sit up, but pain kept her welded to the bed.

'It's all right. You're at the hospital,' the voice said. 'I'm Doctor Nowak.'

'Azriel,' she rasped. 'Adela?' Her mouth was unbearably dry, her tongue scratchy as sandpaper.

'Your friends had to go,' the doctor said, 'but your family are here now; they're waiting outside. You've sustained some very serious injuries,' he continued. 'You have several broken ribs and when you were admitted, you were suffering from internal bleeding.'

Everything felt so hazy, it was as if he was speaking another language.

'Would you like to see your family?'

No! she wanted to cry, but she appeared to have been rendered mute as well as motionless.

She heard the door open and footsteps cross the floor.

'Oh, Izabel, how did this happen?' her mother said.

'Who did this to you?' her father asked.

She kept her eyes closed and then she felt a hand taking hers. It was small and warm. Kasper. His fingers squeezed hers gently.

'I love you, sister,' he whispered in her ear, and a tear spilled onto her swollen face.

24

Azriel raced through the square and into the dead-end street, sweat trickling from his brow and his heart pounding. The battle against the pogromists had been raging all day and his body ached from the exertion. But now he had one of the hooligans on the run. He'd spotted the man throwing a brick through the window of a Jewish home and charged at him, yelling profanities. To his surprise, the man had turned and fled and now he had him cornered.

'Please, young man, don't do it.' Azriel felt someone grasp his arm from behind and turned and saw an elderly man wearing a kippa. 'For every one of them you hurt, they'll punish one hundred of us,' the old man continued.

'They're already punishing hundreds of thousands of us,' Azriel replied, looking back at the man he was chasing, who was trying in vain to scale the fence at the end of the street.

'But can't you see that violence isn't the answer?' the man pleaded.

There had been a time when Azriel would have agreed, but so much had happened since then, he found it impossible. 'It's the only language these hooligans understand,' he muttered.

The old man sighed and slipped away, leaving Azriel to advance on the thug, nervously adjusting the brass knuckles on his fingers.

'Please!' the thug called. He sounded younger than Azriel had imagined and as he drew closer, he realised that he was in fact a boy in his teens. His cheeks were flushed and his pale blue eyes appeared to be swimming with tears. 'Please don't hurt me,' the boy cried.

'What about the people you've been hurting?' Azriel said.

The boy glanced at the piping in his hand and visibly cowered.

Having spent so long being threatened and harassed by the Polish anti-Semites and then the Germans, Azriel had always imagined that it would feel incredible to turn the tables and be the aggressor for once. But as he looked at the boy cowering and practically in tears, he didn't feel anything remotely close to pleasure. Then he thought of how Bernard Goldstein had saved the Polish family whose house had been set on fire. He couldn't attack a teenage boy. Where was the bravery or valour in that?

'Go on, go,' he said, stepping back and gesturing up the street with the piping.

The boy looked at him nervously, as if it might be a trap.

'Go!' Azriel yelled, and the boy raced away.

As he watched him go, Azriel wondered if his act of compassion would pay off and the boy would return to his fellow thugs with tales of the Jew who had spared him from a beating. Somehow, he doubted it and he wondered if he'd done the wrong thing.

Azriel heard footsteps approaching and turned to see that the old man was back and smiling at him.

'May God reward you for your mercy,' he said.

Azriel wanted to ask him what kind of God would allow women like Izabel to be so brutally attacked, but he heard another commotion erupt in an adjacent street. He nodded curtly and sprinted off. He didn't have time to discuss theology; his men needed him.

The following morning, the violence resumed as soon as the curfew ended, until finally the police arrived at lunchtime to disperse the fighters. To Azriel's delight and surprise, they didn't seem to want to arrest the Jewish fighters and there had been no sign of the Germans, so he returned to the store feeling jubilant. He found his parents sitting at the kitchen table, their faces wrought with concern.

'Oh, thank God!' Estera exclaimed as he walked in.

Even Leopold looked happy to see him, getting to his feet and patting him awkwardly on the arm.

'Where's Adela?' he asked, instantly feeling concerned.

'At the orphanage.'

'With that man,' Leopold muttered.

'What man?'

'Jaski, the owner of the orphanage,' Estera replied. 'They've become romantically involved.'

'Oh.' Azriel wasn't sure what to make of this. Adela had always seemed so bookish and serious and never one for matters of a romantic nature. It was hard to imagine her involved with any man, let alone the orphanage owner. Azriel had only met him once, on the night of the play, when he'd been dressed as a crocodile.

'But never mind that for now,' Estera continued. 'What happened?' She came over and stroked his bruised face. 'We've been going out of our minds with worry.'

Azriel sat down, kicked off his boots and rubbed his aching feet. 'The fighting is over. The police broke it up.'

'And now we wait for the German reprisals,' Leopold said glumly.

Azriel prickled at his father's negativity. All the way home through the Jewish quarter, people had been thanking him and clapping him on the back. He was determined not to let Leopold dampen his spirits. 'I wouldn't be so sure. They didn't do anything while we were fighting. And the police hardly made any arrests.'

'Oh, I hope that's an end to it,' Estera said, wringing her hands. 'I don't think I could bear any more trouble.'

'Now do you see why we need to fight back?' Azriel looked Leopold straight in the eyes. 'Maybe now they'll take us more seriously. They'll see that we won't just sit back and accept their punishment, that we're a force to be reckoned with.'

'Hmm,' was all Leopold said in response and Azriel felt himself shrinking right down until he was no longer a man who'd just taken to the streets to fight for his cause, but a hurt little boy, desperate for his father's approval.

25

Adela knocked on the door of Izabel's apartment, nervously repeating her opening line in her head. *Good afternoon, Mrs Stanek, how is Izabel?* Izabel's mother had always made Adela feel nervous. She was always so well put together, in her presence Adela felt scruffy and inelegant, and never more so since the occupation. She looked down at her snagged tights and wooden-soled shoes and sighed.

The door opened and, to her relief, she saw Izabel's kid brother, Kasper, standing there.

'Hello, Kasper, I was just wondering if Izabel was home from the hospital yet?' It had been over a week since the fighting and, miraculously, there had been no German reprisals. Things had returned to normal and, if anything, it was a little better than before. The success of the Bund in fighting back had lifted everyone's spirits.

'Yes, she got home yesterday,' Kasper replied.

'How is she?'

'She has two broken ribs, two black eyes, *and* she had some internal bleeding,' he listed in a grave tone, as if parroting something he'd overheard from a doctor.

Adela's stomach churned at the thought of her friend so seriously injured. 'Would it be possible for me to see her?' she asked, but before Kasper could reply, she heard Krysia calling out from inside the apartment.

'Who is it, Kasper?'

Adela's heart sank.

'Adela,' he called back. Then he stepped closer and lowered his voice. 'Would you like a banana?'

Adela was momentarily thrown, but then she remembered Izabel telling her about his black-market fruit venture. 'Yes, but I don't have any money, I'm afraid.'

'That's all right. I want to give it to you to say sorry.'

'What for?'

'For what happened to your shop, and everything else, you know... Wait here.' He turned and disappeared into the apartment.

Adela felt strangely moved by his unexpected gesture of kindness, but then the door opened wider and Krysia appeared, immaculate as always, in a navy-blue dress and matching Mary Jane shoes.

'What do you want?' she asked, icier than ever.

'Hello. I... I was wondering how Izabel is. Is she home?'

'Yes, but she's not receiving visitors,' Krysia said grandly, as if she was talking about the Queen of England.

Adela's heart sank. 'Oh. Well, please can you tell her that I called and give her my love.'

Krysia pursed her bright pink lips. She'd traced an outline around them in a slightly darker shade of pink, and that, combined with her perfectly drawn-on eyebrows, made her look a little like a cartoon character.

'Tell her I'll come and see her as soon as she's ready to have visitors,' Adela continued nervously.

'Oh no you won't. She's not allowed to see you or your family anymore,' Krysia snapped.

Adela stared at her, horrified. 'But why?'

'Why do you think? It's because of you people she ended up in hospital.'

'But we got her to the hospital.'

'After she was trying to save your precious shop.'

'But—'

'Good day, Adela, please don't come here again.' And with that, the door closed.

Adela stumbled down the stairs, her eyes swimming with tears. How had Krysia managed to twist things so that she and her family were to blame for what had happened to Izabel? What hope did they have if people were so desperate to blame them.

Just as she reached the outer door, she heard someone run down the stairs behind her and for a moment she dared to hope that Krysia had realised how ridiculous she was being and had a change of heart, but she turned to see Kasper, holding out a banana.

'I'm sorry,' he whispered before stuffing it into her hand and racing back upstairs.

Izabel stared blankly at the open page of her detective novel. Normally, she loved losing herself in a murder mystery, but today she couldn't concentrate, and the letters all swam in front of her eyes like tadpoles. Before she'd left the hospital, the doctor had delivered some devastating news. Due to her injuries, she'd never be able to have children. The mindless thugs hadn't just attacked her, they'd stolen the lives of the babies she could have borne. There was a knock on her bedroom door and she groaned. She couldn't face her mother and more of her stupid magazines. She looked at the pile on her nightstand. The cover story on the top was about how to have the perfect wedding dress despite the clothes rations, featuring a gormlessly grinning bride. Who would want to marry Izabel now that she wouldn't be able to give them a family? She shoved the magazine out of sight onto the floor as there was another knock on the door.

'What?' she called tersely.

The door opened and Kasper peered in cautiously.

'Oh, it's you,' she said. 'Since when did you start knocking?'

'Can I come in?' he asked, and she nodded.

He came and stood before her, hands clasped, and gazing at her reverentially, as if visiting a holy site. 'How are you?'

One slight and unexpected advantage of her being attacked was that it seemed to have somehow elevated her to the status of hero in her brother's eyes.

'Just great,' she said drily.

'Your friend Adela was here.'

'Adela?' Izabel sat up and instantly winced. It still hurt to move, even an inch. 'Where is she?'

'Mama made her leave.'

'What? Ow!' Even frowning felt painful. 'Why?'

'She said it was her fault that you got attacked. It wasn't though, was it?' He looked at her anxiously.

'No! Of course not. Why would she say such a thing?'

'She said it was because you were trying to protect their shop.' He took a step closer, eyes wide. 'Is that true? Did you fight the bad men to save the shop?'

She nodded. 'I tried to. Didn't do too well though, did I?' She gave a wry laugh as she glanced down at her injuries.

'You're so brave,' he said solemnly.

She stared at him. She was so unused to receiving compliments from her brother, she thought for a moment that he might have been joking. The last thing she felt was brave; surely he couldn't have meant it. But he was still gazing at her, clearly awestruck. 'Oh, I don't know about that,' she muttered.

'Yes, you are! None of my friends' sisters would be brave enough to fight the bad men.' He fiddled with his sleeve and a small, perfectly ripe banana slipped out into his hand. 'I got you a present,' he said, handing it to her. 'That means you don't have to pay,' he added. 'I'm really glad you didn't die,' he muttered, looking down at his feet.

'So am I, little brother,' she whispered. And for the first time since the attack, she felt as if she meant it.

Adela walked back home, her mind racing and her vision blurred. In all their years of friendship, she never would have imagined being forbidden from seeing Izabel. It was quite possibly the worst thing to have ever happened to her. Krysia had never been the warmest towards Adela, and they'd always spent far more time together at the Rubinsteins' home. As children, this had been mainly for practical reasons as Izabel's mother hated mess. At Adela's, they were allowed to turn her bedroom and the living room into the magical worlds of their imaginations, constructing forts made of bedsheets and dens made from books. Oh, how she wished they could go back to those simpler, innocent days.

Adela wiped her tears and carried on her way, trying to be less pessimistic. But as she neared home, she heard a banging sound coming from further up the street. A group of men were gathered at the junction, standing by a large pile of bricks. Perhaps they were repairing one of the bomb-damaged buildings, she mused. But then she saw something that sent an icy chill right through her. They weren't repairing anything; they were building a wall. But it didn't make any sense. It looked as if they were building it right across the road. Then the terrible truth dawned on her. They'd started building the ghetto.

'Isn't it awful?' a woman said as she passed Adela in the

gutter. Her face was haggard and etched with worry. 'They're building a wall to keep us in, and to keep everyone else out.'

The chill inside Adela erupted in goosebumps on her skin.

'Just when you think things can't get any worse,' the woman muttered, before hurrying on her way.

Adela looked back at the men building the wall and noticed, to her horror, that most of them were wearing the Star of David armbands. She fought the urge to retch. The Germans, in all their cruelty, were making the Jews build their own prison.

26

Izabel looked at her reflection in the mirror and tried not to wince. Her bruising might have finally faded, but she looked so wan her vibrancy seemed to have been worn away too.

'I am brave,' she whispered to her reflection, remembering what Kasper had said to her a couple of weeks previously, and how he'd looked at her with such awe. She *was* brave. She'd confronted those men. She hadn't hidden. She hadn't run away.

She dabbed some foundation onto her face and rubbed it into her skin, blending away the last residue of the bruising and the dark shadows beneath her eyes. Then she applied her trusty kohl, and as her eyes grew larger and more catlike, she felt her spirits lift a little. It was the first time she'd put on make-up since the beating, and it was comforting to see her old face again. She painted her lips ruby red and blotted them on a piece of tissue.

'I *am* brave,' she whispered to her reflection.

Thanks to her convalescence and her mother's ridiculous ban on Adela coming to their apartment, Izabel had had a lot of thinking time and she'd come to the conclusion that once she was better, she was going to double down on her efforts to help rid Poland of the fascists. There was a strange kind of freedom in having something as precious as being able to have children stolen from her, a liberating sense of having less to lose.

She glanced at the little statuette of Saint Brigid on her dressing table and whispered, 'Please give me strength.' Then she stood up and smoothed down her dress. It was her favourite red dress, which used to hug her curves but now hung looser thanks to her loss of appetite over the past few weeks.

She came out of her room to find Kasper loitering in the hallway.

'I hate Papa,' he said, by way of greeting.

She heard the low drone of their father's voice coming from the kitchen. 'What's he done now?'

'He wants us to move. I don't want to move.' He put his hands on his hips and pouted. 'And I don't want to move into someone else's house!'

Izabel frowned. 'Slow down. What do you mean, someone else's house?'

'He said that the Germans are making some of the Jewish people move out of their homes. He said we can move into one of them if we want.'

Izabel shuddered. She hadn't found any evidence of a link between her father and the Germans since discovering the name in his wallet, and when she'd pressed Kasper further, he hadn't been able to offer any tangible proof. Now all her worst fears came flooding back. 'But why would we want to do that?'

'He said they're rich people homes.' He sighed and stuck out his bottom lip. 'I don't want to live in a rich people home. I like my bedroom. I don't want to leave my friends.'

'I don't either,' she said, tousling his hair. 'Let me see if I can talk some sense into him.'

She went into the kitchen to find her father grinning like the cat that had got the cream.

'But what if the family who owned the apartment want to

come back at some point in the future?' her mother was asking, as she filled his cup with tea.

'They won't be coming back,' her father replied. 'They're Jewish.'

Izabel's chest tightened. 'What's that supposed to mean?'

'They're all going to end up in the ghetto,' he replied casually before looking back at Krysia. 'We'll have to move out soon anyway. You've seen where they're building the walls. We're right in the middle of where the ghetto's going to be.' He picked up his newspaper and shook it open, as if declaring the conversation over.

Krysia nodded. 'Well, if you're sure there's no way they'll be able to come back for their property.'

'Is that all that bothers you?' Izabel asked, her voice rising.

Her mother stared at her blankly.

'Don't you care about the people who are having their homes stolen from them, about what's going to happen to them?'

Krysia raised her perfectly plucked eyebrows and sighed. 'I can't believe you're still defending them after what happened to you.'

'Well, I can't believe you're still so incredibly stupid!' Izabel snapped back.

'Don't talk to your mother like that,' her father muttered from behind his paper.

'Why not?' Izabel glowered at the paper. As usual, the headline was about the German advances, above a picture of Hitler. 'It's no worse than the way you talk to her.'

The paper lowered an inch and her father glared at her over the top before disappearing behind it again.

'Izabel!' Krysia exclaimed.

'It wasn't Jewish people who did this to me, Mama, it was Polish thugs, who probably go to mass in the same church as you.'

'Don't talk like that!' Krysia looked at the wooden carving of Jesus on a cross hanging on the wall and crossed herself.

'Why not? It's true!' She stared at her father's paper, her heart pounding. 'How can you agree with what the Germans are doing?'

The newspaper remained still and, behind it, her father remained silent.

Feeling nauseous, Izabel marched over to the door. 'You make me sick,' she muttered.

'Izabel, come back here this minute!' Krysia screeched.

But Izabel ignored her and marched from the room and out of the apartment, trembling with anger.

Azriel stood in the doorway waiting, his cap pulled down low. He knew he was taking a huge risk loitering about so early in the morning – it was the press gangs' favourite time to swoop – but he had to try to see Izabel. In the four weeks since she'd been attacked, he'd seen neither hide nor hair of her and he couldn't stand it any longer. Adela might have resigned herself to Izabel's mother's ridiculous ban on their friendship, but he couldn't take another day of not knowing how she was. So, for the last four days, he'd taken to hanging around outside her building first thing in the morning in the hope that she was well enough to return to work, and he'd catch her en route.

As if on cue, the door to her apartment building swung open and Azriel stepped back into the shadows. His heart sank as a man in a suit strode out, swiftly followed by several women holding shopping baskets, on their way to join the queues for rations no doubt. But still no Izabel. He was about to give up when something in him told him to wait for one more minute. Then the door opened and Izabel walked out. Or, rather, she hobbled out. His heart twinged as he watched her limping slightly, clearly still in pain.

He quickly checked the coast was clear before running across the road to her.

'About time, I've been waiting here for days,' he said.

She gasped in shock. 'What are you doing here?'

'What do you think? I had to see you.' He gently touched her arm. 'How are you?'

Her eyes sparked with indignation. 'I hate my parents! They are the most selfish, ignorant people to have ever walked God's green earth. Even a slug has more compassion.'

'Oh.' He hadn't been expecting this tirade and wasn't exactly sure how to respond.

'I honestly think they took the wrong baby home from the hospital when I was born, and right now there's a family out there somewhere with two loving and kind parents – and a strong, intelligent mother, beautiful on the inside and out – who are looking at their selfish, mean daughter and scratching their heads saying, "Where did we go wrong?" But they didn't go wrong at all because I am their true daughter and I've been trapped in the wrong life with the wrong family for all these years.'

'Oh,' Azriel said again, still utterly lost for words.

'If you can't say anything other than "oh", can you at least kiss me?' she demanded.

'Oh, uh, yes...' He glanced up and down the street anxiously, but before he could do anything, she'd grabbed him by the hand and pulled him into a doorway.

'Kiss me, please,' she urged. 'I need something good to happen to me, or I fear I'm going to give up on life completely.'

He stared at her for a moment, then started to laugh, partly at the theatrics of what she was saying, and partly out of relief that, despite what she'd been through, she clearly hadn't lost her old spitfire ways. He put his arm around her, pulled her close and kissed her.

Adela sat at the kitchen table feeling leaden with sadness. She could hear the men outside putting the finishing touches to the wall that now blocked the street. It was around nine feet tall with rolls of barbed wire on top, and watching it go up she'd felt another wall building around her heart, higher and higher, until she felt as if she could no longer breathe. She was missing Izabel so much, she felt a physical ache, and even though Jaski had remained resolutely upbeat in the face of the ghetto being prepared, she could tell that he was worried too. She put her head in her hands and began to cry.

'*Moj skarbe!*'

A voice jolted her from her tears and, at first, Adela thought she must have been dreaming, but she looked up to see Izabel in the doorway, Azriel standing behind her, grinning from ear to ear.

'Why are you crying?' Izabel asked, hurrying over.

Adela leapt to her feet and, in a second, they were hugging each other.

'What are you doing here?' she murmured into Izabel's shoulder.

'Azriel came and rescued me from the clutches of my evil parents,' she replied. 'Can you believe it? They're planning to move away.'

'What?' Adela pulled back to look at her, horrified.

Izabel nodded.

'Not out of Warsaw?' Adela was unable to keep the panic from her voice.

'No, but it might as well be.' Izabel sighed. 'My father says we'll need to leave because of the stupid ghetto.'

'We'll destroy their stupid ghetto, you'll see,' Azriel said angrily.

'Oh, I hope so!' Izabel exclaimed, stepping towards him and resting her head on his shoulder. She gave Adela a weak smile. 'I've missed you so much.'

'Not as much as I've missed you!' Adela exclaimed.

They all sat down at the table and Adela took Izabel's hand. 'How are you? Kasper said you'd had some terrible injuries.'

Izabel grimaced. 'Yes, but I'm fine now.'

'Are you sure?' Azriel took her other hand.

There was a moment's silence. 'The doctor told me I won't be able to have children,' Izabel muttered, her gaze fixed on the table.

'Oh, *moj skarbe*, I'm so sorry,' Adela cried. Ever since they were little, Izabel had talked about the four children she was going to have. She'd even chosen names for them. Adela had never taken Izabel's baby talk all that seriously, but in the light of this revelation, it was heartbreaking. 'I love you,' she said, lifting Izabel's hand to her lips and kissing it.

'And so do I,' said Azriel, doing the same.

Izabel looked at him anxiously. 'Even though...'

'I love you,' he said again, firmly.

'I thought...' She broke off.

'You mustn't let those thugs break your spirit,' Adela said. 'You're like a beautiful lark. You mustn't allow them to clip your wings.'

'That's really lovely,' Izabel said tearily.

Adela blushed. 'It's actually something that Jaski once said to me, but it applies to you just the same.'

Izabel looked at Adela and Azriel and smiled at them both gratefully. 'I wish you were my family!' she exclaimed.

'We are!' Adela replied.

'I have to admit, I'm glad you're not my family,' Azriel said with a grin and Izabel giggled.

The three of them gripped hands even tighter.

'What if I have to move away?' Izabel said quietly. 'What if we aren't able to see each other anymore?'

Azriel cleared his throat. 'We can still stay connected.'

'How?' Izabel asked.

'We're going to need people on the other side of the wall.' He leaned closer and lowered his voice. 'We'll need things smuggled into the ghetto. Food and... weapons.' He clasped her hand in both of his. 'That's if you want to help? I wouldn't blame you if you didn't – after everything that happened.'

'Of course I do!' Izabel exclaimed.

Adela looked at her, concerned. 'Are you sure? You've been through so much.'

'Exactly!' Izabel exclaimed. 'All the more reason to fight back.' She looked at Azriel. 'Thank you! I was so worried I wouldn't be able to do anything to help you if I moved away. You've given me a purpose again, a reason to keep the fires of hope in my heart burning. And a way to retaliate against my stupid, idiotic parents – or the parents who took me home from the hospital after I was born, anyway.'

'What does that mean?' Adela said with a frown.

Azriel laughed. 'Don't ask!'

'I love you, Rubinsteins,' Izabel declared, grinning at them both.

The poignancy of the moment caused a lump to form in Adela's throat. It was so wonderful to see her beloved friend again, and to hear her back to her normal melodramatic self. But it made the fact that they would soon be separated even more heartbreaking. 'We need to seal this memory in our minds, like a scene from a movie,' she said, 'so we can replay it when things get tough. And let's pray that one day the war will be over, and we'll all be sitting around a table together again.'

'Yes!' Izabel cried and Azriel nodded.

Adela looked at them both and pictured a tiny camera in

her mind, panning around to capture the moment forever. But for some reason she couldn't shake a terrible sense of foreboding, and as her eyes filled with tears, the camera lens became blurred.

27

Adela stared at her arithmetic textbook and sighed. She was supposed to be planning a lesson on angles, but try as she might, she just couldn't concentrate, and the numbers and words kept blurring in front of her eyes like smudges.

'Are you all right?' Jaski asked, looking up from his side of the desk.

'Yes... no.' She put the book down. It had been almost a month since Izabel broke the news about moving to another part of Warsaw and now the fateful day had arrived. 'Izabel will be leaving about now, and I can't bear to think about it. I wish...'

Jaski took his glasses off. 'What?'

'I wish I'd gone to say goodbye to her. She told me not to but...'

'Go,' Jaski said firmly.

'But my lesson?'

'Your lesson can wait; this is more important.'

She gave him a grateful smile and stood up. 'Thank you.'

'There's nothing more important than the people we love, and letting them know that we love them,' he said softly. 'Especially now.'

She nodded and walked around the desk to kiss the top of his head. 'I love you,' she said, then grabbed her jacket and bag and hurried from the room.

As she raced through the city streets, all she could see were processions of people carrying all their worldly goods – or as many as they were able to carry – some in suitcases, some in wheelbarrows and carts and even prams, loaded with teetering piles of belongings. The processions were flowing in two directions – the Jewish moving into the designated ghetto area, and the non-Jewish moving out. She passed a street that had now been blocked off by the wall and shuddered. It felt surreal to think that there would soon come a time when she wouldn't be allowed beyond the wall, when the gates that were also being built would be locked shut. A feeling of claustrophobia squeezed at her ribcage, making it difficult to breathe.

Don't think about that, just think about Izabel, she told herself as she finally arrived at her friend's street. *Please, please, please don't let them have left already*, she silently implored.

She saw Izabel's father's car parked outside their apartment building and breathed a sigh of relief. But then, to her horror, the car rumbled into life and started to pull away from the kerb.

'No!' she cried. 'Izabel!' She raced forwards and managed to bang on the boot. The car came to an abrupt halt and the back door opened and Izabel burst out.

'*Moj skarbe!* You came!' she cried.

'I know you didn't want me to, but I had to,' Adela gasped, breathless.

'I'm so glad you did.' Izabel grabbed her in a hug and squeezed her tight. 'I love you so much,' she murmured in Adela's ear. 'And don't forget, we were meant to find each other when we were eight years old, and we'll find each other again.'

Adela smiled as she remembered Izabel's childhood theory about them being destined to meet. 'Yes, we will,' she replied firmly, although she churned with dread and fear inside.

There was an angry toot on the car horn and Izabel let go of her with a sigh. 'I have to go.'

'I know.'

Izabel kissed her on the cheek then got back into the car.

Adela watched as the car pulled off, Izabel's face pressed to the rear window gazing at her sorrowfully. 'Goodbye, *moj skarbe*,' she whispered, waving forlornly, until the car disappeared from view.

Rather than go straight back to the orphanage after seeing Izabel off, Adela decided to call in at home first as she was craving one of her mother's hugs. But as soon as she opened the door, she heard raised voices. Azriel and Leopold were standing glowering at each other in the middle of the shop. Estera was watching on from behind the counter, clearly distraught. Adela's heart sank as she saw that Azriel was holding a suitcase.

'How could you even think that I'd want to do such a thing,' Azriel said to Leopold. 'Don't you know me at all?'

'No, clearly I don't,' Leopold replied with a heavy sigh.

'What's wrong?' Adela asked.

'Papa wants me to join the police,' Azriel muttered.

'What police?' Adela stared at Leopold, confused.

'The new Jewish police,' Leopold replied. 'The *Judenrat* have been asked to employ a police force of three thousand young men. I was trying to help your brother and get him a job that will keep him safe.'

'But I don't understand.' Adela frowned. 'Jews aren't allowed to be police officers.'

'It's for the ghetto,' Azriel replied. 'Working for the Germans.'

'*No*, working for the *Judenrat*,' Leopold corrected.

'Who work for the Germans.' Azriel's voice grew louder. He put down his suitcase and glared at Leopold. 'I might be your son, but thankfully I didn't inherit your ability to be a traitor to your people.'

'Please, stop this!' Estera cried, but to no avail.

'I'm not a traitor; I'm trying to take care of my people.' Leopold's voice began to rise.

'What about me!' Azriel cried and even though he sounded angry, Adela could tell from the waver in his voice that he was close to tears. 'I'm your son. Why can't you be there for me?'

'Because of the path you've chosen,' Leopold replied. He gave a sad laugh as he shook his head. 'You accuse me of pandering to the Germans, but you're the one who has more in common with them.'

A stunned silence fell upon the room.

Azriel stared at Leopold, clearly horrified. 'What did you say?'

Estera touched Leopold's arm. 'Tell him you didn't mean that.'

'But I did!' Leopold cried, keeping his gaze fixed upon Azriel. 'You've chosen a path of violence, son, and I can never, ever condone that.'

Azriel's face drained of colour. 'Are you saying you think I'm like a Nazi?'

Adela felt sick. She'd never seen them both so angry and upset. 'Please,' she implored. 'Don't you see, this is what the Germans want. They want us fighting with each other.'

But Leopold ignored her. 'You have chosen a path of violence,' he repeated to Azriel, his voice calmer but his expression deadly serious.

'I have *chosen* to fight back against our oppressors,' Azriel replied, his voice taut with anger. 'But don't worry. You will never have to see me again. I should never have come back here in the first place.'

'Don't say that!' Estera cried, clutching at his arm, but Azriel shook her off.

'Papa, stop him, please!' Adela pleaded as Azriel picked up his case and walked out of the door.

Leopold looked at her sadly and shook his head, and a tear trickled down his lined cheek.

Izabel sat on the edge of the bed and looked around the room, tears burning her eyes. The previous occupant appeared to have been a teenage girl. The walls were still covered with posters of famous actors and singers. A large oak wardrobe framed with intricate carvings stood in the corner of the room, with a matching dresser and chest of drawers on the other walls. Next to the window was a bookshelf. The shelves were still full apart from a few gaps. Izabel pictured the girl who'd lived there quickly grabbing her favourite books to take with her to the ghetto. Her heart contracted as she thought of Adela. She would have been heartbroken if she'd had to leave any of her beloved books behind.

Her father had brought them to the kind of apartment building Izabel had dreamed of living in as a teenager. With its ornate stone façade and marble-floored hallway, it was the kind of home she imagined a Hollywood starlet inhabiting. But being there now only made her feel sick. How had her father managed to get a place this grand? Surely these kinds of homes would be taken by the Germans... or their friends.

She heard her father's laugh drifting up from the pavement outside and her stomach contracted. How could he be so callous? How could he steal another person's home without a shred of remorse? Then she heard another man's voice – a German man – and her blood froze. Surely it couldn't be.

She crept over to the window and peeped out from behind the plush velvet curtain. The apartment was only on the third floor so there was no mistaking what she was seeing. She let out a gasp and stepped back out of view, clasping her hands to her chest. Her father was standing there laughing and talking to Dieter.

28

Adela sat at the dinner table, trying to eat her mouthful of bread, but her throat was so tight, she was afraid that if she tried to swallow, she'd choke. She glanced up at her mother, who wasn't even attempting to eat, but staring glumly at her plate instead. Beside her, Leopold stirred his bowl of soup, looking equally distracted.

It had been a month since Izabel had moved away and Azriel had left, and in that time, a terrible sadness had descended upon the family home, eating into the very fabric of the apartment like a dry rot. Thankfully, Azriel hadn't gone far, moving in with one of his friends from the Bund, and Adela still saw him regularly, but Estera remained distraught. Blaming Leopold for what had happened, she now barely spoke at all.

'So, the Germans have announced that all Jews in Warsaw have to have moved into the ghetto by next month,' Leopold said, breaking the silence.

Adela finally swallowed her mouthful of bread. 'How will we all fit? It's barely more than a square mile. It's already feeling so overcrowded.'

Leopold put his spoon down and cleared his throat. 'There's a new law stating that every room in the ghetto has to house four people.' He looked at Estera. 'I was thinking that my sisters could move into the spare bedroom.'

Estera frowned. 'What spare bedroom?'

'Azriel's old room.'

'But what if he wants to move back home?' she exclaimed.

'I can't see that happening,' Leopold said gravely.

'No!' Estera cried. 'Because you drove him away!'

Leopold sighed. 'I didn't drive him away. I offered him a job.'

As they continued arguing, the tightness in Adela's throat spread down to her chest until she felt as if she could barely breathe. It had got to the point where she dreaded coming home and couldn't wait to seek refuge in the relative calm of the orphanage. She hated the Germans for doing this to her family, but she couldn't take any more. She pushed her plate away and stood up from the table, her decision made. Her parents were so busy arguing, they didn't even notice.

'I'm leaving,' she said, her voice trembling.

Finally, they stopped bickering and looked up at her.

'What do you mean?' Estera asked.

'I'm moving into the orphanage. You can use my room to house other people too.'

'No!' Estera cried.

'It's all right, Mama, I'll come and see you every day. I just...' She paused, trying to find the words that would cause the least upset. The last thing she wanted to do was hurt Estera. 'It's just easier for me to do my job if I'm living there. That way, I can teach the older children after curfew. And I'd feel happy knowing my bedroom was being used to give another family a home.'

Estera's eyes filled with tears, but she nodded.

Leopold took the napkin from his lap and stood up. 'Is this really why you want to leave?' he asked softly. He'd always been able to read Adela so well and she felt a wistful pang inside.

'Yes,' she whispered, hoping he couldn't tell that it was only a half-truth. 'And it's only until this craziness is over,' she attempted to say breezily, but her voice came out way too shrill.

Estera stood up and she and Leopold moved in front of her.

'You promise you'll visit,' Estera said, her voice breaking.

'Of course!'

'And let us know if you need anything?' Leopold added.

'Absolutely. Thank you.'

They both opened their arms to her and as she stepped into their embrace, it felt as if her heart was cracking in two. It had been a long time since she been hugged by them both like this, and although it felt comforting, it also reminded her of all they'd lost.

'I'll go and pack my things,' she said, her voice barely more than a whisper.

It was only when Adela arrived back at the orphanage that it dawned on her that Jaski might not agree with her moving in. She'd been so desperate to get out of the family home with its creeping sadness that she hadn't properly thought it through.

She let herself in and walked down the hall. The communal rooms were steeped in darkness and all was quiet, apart from the low murmur of chatter coming from the older children's dormitories. She saw light spilling out from the slightly open door of Jaski's office and her pulse quickened. She cringed at the thought of how foolish she'd feel if he said no to her moving in.

Taking a deep breath, Adela pushed the door open. Jaski was sitting at his desk, his head bowed and a frown on his face. She felt a pang of concern. He was always so resolutely positive, but every so often, when she caught him in an unguarded moment like this, it was as if his cheery mask had slipped.

She coughed softly to let him know she was there.

He looked up and his expression instantly changed to one of surprise, and then delight. 'Adela! What are you doing back here?' His gaze moved down to her suitcase, and he suddenly looked worried. 'What's happened?' He stood up and came over.

'I can't live at home anymore,' she said, fighting the urge to sob.

'Why not?' He took her case from her and placed it on the floor.

'My parents need the rooms for other people to live in – people who've been sent to live in the ghetto.'

'Oh, I see.'

'And I-I...'

'Yes?' He looked at her with such love and concern, it almost caused her to unravel.

'I would rather live here,' she whispered, looking down at the floor. 'With you.' She closed her eyes, preparing for the embarrassment of his rejection, but instead she felt her hands taking hers.

'I would like that very much,' he said softly.

She looked back at him, her eyes filling with tears.

'I love you, Adela.' He pulled her into his embrace, and just like that, her pain was transformed into a warm glow of relief.

Izabel stood in her father's study and looked around. Her parents were out at dinner and Kasper was staying at a friend's. It was the first time she'd been at home alone since they'd moved into the apartment, and she was determined to capitalise on it. She needed to find out how her father knew Dieter and what he might have done for the Germans to have been rewarded with such a plush home. She hadn't seen Dieter since he'd given her the lingerie. After she'd been attacked by the thugs, she'd managed to steer clear of his usual haunts, and as he'd always been too self-interested to ask her where she lived or worked, he hadn't been able to track her down. But now it appeared that he knew her father, it felt as if a net was tightening.

She sat down behind the polished wooden desk. It perfectly demonstrated her father's need for order, with its row of pots containing pencils, pens and a ruler. Even the blotter was neat and tidy, with one perfectly round ink stain in the middle. His mother-of-pearl-embossed cigar box had been placed on one side, directly opposite a framed family photograph on the other. Izabel looked at the picture and grimaced at how staged it had been, with their pristine outfits and rictus grins, and poor Kasper forced to wear some kind of ridiculous sailor boy outfit. Right before they had arrived at the photographer's studio, her mother had accused her father of having an affair with a clerk at the bank where he worked. It was the only time Izabel had seen her mother angry at her father. But as soon as the photographer had posed them all, set the flashbulb and told them to 'smile', they had returned to the ridiculous charade.

Izabel sighed and pulled open one of the deep desk drawers. It was full of files. No doubt containing bank business, but what if one of them hid something else? She took a file out and opened it beneath the light of the desk lamp. It contained a wad of letters, most of them from other branches of the bank, and all equally tedious. She put the file back and pulled out another. What if she'd got it wrong and her father wasn't working for the Germans at all? He might have met Dieter at one of the clubs he frequented. She shuddered. As much as she didn't want her father to be in cahoots with the Germans, the thought that he could have come across Izabel in a bar with Dieter made her feel physically sick.

She opened the file. It contained a large envelope. On the front, her father had written, *For the attention of: Reinhard Muller*. She shivered, wondering what might be inside. She pulled out a sheaf of papers and she heard something jingle. She tipped the envelope upside down and a bag fell out. It was made from black canvas with a drawstring pulled tight at the top. She loosened the string and held the bag upside down and a pile of small silver keys fell onto the desk.

Turning her attention back to the papers, Izabel noticed that each page had a person's name at the top above a list of items and the name and address of a different branch of her father's bank. She quickly flicked through, looking at the names. Bernstein, Abramovich, Rubinstein. Her heart skipped a beat, and she held the page closer to the light. It was for a Saul not a Leopold.

She scanned the other papers. They all seemed to be Jewish names. Then she looked at the lists on each page, all written in her father's immaculately neat handwriting. They were lists of belongings – items of jewellery mostly – with their value denoted beside them. Izabel frowned. Why would her father be listing this information for a German?

As she made her way through the papers, she noticed something else. At the top of each page, her father had written a number in pencil. She looked back at the keys. Each one of them had a number on the fob, corresponding with the numbers on the list. She knew she'd seen keys like these before somewhere, but where? And then she remembered. Her father had a key just like this for a safety deposit box at the bank. Her mother kept her most expensive string of pearls there and a pocket watch she'd inherited from her grandfather.

Izabel put the keys next to the papers and the envelope, as if assembling evidence. Was this how her father had got the apartment? Was he telling the Germans where they could find Jewish treasures stored away in different branches of the bank? Her stomach churned as the reality of her suspicions began to sink in. While she had been working to help the Jewish people, her own father had been helping the Germans steal their property.

29

Azriel joined the crowds waiting by the gate in the fence. A biting wind whipped along Żelazna Street, piercing through his coat and the three layers he was wearing underneath. The ghetto had now been officially closed to the outside world for a week. Even though they'd all known it would be happening for a very long time, he still felt a sickening dread in the pit of his stomach. On the other side of the fence, a tram trundled past along Chłodna Street. Beyond that lay the other part of the ghetto.

Chłodna Street was such an important thoroughfare between east and west Warsaw, the Germans had decided that it should be excluded from the ghetto, so now they were in the bizarre situation of having an artery of freedom cutting right through the heart of their prison. As well as it being a crushing reminder of all they had lost, it was also a huge inconvenience. If you wanted to get from one part of the ghetto to the other, like Azriel did now, you had to wait for the set times the guards would open the gates to let people cross.

He looked at the people hurrying by along Chłodna and felt a sharp stab of envy at their privilege. Some of them kept their heads down, refusing to look at the prison either side of them, but others couldn't help gawping, making Azriel feel as if they were animals in a zoo.

You're not going to meekly accept this new way of life, he reminded himself. But in that moment, it was hard to feel optimistic about the Bund's chances of fighting back. He thought of Izabel, somewhere on the other side of the fence, and his heart contracted. Before the ghetto had been sealed off, he'd put her in touch with some of his Resistance contacts on the other side and she'd promised to help smuggle food and weapons in to him. But as much as he was glad to still feel that connection with her, it also terrified him. After what had happened to her during the pogrom, he'd never forgive himself if she came to more harm while trying to help him.

Izabel boarded the tram and bought a ticket from the conductor. After the Germans had banned Jews from riding the normal trams and forced them to ride in their own segregated trolley cars, Izabel had waged her own one-woman protest, refusing to set foot in one until the law changed back. But the new apartment was miles away from her work and it was bitterly cold, so she'd decided to acquiesce. It wasn't as if her boycott of the trams was going to change anything, she tried telling herself as she made her way along the aisle. There were far more important things she could and would do to help the Resistance.

She shivered as she thought of the enormity of what was to come, and the risks they'd all be taking. She was about to sit down when she felt someone grip her shoulder from behind. Instantly, she froze, filling with dread. It couldn't be – could it?

'Izabel?' The sound of Dieter's voice turned her blood to ice. She took a moment to try to wipe the horror from her face before turning around.

'Oh my goodness, what a delightful surprise!' she exclaimed, clutching her hands to her chest.

'I thought it was you – I'd know those legs anywhere,' he said, with a smirk. 'Where the hell have you been?'

'I was in an accident,' she replied as the tram began to move. Thankfully, she'd prepared for this moment, knowing that sooner or later their paths would probably cross.

'Sit,' he barked, nodding to one of the seats.

She slid in, her spirits sinking.

'What kind of accident?'

'Automobile. I went to my aunt's apartment to convalesce. She lives on the ground floor. I'd injured my leg and broke a few ribs.'

Anyone else would surely express concern at this point, but not Dieter. 'And you weren't able to get a message to me?' He frowned.

'No. I was in pretty bad shape.' She tried not to let her indignation show, but he truly was a contemptible human being.

'You seem all right now.' He looked her up and down, his gaze lingering on her chest.

'I'm almost back to full health,' she said, and then, gritting her teeth, 'So, how fortuitous that we should meet again today. It's as if it was fated to happen.'

He nodded tersely. 'I hope you still have the gift I bought you.'

Her mind was blank for a moment, and then she remembered the lingerie set. 'Of course,' she cried, feeling sick to her stomach.

'Good. Because I didn't pay all that money not to see it on you.'

'And now you'll be able to,' she replied, staring out of the window, praying to Saint Brigid to fill her with grit.

Azriel pulled up his coat collar and stamped his feet against the cold. Surely they wouldn't be made to wait much longer.

He heard one of the guards yell and turned to see him pointing his gun at an elderly rabbi.

'We need some entertainment while we wait,' the guard sneered. 'Why don't you dance for us, old man.'

The rabbi smiled gently, looking confused.

'I said, dance!' the guard screamed, slapping the rabbi across the head with the back of his hand.

Azriel clenched his fists tightly in his coat pockets. He knew it could mean instant death if he did anything to help the rabbi, but how could he stand by and watch such cruelty?

'Dance!' the guard yelled again, and so the old man began to dance, whilst humming under his breath.

A woman standing beside Azriel let out a little wail and turned away. Azriel felt overwhelmed by a sickening combination of rage and hopelessness. How much more of this were they expected to endure?

A man jostled past him, towards the rabbi, who was still dancing. 'You bastards are animals!' he yelled at the guard, causing Azriel's skin to prickle with goosebumps. This man must know that it was pointless to challenge the soldiers, not to mention incredibly dangerous. He watched, motionless, as the man approached the fence.

'Halt!' the guard shouted.

'No!' the man yelled back with a wild look in his eyes. His hair was greasy and dishevelled and his clothes shabby. He threw himself at the fence and began to scramble up.

The crowd fell completely silent and still. The only sound came from the rabbi, who was still singing under his breath as he danced.

'Get down!' the guard yelled, pulling his gun.

Azriel held his breath.

The rabbi started singing louder and dancing faster, as if he was trying to block out the horror about to happen.

'Be quiet!' the guard yelled, spinning round, and pointing the gun at the rabbi. There was a deafening crack as he shot him in the head.

'No!' the woman next to Azriel cried. 'No!'

'Shhh,' Azriel whispered, gripping her arm, terrified that she'd be shot next.

But the guard had turned back to the fence. The man had reached the top and he flung himself down onto Chłodna Street, landing in a heap on the ground. A tram was trundling right towards him.

The guard raised his pistol and took aim as the man began scrambling up. Another piercing crack rang out as the guard shot the man in the chest.

Izabel jumped at the sound of a shot. 'What was that?' she asked, looking out of the window.

The tram jerked to a halt and Dieter leapt to his feet, taking his gun from his holster. 'Stay there!' he barked at her before making his way to the door.

Izabel looked back out of the window. They'd stopped right by the ghetto fence, and a crowd of people were waiting there. All of them were looking, aghast, at something in front of the tram, out of her view.

She heard Dieter calling something, then she saw a couple of German guards come through the gate onto the street. In marked contrast to the watching crowd, they were both laughing. She looked down into her lap, feeling overwhelmed with sorrow. Somewhere trapped behind that fence were Azriel and Adela. What if she never saw them again? It all seemed so helpless. *She* felt so helpless. Then something compelled her to look up again, and she saw a movement on the other side of the fence – a man jostling through the crowd towards her. When he drew level with her window on the tram, he pulled down his coat collar and took off his cap.

'Azriel!' she gasped.

His face broke into that beautiful smile and for a couple of seconds they held each other's gaze, and she felt a jolt of love pass right through her, restoring her hope. And she knew in that moment that she would never give up. She *could* never give up. She would do whatever it took to help free her beloved Rubinsteins.

Izabel put her hand to the window and Azriel raised his. Although they were a few feet apart and separated by glass, it was as if she could feel his hand pressing against hers.

I love you, she mouthed, as the tram rumbled back into life.

I love you, he mouthed back.

Dieter got back onto the tram and said something to the driver and as he walked along the aisle towards her, Izabel felt a knot of determination tighten inside of her. She would do whatever it took to help free Azriel and Adela. *Whatever it took.*

PART TWO

SPRING 1942, WARSAW

30

Izabel placed her hand on Kasper's thin shoulder. 'Not yet,' she whispered as she peered out from the darkened doorway of the store. Two German soldiers were standing at the far end of the street and a flare of light shone in the gathering gloom as one of them struck a match to light their cigarettes.

Kasper fidgeted beneath her hand. Despite having done this regularly for over a year now, he still got nervous, and who could blame him? He was usually so full of bravado, Izabel had to keep reminding herself that he was only ten years old. Or almost eleven, as he liked to tell her whenever she expressed doubt about him working for the Resistance.

The soldiers finally continued on their way, disappearing around the corner, leaving a cloud of smoke in their wake.

'Now,' Izabel said, and they both hurried over to the wall running across the street. Checking once more that the coast was clear, she glanced at her watch and gave a whistle and they both stood motionless and waited.

After a beat of silence, a whistle echoed back from the other side. Izabel felt a shiver of delight as she thought of who it was.

'Go!' she whispered and Kasper dropped to his knees and

began wriggling through a narrow hole at the bottom of the wall that had been left there to drain water out of the ghetto. Izabel stood right in front of him, trying to block anyone from seeing his legs. Oh, if only she were small enough to wriggle through to the other side, she thought wistfully.

She heard another whistle and she crouched down and pulled Kasper's legs to help him back out. He reappeared covered in dust and grime which she tried to brush off, but he wriggled from her grasp, not liking to be fussed over.

'Was he there? Did you see him?' she asked.

'Of course.'

'And did you give him the notes?'

'Yes.'

She breathed a sigh of relief and placed her hand on the wall, thinking of Azriel on the other side and wondering if he was doing the same, or if he'd already run back to safety. After all, if he got caught smuggling food into the ghetto, the punishment would be certain death. It wouldn't be much better for her and Kaspar either. She quickly pushed the thought away. When her fearless little brother had found out what she was doing for Azriel and the Jewish Resistance he'd insisted on helping, leaving her constantly oscillating between feelings of love and gratitude, and terror that he might get hurt.

'Come on,' she said, grabbing his arm. 'Let's go.'

Then she heard someone whistling a tune from the other side of the wall and she wanted to cry for joy. It was the chorus from 'Nisim, Nisim!', a favourite song of hers from Cabaret Warsaw.

'Miracles from heaven,' she sang along. 'Miracles without end!' And her heart felt as if it might explode with gratitude for this precious moment of connection.

'I love you!' she cried. Then, to her horror, she saw a soldier approaching on the other side of the street. Thinking quickly, she grabbed Kasper in an embrace. 'You are the best little brother!' she said loudly. 'I love you so much.' For an awful moment, she thought Azriel might call something back and the soldier would hear, but, thankfully, all remained quiet on the other side of the wall and the soldier walked by.

'He gave me something for you,' Kasper said as they hurried back to the apartment building. They'd been living there for nearly two years now, but Izabel still viewed the apartment as stolen property.

'What was it?' she asked excitedly as they entered the foyer.

He opened his palm to reveal a piece of paper folded into a tiny square. She took it from him and tucked it into her pocket, to read once she was back in the privacy of her bedroom – her *stolen* bedroom.

'Thank you,' she said to Kaspar. They got into the tiny lift and she pulled the lattice door shut.

'That's OK, just don't forget my toffees tomorrow,' he replied gruffly.

'Of course not. I'm going to get you as many toffees as I can find.' She put her arm around his shoulders and pulled him to her as the lift juddered its way up to the fourth floor. The only good thing to have come out of the past eighteen months since the ghetto was sealed off was that she'd become even closer to Kasper. She was in awe of how brave he was and eternally grateful that he was able to provide her with a link to Azriel and Adela via the hole in the wall. It was the only contact Izabel had with Adela and Azriel now.

Of course, they weren't the only ones smuggling things to loved ones. Every day, food was smuggled under or over the wall or thrown from the trams that still ran along Chłodna Street, right through the heart of the ghetto.

As soon as they got inside the apartment, she went to her bedroom, sat down on the bed and carefully unfolded the piece of paper. *Fishermen need rods*, it said in Azriel's writing and then, beneath it, *URGENTLY*.

Izabel's heart began to race as she thought of the coded messages they'd come up with in the days before the ghetto had been closed off and what this one meant. It was the first time it had been used and reading it filled her with a mixture of excitement and anxiety. The Bund needed weapons – urgently – and Azriel wanted her to try to get some for him.

Adela peered around the door of the youngest children's dormitory and checked the rows of beds for any sign of unrest. Recently, several of the younger children had been having nightmares and a couple had started wetting the bed in their sleep. She and Jaski and the rest of the orphanage staff tried to shield them from the growing suffering in the ghetto, but this was proving harder and harder to achieve. The other day, the Germans had shot a man right outside the orphanage during lunch and his dying screams had echoed through the open windows and around the dining hall. Jaski had tried to make light of it, saying that it was just a rare bird screeching for its lunch, but Adela could tell from the children's shell-shocked faces that they didn't believe him. Then one of them had asked if the Germans were going to shoot them too, and a deathly silence fell upon the room.

She heard footsteps behind her and turned to see Jaski approaching, clad in his favourite dark green suit.

'Are they asleep?' he whispered.

'Yes, finally,' she replied.

'Excellent, because you and I are going out.' His eyes gleamed with excitement.

'Where to?'

'Femina, to see a concert. The Jewish Symphonic Orchestra are playing there.'

Her spirits instantly lifted, but then she thought of the children. 'But what if one of the children wakes in the night? What if they need us?'

He took her hand in his. 'The nurses are here. They can take care of them.' His smile faded. 'We need this, Adela. We need to be reminded of the wonders that humans are capable of.'

She saw instantly that he was right. They'd be no good to anyone if they allowed the heaviness to crush them.

The Femina Theatre had been a cinema in the days before the ghetto and Adela and Izabel had been to see many a film there. As she and Jaski entered the foyer, she thought of Izabel and wondered how she was doing. She missed her friend so much, it was like a dull ache that wouldn't go away. The worst thing about it was knowing that they were still in the same city. Sometimes, when she was close to the wall, Adela would swear that she could smell Izabel's magnolia perfume, and she'd imagine her friend walking parallel to her on the other side. The thought was comforting and heartbreaking in equal measure.

She followed Jaski through to the auditorium, her mind bombarded with memories of her and Izabel taking the exact same route, the very same carpet still carrying the ghostly imprint of their footsteps. As they took their seats, she thought she might begin to cry, the sense of loss felt so overwhelming. But then the orchestra began to play. Adela closed her eyes and let the music soak into her.

Ever since the ghetto had been sealed off from the outside world, the Femina had been reopened as a theatre, somewhere for all the actors, dancers and musicians trapped inside to continue to make and perform their art. And, more than that, it felt like an important form of act of resistance, a way of announcing to the world that although the Germans might have been able to physically imprison them, they could not take away their creative spirit.

And it turned out that the Jewish Symphonic Orchestra were intent on an even greater act of defiance. As they reached the end of their performance, they began playing Beethoven's 'Ode to Joy'. The Germans had long ago forbidden Jewish musicians from performing anything other than the work of Jewish composers.

Jaski took hold of her hand and gave it a squeeze and the tears that had been threatening all evening spilled onto Adela's face. *You'll never beat us, because you'll never break our spirit*, the music seemed to be saying, filling the auditorium and their hearts with hope and joy.

31

Azriel plonked the bag of food onto Berek's kitchen table and opened it up. Inside were some potatoes, a couple of apples and two tins of sardines. His stomach gurgled in appreciation.

'Good work, comrade,' Berek said approvingly.

'It's Izabel and her brother you should be thanking,' he replied, and at the thought of Izabel, he took the note Kasper had given him from his pocket and went over to the carbide lamp to read.

My dearest darling, Izabel's looping script began, *I miss you so much, I'm sure I can feel my bone marrow ache. Oh, what I wouldn't give for just another moment with you, although I fear just one moment wouldn't be nearly enough for what I'd like to do!*

Azriel's cheeks burned at the thought, and he checked Berek was nowhere near before continuing to read.

Keep the faith, my darling, and don't forget, my love for you is greater than the entire universe and as limitless as the galaxies.

Feeling a wistful pang, he carefully folded the note up again and tucked it into his pocket. As instructed when she'd been trained by the Bund prior to the ghetto being closed, Izabel had been careful not to say anything that might give away her identity so he was safe to keep it. If only he were able to see her again, to hold the hand that had written the note and wrap his arms around her. His body ached to be with her.

'Are you able to go and meet Binjamin and collect the latest issue of *Bulletin*?' Berek asked as he set about peeling one of the potatoes.

'Of course.' Binjamin was one of the clandestine printers for the Bund – a quiet, unassuming man with a huge heart, who Azriel had really grown to admire and respect. 'Where should I meet him?' he asked.

'The usual place,' Berek replied.

Azriel picked up the satchel he used for such jobs, which had a secret compartment to hide the papers in. 'I'll see you later.'

'Yes. Be safe.'

'Thank you, comrade.'

As Azriel ran down the stairs of the apartment building, he mused on how they always urged each other to be safe these days, even if they were just popping out to get some rations. It seemed hard to imagine that there was once a time when people didn't feel the need to pray for each other's safety almost every second of every day.

Outside, twilight was gathering, and the air was cooling. Azriel skulked along in the shadows. Since the formation of the ghetto, there was no more need to walk in the gutter – the whole place was like a gutter now. But there was a new scourge to be on the lookout for – the Jewish police, and most especially the Jewish secret police, or the Thirteeners as they were known, due to the address of their headquarters at 13 Leszno. They'd been hand-picked by the Gestapo to stop the smuggling and crack down on Resistance groups like the Bund. It made his skin crawl to think that his father had seriously suggested he join them. It was as if he'd never known or understood Azriel at all. And if all that wasn't bad enough, lately the Germans had taken to turning up in the ghetto unannounced after dark and shooting people randomly, as if for sport.

As Azriel approached the junction, he heard raised voices and instinctively drew back. His heart sank when he heard a German voice asking, 'What are you doing here?'

'I'm just going to get some bread for my children,' he heard Binjamin reply.

'Oh really?' the German said, coolly. 'Then you won't mind showing us what's in that bag of yours.'

Azriel felt sick. He knew that Binjamin would have a secret compartment in his bag, but what if they found it? What if they found the copies of *Bulletin* inside?

'I can't believe they played Beethoven at the end,' Adela said breathlessly, as she and Jaski made their way along the dark-ened street back to the orphanage.

'Wasn't it wonderful!' Jaski stopped walking and took both her hands in his.

'And so brave...' Adela added, lowering her voice. 'Given that the Germans have forbidden Beethoven.'

'How can you forbid Beethoven?' Jaski exclaimed. 'It's like... it's like...' He looked up at the sky. 'It's like trying to forbid people from looking at the moon. It's a thing so beautiful, it transcends all petty human rules.'

Adela gazed up at the pearly moon. In these days of mounting loss, it felt so good to be reminded that there were some things the Germans would never be able to take from them.

'I think we should put on another play,' Jaski said as they continued on their way. 'It will do the children good, lift their spirits.'

'Yes!' Adela exclaimed, linking her arm through his. The street went suddenly dark. Adela looked up and saw that a thick bank of cloud had drifted over the moon. Her breath caught in her throat. It felt symbolic somehow, as if the sky was warning her of more darkness to come.

The Germans can't take everything from us, she reminded herself as they walked along the street, but now the question *Can they?* had added itself to the end of the sentence. She shivered and clutched Jaski's arm tighter.

Azriel stood, pressed to the wall, the only sound the pulsing of blood in his ears. Then the German began yelling.

'What the hell is this?'

Azriel took a breath and peered round the corner to see Binjamin standing with his hands in the air, one soldier holding a bundle of *Bulletins*, the other aiming a gun at his head.

Azriel darted back behind the corner, and leaned against the wall, his heart racing. He thought of the gun tucked inside his boot. With the element of surprise on his side, he knew he'd be able to take out at least one of the soldiers, but then there was the risk that the other would shoot Binjamin. And there could be more lurking close by, ready to swoop at the sound of gunfire. With any luck, they wouldn't shoot Binjamin; they'd arrest him. Yes, they'd probably—

A gunshot rang out, slicing through his thoughts, and instantly all the background hubbub from the surrounding apartments faded to silence.

Please, let it have been a warning shot, Azriel silently implored, praying he'd hear Binjamin's voice. But instead he heard one of the soldiers say something in German and then both soldiers began laughing.

Azriel remained rooted to the spot, frozen by a mixture of

anger and horror as the soldiers' boots clipped off into the distance. He thought of the last time he'd seen Binjamin, laughing with his wife and bouncing his new baby daughter on his knee. Hopefully, he wouldn't be dead, he'd be wounded. Maybe he'd be able to save him. But as he made his way over to the body, he saw blood pooling from his head all over the ground.

Azriel crouched down beside him and he felt a hardening in his heart. He hadn't killed anyone yet, but he knew now without a shadow of a doubt that it was only a matter of time. He didn't care what his father thought. He wasn't the same as the Nazis. They used violence to terrorise and oppress; he was fighting for freedom.

He placed his hand on his dead comrade's shoulder. 'I promise, you won't have died in vain,' he whispered.

High above them, the moon came out from behind a cloud and bathed them both in its silvery light. It felt like a particularly cruel piece of timing, a spotlight being thrown on this latest event, as if to emphasise the horror.

32

Izabel took a sip of her gin fizz. And another. And another. In the nineteen months since Dieter had come back into her life, she'd come to increasingly rely upon alcohol to numb the pain of time spent in his company. Everything about him made her stomach churn and her skin crawl, from his arrogant smirk to his condescending nod. Even his fingernails had begun to annoy her, she realised, as she watched him pick up his beer. They were too long, and weirdly pointy.

She looked at the gun on his holster and sighed. If she could only steal it without being caught. The thought of being able to smuggle German weapons into the ghetto to help the Bund was a thrilling one, but perhaps she wouldn't need to steal it. It was time to see if her plan would work.

Dieter lit a cigarette for her and passed it across the restaurant table.

'*Danke*,' she said, knowing how he liked it when she spoke in his mother tongue.

'You're welcome,' he replied with a cold smile. 'What are you thinking?' he asked.

How to steal your weapon and use it against you, she thought, smiling back sweetly.

'I'm thinking that I wish I had a gun,' she said wistfully.

He laughed. 'Why would you want a weapon?'

'These are such dangerous times and you can't always be there to protect me.' She lowered her stare and gazed up at him coquettishly.

As predicted, he puffed up his chest and nodded. 'Don't worry, you're safe now we're running this country and all of the *undesirables* are behind the wall.' He uttered the word 'undesirables' as if it were something sour to be spat out, making Izabel long for his gun even more.

'But what if they break out?' She faked a look of horror.

He gave another arrogant laugh. 'They won't. And, anyway, they won't be here for very much longer.'

'What do you mean?' she asked, hoping he couldn't detect the sudden dread she was feeling.

He beckoned the waiter over and ordered more drinks.

'We're sending them away.'

Izabel's stomach clenched. 'To a labour camp?'

'Don't you worry your pretty little head about it.'

'Oh, but I do worry. What if they fight back?' She held her breath, hoping he'd give something more away.

'Trust me, they won't be fighting back where they're going. They won't be doing anything.' He smirked.

Adela watched as a man pasted a poster to an apartment building wall. What poisonous things would it be saying about the Jewish people this time? she wondered, feeling a mixture of anger and dread rise inside her. She wasn't sure how much more of this endless campaign of degradation she could take.

She glanced around at the bodies lying in the street. Typhus and dysentery had torn through the ghetto due to the over-crowding, and the cemetery next door now overflowed with bodies. She'd thought that the first year of the occupation was unbearable, but it was nothing compared to this. The ghetto had made this part of Warsaw a hell on earth. Thankfully, her parents were bearing up. Leopold was busier than ever with his work for the *Judenrat* and Estera had started volunteering at a soup kitchen, which seemed to have given her a much-needed sense of purpose.

The man finished sticking up the poster and continued on his way. To her surprise, she saw that this one wasn't displaying any kind of grotesque caricature. Instead it was announcing a '*Grossaktion*' and asking for volunteers to be transported else-where to work. In exchange, anyone who volunteered would receive three kilos of bread and a kilo of marmalade. She instantly drooled at the thought, but just as quickly felt over-whelmed with guilt. They'd been starved for so long now, the Germans knew they'd do almost anything for the promise of food. Well, she refused to be humiliated in that way. She wouldn't be that weak. For a start, there was no way she would ever leave Jaski and children, no matter how hungry she was.

Izabel felt bile rising and burning at the back of her throat. But she mustn't let Dieter see her concern; she had to keep her cool. If what he was alluding to was true, and the Germans were planning on sending the Jewish somewhere they 'wouldn't be doing anything', Azriel and the Bund needed weapons more urgently than ever. She had to get Dieter to give her one.

'I'm sorry, I shouldn't have asked. I suppose you don't have the authority to give guns to just anyone.' She leaned across the table and lowered her voice. 'Not even to your very special friends.'

As she'd hoped, he looked personally affronted that she should suggest such a thing. 'Of course I have the authority.'

'Do you?' She widened her eyes and looked at him with what she hoped was longing rather than loathing.

'Yes. As a matter of fact, I could get you one right now if I wanted to.'

'Oh my! I didn't realise you had quite so much power.'

He nodded smugly. 'In fact, I quite like the idea of you with a pistol.'

'Me too,' she cooed.

'Perhaps I'll have a gift for you then, the next time we meet.'

She grinned. 'That would be wonderful.'

'But, of course, I would expect a gift from you in return.'

'Naturally,' she said, instantly feeling sick.

He put his hand under the table and squeezed her knee the way you might test a fruit for ripeness. 'So maybe next time we should meet at the Crescent Hotel?'

Her heart sank. This was the first time he'd mentioned meeting in a hotel since he'd come back into her life, and she'd been hoping that in their time apart he'd decided to remain faithful to his wife.

'I'll bring the dress I bought you in Paris too. You can model it for me.'

She thought of being able to smuggle a weapon to Azriel, and of what he might be able to do with it. There was no way she was going to sleep with Dieter, but perhaps if she got him to the hotel with the gun, she could feign illness at the last minute and still walk away with it. It had to be worth a try. How were the Bund and the other members of the ghetto Resistance ever going to beat the Germans and whatever horrors they had planned for them if they weren't armed?

'I can't wait,' she replied, placing her hand on top of his and praying to Saint Brigid that she wouldn't regret it.

33

Adela watched as the children chattered excitedly. They'd just finished their performance of another play and it had gone remarkably well, especially considering the fact that Jaski had unexpectedly brought it forward by a week. Now they were all gathered around the dining tables sipping water and eating porridge prepared by Marta, still in their costumes, so it was quite the scene. They'd created a weird and wonderful mixture of fairy tales in the end, so the hall was full of dwarves and woodland creatures, Snow White, the big bad wolf and Beauty and the Beast.

'Weren't they wonderful,' Adela said, as Jaski joined her. This time, he'd cast himself as a wizard called The Great Grolin, who narrated the tale, and he was clad in a black velvet cloak dotted in stars made from gold paper.

'They are indeed,' he replied, but she knew him well enough by now to be able to detect a sadness in his smile.

'Are you all right?' she asked.

'Yes, yes, of course. I'm just tired.' He cleared his throat and clapped his hands. 'Children, if I could just tear your attention away from your porridge, please.'

They looked up but continued eating.

'I want to thank you all so much for all your hard work on the play. Your performance was magnificent, fantastic, fabulous.' He paused, and Adela smiled as she saw him start to fill with light again. 'In short, your performance was mag-tasticulous!'

The children started to giggle.

'And now you all have magic powers,' he continued, clearly warming to his theme as he began striding around the room, twirling his cloak.

'Can we turn ourselves invisible?' a little boy named Aaron called.

'Oh, I wish,' Marta muttered beside Adela. 'Then they could all escape the Germans.'

'Sadly no, but the magic powers you have are even better than invisibility,' Jaski replied. 'Because now you have mastered the art of your imaginations.'

'What does that mean?' a girl called Ronia asked.

'It means you're able to pretend to be different people and things,' Adela said.

'Yes indeed,' Jaski said, smiling at her. 'Which means you're able to be whatever you want to. All you have to do is use your imagination and, hey presto!' He waved his wand. 'You can be a dinosaur, or a princess, or even a pea.' He pointed at the child in a round green pea costume, and they all started to giggle. 'So never forget that, please,' he said, and his smile faded. 'If you're ever feeling sad, or scared, or alone, use the magic of your imagination and pretend to be something or somewhere else.'

Adela gulped. She understood now that there was a subtext to his speech, but what was it, and why?

～

That night, once the children were all in bed, Adela perched on the arm of Jaski's chair and stroked his hair. 'I really liked your speech to the children tonight,' she said, planting a kiss on top of his head.

'Thank you, my love,' he replied.

'It felt as if you were preparing them for something.'

'Maybe I was,' he replied softly.

She slid down beside him in the chair. 'What do you think is going to happen?'

'I don't know, but there's no doubting things are getting harder.'

Adela shuddered. In the month since the posters about the *Grossaktion* had appeared, thousands of people had been rounded up by the Germans and the Jewish police and sent to the Umschlagplatz, a fenced-off area at the Gdańska freight station, where they were put on trains as part of what was being called a 'resettlement to the east'. Everyone knew this was code for being sent to a labour camp and some of the rumours circulating the ghetto were even worse – that the people on the trains leaving Warsaw every day were being sent to their deaths. Izabel had smuggled intelligence to Azriel saying as much, although Adela wasn't sure who her source was, or if it was reliable.

'Surely they wouldn't send the children to their labour camps,' she said, hoping she didn't sound ridiculously naive.

'You're right,' Jaski replied, squeezing her hand. 'Of course they wouldn't.' He looked up at her and smiled, but, to her dismay, she saw that his eyes glimmered with tears.

The next morning, Jaski seemed back to his normal self, regaling the children with a tale from his childhood over breakfast. As always, Adela marvelled at the way he was able to keep an audience ranging in age from four to thirteen completely rapt.

As soon as they'd finished eating, she prepared to give them their history lesson, but Jaski announced there'd been a change of plan.

'We're going to have a games party instead,' he said. 'I think you all deserve to have some fun after your hard work in the play.'

Adela gave him a pointed stare.

'Not that history with Miss Rubinstein isn't fun,' he added quickly.

'Would you like to borrow my rolling pin to whack him with?' Marta asked Adela as she gave Jaski a pantomime-style glare. The dining hall rang with laughter. Then, as the children cleared their bowls away, Jaski came over to Adela.

'Your mother left a message at the office,' he said, fiddling with the cuffs of his velvet jacket. 'She asked if you can go and see her at home.'

Adela frowned. 'Did she say what it was about?'

He shook his head. 'It's all right. Take the day off. Go and be with her. We'll be fine.'

'Are you sure?' She stared at him. He was looking really anxious and once again she couldn't shake the feeling that something was wrong.

He kissed her and smiled. 'Of course, my love.'

All the way home through the ghetto, the feeling of foreboding that had taken root in Adela began to grow. And then something terrible occurred to her. What if Estera had been summoned to leave on the trains headed east?

As if on cue, a procession of people made their way along the other side of the street, shepherded by the Jewish police. They were all clutching small cases, their faces etched with worry as they headed for the station square. Estera wouldn't be among them, Adela reassured herself. As someone who worked in a shop, Estera had a number: a precious piece of paper signifying that she was still needed in the ghetto. And, in addition to that, the *Judenrat* were exempt from the great deportation, so being married to Leopold would surely spare her from being deported too.

Over the past couple of years, Adela had come to agree with Azriel that the *Judenrat* were just puppets for the Nazis, but now she couldn't help feeling huge relief that it would keep her parents with them in the ghetto.

When she reached the store, she found Estera pacing up and down looking ashen-faced.

'Mama, what is it, what's wrong?' Adela asked, hurrying over to her.

'Oh, my darling, you came!' she exclaimed.

'Of course I came. Jaski told me you'd left a message. What's happened?'

'We, uh, we're short staffed in the soup kitchen,' Estera replied. 'I was wondering if you could help us for a few hours.'

'Of course, but why didn't you just say that in your message? I could have met you there.'

Estera picked at the raw skin on her knuckles. 'I don't know. I'm not thinking straight these days.'

'Oh, Mama!' Adela flung her arms around her and hugged her tight. 'It's all right. None of us are thinking straight anymore. Come on, let's go and make some soup.'

The next few hours passed by in a blur. The soup kitchen was busier than ever, but Adela was thankful for the opportunity to lose herself in a haze of chopping vegetables and cooking and serving. She couldn't help noticing the tension in the air as people huddled together in groups, talking in hushed tones. Of course, all talk was of the deportations – who'd gone, and where they'd been sent to.

'I've heard that the camp in Treblinka never receives deliveries of food,' Adela overheard one woman say, as she collected her empty soup bowl. 'Why would they not bring food? Are they planning on starving us all to death?'

Adela's mouth went dry. She'd heard the exact same rumour from Azriel. The Bund had managed to smuggle someone out of the ghetto who'd followed the trains to their destination in the east, Treblinka. He'd returned with the news that no trains containing food ever arrived at the station there.

She glanced across at Estera, who was standing behind a trestle table, ladling soup into tin cups, all the while glancing around anxiously. Adela went over and placed her hand on her shoulder.

'I love you, Mama,' she whispered in her ear.

'Oh Adela!' Estera exclaimed and she burst into tears.

'What is it? What's wrong? Has something happened?'

The apprehension Adela had felt that morning stirred back into life. Both Jaski and her mother were acting strangely and it was unnerving. Did they both know something she didn't?

'I can't... I'm not...' Estera stammered.

'I think I should get back to the orphanage,' Adela said, taking off her apron. If her mother couldn't tell her what was wrong, maybe Jaski could.

'No!' Estera cried.

'Mama!' Adela frowned. 'What's wrong?'

'I need your help here.' Estera wiped away her tears but more kept coming.

Adela looked around. The crowd for the soup was thinning and there were plenty of volunteers. Did Estera really still need her? Adela couldn't shake her creeping sense of dread.

'Mama?' she said again. 'What's going on?'

'You need to stay here. Please, Adela, I'm begging you.'

Adela put her apron on the table. 'I need to go back to the orphanage,' she said firmly. Estera grabbed her arm, but Adela easily shook her off. 'Do you know something that I don't?'

'No,' Estera murmured, but she wouldn't meet her gaze.

'Don't lie to me. Please.'

'He told me not to let you go back,' Estera said helplessly.

'Who did? Jaski?'

Estera nodded.

'Oh no!' She clapped her hand to her mouth in horror. There was only one reason she could think of for him doing this. 'Are they... are they being deported?'

Estera began to openly weep.

'Oh, Mama, how could you have kept this from me?' Adela began making her way out from behind the table.

'Please, Adela. Please don't go. I'm begging you,' Estera cried.

But Adela could hardly hear her over the pounding of her heart. She jostled her way through the crowd and she began to run and run.

34

There were many horrific things that had happened since the start of the war, Azriel thought to himself as he lay stiff as a board in the back of the cart, but being surrounded by corpses surely had to be one of the very worst. He kept his eyes shut tight and tried not to breathe, but the strange, sweet odour was too pervasive and seemed to cling to him like a putrid fog.

Remember what you're doing this for, he told himself as the cart jerked forwards. If the ghetto Resistance were to have any chance in their fightback against the Germans, they urgently needed weapons – and a lot of them. When Azriel had volunteered to be smuggled out of the ghetto to collect a cache of guns, it hadn't been clear how it was going to happen. But, gruesome as it was, using the undertakers, who were sympathetic to the Resistance, made sense. Sadly, dead bodies were now the main export from the ghetto, sent out on a daily basis. And at least there wasn't far to go – the cemetery that was now being used as a mass grave was just the other side of the wall. They just had to make it through the checkpoint.

As if on cue, the cart juddered to a halt and he heard German voices. *Time to play dead*, Azriel told himself, and felt the most inappropriate nervous urge to laugh. He tried to relax his body as best he could and he became aware of a burst of light through his shut eyelids. His pulse quickened as he felt the body next to him being prodded. Then he heard the guard gasp in horror, no doubt at the smell, and all went dark again as the tarpaulin was thrown back over.

He breathed a sigh of relief and instantly gagged. *Think of something else*, he urged himself, and, instantly, Izabel appeared in his mind, like a beautiful Hollywood actress, smiling at him from the silver screen. Oh, how he wished he had the power to conjure her up in real life – although obviously he wouldn't want to conjure her up here; she'd be horrified. Again, he felt the near hysterical desire to laugh. *Oh please, let this hell be over with!* He silently implored as the cart began moving forwards again.

∼

Izabel picked up her little statuette of Saint Brigid and clutched it tightly.

'Please grant me a miracle and let me get out of this in one piece,' she whispered. 'And with a gun,' she added. Saint Brigid's painted-on mouth smiled up at her. Izabel wasn't sure if it was her imagination, but it seemed as if the saint's gaze was a little more judgemental than before. 'I have to do *something*,' she hissed, putting the figurine back on the dresser. 'I can't let Adela and Azriel be deported to their deaths.'

She checked her appearance one last time and patted her perfectly rolled hair. Never in all her born days could she have imagined meeting a Nazi for a liaison in a hotel, but there were now so many unforeseen horrors occurring on a daily basis, it was almost becoming normal.

She applied a spritz of perfume and stood up. *I'm doing this for Azriel and Adela*, she reminded herself and instantly felt fortified.

With that thought she left her bedroom to find Kasper loitering in the hallway, playing with a spinning top.

'Die, Germans, die!' he muttered as he spun the top faster. Then he looked up. 'Why are you dressed like Mama?' he remarked. 'Where are you going?'

'Never you mind,' she replied. Then, seeing a flicker of hurt pass across his face, she reached into her bag and pulled out a toffee. 'Here, chew on this while I'm gone.'

He snatched it from her eagerly and she bent down and kissed him.

'Urrgh, lipstick.' He grimaced, wiping his cheek.

'I'll see you later,' she said.

'Yes.' He unwrapped the toffee and shoved it into his mouth. 'Be careful,' he mumbled.

Izabel entered the hotel lobby to find Dieter standing at the bar, smoking a cigarette and nursing a large glass of whisky.

'Very nice,' he said by way of greeting, looking her up and down. She'd worn her tightest dress and highest heels and a pair of her mother's sheer stockings with a piped back line running up the back. 'I say we go straight to the room.'

She looked him over. There was no sign of a gun apart from his own. 'What about my present?'

'Oh, you'll get your present,' he replied in a knowing tone, sending a surge of fear right through her. What fresh hell had she let herself in for?

Adela tore through the narrow ghetto streets, past the beggars and the poor souls trying to sell what little possessions they had left in the world. All she could think about was the orphanage and the terrible truth that had finally dawned upon her. Jaski had known something bad was about to happen. It was why he'd brought the play forward a week, why he'd given the children the pep talk about using their imaginations that morning. And why he'd asked Estera to keep Adela out of the way. But why would Estera agree to such a thing? And why would Jaski want her to leave him? Why wouldn't he want her there with him, to help him take care of the children? On and on the panicked questions plagued her, racing in time with her pounding heart and feet.

Finally, she sped round the corner and the orphanage loomed into view. The main door, normally always locked shut, was hanging open, but there wasn't a soul in sight.

She raced up the steps and into the empty hallway, looking around frantically.

'Hello!' she cried at the top of her voice. 'Is there anyone there?'

All was deathly silent, and then she heard a sob coming from the dining room. Adela raced inside and found Marta sitting on the floor, rocking back and forth, her body heaving with great sobs.

'Marta, what's happened?' she cried.

'They came for the children!' she gasped. 'Those poor innocent babies.'

'When?'

'They left about ten minutes ago.'

'And Jaski?'

Marta looked up at Adela through tear-filled eyes. 'He's with them. He refused to leave them.'

Marta's words hit her with the force of a train. 'I have to go. I have to be with them too.'

Marta grabbed her wrist. 'He wanted to save you. Me too. He told me to hide in the cellar.'

'But I can't be here without him. Without the children. They need me.' She tugged herself free from Marta's grasp and raced back out of the door.

As a child, Adela had always been the slowest when it came to running, but it was as if her determination to be with Jaski was giving her some kind of superhuman strength. Faster and faster, her feet pounded, and when her stupid wooden shoes became too cumbersome and painful, she kicked them off and ran on in bare feet. *Please God, help me to catch up with them,* she silently implored as she raced on, her lungs burning. Finally, she reached the road leading to the station square, to be greeted with the most heartbreaking sight she'd ever seen in her life. The orphans, all dressed in their smartest clothes and wearing their blue knapsacks, were marching in rows of five, holding hands.

'No!' Adela cried as she raced to catch up with them.

Several of the orphanage nurses were walking at the rear of the procession, but where was Jaski? As she ran past the children, she heard some of them call her name.

'We're going to the countryside, Miss Adela,' one of them cried excitedly.

'I've never been to the countryside before,' another said. 'I hope I see a sheep!'

'No, no, no,' Adela muttered as she hurried past. They all looked so happy and excited, so innocent, many of them clutching their favourite toys. No doubt Jaski had filled their heads with tales of adventure to stop them from fearing the worst. But this *was* the worst, the absolute worst.

Finally, she saw Jaski, marching at the head of the procession, like the Pied Piper of Hamelin. He was holding hands with Tomas, the youngest of the orphans, who had just turned four.

'Jaski!' she cried as she drew level with him.

As soon as he heard her, she saw his face light up, then

immediately fall. 'What are you doing here?' he asked. 'I thought you were helping your mother.'

'Why did you send me away?' Her voice was feeble with fear.

'One of us needs to stay here,' he replied breezily. 'To take care of the orphanage, while I'm gone.'

'Didn't you even want to say goodbye?' she cried.

'Why is she sad?' Tomas asked, looking frightened.

'Because she isn't able to come with us,' Jaski said. 'But we'll see her again soon.' He looked at her imploringly and mouthed the word *please* over Tomas's head.

'But... but I love you,' she stammered.

'Exactly. And I love you. More than anything,' he replied. 'Knowing you're still here will keep me going.' He looked back at the other children. 'We're nearly there,' he called to them in a sing-song voice. 'It's nearly time for our train ride!'

A cheer rang out from the children, and Adela wanted to wail, but instead she looked at Jaski and as he met her gaze, she nodded. She had to stay strong for him. She had to stay strong for the children. 'I love you,' she cried again, as he reached the station square and the SS guard on duty opened the gate.

'I love you too,' he called back. 'There's a letter for you on my desk.'

She stood and watched as the children all filed past, calling out to her, full of excitement. She owed it to them and Jaski to do this one last thing. So she forced a smile onto her face and she began to wave. 'Goodbye!' she cried shrilly. 'Have a fun adventure in the countryside.'

It was only when the gate clanged shut behind them that she bent over double and allowed the tears to slide onto her face.

35

Izabel lay on the bed looking up at Dieter. *I hate you,* she thought as she watched him get dressed. *I hate you, I hate you, I hate you.*

She'd been hoping they would spend some time in the hotel bar, enough time for her to feign some kind of illness, but he'd brought her up to the room straight away, and he'd let her know that he was expecting his gift first, with no mention at all of the gun. She'd tried resisting his advances, but this had only seemed to work him into more of a frenzy, and so she'd found herself detaching from her body, just as she'd done in the alleyway with the pogromists, and disappearing into a walled secret garden in her mind where he couldn't reach her, praying it would be over soon.

'I've wanted to do that for so long,' he said now, as he adjusted his collar. 'And it didn't disappoint.'

Her stomach churned. Would that mean he'd want more? Panic began rising inside of her, but she managed to shove it down. She'd come here for a reason. This couldn't have all been in vain.

'So, what about my present?' she said, propping herself onto her elbow and gazing up at him.

For a terrible moment, he looked blank, and she thought he might have actually forgotten. But then a smile crept across his face. 'Ah, yes,' he said, and he opened the top drawer of the dresser.

Her heart rate quickened as he took out a package wrapped in a silk scarf.

'Here.' He handed it to her.

She hoped he couldn't see her fingers trembling as she unwrapped it to reveal a gun. Although she was hardly an expert on such matters, she could tell it was a good one. Sturdy and compact.

'It suits you,' he said with another sickening smile as she turned it over in her hands.

She pictured aiming it at him and pulling the trigger. Shooting him right in the middle of his stupid puffed-up chest. And then again, right between the legs.

Stay focused, she reminded herself, thinking of Azriel and Adela. Oh, Azriel! How could she ever face him again after this? And what if Adela ever found out! She'd flipped her wig when Izabel had flirted with Dieter. She'd probably disown her if she found out what she'd done to get the gun. She swallowed hard and concentrated on keeping the smile on her face.

'Thank you,' she cooed.

'I doubt you'll ever need it,' he said. 'We've got rid of thousands of Jews this past month alone.'

Again, she had to fight the urge to pull the trigger.

'To the labour camp?' she asked nonchalantly.

He laughed. 'If that's what you want to call it, although the only labour happening there is in the crematoriums.' He looked at his watch. 'I've got to go.' His eyes lingered all over her, making her skin feel dirty beneath his gaze. 'We'll do this again,' he said before turning to leave. *Over my dead body*, she thought bitterly.

She lay there for a moment, horror gathering like a storm in the pit of her stomach. He'd all but admitted to her that Treblinka was a death camp.

Don't think about it, you can't think about it, she urged as she forced herself to get up. *You got what you came here for.*

A fantasy began playing out in her mind, in which Azriel shot Dieter stone dead with the very same gun he'd given Izabel. But it didn't bring her any pleasure; she only felt hollow.

She scrubbed herself clean in the bathroom, before getting dressed, hiding the gun in the bottom of her bag and going downstairs. As she walked through the lobby, she imagined everyone staring and pointing at her, somehow knowing what she'd just done, but when she glanced around, she saw, to her relief, that they were all reading newspapers or engaged in conversation. She stepped outside and took a breath of the hot summer air. It felt oppressively humid all of a sudden and she felt nauseous as hot, sticky shame crept through her, burning at her from her toes to her scalp.

You had to do it. You had to get the gun, she told herself as she kept putting one foot in front of the other. *When I get home, I'll have a long soak in the bath*, she told herself. *Clean all traces of that animal away.*

She saw a group of women walking towards her. They were all dressed in the latest fashions, in rich shades of damson, pink and fern green. She thought of the Jewish people suffering on the other side of the ghetto wall, stripped of all colour and all hope, and suddenly the women's clothes seemed garish and offensive.

What if the Resistance doesn't succeed? she thought fearfully. *What if the Germans win? What if it is all in vain?*

But just as she was about to spiral into despair, an arm reached out from beside her and pulled her into an alleyway.

~

Adela pulled herself upright and wiped her face. She couldn't give up; there had to be something she could do. The train hadn't left yet. The children and Jaski were still in Warsaw.

And then she thought of Leopold. He was on the *Judenrat*. Surely there was something he could do. She took off running again, her bare feet being torn to shreds on the stony ground, but she didn't care. The horror she was feeling numbed her to any pain.

Thankfully, the office where Leopold worked wasn't too far away. She crashed through the door and when she saw her father behind his desk, she wanted to sing with relief.

'Adela, what's happened?' he exclaimed. Clearly he hadn't been privy to Jaski and Estera's plan.

'You have to help!' she gasped. 'They are going to deport Jaski and the orphans. Please! You have to do something to stop them.' She grabbed at his arm, fresh tears streaming down her face.

'Oh my goodness!' Leopold's eyes widened in horror and he stood up and hurried over to the door.

She followed him as he made his way to the office of Adam Cherniakov, the president of the *Judenrat*.

'Wait here,' he told her, before heading inside.

She paced up and down, praying harder than she'd ever done in her life before that he could work some kind of miracle.

Finally, Leopold reappeared with Cherniakov, a balding, middle-aged man, wearing a bowtie and glasses.

'Don't worry,' Cherniakov said to Adela. 'I'll get them to stop this madness.'

The three of them made their way to the station square, Adela's heart pounding. Perhaps there was still hope after all.

When they got to the gate, Cherniakov began pleading with the SS guards on duty, but to no avail. He returned to Leopold and Adela, ashen-faced. 'I'm so sorry,' he said softly, his eyes shiny with tears.

'No!' she cried. 'Please!'

Leopold wrapped his arms around her and held her tight. It was something he'd done so many times throughout her childhood and it had never failed to console her. But now she was way beyond consoling.

'How can they do this? They're innocent children,' she sobbed into his chest. She felt his body stiffen and she looked up at him.

'They're monsters,' Leopold replied, his normally calm voice taut with rage. 'And they're drunk on their own evil.'

'Get off me, you fiend!' Izabel yelped as her assailant pulled her further into the darkened passageway. If only she was able to get to the gun. If only she hadn't hidden it so well.

'Well, that's a fine way to greet me.' The fiend spoke, and she froze in shock.

It couldn't be. She had to be hallucinating. The stress of what had happened with Dieter had sent her crazy.

'I thought you'd be happy to see me,' he continued, causing her mouth to gape open. Azriel laughed. 'I don't believe it. I've finally made you speechless.'

'How is it you?' she gasped, reaching out to touch his face. His cheeks were hollow and his jaw rough with stubble, but in that moment he seemed like the most beautiful thing she'd ever laid eyes on. 'How are you here?'

'I was smuggled out,' he whispered in her ear and the sensation sent a shiver through her. 'I've been sent on a mission to collect weapons to smuggle back in. I can't stay long, I'm afraid, it's too dangerous, but I had to try to see you. Kasper told me where you were living, so I waited here on the off chance.'

'Oh, Azriel!' Her knees almost buckled from the shock and relief. 'You have no idea what this means to me. I asked Saint

Brigid to grant me a miracle and I thought she'd let me down, but she was clearly saving her miracles for something truly special.' She raised her eyes heavenward. 'Oh, Brigid, I'm so sorry I doubted you!'

Azriel laughed. 'I should have known you wouldn't remain speechless for long! I've missed you and your crazy talk so much!' He hugged her to him, then immediately pushed her away. 'I'm sorry I smell so bad. I had to be smuggled out in quite unpleasant conditions.'

She pulled him back towards her. 'I don't care. I just want you to hold me. Please!'

As he held her, she felt hope returning to her body, fizzing through her veins and chasing away the shame she'd been feeling. This was why she'd gone to the hotel room with Dieter, she reminded herself, to help Azriel. Somewhere above, an apartment window opened, and a tune wafted down on the breeze.

'Would you care to dance?' Azriel asked.

'Why, I would be delighted,' she replied.

He took hold of her hand and put his arm around her waist and as she felt the music moving inside of them, it was as if the darkened passageway melted away and they were on a dance floor, illuminated by a spotlight's golden glow. And nothing could penetrate that glow. It shone around them like a protective shield.

And then the song came to an end.

'I'm going to have to leave,' he whispered.

'Please tell me this isn't a dream,' she replied.

He took her face in his hands and kissed her passionately, and it was as if his kiss had magical powers, removing all trace of what had happened with Dieter from her body.

'I have something for you!' she exclaimed, fumbling in her bag and pulling out the gun.

He gave a low whistle of appreciation as he unwrapped the scarf. 'Where did you get this?'

'A source in the city,' she replied, cringing inside.

'Thank you!' He tucked it into his belt, beneath his shirt, then pulled her close again. 'I miss you so much.'

'I miss you too. Oh, Azriel, life is so hard without you.'

'I think about you all the time,' he said. 'From the moment I wake up until I fall asleep, I'm always wondering where you are and what you're doing and reminiscing about the times we had together.'

'Me too!' she exclaimed. It made her so happy to know that he thought about her so much.

'So, in a way, we're together always,' he continued, gently touching the side of her face.

'In our thoughts and dreams,' she said, and he nodded before kissing her tenderly on the lips.

'I love you.'

'I love you too.' But as she said the words, her stomach churned. Would he still love her if he knew what she'd done to get the pistol?

He kissed her once more, then melted off into the shadows. She stood there gazing after him, unable to move.

Adela returned to the orphanage feeling utterly broken. She wouldn't have gone back there at all if it hadn't been for Jaski telling her about the letter. Walking through the empty hallways, the silence was deafening. Oh, how she longed to hear the laughter and chatter of the children. How could it be that only a day ago they were celebrating the play? Everything made sense now. But how had Jaski known they were about to be deported?

She hurried into his office. There was his chair exactly as he'd left it, pushed halfway back into the room. Just like everything else he did in life, Jaski would always leave his desk in the most dramatic fashion, pushing his wheeled chair back at full force. And there was his pen lying on the blotter, drops of ink like black blood trailing across the page. *Just find the letter*, she told herself. *Then go.*

An envelope had been propped against the ink pot with her name written on it in his flamboyant handwriting.

My dearest Adela,

By the time you read this, the worst will have happened, and the children and I will be gone. It breaks my heart to leave you without saying goodbye, but I'd be even more heartbroken if the Germans took you too. Please forgive me, I hope you understand. A friend of mine informed me that the SS would be coming for the children. He even offered me the chance of escape. But how could I ever leave the children, especially to such a perilous fate? I pray that we'll survive this, but I've heard the rumours and I know you have too. I couldn't save my own life, but it brings me such joy to think that you might survive all this. You have brought me so much joy, ever since that day you walked into the orphanage, demanding to help the children. We achieved such a lot together. We brought the children so much happiness. Never forget that. And never forget that you are made of water and stardust, proof that magic really does exist. Thank you for weaving my life with your magic. I shall be thinking of you every moment we're apart.

With love always,

Your Jaski

Adela read and reread the words until they swam in front of her eyes, blurring her vision, and a sorrow, the like of which she'd never felt before, caused her heart to splinter into pieces.

36

Azriel lay in the coffin trying not to think that this could be some horrible kind of premonition. He'd been hidden at the bottom of a huge pile of coffins along with the weapons. Some of the other coffins contained food. Hopefully, the guards wouldn't check all of them, but if they did... He shuddered. He supposed there was a certain dramatic quality to a man being killed inside a coffin; it was the kind of thing he could imagine Izabel coming up with on one of her flights of fancy.

He thought of Izabel and their impromptu dance in the darkened passageway. What a gift that had been, and to hear that she thought about him constantly too.

Suddenly, he heard men's voices outside and the truck door being opened, and he remained frozen stiff – *as stiff as a corpse*, he thought, and again felt the inappropriate urge to laugh. There was the sound of a couple of the coffins being opened, but then, thankfully, the men's voices faded and the truck door slammed shut. Relief flooded his body. He'd lived to see another day.

. . .

Azriel got back to Berek's apartment later that night.

'Well?' Berek said, his expression full of hope.

Azriel nodded.

'Excellent!'

They went into Berek's bedroom and Azriel placed the cache of weapons on the bed.

'Very good.' Berek nodded his approval. Then his gaze fell upon the pistol Izabel had given him and he picked it up, staring at it in shock. 'Where did you get this?'

'From one of my other contacts on the outside,' Azriel replied. 'Why?'

'It's a Walther PPK. Standard issue for the Gestapo.'

Azriel's blood ran cold as he thought of Izabel's breezy reply when he'd asked where she got it. 'Oh.'

'I'd heard that some of those Nazi swine were selling weapons on the black market,' Berek continued, turning the gun over in his hands. He looked at Azriel and laughed. 'Well, their greed is our gain. This is one of the best concealed carry weapons on the market. Whoever sold this one is going to live to regret it.'

Azriel smiled weakly, his stomach knotting with worry. What if she'd got it from the soldier she'd been fraternising with before? And what had she had to do to get it? But before he was able to dwell on it any further, there was a loud knock at the apartment door. It was the coded knock that the Bund members had been given, but still, they couldn't be too careful.

'I'll hide these; you get it,' Berek said, swiftly removing the weapons from the bed.

Azriel approached the door apprehensively. 'Who is it?' he called without opening it.

'Azriel, it's me.'

He started at the sound of Adela's voice. When he'd given her Berek's address, he'd made it clear that she was only to come to him in the most dire of emergencies. His pulse quickened. Had something happened to their parents?

He opened the door to find Adela standing there, out of breath. Her hair was messed up and her eyes looked wild.

'What's happened, little bookworm?' he asked, quickly ushering her inside.

'I've come to join you,' she said, her bottom lip quivering.

'What do you mean?'

'I want to join the Bund.' She lowered her voice. 'The Bund militia.'

'But... I don't understand.'

'The Germans have taken Jaski and the orphans. They've deported them to their death camp in Treblinka. All of them.'

'What?' He stared at her in horror.

'Papa went to the head of the *Judenrat* and he begged the Germans to show some mercy, but they refused.' She stared at him defiantly. 'You were right all along. The *Judenrat* are a joke. They have no authority.'

He nodded sadly, but oh how he wished that in this case he was wrong.

'So I want to join you,' she continued, her brown eyes sparking with anger. 'And I'll do anything – *anything* – to defeat the Germans.' She clutched his hand. 'I mean it, Azriel. I'll even kill them if I have to.'

37

Izabel hurried along the street. It was almost time for their next designated smuggling drop, but she'd been kept late at work, so she needed to be quick if she was going to make it on time. Kasper had the bag of food in his room, but she'd given him strict instructions to never go through the wall alone; it was far too dangerous without her there to act as her cover and lookout. But just as she was crossing the square, she heard someone call her name and she turned to see Dieter with one of his fellow soldiers.

'Damn!' she muttered, while forcing her expression into one of delight.

'Where are you off to in such a hurry?' he asked, striding over. It was the first time she'd seen him since the fateful night in the hotel and it still felt way too soon.

'Back home,' she replied. 'I... I need to help my mother with something... Dinner.'

'Hmm, that's a shame. I was thinking it would be nice if you had dinner with me.'

Panic surged through her. If she had dinner with Dieter,

there was no way they'd be able to do the food drop, and she wouldn't find out if Azriel had made it back to the ghetto safely.

'How about tomorrow night?' she asked.

'I can't,' he replied. 'Never mind. We can go for a quick drink now instead.'

'But...'

He took hold of her arm. 'What's wrong? Don't you want to have a drink with me?' Everything he said came out sounding like a veiled threat. She needed to get a grip, regain control of the situation.

'Of course I do!' she exclaimed. 'Always!' His grip on her arm lessened slightly. 'It's just that...' His grip tightened again.

'What?'

'Nothing. Let's go.'

Azriel made his way through the ghetto, his shirt collar pulled up against the rain. All day long, a storm had been brewing and now it had finally broken. As he approached the wall, he thought of Izabel waiting on the other side with her brother. He put his hand in his pocket and felt for the note Adela had given him to pass on along with a note of his own.

There was a loud rumble of thunder and he glanced down at his watch. He was a minute late. He checked the coast was clear and hurried over to the hole, kicking aside the pile of rubble he'd put there to hide it. He checked again that no one was coming, then gave a long low whistle. He waited for Izabel to whistle back, but all remained silent. Perhaps she hadn't heard him over the rain.

He whistled again and he heard the scrambling sound that always signalled that Kasper had begun burrowing his way through. He frowned. Why hadn't Izabel whistled? What if it was a trap?

He hurried across the street and took cover in a doorway to wait and watch. After a few seconds, a pair of small hands appeared holding a sack, followed by Kasper's tousled blonde head. Azriel ran back over.

'Why didn't your sister whistle?' he asked, crouching down and taking the sack. Then he pressed the notes into his hand.

'She's not here,' Kasper replied, wriggling so that he could tuck the notes inside his shirt pocket. 'She... Ow!' he yelped suddenly. 'Ow!'

Azriel stared, horrified, as the boy began writhing in pain. On the other side of the wall, he heard a man yelling and the sound of something cracking.

'Ow!' Kasper screamed again and his body started disappearing back through the hole.

Azriel caught his hands just in time and started to pull. But clearly whoever was on the other side was pulling too and the boy cried out in agony. Azriel didn't know what to do. If he kept pulling, Kasper might be torn in two, but if he didn't try to pull him to safety who knew what would happen to him.

The sound of beating continued and Kasper's eyes began to glaze. Unable to witness any more of his suffering, Azriel let go.

'Smugglers!' a man on the other side of the wall yelled, blowing a whistle. 'Smugglers!'

Shit! Azriel heard footsteps pounding up the road towards him.

'Kasper!' he heard a woman scream from the other side of the wall. 'Let go of him, you bastard! Let go!'

'Iz?' he cried as the footsteps got closer.

'Stop it!' she cried.

'Is he OK?' Azriel called.

'Go and get a doctor!' she heard Izabel yelling at someone.

Oh, if only he could fit through the hole or scale that damned wall and help.

The footsteps behind him grew louder and then a shot rang

out and a bullet ricocheted off the wall. Azriel started to run as another shot was fired. Was this how it was going to end? he wondered as he raced around the corner. After all this, was he going to die before he saw the Germans defeated?

Izabel stared at Kasper lying motionless on the ground.

'He's just a child,' she screamed at the policeman she'd found battering him with his truncheon. 'He's just a child,' she repeated, collapsing to the floor beside her brother.

'Iz?' she heard Azriel call out from the other side, but all she could think of was Kasper.

'Please, please don't die,' she begged, holding him close to her.

To her huge relief, he let out a moan and his eyelids fluttered.

'I caught him smuggling,' the policeman whined, his nasal voice grating on her every nerve.

'Shame on you!' she cried. 'He's ten years old.' Oh, if only she hadn't given that gun to Azriel, she would have shot him right there on the spot.

'Is he OK?' she heard Azriel call.

Kasper let out another moan. 'Don't you go dying on me,' she said to him, in her sternest big-sister voice. 'Go and get a doctor!' she yelled at the policeman. 'Somebody please, get a doctor!' she screamed.

The policeman turned on his heel and ran off.

On the other side of the wall, she heard the sound of pounding footsteps, followed by the piercing crack of a shot.

Izabel gasped and clutched Kasper tighter. 'Azriel?' she whispered.

Another shot rang out, and another. Feeling sick to her stomach, she scooped Kasper into her arms and ran for cover.

'Am I going to die?' Kasper murmured as she held him tight, half running, half stumbling along the street towards the hospital.

'No, of course not,' she replied. But how could she know? He was white as a sheet and clearly in agony. 'Why did you go without me?' she asked.

'I don't want them to starve,' he replied. 'And I wanted my toffees,' he added and she didn't know whether to laugh or cry.

'Oh, Kasper! I would have given you your toffees anyway!'

'The notes,' he murmured. 'In my shirt.'

She saw some paper poking out of his shirt pocket and quickly pulled the notes out and tucked them into her bag just as they reached the hospital. 'If anyone asks you what happened, just say a bigger boy beat you trying to steal some food,' she whispered.

'I'm not stupid,' he replied crossly, and once again she didn't know whether to laugh or cry.

A nurse came running over and helped Izabel place Kasper on a bed. While she watched the nurse gently examining her brother for injuries, she thought of Azriel and the gunshots. What if he'd been killed? What if Kasper was going to die? It would all be her fault.

No, she told herself, it would be Dieter's fault. He was the one who had stopped her, who had practically frogmarched her into the bar and made her have a drink. She felt fury lying heavy in the pit of her stomach like a cold, hard stone. She was sick of the Germans and the Polish police and the pogromists and their incessant violence and hate. What was the point of all this suffering? What did they hope to achieve? Why couldn't they just let people get on with their lives?

She clenched her fists tightly in her lap. If Azriel had been killed and if her brother didn't fully recover, she was going to avenge them if it was the last thing she did. After all, what would she have to lose?

She looked at Kasper lying there so helpless on the hospital bed. She was going to use that quick wit of hers and her lioness courage and she was going to come up with a plan that would wipe that smug smirk off Dieter's face once and for all.

38

The Friday after Jaski and the orphans were taken, Adela arrived home for Shabbat dinner feeling heavy-hearted and in no mood for saying blessings of any kind, but Estera had been insistent that she and Azriel attend. Azriel hadn't seen Leopold since their terrible argument and Adela had been afraid he'd refuse to attend, but the news about the orphanage had shaken him to the core too and he seemed to want to do anything to keep Adela happy.

'Please try not to argue with Papa,' Adela said to him as they climbed the stairs to the apartment.

Azriel sighed in response, but Adela didn't push. It was a minor miracle that he'd agreed to come at all, and besides, he was worried out of his mind about Izabel's brother, as she had been too, ever since he'd told her what had happened.

They found their parents sitting holding hands at the table, grave-faced.

'What's wrong?' Adela asked.

'Oh good, you both came,' Estera said, but rather than bustle around fixing them something to eat or drink, she remained seated and looked at Leopold.

'I can't stay long,' Azriel said, sitting down. 'I have some business to attend to later for the Bund.' He looked at Leopold defiantly, but their father didn't flinch.

'Your father has something to tell you,' Estera said, and Adela felt fear growing in the pit of her stomach.

'I resigned from the *Judenrat*,' Leopold said quietly, looking down at the tablecloth.

'Why?' Adela sat down. She'd never seen her wise, strong father look so defeated.

'After what they did to the orphans, how could I continue?' He gave a weary sigh. 'I took the job because I truly believed I'd be able to help people, but if I can't even save innocent children, I'm of no use at all.'

'Don't say that!' Adela exclaimed. 'It's not your fault.'

'I've tried so hard,' he continued, his voice cracking, 'so hard.' He looked at Azriel. 'I know you think I've been no more than a puppet, but I need you to know that I never took the job to help the Germans – or myself – I thought it was an opportunity to do good.'

Adela looked at Azriel and held her breath, praying he wouldn't use this opportunity to crow. It couldn't have been easy for Leopold to admit that he'd made a mistake and to humble himself like this.

Azriel stood up and Adela's breath caught in her throat. Surely he wasn't going to walk out? She watched as he walked around the table, coming to a halt behind Leopold. Then he placed his hands on his father's shoulders.

'I'm sorry, Papa,' he said softly.

'Oh son!' Leopold got to his feet and the two men clung to each other in a hug.

'I'm so sorry,' Azriel mumbled.

'So am I.' Leopold held him at arm's length and looked him in the eye. 'So am I.'

Adela's eyes filled with tears. After the horror of the past week, it felt so good to see such a display of love.

After a moment, the men sat down.

'Of course this has certain implications,' Leopold said, glancing anxiously at Estera.

'What do you mean?' Adela asked.

'Now I'm no longer a member of the *Judenrat*, I'm no longer exempt from deportation.'

'But what about the shop?' Adela looked at Estera. 'You have a number.'

'Not anymore,' she replied. 'We're no longer allowed to trade.'

Adela looked at Azriel.

'It's all right,' he said. 'I can find you somewhere safe to stay. The Bund have been building hiding places all over the city in preparation.'

'In preparation for what?' Leopold asked.

Azriel looked at him and smiled. 'For when we fight back.'

39

Azriel made his way down the narrow staircase into the basement kitchen of the old bakery. Like so many other Jewish businesses in Warsaw, the bakery had ceased trading a long time ago and the kitchen was dirty and cold. He headed over to the huge oven and opened the door. He pictured the baker who'd once worked there, loading the oven with tray after tray of bagels and bread, and gave a wry smile as he climbed inside.

Fumbling in the dark, he found the catch on the false wall at the back and pulled it open, then crawled through the hole beyond and into a concealed room. It was freezing cold and the walls were damp, but if it kept his parents safe that was all that mattered.

When his father had apologised, he'd felt no sense of elation or self-righteousness; all he could think of was how much time they'd wasted being estranged. All the more reason to get his parents to a place of relative safety immediately, he mused as he placed some blankets on the makeshift camp bed he'd set up in the corner.

He looked around at the rest of the cellar. A fold-away table stood propped against the wall along with three deckchairs.

He'd managed to acquire a portable gas stove, which sat beside a couple of pots and pans on the floor in what would be the kitchen area. He wasn't sure what Estera would make of their new living arrangements and he felt a burst of anger as he thought of his parents being made to live underground like rats. But if it kept them safe, he reminded himself again, it had to be worth it.

And besides, they were hardly alone. For months now, the Bund and other Jewish Resistance groups had been creating hiding places all over the ghetto. There was now a whole subterranean town, connected by tunnels and the sewer canals, that the Germans and Jewish police knew nothing about. Slowly but surely, weapons and grenades were being smuggled in, turning the buildings lining the narrow streets into a powder keg. He wasn't sure how and he wasn't sure when, but one day they were going to take the Germans by surprise and let them see that they weren't just sheep who could be led to the slaughter.

Of course, he understood that, ultimately, they would be no match for the German army, but if they could just hold out for an Allied victory, then maybe they'd be saved. And even if they couldn't, Azriel would rather die knowing that he'd taken some Germans with him and that his life, and death, hadn't been in vain.

He took one last look around the place, then set off to get his parents.

～

Izabel looked across the table at Dieter. He'd been chewing on a piece of steak for several seconds now and a strand of drool was trickling from his mouth onto his chin. She'd never felt more repelled by another human being, but she'd also never felt so intent upon revenge. Thankfully, Kasper was recovering from his injuries – much to his disappointment, he hadn't sustained any lasting war wounds – but Izabel couldn't shake the image of seeing him being beaten senseless by a grown man and the seed of hatred it had planted was growing like a gnarly vine inside of her. Sometimes it felt as if it would choke her alive. And then there was not knowing whether Azriel was alive or dead, which was almost too much to bear.

She watched as Dieter finally swallowed the piece of meat and smacked his greasy lips together. He looked so smug. So self-satisfied. It was so unfair that while he feasted on the finest meat, on the other side of the wall, thousands of people were deliberately being starved. That's if there were thousands left. According to her father, most of the ghetto had now been deported already. What if Adela was one of them? Panic began building inside of her. What if Azriel had been shot and Adela and her parents sent east?

'Why the frown?' Dieter asked.

She forced her mouth up into a smile. 'I'm sorry. I suppose I was wishing I was able to spend more time with you.'

Instead of looking surprised or happy at this, like a humbler person would, he nodded knowingly as if it was a given that everyone would want to spend more time with him if given the chance.

'I'd give anything to spend a whole night with you rather than just a couple of hours,' she continued, as she'd practised many times before coming to meet him that evening. Lord knows, she'd had to. She'd never meant anything less.

His smug smile grew. 'Is that so?'

'But I know you probably aren't allowed.' She held her breath, hoping that by questioning his authority he'd feel determined to prove her wrong, just as he had with the gun.

'I can do whatever I want,' he stated, falling hook, line and sinker.

'Don't you want to spend the whole night with me then?'

She took a breath to steel herself, then slid her hand under the table and onto his leg.

A little gasp of pleasure escaped his lips. 'Of course!'

She moved her hand higher, and his expression glazed slightly. And in that moment, she realised that she wasn't entirely powerless and it almost gave her a thrill.

'How about tomorrow night, at the hotel,' he murmured.

'I think that would be wonderful.' She slid her hand higher, quickly caressed him and then withdrew. The gnarly vine of hatred growing within her seemed to be made of steel.

Adela tried not to gag as the smell of bleach filled her nostrils. It didn't help that they were down in a cellar so there was no ventilation. She was now living in one of the many underground hiding places the Bund had been creating in Warsaw. When Azriel had brought her there, she'd been amazed at the ingenuity and the effort they'd gone to; to get to the cellar, you had to go through a secret door hidden behind a bookcase.

'OK, I think it might be time to wash it off,' Azriel said, looking at her hair.

She couldn't help giggling, partly from nerves and partly from the surreal nature of the situation. 'I bet you never thought you'd end up in hairdressing when you joined the Bund,' she quipped as he fetched a basin and a large jug of water.

He laughed. 'No, absolutely not!' He placed the basin on her lap and she tipped her head forwards. 'And I bet you never thought that the war would turn you blonde.'

'No, grey more like!' She winced as he tipped the icy cold water over her head. 'Are you sure it will work?' She regretted asking the question as soon as she'd uttered it. She'd meant what she'd said when she'd told him she'd do anything to fight the Germans. She didn't want him to see her fear.

'Of course,' he replied confidently. 'How many Jewish women do you know with blonde hair?'

She laughed, but inside she felt a little sick at the thought of having to disguise her heritage.

'Don't worry, little bookworm, you're going to be fine. And you're going to be out of this place for a while!'

She nodded.

'And you're going to see Izabel, hopefully.'

At this, her nervousness turned to excitement, although she couldn't help noting his use of the word 'hopefully'. She'd have to get out of the ghetto first, and then pass the different checkpoints on the other side.

'Are you sure my false papers will stand up to scrutiny?'

He nodded. Then he put down the jug and crouched in front of her, taking hold of her hands. 'I'd never let you go if I thought it was too dangerous.'

She nodded. 'I know.'

'We've reached the point where there's nothing left to lose.'

She thought of Jaski and the orphans and nodded again.

'And remember what we told you in your training,' Azriel continued. 'When you get to the other side, you must make sure that you look confident and happy. No frowning, and no looking down at the ground.'

'Of course,' she agreed. Surely, being on the other side of the cursed ghetto wall would make that easy.

As soon as her hair was dried and styled, Azriel took Adela to a tenement building next to the ghetto wall. The Bund had dug a tunnel from the cellar of the building into the cellar of a store across the street on the other side of the wall, belonging to a member of the Polish Resistance. Her pulse quickened as Azriel led her down the cellar steps. She tried not to think about the enormity of what she was about to do, or what would happen to her if she got caught.

'You have the map?' Azriel asked, even though he was the one who had put it in the sole of her shoe.

'Yes.' She shivered as she thought of the map of the camp at Treblinka hidden beneath her foot. A Bund member had recently been sent there undercover and they'd returned with a plan of the layout, and, more importantly, potential places where the fence could be breached. She clenched her fists tightly as she thought of Jaski and the orphans, praying that by some miracle they were still alive.

Azriel moved a large set of shelves from the wall, to reveal a jagged hole, a couple of feet wide. 'Filip, our contact in the Polish Home Army, will be waiting for you at the other side,' he said. 'All you have to do is give the coded knock and he'll let you out. If he isn't there, come straight back. I'll wait here until I know you must have made it there safely.'

She nodded, feeling slightly sick as she peered into the pitch dark of the tunnel.

'Good luck, little bookworm.' He hugged her tightly. 'I love you. Be safe.'

'I love you too... and Azriel?'

'Yes?'

'If anything happens to me and I don't make it back please tell Mama and Papa I love them. And tell them that I had to do this – for Jaski and the orphans.'

'Nothing's going to happen to you,' he replied firmly before hugging her again. 'But I will,' he whispered in her ear.

Adela scrambled into the tunnel and began to crawl. After a few seconds, Azriel pushed the shelves back over the hole and she was plunged into total darkness.

'I am made of water and stardust,' she whispered over and over, her voice quivering, as she slowly moved along the cold, earthy floor. 'I am proof that magic exists.'

After what felt like an eternity, but could have only been a few minutes, she reached a dead end. Her hand trembling, she reached out and gave the coded knock. Panic began rising inside of her. What if Filip wasn't there? What if she crawled all the way back and Azriel had gone too? What if she was trapped down there in the cold and dark?

40

Izabel checked the pocket in her bag and felt a bolt of adrenaline as she saw the silver glint of the knife's blade. Her plan, such as it was, was a simple one, fuelled by a burning desire for vengeance. She would seduce Dieter and then, when she'd got him in a moment of vulnerability, she would reach for the knife and stab him in the throat. She grimaced at the thought. Then she would get dressed – she'd packed a change of clothes in her overnight case just in case the clothes she was wearing became stained with his blood – and return home. Presumably, Dieter would have told his fellow soldiers that he wouldn't be back that night, so she'd have several hours before anyone raised the alarm. Dieter still didn't know where she lived or worked, so hopefully his death wouldn't be traced back to her, but even if it was, she'd reached a point where she no longer cared. The more she replayed the night Kasper was beaten, the more she became convinced that Azriel was dead. And the news about the camp in Treblinka was so relentlessly grim, it was becoming impossible to believe that she'd ever see her beloved Rubinsteins again.

She zipped up the compartment on her bag, closed the lid

on her case, and applied a spritz of perfume. Then she picked up her Saint Brigid figurine and clutched her tightly.

'Please forgive me for what I'm about to do,' she whispered. 'Please grant me a miracle.'

Brigid smiled up at her serenely.

Down in the tunnel, Adela heard something being dragged across the floor above her, and then a shaft of pale light fell upon her face. Blinking as her eyes adjusted, she felt a pair of hands reaching out to help her out of the tunnel. She emerged into another cellar, much smaller than the one she'd just come from, and saw the outline of a thin man silhouetted in the lamplight.

'Come,' he said, beckoning her to follow him.

He led her up a flight of stone steps into a room where two other men were sitting at a table. The air was thick with cigarette smoke.

Adela brushed herself down and patted her hair.

'Greetings, comrade, I'm Filip,' one of the men said. His voice was deep and gravelly, and despite being the size of a bear, he had a warm smile that instantly put her at ease. 'Do you have the document?'

'I do.' She sat on one of the chairs and carefully took the folded paper from the hiding place in her shoe.

'Excellent, thank you.' He took the paper from her. 'I under-stand you're going to courier something for us.'

She nodded and he passed her an envelope. 'We've coded the message into a piece of sheet music. So if you're stopped and questioned, you're to say that you're on your way to a piano lesson.'

'OK.' Her heart raced as she put the envelope in her bag. Coming through the tunnel was the least scary part of her mission. Once she was outside, she could be stopped and questioned by the Germans. She had to trust that the Bund had done a good job forging her papers.

Once she'd freshened up, she got changed into the outfit Azriel had given her – a lilac dress and a grey fur stole. As she put on the clothes, she practised smiling, ready for her new carefree role on the Aryan side of the wall. Then she was shown out of the apartment by Filip. 'Good luck,' he whispered as he pointed her in the direction of the main door.

'Thank you,' she whispered back.

Although she'd studied a map with Azriel before coming and knew exactly where she'd be coming out and where she had to go, she still felt disorientated when she emerged into the sunny street. The pavement was bustling with people, all looking so healthy and happy. She glanced up at the ghetto wall looming over them, shocked at the stark contrast between life on either side.

As she made her way along the street, she didn't feel any joy at momentarily being free. All she felt was anger and resentment. Did nobody care about what was happening on their side of the wall? Was it really that easy to forget all about them? But then she thought of the Resistance contacts she'd just met and the person she'd be delivering the coded message to. There were plenty of people on this side of the wall who cared about their plight, and who were risking everything to try to defeat the Germans. Including Izabel, who, if all went according to plan, she'd get to see that very evening. Smiling at the thought of surprising her beloved friend, she continued on her way.

Izabel opened the bedroom door and listened. She could hear her parents talking in the living room and made a break for it, while she could. She slipped out of the apartment, her heart thudding. If they heard her and came after her, she'd have no way of explaining why she was leaving with an overnight case. She slid the lift door shut and, after what felt like forever, it began its slow juddering descent.

Outside, the sun was beginning to set behind the buildings and the sky was streaked crimson and tangerine. It was the kind of sunset she usually loved, so fiery and dramatic, but today the red only reminded her of blood. Would there be a lot of blood? she wondered. Would she end up covered in it? Her stomach churned.

It's not too late to change your mind, she told herself. *You could turn around right now and go back home.*

But the new apartment wasn't her home and never would be. Her father was a traitor and the people she cared about the most were gone and, for all she knew, dead. She realised that killing one Nazi would hardly win the war, or change things for the better in Poland, but at least she would have done something to try to even the score.

By the time she reached the hotel, Izabel was filled with a sense of finality.

She found Dieter at the bar, sipping on a whisky. He looked her up and down and nodded approvingly.

'I've been thinking about this all day,' she said breathlessly in his ear as they embraced.

'Oh, me too.' He groped her buttock and squeezed it tightly. 'Would you like a drink?'

She shook her head. 'I just want to be alone with you.' She leaned closer and took a breath before whispering what she wanted to do.

He turned and slapped some money down on the bar and steered her back out into the lobby.

A woman was standing watching them from beside a huge vase of flowers and, for a moment, Izabel felt a wave of shame.

You have nothing to be ashamed of, she reminded herself.

But now she was standing beside Dieter, waiting for the lift, he seemed a lot bigger and stronger than before. In her fury-fuelled fantasies, she'd stabbed him so effortlessly. But what if he was able to overpower her? He was a soldier after all; he'd be trained in how to fight off an assailant.

She glanced over at the woman by the flowers again. There was something weirdly familiar about her and her panic grew. The last thing she needed was a witness able to place her at the scene of the crime. Izabel studied the woman as the lift began clanging its way down to the ground floor. She was thin with short, bright blonde hair and wearing a lilac dress, with a grey fur stole. Then she realised why she thought she knew her; she looked a little like a blonde version of Adela.

The lift arrived and Dieter pulled the lattice door open. 'I've treated us to a room on the top floor,' he said. 'It has the best views of Warsaw... because you can't see the ghetto,' he added with a snort of laughter.

The woman by the vase gave a loud cough and Izabel froze. She even coughed just like Adela. Izabel got into the lift and stared at the woman through the lattice door. The woman stared right back. Izabel felt as if she was about to pass out. She'd know that gaze anywhere. She was looking right into the eyes of her beloved friend!

41

Adela stared after the lift as it whirred and clanged upwards. When she'd come up with her plan to try to find Izabel, she'd pictured a joyful reunion at best, and not being able to find her at worst. Never in her wildest dreams had she imagined following Izabel to a hotel, for a rendezvous with a Nazi! And, even worse, the Nazi who had antagonised Adela that awful day outside the orphanage. She'd recognised his mean little eyes instantly. What on earth was Izabel doing with him?

She took a breath to try to calm herself. When she'd seen Izabel leaving home holding a small case, she'd been afraid that she might be going away somewhere. She'd been hoping to attract her attention quietly and discreetly, but there'd been so many people about, she'd had to hang back. Seeing Izabel's familiarity with the Nazi at the hotel didn't make sense. She knew that Izabel had been smuggling information into the ghetto to the Bund for months. Had she been getting it from the soldier? Had she been... sleeping with him?

Feeling numb with shock, Adela hurried through the lobby. After the gloom and misery of the ghetto, the sights and sounds and smells of the hotel felt like an assault upon her senses. A giggling group of women reeking of perfume and dripping with jewellery walked past and anger prickled her skin.

Remember to look happy, she told herself and she plastered a stupid smile on her face before stepping outside. The evening was becoming chilly, and she could smell the earthy scent of autumn on the air. Autumn had always been her favourite season. But would she live to see another, she wondered, and a shard of sorrow pierced her heart.

She pulled her fur stole tighter around her. Rather than feeling like a treat, being allowed to escape the ghetto for a few hours was starting to feel like torture. And now she'd have to return with this new knowledge about Izabel. What on earth would she say to Azriel?

She was about to go down the steps leading to the street when she felt a hand clamp her shoulder, and her heart leapt right into her throat. Then she caught a waft of perfume that instantly conjured a wealth of happy memories.

'*Moj skarbe*, is it you?' a voice whispered from behind her.

Adela turned to see Izabel staring at her, wide-eyed. 'You recognised me!' Adela exclaimed.

'Yes. The blonde hair threw me off at first, but there was no mistaking that stare.' Izabel shook her head in disbelief. 'How did you get here? What are you doing here? I thought I was hallucinating!'

It took everything Adela had not to fling her arms around her friend, but she had to find out what on earth she was doing with the German first. 'I wanted to ask you the exact same thing,' she whispered back.

Izabel clutched her hands to her chest. 'Every time I pray to Saint Brigid for a miracle, she sends me one. She sends me a Rubinstein!'

'Shh!' Adela hissed, looking around, but, thankfully, there was no one within earshot.

'I'm sorry, I'm just too overcome with joy.' She shook her head in disbelief. 'And to think of what I was about to do.'

'What are you doing here with *him*?' Adela whispered, looking back into the hotel.

'Oh Lord, if I told you, you'd never believe me.' Izabel clasped Adela's arm. 'Azriel – is he... is he dead?'

'No! Why would you think that?'

'He's not! Oh, Joseph, Mary!' Izabel raised her gaze heavenwards. 'I thought I heard him get shot.' She led Adela over to the side, out of the light spilling from the hotel door. 'The night Kasper was beaten, I thought he'd been killed. I heard a shot.'

'No, he's very much alive.'

'Oh my goodness, that's wonderful!' She beamed at Adela. Then, as quickly as it had appeared, her smile faded. 'Now I don't know what to do!' She looked at the hotel door, panic-stricken. 'I told him my watch had fallen off in the hotel lobby.'

Adela frowned. 'The soldier?'

'Yes. He'll be expecting me back any minute.'

'Were you... were you about to sleep with him?' Adela asked, unable to contain her horror.

'No!' Izabel shook her head, looking appalled by the mere thought. She leaned closer and whispered in her ear, 'I was going to kill him. And now I think we need to get away as quickly as possible.'

'What?' Adela gasped.

'Quickly!' Izabel hissed. 'There's no time to lose!'

As they hurried off along the street, Adela's mind buzzed as she tried to make sense of what she'd just been told. How and why had Izabel been planning to kill the soldier? Was this something the Bund had put her up to, without Adela knowing?

They raced along the city streets until they finally reached the park. Adela winced as she saw the carousel going round and round, filling the night air with music and laughter. The contrast with life in the ghetto was so painful.

'Do you remember when we used to ride the carousel as children?' Izabel asked.

'Of course.'

'And we'd pretend that our horses were able to fly.'

Adela laughed. 'Yes, and while all the other people went round and round, we were flying to the moon and stars.'

Izabel grabbed her arm. 'Let's ride it again, now.'

'Now? But...'

Izabel stopped walking and stared at her. 'But what? We've somehow been reunited, *moj skarbe*. This is a magical night of miracles, and we need to celebrate. I bet Jaski would want you to.'

'Jaski is...' Adela broke off, a lump forming in her throat.

'What?' Izabel clutched her arm. 'What?' she asked again, more insistently.

'They deported him to the death camp in Treblinka. All the orphans too.'

'Oh no!' Izabel bit on her bottom lip, the way she always did to prevent the onset of tears.

Adela gazed at her friend, this person she knew almost as well as herself. Even though they hadn't seen each other for almost two years, it was as if no time had passed at all. Perhaps that was the measure of a true friendship. Just like a favourite book that's been read so many times it's committed to memory, you know all the chapters that make that person whole.

'Oh, *moj skarbe*, I'm so sorry.' Izabel put down her case and clutched Adela's hands. 'I'm so sorry for everything you've been through. I've tried my hardest to help from out here, but it never feels like enough. I wish I could do more. I've tried everything I can think of, trust me.' She gave a shudder.

'I can't believe you were planning to kill that soldier!' Adela exclaimed. 'Was he the one who harassed me that day outside the orphanage?'

Izabel looked away for a moment before nodding. 'I've been

using him to get intelligence for the Bund, and then, when I thought Azriel had been killed, I decided to take my revenge.' She gave her a sheepish smile. 'I admit that it wasn't one of my finest plans. I was just so angry about everything that had happened. I had to do something.'

'Well, maybe it would be safer if you stick to working for the Bund instead of striking out on your own.' Adela smiled and squeezed her hands, delighted once more to see her impetuous, loyal friend.

'Yes!' Izabel exclaimed with a grin. 'And now I've seen you and I know Azriel is alive, I have something to live for again.'

'Exactly!' Adela smiled back at her. 'Come on, *moj skarbe*, let's fly to the moon.'

They walked arm in arm to the carousel and just as they did when they were kids, they chose horses next to each other.

As the carousel began to move, Adela placed her hands on her horse's shiny golden mane. Up above, the sky was darkening and the first of the stars were starting to appear. She noticed one twinkling far brighter than the others and immediately thought of Jaski. *Please still be alive*, she silently whispered.

As the ride picked up speed, the breeze ruffled her hair and it was as if he was there, sitting behind her on the horse. The music from the organ reverberated through her body and after years of hardship, it felt like the sweetest, most freeing feeling.

'To the moon!' Izabel cried from the horse beside hers and Adela threw her head back and sucked in lungfuls of air.

It was the saddest, yet most beautiful feeling. Despite everything she'd been through, and everything yet to come, Adela still so badly wanted to live.

42

Azriel waited anxiously at the mouth of the tunnel. Adela was meant to have returned a couple of hours ago. Something had clearly gone wrong, but what? He wrung his hands together and began pacing the cramped room. If anything had happened to her, he'd never forgive himself. He never should have sent her to the other side. She was too inexperienced for this kind of work, too nervous. The problem was, women made far better couriers because they aroused less suspicion. Unlike the Bund, and other Jewish Resistance groups, the Nazis seemed to believe that women were simple creatures, incapable of anything as daring and underhand as spying or sabotage. He gave a wry smile, as he thought of Izabel and Adela. Well, more fool the Germans.

Finally, he heard a noise from inside the tunnel and he quickly drew his weapon, standing with his back pressed to the wall by the entrance. The scrambling sound grew louder and, to his relief, Adela appeared.

'Little bookworm!' he exclaimed, hugging her tightly. 'Did you deliver the messages?'

'Yes!' Adela's eyes sparkled in the lamplight and, to his delight, he saw that the sadness that had clouded her gaze ever since Jaski and the orphans had been deported seemed to have lifted. In fact, she looked more animated than he'd seen her in a long time. 'And I saw Izabel!'

'You did? That's wonderful!' He felt a weird blend of excitement at the mention of Izabel and wistfulness that it hadn't been him who had seen her. 'How was she?'

'Well, she thought you were dead.'

'Why would she think that?' He frowned, shocked.

'She thought she heard you being shot the night her brother was attacked.' Adela glanced around the darkened basement. 'Is there anyone else here?' she whispered.

He shook his head.

'She was going to kill a soldier to avenge your death!'

'What?' He stared at her, certain he must have misheard.

'Yes.' Adela laughed. 'Thankfully, I found her in the nick of time. She's been fraternising with a soldier to try to get information for the Resistance. She told me she got a weapon from him too.'

Azriel winced. He wondered if it was the same German soldier from before. But he couldn't let on to Adela that he'd known about that, so he forced himself to look surprised.

'Was she OK?' he asked.

'Yes, especially when she learned you were still alive. I'd say she was positively elated!' Adela grinned.

'Oh good.' He gave a relieved smile, but inside he felt conflicted. The thought of Izabel going to such lengths to help them filled him with awe and gratitude for her bravery, but equally he felt terrified for her safety.

'And Filip gave me this to give to you.' She opened her satchel and undid the secret compartment, producing a jar of jam and two rectangular packages wrapped in greasy paper.

'Butter?' he asked, confused.

She laughed. 'I wouldn't want to put it on my bread.' She

moved closer and whispered in his ear. 'It's gunpowder. And there are bullets in the jam.'

He felt a shiver of excitement run up his spine. It felt so good to finally be doing something more to fight back after all this time. And after so many had been deported. Now they knew the truth about the death camps, those remaining in the ghetto were ready to join the fight too. The *Judenrat* and the Jewish police no longer had any authority. It was the Jewish militias who were in charge now, and people were mobilising for the fight. He didn't know how and when it would happen, but one day soon, the time would come for them to emerge from their hiding places and give the Nazis a taste of their own medicine. They might not be as well armed as the Germans, but they had weapons and explosives and ammunition, and they would have the element of surprise on their side. But perhaps their greatest advantage was that the Germans would be fighting a band of people who knew they had nothing left to lose. People who believed it was better to die fighting than to lie down and accept their defeat.

43

'Happy Christmas,' Dieter said, handing a Izabel a pink box, tied with a shimmering silver ribbon. 'I want you to wear it for me,' he continued before she had time to respond.

So, really, you've got me a present for you, Izabel thought to herself as she undid the bow. It was an act of selfishness that summed Dieter up so perfectly.

A waiter drifted by and topped up their glasses and she lifted the lid and looked inside. Nestled on a bed of silver tissue paper was a red satin lingerie set. Bile rose to the back of her throat as she thought of Dieter pawing away at her while she wore it. Her disappearance from the hotel the night she'd seen Adela had left Izabel with a lot of explaining to do. In the end, she'd decided to tell Dieter that she'd had a sudden panic, worrying that she might fall pregnant, even though this was no longer possible thanks to the pogromists. Thankfully, he'd fallen for it and, since then, they'd resumed meeting for drinks and meals so she could try and wheedle more information for the Bund from him, but never in a hotel room. She'd been hoping that the thought of her falling pregnant had been just as fright-ening a prospect for him too, but now it seemed it was no longer so.

'Wear it for you when?' she asked, trying to sound calm.

'Tonight.' He smiled across the table. 'I've booked us a room.'

'A room? But I thought...' Panic began rising inside of her. She hadn't anticipated this turn of events and she didn't know what to do.

'What?' His smile hardened.

'I thought we weren't going to do that anymore.' She leaned forward and lowered her voice. 'I don't want to fall pregnant.'

'You won't. I'll be careful.' He downed the rest of his drink. 'It's Christmas Eve. I want my present from you.' He stood up and held out his hand. 'Come.'

'But I haven't finished my drink,' she said lamely, trying to buy more time.

'Bring it with you,' he barked.

She stood up and he clamped his hand to her arm like a vice and steered her out into the lobby towards the lifts.

'I've been looking forward to this for a very long time,' he murmured in her ear as they waited for the lift to arrive.

Izabel gazed wistfully across the lobby, wishing Adela would magically appear again. But all she saw were Christmas revellers, blissfully unaware of the horror she was about to endure.

Adela gazed up at the night sky, searching for the brightest star, which she always saw as being symbolic of Jaski.

'I miss you,' she whispered, fixing her gaze upon its twinkling light.

The star flickered, as if Jaski was saying, *I miss you too.*

Then she looked at the other stars and thought of the

orphans. *I hope Jaski has you all acting in the most incredible play*, she thought, gulping down the onset of tears.

She turned her gaze to the moon and thought of Izabel. Although the ghetto had been in existence for two years now, she still hadn't got used to the fact that her beloved friend was just a couple of miles away. Oh, how she hated that wall and how it had turned her part of Warsaw into a prison. But at least the Germans had stopped their deportations. Perhaps soon the Allies would claim victory and the wall would be torn down.

'Happy Christmas, *moj skarbe*,' she whispered, hoping that somehow the moon would transmit her message like a magical radio signal.

Izabel emerged from the hotel bathroom in the new lingerie set. It was a lot skimpier than the one Dieter had bought her before and she felt vulnerable and exposed beneath his stare.

'Very nice,' he murmured from the bed. 'Very nice indeed.' He beckoned to her. 'Come.'

An image of Adela popped into Izabel's mind. *Don't be scared*, moj skarbe, she imagined her whispering. *You're just doing your job. You're doing this for the Resistance.*

Izabel gritted her teeth and walked over to the bed.

Thankfully, Dieter was so excited by the sight of her in his Christmas gift that the whole thing was over in less than a minute. When he'd finished, he rolled off her and lit a cigarette.

'That was incredible,' he said, through wisps of smoke.

'Yes!' she exclaimed, emboldened by the relief that it was over. Now, it was time for her to get her real gift and, more importantly, a gift for the Resistance. The prospect of gathering some information for them was the only thing that had kept her going throughout the sorry ordeal. 'I hope the war doesn't end soon,' she murmured, trailing her fingers up his arm.

He frowned at her. 'Why?'

'Because then you'd have to go back to Germany.'

He smiled. 'Don't worry. I have plenty of work to do here. And, anyway, soon the whole of Warsaw will be German.'

'What do you mean?' she asked, trying to keep a lid on her anxiety.

'Once we've got rid of the ghetto.'

She leaned on her elbow and looked at him. 'How are you going to do that?'

'We're going to finish what we started back in July.'

She stared at him blankly. Her stomach churned. This was going to require all her acting skills.

'We're going to rid this city of the Jews once and for all.'

She feigned an expression of delight.

'It's high time we cleansed Warsaw of the vermin and their disease.'

They're only falling sick because of the conditions you're keeping them in, she wanted to scream, but she bit her lip. 'That's wonderful. So, when are you planning to do this?'

'Why so many questions?' He put his cigarette in the ashtray on his nightstand and rolled over to face her.

'I just can't wait,' she said with a giggle, then, fighting the urge to retch, she leaned closer and planted a trail of kisses on his neck.

He let out a moan of pleasure and gripped her face in his hands. 'We begin another deportation in the middle of January,' he said breathlessly. 'We should be rid of them all by the end of the month.' He pulled her face towards him and clamped his mouth to hers, adding to her suffocating feeling of fear.

44

'The Germans are planning another deportation,' Azriel said, as he read the coded note from Izabel. When he'd seen a note from her, smuggled into the ghetto along with some knives and food, he'd hoped it had been one of her personal letters. This was the news that he'd been dreading.

Berek looked up from the grenade he'd been making from some gunpowder and an old shoe polish tin. 'When?'

'Mid-January, and it will come without warning.'

Berek put the grenade down on the table. 'Well, we'll be ready and waiting for them.'

'Will we be able to repel them though?' Azriel looked at the handmade grenade. They'd been smuggling weapons and ammunition into the ghetto for months now, but what match would their Molotov cocktails and home-made grenades be for the might of the German army?

Berek nodded. 'Yes, because, thanks to your informant, the element of surprise will be on *our* side, and we will take full advantage of that.'

'How so?'

'The Germans think they're going to surprise us, but now we know their plans, we can prepare to surprise them.'

Azriel felt his tension ease a little. 'I like the sound of that.'

Berek nodded. 'Oh yes, we'll give them a welcome they won't be expecting.'

~

The new year arrived, bringing with it good news from Stalingrad, where the Russian army had managed to completely encircle the German forces.

'Do you really think the Russians will be able to defeat the Germans?' Adela asked Leopold over breakfast in the dim lamplight of the cellar. It was three weeks into January and, following Azriel's advice, she'd moved into her parents' hiding place. According to Azriel, another deportation could be imminent and he thought it was safer for them to stick together.

'Oh yes,' Leopold replied. 'And once they've done that, they'll be able to liberate Ukraine and then Poland.'

'We can only pray.' Estera smiled sadly.

'We just have to hold out for a few more months.' Leopold gave her a reassuring smile.

'I'd better get to work,' Adela said, drinking the last of her tea. She'd started work in one of the ghetto schools a couple of months before, and although it wasn't nearly as magical as Jaski's secret school, it felt good to be teaching again, and she welcomed the distraction.

'Me too. I'll walk with you,' Estera said, dabbing her lips with her napkin. She had recently been drafted to work in one of the armament factories the Germans had set up in the ghetto and although it made Adela sick to think of her mother making weapons for the Nazis, at least having a factory job should keep her safe from any further deportations. 'It will be good to get outside,' Estera said as she stood up from the table. 'I'm starting to feel like a mole, spending so much time underground.'

'You will always be my beautiful princess,' Leopold said, reaching for her hand and kissing it passionately.

'And you will always be my handsome prince.' Estera took his hand and held it to her heart.

'Oh, please!' Adela pretended to grimace, but really it delighted her to see her parents so playful and loving again. Oh, how she wished her father's prediction would come true. Could she dare to believe that they might survive the horror of the ghetto after all?

Adela and Estera emerged from the building and instantly gasped. The air was so cold, it felt as if it had teeth, gnawing into Adela's skin. She lifted her scarf up to her eyes and linked her arm through her mother's.

'Do you think Papa is right?' she asked as they began walking. 'Do you think the Russians will be here soon?'

'I hope so,' Estera replied. 'But whatever happens, I'm so glad that we're living together again – even if it is in a burrow like moles.'

Adela laughed. 'Yes, and all in one room!' It was funny, before the ghetto, she would have hated the thought of sharing a room with her parents, but now she found it comforting to be at such close quarters, especially at night. It was soothing falling asleep to the low rumble of her father's snores and waking to the sounds of her mother making breakfast.

When they reached the junction where they had to part ways, Adela hugged Estera tightly. Living together in the cellar seemed to have eased Estera's anxiety too, and it had been wonderful catching glimpses of the person she'd been before the war – humming tunes as she cobbled a meal together from their meagre rations and reminiscing about fun family memories.

Some nights, at Adela's request, she'd tell her a bedtime story, sitting on the edge of Adela's camp bed and stroking her hair as she brought to life the fairy tales Adela had so loved as a child.

'I love you, Mama,' she whispered in her ear.

Estera kissed her. 'Oh, darling daughter, I love you too.'

Adela continued on her way, mentally preparing her first lesson for the day. She'd been planning on teaching the children about verbs and adjectives, but after Leopold's optimistic prediction over breakfast, she felt the desire to do something fun. Perhaps she could ask the class to write a play together instead. Then, if it worked out well, they could perform it too. Her mind started buzzing with ideas. But just as she reached the street leading to the school, she heard the dreaded sound of soldiers' jackboots on the pavement and turned to see a large group of SS soldiers, in their black uniforms and red swastika armbands, marching towards her. A grey army truck crawled down the road behind them. Fear coursed through her veins. Was this the start of the deportations Azriel had warned her about? The other people on the pavement looked equally horrified.

'Jews!' one of the soldiers yelled through a loud hailer. 'Today, you will be leaving Warsaw. We need you to make your way to the Umschlagplatz immediately.'

No, no, no! Adela thought and she turned back and began hurrying away. She heard footsteps running behind her and someone grabbed her shoulder.

'It's time to go,' the soldier said.

'But what about my belongings? Don't I need to get some clothes?' she asked, desperate to buy herself an opportunity to escape.

'There's no time for that,' he said, as the other soldiers began rounding up everyone on the street and making them stand in a line.

Adela thought of her mother and prayed that she'd made it

to work safely. And what about Azriel? What if he got caught up in this too? Her heart began to race as the enormity of what was happening hit her. This was it, the moment she'd been dreading and trying to avoid for so long. She wouldn't get to see the Russians liberate Poland. She wouldn't get to see her beloved Izabel again. She might not even get to see her family. She was about to be deported to her death.

45

Azriel watched from the doorway as the procession of people silently made their way towards the Umschlagplatz, with pairs of SS soldiers guarding them on the flanks. Even though he'd been prepared for this moment for a month, it didn't make it any less sickening.

But it isn't over yet, he reminded himself, feeling in the inside pocket of his jacket for his pistol. He turned to look at his comrades. There were ten of them gathered behind him in the doorway and members of the other Jewish military groups were also preparing to strike in a neighbouring street.

'Ready?' he asked.

They nodded, grim-faced. They all knew that, even if their plan worked, they probably wouldn't all make it back alive. Perhaps none of them would. Azriel became filled with a grim sense of determination. At least if he died today, it would be fighting for freedom, and hopefully he'd take one or more of the Germans with him. At least he wouldn't be dying in vain.

'We'll leave one at a time and join the crowd,' he instructed the others. 'Then, once we're at the Umschlagplatz, I'll give the signal and you know what to do.'

Again, they all nodded grimly.

'Good luck, comrades,' Azriel whispered. 'It's an honour to fight alongside you.'

They all hugged and slapped each other on the back, and then, one by one, they slipped through the door.

Azriel thought of his parents and Adela. He hoped they'd managed to escape the round-up. He'd warned them after he got Izabel's note to always be on their guard. He took a breath to regain his focus, then stepped out onto the street.

As Adela was shepherded into the cordoned-off section of the station yard, she fought the urge to panic. The last time she'd been there, it had been to try to save Jaski and the orphans. She'd studiously avoided going anywhere near the Gdańska freight station ever since. And now it was only a matter of time before she'd be ushered across to the other side where the trains were waiting to take them to their deaths.

She looked around the crowded yard to see if she recognised anyone. Not that she wanted to. She wouldn't wish this fate upon anyone. She thought of Izabel and sorrow engulfed her. Could this really be it? Would she never see her friend again?

The guards began moving one of the columns of people across the yard towards the trains and Adela's heart broke for them all. They looked shell-shocked, and understandably so. This wasn't like the great deportation of before, when most people had fallen for the lies the Germans told them and believed that they were being sent somewhere to work. Now they all knew the terrible truth about Treblinka and the fate that awaited them there.

Adela continued scanning the row of frightened faces until she saw something that made her stomach drop. Estera was in the column of people heading for the trains.

'Mama!' she cried.

Estera stopped and turned and their eyes locked. Although she was too far away for Adela to hear what she was saying, she was able to read her lips.

'Oh, Adela! Oh no!' she gasped.

Adela took a couple of steps towards her, but, quick as a flash, a guard was at her side.

'Stay in your line!' he barked.

'But my mother's over there about to get on a train; can't I go with her?' Adela pleaded.

He looked at her coldly. 'Stay in your line.'

'Mama, I love you,' she cried at the top of her voice. There was nothing else to say.

'I love you too,' Estera called back. 'I'll see you at the other end.'

'But...' Adela broke off, not wanting to speak her worst fears out loud. What if they never saw each other again?

'I'll see you at the other end,' Estera called again, in the same firm tone she used when Adela and Azriel were children and she wanted them to do as they were told.

'I love you,' Adela called as Estera approached the waiting train.

'I love you too,' Estera replied, her voice now wavering. 'So very much.'

As Adela watched her disappear from view, she clenched her fists so tightly, her nails dug into her palms. She *would* see her mother again. She *had* to.

She looked back at the guard who had forbidden her from switching lines and felt a hatred so intense, it practically choked her.

~

Azriel's pulse quickened as the Umschlagplatz came into view. He'd successfully managed to infiltrate one of the columns of people being marched inside, but would their plan work, or had he just helped the Germans by offering himself up for deportation? One thing was for certain, it was too late to do anything about it now; he was just moments away from being herded into the yard. And then it would be time to put the plan into action.

He trudged, head down, through the gates, then glanced up and scanned the crowd. He could see one of his comrades up ahead looking at a German guard and reaching into his pocket for his pistol. Azriel did the same.

This was it, the moment of truth.

Adela stared glumly at the floor, trying desperately to think of something, *anything*, that might stop the crushing weight of despair bearing down upon her. But not even Jaski's mantra could help her now. What use was it being made of stardust, when the Germans could just march in and sweep them away? Where was the proof of magic when she needed it most? Just as she was about to lose herself in sorrow and fear, the loud crack of a gunshot pierced the air and the whole crowd flinched and cowered.

'Run!' someone yelled from the gate behind her. 'Run!'

She turned, confused, and saw that some of the prisoners were fleeing back out through the gates.

Another shot rang out and, to her surprise, she saw that it had come from one of the prisoners inside the yard. He was standing at the top of some steps, waving a pistol in the air.

'Escape while you can!' he yelled down at them.

Another shot was fired, and he clutched his side and toppled to the ground.

The prisoners around Adela started to flee, but she stood

motionless. How could she run when Estera had just been led through to the trains? But then she felt someone grab her arm and turned to see Azriel.

'Go!' he yelled. 'Get out of here.'

'But—'

'Go!' he yelled again, and she saw that he too was holding a gun.

Dazed, she turned and started to run. When she reached the gates to the yard, she saw that they were unmanned. As she raced through them, she felt no joy at having escaped. All she could think about was her mother and her heart ached as she ran further and further from her.

46

Izabel sat at her desk pushing a pile of papers from left to right and back again. She still couldn't shake the feeling of unease that had plagued her all morning, and it had been impossible to concentrate. Thankfully, Mr Bolek had been out at a meeting, so she'd been able to get away with doing nothing.

She noticed someone running by outside and her heart skipped a beat.

'Stop fretting!' she told herself crossly, pushing the papers back across her desk.

But just as she was feeling calmer again, the door to the office burst open and Mr Bolek bustled in.

'Something's happening in the ghetto,' he said, breathless.

'What do you mean?' Izabel leapt to her feet, sending her chair teetering backwards into a filing cabinet. 'What's going on? Are they OK?'

'I'm not entirely sure, but shots have been heard.'

'But shots are often heard in there.' She set her chair straight, her heart sinking. These days, the Germans regularly went into the ghetto to take potshots at people, especially if they'd been drinking. Dieter once joked about it, calling it 'target practice'.

'True,' Mr Bolek said, taking off his hat and coat and hanging them on the stand. 'But this time I think it might have been the Jews doing the shooting.'

'What?' Her gloom instantly gave way to excitement. 'How do you know?'

'Why else would the Germans be beating a hasty retreat?' He went over to the drinks cabinet in the corner and poured himself a vodka. 'I just saw them leaving the ghetto. It looked like they couldn't get out of there fast enough, and one of them appeared to be injured.'

Izabel clasped her hands together to try to stop herself from cheering out loud. Mr Bolek seemed harmless enough, but these days you just didn't know who could be trusted. She sat down and gazed blankly at the papers on her desk. If what he was saying was true, this was wonderful news – as long as the Rubinsteins were still safe, of course. She bit on her lip anxiously, worried her excitement might have been premature. If the Germans had been forced to retreat, they wouldn't take it lying down. In fact, there was bound to be all hell to pay.

Please, please, stay safe, she silently prayed, conjuring an image of Adela and Azriel and their parents in her mind and picturing the protective arms of Saint Brigid wrapping around them.

Adela crawled through the oven and into the cellar. It was so dark after the light outside that at first she thought there was no one there and she wanted to wail. If she'd lost both her parents to the deportation, it would feel like the end of the world. But then she heard the gentle rasp of her father's snores.

'Papa!' she cried, scrambling over to her parents' bed in the corner.

'What is it? What's wrong?' he said, waking with a start.

'Oh, Papa, there's been another deportation. They've taken Mama. They were going to take me too, but then the shooting started and Azriel's there and I'm worried that they're going to kill him. He told me to run. He told me to leave. He—'

'Hey, slow down,' Leopold interrupted, and he sat up and held her tight. She pressed her face into his shoulder and began to sob. 'Take a breath,' he said softly.

She took a breath, and another.

'Tell me what happened,' he said, stroking her hair. 'Take it slowly.'

She took another breath and then, voice cracking, she told him everything. When she got to the part about seeing Estera being led onto the train, she felt him flinch, but, as always, he remained calm and kept holding her and stroking her hair. 'What if we've lost them both?' she cried.

'Your mother and I prepared for this,' he said sadly. 'We always knew this could happen. Ever since last July, I've felt as if we've been living on borrowed time.' He shifted back slightly and wiped his eyes. 'And because we knew that, we did a lot of talking.'

'About what?'

'About what we'd do if we were separated and one of us was taken.'

Adela stifled another sob at the thought of her parents being torn apart.

'As long as you and Azriel were still here, we had to keep going. And we had to keep the faith that we'd all be together again one day.'

'But...' Adela broke off, not wanting to make him feel worse.

'We have to keep the faith, Adela; that's all we have left to hold on to.'

She nodded and nestled into him. Just because Estera had been taken, it didn't mean she was going to die, she tried telling herself. Maybe these new deportations were to a labour camp. She had to keep the hope alive or she didn't know how she'd go on.

The sound of the oven door being opened broke the silence. She and Leopold exchanged frightened stares.

'Do you think it's the Germans?' she whispered.

He didn't reply but took hold of her hand and squeezed it tightly. They both sat motionless on the bed, staring at the hole in the wall as someone came scrambling through. Adela was so scared, she could hear her heart pounding.

'Hello?' a voice said in the dark.

'Azriel!' she cried, flooded with relief.

Azriel heard the sound of a match being struck and lamplight filled the room. Adela was sitting on the bed with Leopold, hunched together like a pair of frightened rabbits.

'We made the Germans leave the ghetto!' he exclaimed. 'They stopped their deportation and fled.'

To his surprise, Adela and Leopold remained glum-faced.

'Did you hear what I said?' He went over and crouched down in front of them. 'We took them by surprise, and they panicked and left.'

'Yes, but not before they deported some,' Adela muttered.

His heart began to sink. 'What's wrong? What's happened?'

Leopold leaned forward and touched him on the arm. 'It's your mother,' he said softly.

The panic in Azriel grew. 'What about her?'

'The Germans took her,' Adela said, her voice breaking. 'They've sent her away.'

Azriel sank onto the floor, his head in his hands. 'No!' he cried. 'How did I not see her? Why didn't I save her?'

'It isn't your fault, son,' he heard Leopold say and he felt his hand on his shoulder.

'There was nothing you could have done,' Adela said. 'They'd already put her on the train.'

But Azriel was beyond consoling. The Germans had taken his mother, and it was as if they'd torn away a part of his soul.

47

Adela looked down at the Molotov cocktail she was making from a burned-out light bulb and gave a wry smile. She never could have foreseen that she'd one day end up making explosives, but that was the thing about having nothing left to lose: it prompted a wild, almost reckless abandon you didn't know you possessed.

During the three months since Estera had been deported, Adela was continually reminded of the opening line from the Dickens novel *A Tale of Two Cities*. Without her mother, it felt like the worst of times, but, to everyone's shock, the surprise attack by the Jewish Resistance seemed to have really rattled the Germans and they hadn't attempted any deportations since. Buoyed by this success, the Resistance had gone from strength to strength, and in that way, it felt like the best of times. Almost everyone in the ghetto wanted to be involved, and membership of the Jewish Fighting Organisation – a coalition of Jewish youth groups and organisations like the Bund – boomed. There was a terrific sense of community as they all came together to prepare for another German assault, digging tunnels and bunkers and amassing home-made ammunition and weapons.

Adela stuffed a piece of rag into the top of the light bulb, then went over to the window and peered outside. She was in the apartment where Azriel was staying and as well as being a makeshift munitions factory, it had an excellent view of one of the ghetto gates. She looked down at the guards on duty. Azriel had received a tip-off from Izabel that a new German assault on the ghetto was imminent and it was almost Passover. She wouldn't put it past the Germans to attack on such an important date in the Jewish calendar.

She opened the window and gazed up at the sky. She still looked at the stars every night and whispered her prayers to Jaski, but she refused to find a star that made her think of Estera; she had to cling to the hope that her mother was still alive.

Her thoughts turned to Izabel somewhere out there in the darkness on the other side of the wall. 'I love you, *moj skarbe*,' she whispered before closing the window and putting on her coat. It was getting late and she needed to get back to Leopold in the cellar. Although he'd remained his calm, stoic self since Estera was taken, she didn't like leaving him on his own for too long.

Azriel was dreaming that he was walking down a Warsaw street and he could see Izabel on the other side, but try as he might, he couldn't get her to hear him. 'It's me!' he yelled over and over. 'Izabel, it's me!' The street filled with the sound of men singing and he shouted even louder to try to make himself heard.

'Izabel!' he cried, waking himself up with a start. He sat up and rubbed his eyes. Milky white dawn light was creeping in through a chink in the blinds. He frowned. He could still hear the men from his dream singing, and their voices were growing louder and louder.

He got out of bed and padded over to the window. As he peered outside, his blood ran cold. Hundreds of SS troops were amassed outside the ghetto gates, stretching back as far as the eye could see, all singing in German.

Azriel raced through to Berek's room.

'It's happening!' he gasped. 'They're here! They're at the gates!'

Berek sprang from the bed, fully clothed. 'Wake the others,' he hissed.

Azriel nodded and went through to the living room, where five other comrades were sleeping in a row on the floor.

'Wake up,' he called. 'The Germans are here.'

Quick as a flash, the men scrambled into action, fetching pistols, Molotov cocktails and grenades from the cupboards and taking their positions by the windows.

Azriel watched as, down below, the guards swung the gates open, and the singing reached a crescendo.

'Do you think it'll work?' he asked Berek as the soldiers began marching six abreast through the narrow ghetto gates.

'Absolutely,' Berek said and Azriel felt a wave of gratitude for his friend. It was no surprise that the Bund had chosen Berek as a commander of their youth militia. With his optimism and calm confidence, he was a truly inspirational leader. 'OK, get ready,' Berek instructed, as they watched the soldiers make their way up the street.

Azriel held his breath. Any minute now, they would stop their smug singing.

A loud boom echoed through the air, sending the first of the soldiers flying.

'Yes!' Berek exclaimed and the other men exchanged nervous smiles. The Jewish Fighting Organisation had planted improvised explosive devices in the street just inside the ghetto gate. The singing Germans had swaggered straight into a trap.

Azriel opened his window, raised his pistol and took aim.

From the other windows in the apartment, and other apartments across the street, fellow Resistance members did the same. A hail of bullets and grenades made from pieces of drainpipe showered down upon the Germans, who scattered like ants fleeing a bucket of scalding water.

Adela woke with a start as a loud boom reverberated through the cellar. She sat up in her camp bed to see Leopold sitting at the table, reading his Torah.

'What was that?' she whispered.

He put the Torah down and clasped his hands. 'I think the Germans might be back again.'

Adela scrambled out of bed. She'd taken to sleeping in her clothes in preparation for the rumoured assault on the ghetto, so she only had to put on her boots. She fetched them from the corner and joined Leopold at the table.

'What are you doing?' he asked, looking concerned as she pulled them on.

'I have to go and help.' She placed her hand on his arm and gave it a squeeze. 'I promised Azriel,' she added, hoping he wouldn't try to prevent her from leaving.

To her relief, Leopold nodded, then he stood up and put on his jacket.

'Where are you going?' she asked.

'I'm coming with you.'

'But there's going to be fighting. It'll be too dangerous.'

He looked at her, his face deadly serious. 'I want to help too. I need to. They took your mother.' His voice cracked. 'I have to do something. And I won't leave my children to fight alone.'

She threw her arms around him and hugged him tightly. 'I love you, Papa.'

'Enough of that soppy stuff,' he said gruffly. 'We have work to do.'

48

'Do you think the war will ever end?' Kasper asked as he handed Izabel half of his orange.

'Of course it will,' she answered, although privately she'd been asking herself that very same question every day for months.

'I can't remember what it was like before the war,' Kasper said, and the matter-of-fact way in which he said it broke her heart.

She put her arm around him and pulled him close. For once, he didn't try to wriggle from her embrace. 'I suppose that's because the war's been going on for a third of your lifetime,' she replied, breathing in the scent of his scalp.

Down the hallway, she heard her father talking and she felt the familiar twinge of hatred she experienced every time she heard or saw him now.

'Let's get out of here,' she said, standing up and popping her half of the orange into her bag. 'Let's go to the park.'

'Yes!' Kasper exclaimed, leaping to his feet.

As soon as they stepped outside, Izabel could tell something sinister was afoot. A convoy of German army trucks streamed past and, in the distance, she could hear a dull thud, thud, thud, followed by a loud boom.

'What's happening?' Kasper asked, eyes wide.

'I don't know. But it doesn't sound good.' Fear began percolating inside her. 'Let's go and investigate.' She took his hand and led him after the trucks, her heart pounding.

As they drew closer to the ghetto, the air boomed and cracked with the sound of explosions and gunfire.

'Is it a war?' Kasper asked in hushed tones.

'I don't know – but I hope so,' she replied.

They turned onto a street leading to one of the ghetto gates and found it full of SS soldiers. An agitated-looking officer was barking orders at some of the men, who were looking distinctly nonplussed. More gunfire and shouting rang out from inside the ghetto walls and the smell of gunpowder hung heavy in the air. Izabel thought of the weapons she'd helped smuggle in over the past year. The thought that the Jewish Resistance might now be using them against the Nazis filled her with hope.

'We should get out of here,' she said to Kasper, clasping his hand tighter and preparing to go.

A cluster of SS men marched past. Then one of them stopped and grabbed her arm. She recognised the small, closely set eyes immediately.

'What are you doing here?' Dieter asked, sending a chill right through her. Then his gaze fell upon Kasper. 'And who is this?'

Azriel reloaded his pistol with what was left of the ammunition.

'We need more bullets,' he called to Berek. 'If we don't get them soon, we'll be sitting ducks! Can't Filip send us any?'

'I'll try to get a message to him,' Berek replied.

Azriel breathed a sigh of relief. The Germans might have

retreated after the surprise ambush, but they wouldn't be gone for long, of that he was sure, and they were certain to return armed to the teeth.

He heard the coded knock on the apartment door and watched, pistol at the ready, as one of his comrades went to answer it. He put the gun down and gave a relieved smile as Adela walked into the room.

'Little bookworm!' he exclaimed, standing up to greet her. 'Did you hear what happened? We sent the Germans...' He broke off, staring past Adela at his father standing in the doorway. 'Papa!'

He held his breath and waited for Leopold to speak, hoping with all his might that he hadn't come here to give him a lecture on the wrongs of violence. It was definitely not the time nor the place.

'Son.' Leopold strode over and took his hands in his. 'I heard what happened. How you managed to repel the Germans. It's incredible, well done!'

'Do you mean it?' Azriel said, feeling awash with emotion.

Leopold nodded and hugged him tightly.

'Thank you,' Azriel stammered.

'We've come to help,' Adela said, putting her arms round them both.

At that moment, Berek came back into the room. 'We need you to get a message to Filip,' he said to Adela. 'We need more ammunition.'

'Of course,' Adela replied.

'I'll take her to the tunnel,' Azriel said.

'The tunnel?' Leopold's eyes widened.

'It's all right, Papa, it's perfectly safe,' Adela said. 'I've done it loads of times before.'

'Done what, exactly?' Leopold asked.

'Smuggled things in and out of the ghetto,' Adela replied.

Again, Azriel worried that his father might get upset and try to stop them, but, to his surprise, Leopold gave them both a tearful smile. 'How did I get to have such brave children?' he murmured. Then he cleared his throat and looked at Berek. 'How can I help?'

'Maybe you could give one of the men a break and be lookout,' Berek said.

'Of course.'

Azriel shook his head and smiled as he watched them go over to the window. First, they'd forced the Germans to retreat and now his father had come and offered his services to the Resistance. This was indeed a day of miracles. He only hoped they'd last.

He smiled at Adela. 'Come on, little bookworm, let's go.'

Izabel looked at Dieter, her mind whirring. 'This is my... my neighbour's son,' she stammered. In all this time, she'd managed to keep Dieter separate from her home life. The two worlds colliding like this sent terror coursing through her veins.

'But I—' Kasper muttered.

'I'm taking him out for the morning,' Izabel continued, squeezing his hand tight.

Dieter's thin lips pursed into a scowl. 'Why on earth would you bring him here?'

'We heard the commotion and wanted to know what was going on.' She somehow managed to compose herself enough to give him a concerned smile. 'Is everything OK?'

'No, no it's not,' he snapped. 'And it's not safe for you to be here, so go.'

'Yes, of course.' She tugged on Kasper's hand, and they started hurrying back along the street.

'Are you friends with a German?' Kasper asked, clearly horrified, as he ran to keep up with her stride.

'No!' she exclaimed. 'I most certainly am not!'

She glanced over her shoulder. Dieter had rejoined the soldiers, and they were making their way to the others amassed outside the ghetto gate. A chill pierced her to the core as she thought of him going into the ghetto. What if his path crossed with Azriel's or Adela's? What if he killed one of them?

~

Adela watched as Azriel moved the bookshelf to reveal the entrance to the tunnel.

'Good luck,' he said, turning back to face her. 'I'll have to go back to the others, but I'll leave the bookshelf away from the wall, so you have enough room to slip out.'

'I'll be fine,' she said, with a lot more bravado than she felt. 'I'll be back before you know it – and hopefully with bullets.'

'Yes!' He pulled her into a hug, and she wished for a moment that she could freeze time, and stay there like that with him forever. But time kept moving and he let her go.

This time, when she made her way along the tunnel, she didn't feel any claustrophobia. She was too intent upon her mission. It was too important. When she reached the other end, she gave the coded knock and waited. Filip didn't know she was coming, but presumably he was fully aware of what was happening in the ghetto so he'd be prepared for something.

Adela waited and waited, but there was no response. The darkness of the tunnel started closing in on her and she took a long slow breath. It was OK. There was no need to panic. She just needed to stay calm and work out what she should do. Wait there in the hope that he'd eventually hear her, or return, empty-handed, to the ghetto?

~

Azriel followed Berek along the narrow passageway between two tenement buildings. The crackle of gunfire and smell of smoke filled the air. It was mid-afternoon and the Germans had launched a new assault, beginning with an artillery barrage, followed by smaller units of soldiers entering the ghetto. They had raided a warehouse and built a barricade from hundreds of mattresses. Azriel gripped the Molotov cocktails tighter in his hands. The good thing about a mattress barricade was that it was likely to be highly flammable.

He and Berek exchanged glances, lit the rag fuses and hurled the explosives before beating a hasty retreat. Other Resistance members in the overlooking buildings began throwing Molotovs from the windows. Azriel glanced back before disappearing into the passageway and saw the first of the mattresses going up in flames. He and Berek raced back to the relative safety of a nearby bunker beneath a deserted butcher's shop. It was time to regroup.

Once there, they received word of a fight going on in Muranów Square, where the Germans had encircled the Jewish Resistance fighters and had them under siege.

'We need the element of surprise again,' Berek said, looking thoughtful. Then his eyes began sparking with excitement. 'I have an idea!'

Adela lay in the tunnel humming Beethoven's 'Ode to Joy' to try to drown out the scurrying sound she was sure was coming from a rat. She'd decided to wait and see if Filip showed up; surely he wouldn't be much longer. As she hummed Beethoven, she remembered the concert Jaski had taken her to, what felt like another lifetime ago.

'If only you could see me now,' she whispered to him in the dark.

Oh, but I can, she imagined him whispering back and instantly she felt calmer.

Finally, she heard a sound from the other side of the tunnel door.

'Thank goodness!' she exclaimed, scrambling upright, and giving the coded knock.

There were a few moments of silence and she felt a burst of fear. What if it wasn't Filip? She decided to wait and not knock again and then, to her relief, she heard the door being opened. She crawled forwards, blinking as she made her way into the light of the room. And then she looked up, right into the frowning face of a German soldier.

49

Azriel looked down at the SS uniform he was wearing and fought the urge to retch. Never in his wildest dreams would he have imagined one day wearing such a symbol of oppression and terror, but he had to admit that Berek's idea was genius. What better way to catch the Germans off guard than dressing as them? They'd got the uniforms from two of the soldiers who'd been killed in the morning's fighting. Azriel tried not to think about the dark blood stain on the side of his jacket.

As they approached Muranów Square, they saw a group of German soldiers guarding one of the exits and they looked at each other and nodded. They drew closer and closer, but because of the uniforms, the soldiers didn't bat an eyelid.

It felt so strange to be walking right up to the lion's mouth like this. After years of torment due to the wretched armband they'd been made to wear, Azriel finally felt invisible to the German gaze. It was a strangely intoxicating feeling.

He and Berek approached a building on the corner of the square they knew to be a Resistance stronghold and as they reached the door, they turned and fired before disappearing inside. Pandemonium broke out as the soldiers scattered and, taking advantage of the mayhem, Resistance fighters who'd been stationed on the roof above began opening fire. Berek and Azriel looked at each other and grinned before racing up to join them.

'Who would want the Germans' luck today.' Berek laughed as they took the stairs two at a time.

'Not me, and I don't want their uniform either,' Azriel said, tearing off the jacket and its cursed swastika.

They got to the roof just in time to see two boys hoisting a flag on one of the poles on top of the building. The Resistance fighters stationed around the roof raised their weapons and cheered and Azriel's spirits soared as he saw the red and white of the Polish flag fluttering in the breeze. Then the boys hoisted a white flag featuring a blue Star of David – the flag of the Jewish Resistance – and he joined in the cheers. It felt so wonderful to see the blue star from their armbands being reclaimed on a flag of victory. He couldn't wait to tell Leopold and Adela. He wondered if his sister was back yet. Hopefully, she would have good news of her own, in the form of more ammunition. Then he thought of Estera. He had to keep hoping that by some miracle she was still alive, and one day he'd be able to tell her all about the day they fought and beat the Germans. Izabel too.

He gazed across the rooftops of Warsaw to the other side of the wall. He wondered if she'd heard what had happened in the ghetto. If she had, he hoped she was proud.

Izabel looked at Kasper and sighed.

'I suppose we ought to go home.'

They'd been out for most of the day now. What with seeing Dieter and all the sounds of fighting coming from the ghetto, she'd been far too anxious to be cooped up in the apartment, so they'd spent hours roaming the Warsaw streets and parks, trying to glean news from passersby.

'OK,' Kasper muttered. Clearly the day's drama had taken its toll on him too. His usual zest had vanished, and he trudged along beside her, pale-faced. 'Do you think Adela and Azriel are OK?' he asked as they reached the park gates.

'I hope so. I wish I had a way to find out. Oh, it's so frustrating!' She glanced down a side street where the ghetto wall loomed at the end. 'They're so near and yet they might as well be in another country.'

She contemplated going to one of her contacts in the Polish Home Army, Filip's place. He had a tunnel to the ghetto in his basement, the closest thing to a direct line of communication. If anyone knew how Adela and Azriel were, it would be him. But it would probably be too risky to go there today.

Her head began to spin from fear and confusion. It was so hard to know the right thing to do. And so irritating to realise that the safest course of action was to do nothing.

'Look!' Kasper cried excitedly, pointing to the ghetto wall.

'What? Oh my...' She broke off, overwhelmed with surprise and delight. There, fluttering from the top of one of the buildings inside the ghetto, was the Polish flag. And next to it, a flag bearing a blue Star of David.

'What does it mean?' Kasper asked her, eyes wide.

'It means that they're beating the Germans,' she whispered. 'The Jewish Resistance are actually beating the Germans!'

'So your friends are going to be OK?' he asked her hopefully.

'I don't know. But I hope so.' She felt like dropping to her knees and crying with joy. But at that moment, a German tank screeched around the corner, instantly dampening her excitement.

She took one last long look at the flags – it was a sight she wanted to remember forever – then she clutched Kasper's hand and they hurried on their way.

No matter how hard she tried, Adela couldn't stop her body from trembling. The soldier's intense stare seemed to pierce right through her. Whatever excuse she came up with for suddenly appearing out of the tunnel, she was certain he'd be able to tell that she was lying.

'Well?' he said. 'What are you doing here?'

'I... I was hiding from the fighting that's going on in the ghetto. I went down to a basement and I... I found a hole in the wall.'

'Oh, really?' He sighed and shook his head.

'Yes. I was scared I might get injured. There were so many explosions going on and people shooting. I wanted to hide. And then, when I got inside the hole, I was curious to find out where it went.'

'And I'm curious to find out whether you're lying to me,' he replied. He beckoned at her with his gun to come closer, then grabbed her arm.

'Where are you taking me?' she asked, her voice barely more than a squeak.

'I'm taking you to see some colleagues of mine who are experts in finding out the truth.' He gave a sinister smirk. 'They're currently talking to the man who owns this place – a known member of the Polish Home Army. Perhaps you know him? I suppose we'll soon see if he knows you.' He gripped her arm tighter and led her from the room.

Adela gulped. If they discovered she was a member of the Resistance, she would probably be killed on the spot. She thought of her parents and Azriel and Izabel and something inside of her hardened. Wherever the soldier was taking her, one thing was for certain, she would never, ever betray her people and she would make her family proud.

50

Azriel watched, barely able to breathe, as two German soldiers advanced into the ghetto holding white flags.

'We want to bring an end to the fighting,' one of them called, his voice echoing along the empty street. 'We come in peace.'

'Liar,' Berek whispered from beside Azriel. They, like so many other Resistance fighters, were hiding inside one of the nearby buildings, watching and waiting. It was now the fourth day of fighting and, unbelievably, the Resistance had managed to quell repeated German assaults. In a tactic borrowed from the Russian army in Stalingrad known as 'hugging the enemy', the Resistance fighters had stayed close to the Germans, rather than running away, ambushing them with grenade and Molotov attacks, and even closer-quarters street fighting.

'Let's agree to a surrender,' the soldier shouted. 'We will honour your wishes.'

Azriel gave a low, wry laugh. The day the Germans honoured any wishes of the Jewish would be a cold day in hell. 'Go to hell,' he whispered and, as if on cue, a volley of gunfire erupted from one of the nearby buildings and the German soldiers collapsed to the ground, their false white flags landing beside them.

A cheer went up from the Resistance fighters, but Azriel couldn't join in. Ever since Adela had left through the tunnel never to return, he'd been consumed by anxiety. The Resistance hadn't heard anything from Filip either, which strongly suggested the Germans had captured them both. Not wanting to worry Leopold, he'd told him that Adela had probably chosen to stay in the safety of the other side of the wall until the fighting ended, but he was almost certain Leopold realised the truth, which made him feel even worse. What if he'd sent his sister to her death? It was a question that plagued his every waking moment.

'Come,' Berek said. 'The Germans aren't going to be happy with what happened to their phoney peace brigade. We need to get underground.'

Azriel went into the other room, where Leopold was sitting reading in the corner. Only his father could be calm enough to read while all hell was breaking loose around him.

'We need to move, Papa,' he said, going over and placing his hand on his father's shoulder. 'Go underground.'

'OK,' he said, snapping his book shut. 'I don't suppose there's been any word about your sister?'

Azriel shook his head, again feeling overwhelmed with guilt. 'I wish I hadn't let her go.'

'Oh son, you mustn't torture yourself.'

Azriel looked at him in surprise. He'd been so sure Leopold would blame him.

'We have to remember that it's the Germans at fault here,' he continued. 'I could just as easily blame myself for allowing your mother to go to work the day she was deported.'

Azriel wasn't entirely sure it was the same, but he nodded, relieved for his father's support.

'And your sister wanted to go. I was there, remember?' He

gave a sad smile. 'I haven't seen her that enthusiastic to go some-where since I used to take her to the library as a kid.'

Azriel nodded, filling with love for Adela at the memory.

Leopold put his arm around his shoulders. 'Come, let's go to our new burrow.'

Azriel pulled his father to him and hugged him tight. After their falling out, and all they had lost since, he was so grateful Leopold was able to find it in his heart to forgive and support him. 'Thank you, Papa,' he murmured into his shoulder.

The next morning, after barely any sleep in a Bund bunker deep in the heart of the ghetto, Azriel was woken by one of his comrades shaking his shoulder.

'We have to move!' he cried. 'The Germans are back and they're setting fire to everything.'

Azriel staggered up from his makeshift bed on the floor and went over to wake Leopold.

Berek hurried into the room looking anxious. 'They're trying to smoke us out,' he said. 'We need to get down to the sewer.'

'The sewer?' Leopold looked at Azriel questioningly.

'It's all right, Papa, the Resistance have been using the sewage system for months now. We know our way around.'

Leopold frowned. 'Maybe I'll take my chances and stay here. I'm an old man. I don't want to slow you down.'

'No!' Azriel exclaimed. 'There's no way I'm leaving you behind.'

Leopold looked at him and smiled. Azriel couldn't be sure in the dim lamplight, but it looked as if his eyes were gleaming with tears. 'Come on then,' his father said. 'Take me to my lovely new home.'

The group of men crept out of the building and onto the

deserted street. The air was heavy with the smell of smoke, instantly triggering a memory in Azriel of the day the store was firebombed. He thought of Izabel and how she'd appeared at the store so battered and bruised and how brave she'd been, and he wondered what she was doing now. It was crazy to think that she wasn't all that far away. And yet, they were worlds apart.

A rattle of gunfire broke out, followed by the shouting of German soldiers.

'Quick!' Azriel said, and they began running in the direction of the nearest drainage cover. One of the other men cranked it open and Azriel looked at Leopold. 'I'll go down first then help you down,' he said.

Leopold nodded.

Azriel lowered himself into the hole. 'OK, Papa, come down, I'll guide you.' He reached up and clasped his father's hand.

Up on the street, the shouting grew louder. Thankfully, they all made it down safely and the last man replaced the cover, plunging them into darkness.

'We need to get moving,' Berek said, the tunnel giving his voice a ghostly echo.

Slowly, they made their way through the cold, damp dark, Azriel keeping hold of Leopold's arm to stop him from slipping.

After a while, they heard voices up ahead of them and came across another group of Bund fighters.

'The Germans are setting fire to everything in sight,' one of them said. 'Then they're shooting anyone who tries to escape.'

Azriel's stomach churned. They'd done so well to keep the soldiers at bay for as long as they had, but it was inevitable that they'd keep going until they got their revenge and that when they did it would be brutal.

'The Polish Home Army are offering to smuggle us to safety,' one of the other Bund men said. 'We can use the sewage canal to escape from the ghetto and into the forest.'

Azriel thought of the other Resistance fighters holed up in the cellars and bunkers. He couldn't leave them in their hour of need, but the thought of Leopold being able to escape filled him with hope.

'Can you take my father with you?' he asked. 'He's one of us.'

'There's no need for that,' Leopold said. 'I can—'

'Please!' Azriel interrupted.

'Of course,' the Bundist replied. 'But we have to hurry.'

Azriel clasped Leopold's hand in the dark. 'Go with them, Papa. I'll come and join you soon.'

'Are you sure?'

Azriel put his arms round him and hugged him tightly. 'I'll see you soon,' he whispered in his ear.

He stood with Berek and watched as Leopold and the other men made their way along the tunnel and out of view. After losing his mother and then Adela, watching Leopold go felt like losing a limb. What if he never saw any of them again? How had it come to this?

He clenched his hands into tight fists. He had to keep going. He had to keep fighting. Right until the end.

51

For the next few days, Azriel lost all sense of time. The sun rose and set, and darkness came and went, but all he could think about – all any of the Resistance fighters could think about – was survival. Having learned from their previous mistakes, the Germans adopted a new tactic of sending smaller units into the ghetto, armed with rifles and flame throwers, and slowly but surely, they took control of pockets of the ghetto at a time, razing buildings to the ground in their wake. Tanks followed the units, firing upon those who fled the burning buildings.

By May, all the fighting spirit in the Resistance had gone, replaced by a grim sense of inevitability. They'd been fighting for almost a month now, and Azriel tried to console himself with thoughts of those first few days, when they'd inflicted such startling losses upon the Germans. But the victories they'd enjoyed had come at such a high price. He still hadn't received any word about Adela, although he had learned that Filip had been arrested. The implications of this were terrifying and he was plagued by thoughts of his sister being taken too. He had no idea what had happened to Leopold either. The only one of his loved ones he could be fairly certain was all right was Izabel.

Oh, how he wished he could fly over the wall and find her, just to have another moment in her presence. To hear her laugh and listen to one of her theatrical stories, rather than sit cowering in a sewer, choking from the stench and waiting for his death. He glanced at his comrade beside him, sitting slumped, head in hands. And then, up above, he heard the drain cover being prised open. Azriel stood to make room for the new arrivals coming to hide, but then he heard a sound that chilled him to the core – a man muttering something in German. He caught a glimpse of something being thrown down towards him, and then the tunnel filled with a choking smoke.

Izabel sat in the corner of the hotel bar nursing her drink. Every time someone came through the door, her heart leapt into her mouth, but there was still no sign of Dieter. She hadn't seen him since the day outside the ghetto with Kasper, but it was Wednesday, the night they normally met for a midweek drink, and so she'd come to the hotel, against all her better instincts. As much as she dreaded seeing him, her desperation to learn about what was happening in the ghetto was greater. Fires had been raging in there for days and not knowing what had happened to Azriel and Adela was driving her out of her mind with worry.

She was about to give up and go home when the door burst open and a group of soldiers stumbled in, singing a German song. Dieter was in the middle of them, bleary-eyed and flush-faced from drinking. When he saw her sitting at their usual table, his smug smile grew. As the other soldiers made their way through to the restaurant, he came staggering over.

'I was hoping you'd be here,' he said as he reached the table. His voice was slurred, and he reeked of alcohol. 'You can help me celebrate.'

'Celebrate what?'

'Ridding Warsaw of the vermin.' He crashed down into the seat opposite her, knocking the table and causing her drink to slosh over the rim of the glass. 'We've been burning them out of their bunkers and smoking them out of the sewers. It's only a matter of time now.'

She tried really hard to smile, but the terror she felt was too vast and her mouth wouldn't co-operate.

'What's wrong?' His smirk faded and he leaned closer. 'Why so glum?'

She took a sip of her gin fizz, desperately trying to compose herself, but all she could think of were her beloved Rubinsteins being burned to death. 'I'm not feeling very well,' she muttered, picking up her bag. 'I think I ought to leave.'

'But I want you to stay.' He shifted slightly so he blocked her exit from the table. 'I told you, I want to celebrate with you. I must have killed at least fifty Jews today.' He leaned forward and put his hand on her knee. 'Come on, let's go up to my room.'

She stared at him, horrified, as he swayed to his feet and held out his hand.

Feeling powerless, she walked with him numbly into the lobby. Her blood was racing so fast, she could hear it pulsing in her ears. 'Are there any survivors?' she said as they got into the lift.

'In the ghetto?' He smiled at her and shook his head.

Panic surged through her, blurring her vision.

As the lift made its way up through the floors, she thought of the time she'd come there before with the plan to kill him, until she'd seen Adela standing watching in the lobby. That night had been the last time she'd seen her friend. The realisation that it had been the last time she'd ever see her was crushing. Izabel thought of how they'd laughed as they'd ridden the carousel, reliving such precious escapades from their childhood. And now, thanks to monsters like

Dieter, Adela and Azriel and Leopold and Estera had been burned alive.

A cold, white rage descended upon her, unlike anything she'd ever felt before. Usually when she got angry, Izabel felt fiery and impetuous and slightly out of control, but now her anger was so intense, it felt as if every muscle and sinew in her body had clenched rigid. She followed Dieter into the room, her rage growing with every step.

'Oh, I'm looking forward to this,' he said, taking off his jacket and unbuttoning his fly.

'Me too,' she said, and for once, she actually meant it. 'I'll just go and freshen up.'

She went into the bathroom and stared at her reflection in the mirror. There was a wild intensity to her gaze she'd never seen before. It was as if she'd been possessed by something. Perhaps it was the devil. But, no, surely Dieter was the devil.

'Forgive me, Saint Brigid,' she whispered, before turning and going back into the room.

Dieter was lying spread-eagled on the bed. He was still wearing his holster. Izabel kicked off her shoes and climbed on top of him.

'I need you to celebrate,' he murmured, his eyelids drooping.

'Oh, don't worry, I will,' she replied, kneeling over him.

He gave a groan of pleasure and groped at her chest. The steely anger inside of her grew even stronger.

'Oh yes,' Dieter murmured as she leaned over him. 'Yes!'

She brought her lips to his, trying not to grimace at the sour taste of his tongue as it poked and prodded its way between her teeth.

'Let me just move this out of the way,' she said, easing the gun from the holster.

'Of course,' he gasped, his eyes glazed with lust.

She leaned forward again, kissing him full on the mouth, the gun in one hand and reaching for a pillow with another.

'Oh!' he groaned, closing his eyes as she moved her hips. 'That feels so good.'

She sat up and swiftly brought the pillow down over his face. Before he had time to respond, she buried the end of the pistol into it and pulled the trigger. There was a muffled bang and his body jerked, then fell still. Heart pounding, Izabel steadied her breath before moving the pillow away and saw, to her horror, that he was still staring up at her. But then she noticed a dark trickle of blood running from a hole in his forehead. And she realised that his stare was completely vacant. She placed her fingers on the side of his neck. There was no pulse.

Feeling completely numb, she put the pillow back over his head and got off the bed. She put on her shoes and tucked the gun into her bag, then made her way down the stairs and into the lobby, slipping through the revolving doors and into the darkness. The smell of smoke filled the air and the sky above the ghetto burned red. It was so bright, it was impossible to see the stars. It was as if heaven itself was on fire.

Izabel pictured Saint Brigid clutching her head in despair. But still, she felt nothing. Adela and Azriel were gone, and hopefully soon she would be able to join them. She thought about taking Dieter's gun and shooting herself, but that would be a waste of her death. As she walked on, she felt the seed of an idea begin to germinate. She would take what was left of her life and give it to the Resistance. She would avenge her beloved Rubinsteins and fight the Germans – hopefully to the death.

PART THREE

AUSCHWITZ, 1944

52

Adela gazed up at the tiny patch of blue just visible through the barred window in the corner of the cattle truck. If she could keep focusing on the sky, she could remind herself of the stars waiting to shine there as soon as night fell. She could remind herself that she too was made of stardust and water, and proof of that magic existed – even if all around her there was nothing but proof of inhumanity.

'I need to go to the toilet,' a young girl somewhere to the left of her cried. It was impossible to see her, they'd all been jammed in so tight. 'Mama, please, I can't hold it in,' the girl wailed.

'Just let go, pet, it's all right,' her mother replied. 'We can get you some clean clothes once we arrive.'

The one bucket that had been slung in after them to use as a toilet had soon filled and now the truck stank of urine. Adela had been trying to ignore the burning sensation in her bladder for the last couple of hours, part of her praying they'd reach their destination soon, but another, bleaker part, praying that the train never stopped.

Look at the sky, she imagined Jaski whispering in her ear, and she looked back at the tiny window. Every so often, she felt the breeze caress her face and it felt like the sweetest of kisses. How curious that, even in these circumstances, she should be able to find a simple pleasure like this. She couldn't decide if it was the loveliest or most tragic of things. *It's more proof of magic*, she heard Jaski whisper, and she shivered as she remembered that day in the storeroom, when he'd first shared his magical motto with her. It had helped her so much since, and now she would need it more than ever.

The clatter of the train on the tracks started to slow and her stomach lurched.

'Nearly there,' she heard the mother soothe her little girl and it reminded her of how Estera would speak to her and Azriel when they went on childhood vacations to see their grandparents in the countryside. 'Nearly there,' she'd say in her sing-song voice, leaning over to smile at them in the back seat of the car. The memory of her family all together and happy felt like a shard of glass stabbing her heart. For so long now, they'd all been scattered like seeds on the wind; she didn't even know if the others were alive.

A terrible thought occurred to her. What if she was the only one left? What if everyone she loved the most – Azriel, Estera, Leopold, Izabel, Jaski – had now perished? After the Germans had found her in Filip's basement, she'd stuck to her story of simply trying to escape the fighting in the ghetto, and Filip hadn't betrayed her either, so she'd been sent to a labour camp. Every day she'd been there, she'd searched the other prisoners' hollowed-out faces in the hope that she might see Estera, but to no avail. And now they'd been crammed like cattle onto another train to be sent who knew where to face who knew what.

Look at the sky, she heard Jaski whisper again.

But as she looked through the gap in the wooden slats, tears blurred her vision and the blue disappeared. The train ground to a halt and silence fell upon the crowded truck. No doubt they were all thinking the same thing. Where had they been brought? And would they live to tell the tale?

Adela wiped away her tears. For all she knew, her loved ones could still be alive, and until she knew differently, she couldn't give up.

Outside, she heard men shouting in German and a dog barking. Then came the sound of the large iron bolt being unlocked and the train door was flung open. They all squinted in the sudden dazzling sunlight. Something was yelled at them in German, and as Adela's eyes adjusted, she saw two soldiers, rifles drawn, standing at the open door, gesturing at them to get off.

Like a great lumbering organism rousing itself from sleep, the truck's occupants shuffled as one in the direction of the door, stumbling as they dropped down to the floor. There was a collective murmur as they looked around. The train had come to the end of the line, and up ahead was a camp, surrounded by watchtowers and a barbed wire fence. More guards were standing beside the track, some of them holding large, snarling dogs, straining on the leash.

They were all ushered into lines, men on one side, women and children on the other, and then they started shuffling towards more guards. As they drew closer, Adela saw that the guards were directing people to the left or to the right. At first, she thought they were being divided according to sex, but then she realised that some men were being sent to the left with the women and children, and some women – mainly young women, it seemed – were being sent to the right with most of the men. Perhaps it was for the best that she wasn't with her family, she mused, as she drew closer to the guards. It would have been heart-wrenching to have been torn apart here. She watched, heart in mouth, as a mother was forced from her two teenage daughters.

'Don't worry, my loves, I'll see you soon,' she called, her

voice shrill from poorly disguised fear, as one of the girls began to cry.

Adela took another step closer. Which way would she be asked to go? she wondered. With the mother or with her daughters? She stepped in front of the guards, trying not to show the hatred and fear swirling inside of her. One of the guards muttered something to another and he gestured at Adela to go right, after the girls.

Once again, they were split into men and women and marched inside the camp, through a large wrought-iron gate. Some words in German had been forged into a banner above.

'What do you think that says?' she muttered to a young woman with beautiful auburn hair walking beside her.

The woman shrugged. 'Welcome to hell?'

Adela gave a small laugh. 'I'm Adela,' she said.

'Hanna,' the woman replied with a small smile.

Adela imagined catching the smile in the palm of her hand and pressing it to her heart, a welcome spark of warmth against the growing chill.

53

Izabel stood at the window and watched as a new procession of prisoners made their way into the camp. She'd seen so many arrive now, she thought she might have been immune to the sight, but each time, it was the same. Each time, she relived that same dreadful memory, trapped it seemed, within every cell of her body, as she remembered the terrible day she too had been marched through those gates. If she'd known then the fate that awaited her, she probably would have begged the guards by the train to make her go to the left. Better to have disappeared in the plumes of foul smoke coiling from the chimneys that loomed over the camp than be made to die over and over again every day.

But it seemed that, just like a cat, Izabel had many lives. She'd got away with killing Dieter and when she'd been captured delivering leaflets for the Resistance after the obliteration of the ghetto, she'd managed to evade execution and the Germans had sent her to a labour camp in Majdanek instead. Then, several months ago, she'd been put on a train to Auschwitz, and again she'd escaped death.

She noticed a teenage girl sobbing as she walked past and

Izabel wanted to call out to her, 'Stop crying, please! If you show that kind of weakness, you'll be dead within a week.' But she remained silent. Something was compelling her to stay alive, a feeling that she'd been kept alive for a reason, even if she didn't know what that reason was yet. It was so hard though. After seeing the Nazis raze the ghetto to the ground and knowing that her beloved Azriel and Adela had been killed, it was difficult to find a reason for being.

Perhaps that was why she was still alive, she mused as she looked back at the new arrivals. Maybe it was her punishment for having survived when they didn't. Lord knew, she felt guilty enough.

She saw a woman passing by outside, her long auburn hair gleaming in the sunshine, and she felt a pang of sorrow for the fate that was about to befall her. Izabel thought back to the brutish woman who'd hacked off her hair when she'd first arrived. She'd been so despondent by then that she hadn't cared one bit.

Izabel reached up and stroked her hair. It had grown back thicker than before and was now cut into a short, flapper-style bob. Bozena, one of the other girls in the doll's house, as the guards called it, had been a hairdresser before, and a very talented one at that, it turned out.

Izabel sighed. She bet Bozena had never dreamed she'd one day be cutting hair in a place like this. She went over to the dressing table and applied a spritz of perfume to her neck and wrists, anything to help drown out the stench of what was to come. Then she stood up and looked at her reflection in the mirror, adjusting the belt on her striped dress and cinching it in a notch. She felt another stab of guilt as she looked at the slight curve of her hips. It wouldn't be long before the women marching by outside would be thin as skeletons, their curves all melting away along with their hope.

When Izabel had first arrived at Auschwitz, she'd wanted to

waste away to nothing, but as soon as she'd volunteered to work in the doll's house, the guards had sent her to the infirmary to be fattened up like a goose for Christmas. She shuddered as she recalled the calcium injections and the disinfectant baths and being made to sunbathe beneath quartz lamps.

She heard men's voices outside and took a breath to try to calm her racing pulse. They were only supposed to work between eight and ten at night and on Sunday afternoons, but some of the soldiers saw the doll's house as their own private playground and would bribe the guards to look the other way when they paid a visit. Izabel heard the door open behind her and steeled herself before turning around. An SS guard came in and carefully closed the door behind him. Then he looked her up and down, his pale face completely expressionless. As Izabel prepared to greet him, she mentally recited the line she always told herself before a liaison – Adela and Azriel were dead, therefore nothing else really mattered.

54

Azriel approached the wood pile and felt in his pocket for the knife. He'd made it from a large shard of glass, binding a strip of fabric around the blunt end to form a handle. One of his Resistance contacts had told him where to hide it during their work detail digging ditches earlier that day. But what if he'd got the instructions wrong and he wasn't able to find the hiding place?

He reached the pile of logs and took four steps as instructed, then glanced over his shoulder to check the coast was clear before crouching down and pretending to adjust the lace on his relic of a shoe. He leaned forward slightly and peered at the bottom log. Sure enough, there was a small gap beside it. Quick as a trice, he took the knife from his pocket and slipped it through the gap and into the hiding hole that had been dug into the ground below. Then he stood up and took another look around, his heart pounding, and trying not to think of what would happen if he was caught.

The guards seemed to need less and less of a reason to mindlessly kill these days. In the four months Azriel had been in Auschwitz, he'd lost count of the men who'd been shot right in front of him, or dragged off by the guards, never to be seen again. Of course, they all had a good idea where those men ended up, and were reminded every time they saw the flames leaping from the crematorium chimneys, not to mention the horrific smell. He had a sudden flashback to Warsaw and the sweet floral scent of Izabel's perfume. He'd give anything to smell her again, to see her and hold her.

When the Germans had tried to smoke the Resistance members out of the sewage system, Azriel had realised that his only option was to try to escape. So he'd followed the sewage canal outside of the ghetto, where he'd been spirited away by the Resistance to a forest in the countryside. He'd finally been caught in Krakow, when he'd been sent there to courier a message. Thankfully, the Germans didn't realise what he was doing and so they'd arrested him for the crime of being Jewish and deported him to Auschwitz.

When he'd first arrived at the camp and realised the depths of the depravity at this new hell on earth, he'd tried to block all thoughts of his loved ones from his mind. He was afraid that thinking of all he'd lost would crush his spirit, but he'd come to realise that the opposite was true. He needed to hold on to his memories of them to give him a reason to keep going. He needed to relive them every day, just like polishing precious jewels to keep them shiny.

One day, he would smell that perfume again, he told himself as he hurried back to the barracks. One day, he'd be listening to Izabel's dramatic diatribes and he wouldn't internally groan, he'd revel in her theatrics. And one day, he and Izabel and Adela would be reunited, just as they'd vowed, sitting around that kitchen table over three years previously.

Later that night in the hut, just before lights out, one of the older men started praying and Azriel thought of his father. He shifted in the crowded bunk, trying not to think the worst. He had to hope that Leopold had somehow managed to survive and evade deportation. He knew from the selection process at the camp gates that virtually no one of Leopold's age was sent to the barracks to work. Rumour was that those told to go left were sent straight to their deaths. He had it on good authority from someone who'd talked to a member of the *Sonderkommando* – the men who worked in the crematoria – that those poor souls instantly perished. Despite the summer heat and the fact that he was surrounded by other men, Azriel couldn't help shivering.

The *Sonderkommando* was yet another depraved way in which the Germans sought to torture the Jewish people and pit them against one another. He couldn't imagine what it was like to have to work in the place where so many of your people were murdered. How anyone could do such a job was beyond him, but then, the men selected for the *Sonderkommando* weren't exactly given much choice – work in the crematoria or be incinerated there. And the worst thing was, the *Sonderkommandos* always ended up being killed too. Every three months or so, the Germans would recruit a new batch, with no mention of what had happened to the previous lot, who were never seen again.

'You all right?' his friend Stanislaw asked, as Azriel shifted in the bunk again.

'Yes. I'm sorry, I can't settle.'

'It's this feather eiderdown, it's just too comfortable,' Stanislaw joked, adjusting the threadbare blanket, his laughter triggering a hacking cough.

'Not to mention these new-model wooden mattresses,' Azriel joked back, knocking on the wooden slats of the bunk.

A fellow Bundist from Gdańsk, Stanislaw was one of his closest allies in the camp and he was grateful every day for his friendship and dry humour. Hearing his rattling cough filled Azriel with concern.

'Here, take this,' he said, passing Stanislaw his paper-thin pillow. 'It'll help your chest to be propped up a bit.'

'Thanks, comrade,' Stanislaw wheezed in between coughs.

Azriel thought of how his mother had always given him an extra pillow when he had a cough as a kid, and he felt a pang of sorrow. Estera had made him warm honey and lemon drinks too and would stroke his hair as he took sips. As he'd grown older and started dreaming of a career in medicine, Azriel had vowed to treat his patients with the same care and attention Estera had shown him whenever he was ill. If the war ever ended and he made it out of Auschwitz alive, perhaps he could return to university and resume his dream. After so much death and loss, the thought of spending the rest of his life focusing on healing others was hugely appealing.

But the war wasn't over, he reminded himself, and before it was, there would be other battles to fight, of that he was certain. He thought of the knife he'd hidden earlier, and the other weapons the Resistance had been smuggling into the camp through holes in the fence from partisans on the outside, and he clenched his hands into tight fists. The Auschwitz guards might think that they were all-powerful, but one thing was for certain, he wasn't going to be led to his death like a lamb to the slaughter. He was going to fight for his life with everything he'd got.

55

Adela stood in the early-morning sun trying not to flinch beneath the guard's glare. She'd barely slept a wink during her first night at this new camp and the combination of tiredness and acute hunger was making her dizzy. The guard, a stocky woman with closely cropped hair, was making her way along the line, stopping every so often to gesture at someone to fall out – for what, it wasn't certain. As she drew closer, Adela took a breath and stood taller. *I am made of water and stardust; I am proof that magic exists*, she silently chanted, and she felt herself grow a little stronger.

The guard stopped in front of her. She smelled of a mixture of soap – *oh soap!* – and cigarettes. As they met each other's gaze, Adela's heart almost stopped. She'd never been on the receiving end of such a cold, hard stare.

After what felt like forever, the guard moved on and, despite the heat, Adela could have sworn she felt an icy breeze in her wake. The women who'd been told to leave the line were ordered off along the long pathway between the barracks.

A kapo barked at the others to pay attention. 'You've been

chosen to work at a munitions plant,' she called. 'After breakfast, you will report for your first shift.'

The word 'breakfast' echoed around Adela's mind, sending
her stomach into a frenzy. The image of one of Estera's bagels
appeared in the air before her, like a mirage, causing her to
drool. But then she pictured Estera kneading the dough,
shaping the bagels and placing them in the oven, and her
appetite disappeared. What had become of her parents? She
hardly dared contemplate the answer.

Breakfast turned out to be the same as dinner the night
before, a thin, watery soup, with a piece of rock-hard black
bread and an insipid brown liquid that was supposed to be
coffee. Then they were summoned back outside, and a team of
guards corralled them into formation, walking in pairs out of the
camp and across the fields. After what felt like forever, owing to
the pain caused by the ill-fitting shoes she'd been given, they
arrived at a large building. The sign by the door read, *Weichsel
Union Metallwerke.*

A factory official wearing a white lab coat over her clothes
was there to greet them. 'You will be working making detonators
for artillery shells,' she said. 'All Jews are to come with me.'

Adela looked at the yellow triangle that had been pinned to
her raggedy uniform the day before and she followed a couple
of other Jewish women along a corridor to a room at the very
end. They entered to find a small group of women working
away at two rows of tables.

'You will be making the gunpowder for the shells,' the official told them. 'Your supervisor will explain what you have to
do.' She turned on her heel and headed back through the door.

One of the women got up from a table, smiling at them. 'I'm
Jemima,' she said, before explaining the details of the job, carefully measuring and grinding the saltpetre, charcoal and
sulphur that was to be blended together to form the powder.

Once Adela had settled down to begin work, she felt

conflicting emotions. On the one hand, it was refreshing to get out of the barracks and have something to distract her, but she also felt sick at the thought that the gunpowder she was making would be used by German soldiers to kill the Allies. She pictured the Nazis sniggering with glee as they cooked up their plan to make their prisoners help kill people on their own side. It was so hard not to become brittle with bitterness in the face of such cruelty, and she prayed that she might hear Jaski whisper some sunny words of wisdom in her ear, but all she heard was the whir of machinery next door and the low hum of women's voices.

Hours passed and as the end of the shift finally drew close, Adela asked for permission to use the washroom.

At least I now have the luxury of a toilet, she thought to herself wryly as she entered the room.

Two women were standing, huddled together in murmured conversation, by the sinks. When they saw Adela, they sprang apart as if they'd been caught committing some kind of terrible misdemeanour. Adela smiled faintly at them before going into one of the stalls. She guessed that in this place it probably was a crime to talk to one another on a toilet break.

'See you, Asna,' she heard one of the women say. 'Take good care.'

'And you,' the other woman replied.

There was such obvious warmth in their voices, it made Adela think of Izabel. 'I miss you, *moj skarbe,*' she whispered, gazing at the air vent above her, and praying her words might find their way to her beloved friend, back home in Warsaw.

56

Izabel fought to contain her surprise as the door to her room opened and the soldier walked in. His visit the day before had been so strange, she'd assumed she'd never see him again. He'd spent the entire time sitting on the end of the bed with his back to her, not saying or doing a thing, and then, after about fifteen minutes, he'd upped and left. And whilst Izabel had been hugely grateful that he hadn't touched her, she had found the whole thing quite unnerving.

'Hello,' she said, fiddling with the belt on her striped dress.

'Sit,' he replied, gesturing at the bed.

She perched down as instructed, adjusting the pillow behind her. And then, just like the day before, he sat at the end of the bed with his back to her. She wondered if she ought to say something, but not wanting to do anything that might elicit an angry response, she focused instead on her breathing, inhaling slowly for a count of three, then exhaling. Then she said a silent prayer to Saint Brigid. *Please, Saint Brigid, keep me safe from this monster.*

The soldier cleared his throat, causing her to jump.

'It's my son's birthday today,' he said, so quietly Izabel wasn't sure she'd heard him correctly.

'Oh,' she replied.

'He's seven.'

'Oh,' she said again, unsure how else to respond. She pictured a seven-year-old version of the soldier, blonde and thin, somewhere in Germany, and then an image of Kasper came into her mind, and she had to fight the urge to cry.

'Wilhelm.' The soldier shifted slightly but still didn't look at her. 'That's his name.'

I have a brother just a few years older than your son, she wanted to tell him, tears stinging her eyes. *His name's Kasper and I might never see him again, thanks to you.* But she remained silent and wiped her tears away.

'Do you believe in hell?' he asked after a minute or two.

'Yes,' she answered without hesitation. As far as she was concerned, Auschwitz was all the proof she needed that hell existed right there on earth.

She watched the back of his head as he nodded. His blonde hair neatly tapered into a V-shape at the nape of his neck.

'Does it frighten you?' he asked.

She thought carefully before answering. 'Yes, it does,' she said softly.

He turned his head slightly. 'Me too.'

She stared at him in shock. It was hard to imagine an SS soldier being frightened of anything, let alone admitting to it.

'I didn't want to do it,' he whispered, or at least that's what she thought he said.

'Do what?' she whispered back.

'Sometimes I feel as if I'm trapped in a bad dream,' he continued, seemingly not hearing her.

She wanted to reply, *You and me both*, but thought better of it.

They sat in silence for a while, with Izabel hardly daring to move. Then he stood up.

'Thank you,' he muttered, still with his back to her, then headed for the door. He stopped just before leaving and he felt in his pocket for something, which he placed on her dressing table. And then he was gone.

Izabel hugged her knees to her chest, trying to make sense of what had just happened. Why had he asked her if she believed in hell? And why was he, of all people, frightened of it when he was one of those responsible for creating this hellish prison camp?

She heard the shuffling feet of the prisoners returning from their work details outside and it jolted her from her musings. It wouldn't be long before her evening shift began and the doll's house would fill with those prisoners *lucky* enough to have been issued with a brothel permit.

Having a brothel at Auschwitz was supposed to increase productivity, enticing the men to work harder in exchange for the possibility of a ticket to come and visit. Although most of the prisoners who visited seemed far from enthusiastic, with barely enough energy to blink, let alone do anything else. The kapos were the worst of the prisoners, as they were given more food than the others and had more energy. It also seemed as if their privileges had gone to their heads, making many of them as sadistic as their Nazi bosses. Izabel had developed her way of coping, though, retreating into the walled secret garden inside her head until it was over.

She got up from the bed and went over to the dresser. The SS man had left a small package wrapped in brown paper. As she picked it up, she caught a waft of roses. Inside was a pale pink bar of soap. She felt simultaneously thrilled and sickened. As much as she didn't want to accept his gift, the scent was intoxicating. She brought it to her nose and inhaled. She would take it to the washroom and share it with the other women; that way it wouldn't seem so bad.

There was only one bathroom in the building and Izabel had come to see it as something of a haven, especially if she ran into Bozena there. But today when she reached the bathroom, it was empty. Izabel filled the basin with water and rubbed the bar of soap into a creamy lather, feeling guilty again. Soap was one of the many things the prisoners at Auschwitz were deprived of and the scent of roses drifting up on the steam suddenly seemed cloying and sickly. She looked at her reflection as she washed her face and it was like seeing the ghost of herself, she looked so pale and drawn.

The door crashed open and Bozena marched in, a look of horror upon her face.

'Have you heard about Zosia?' she said, coming over to join Izabel at the sink.

Zosia was another of the women in the doll's house, a German who had been a prostitute before, and as such was seen as the boss and responsible for training the inexperienced new recruits.

Izabel shook her head.

'She caught a disease – you know – down there.' She nodded to Izabel's crotch. 'They've taken her to the infirmary.'

Izabel shuddered. They'd all heard the rumours of what went on in the infirmary, and the experiments that were carried out on women by German doctors trying to find miracle cures for sexual disease.

'I hate it here,' Bozena whispered, meeting her gaze in the mirror.

'Me too,' Izabel whispered back.

'I'd never have agreed to work here if I'd known what it was. They told me it was a job that offered more food, and I was so hungry that was all I could think of.'

Izabel nodded.

'Is that what they said to you too?' Bozena asked.

Izabel wondered if she ought to lie and say yes, but she didn't have the energy. 'No. I knew what it was.'

Bozena frowned, clearly confused. 'Why did you agree then?'

'I was trying to protect someone, a younger girl in my hut. They were going to take her unless they had another volunteer.' Izabel shuddered as she thought back to that terrible night. The girl, Natalia, had been so sweet, so innocent. Izabel couldn't bear the thought of her being defiled by countless men. When she'd offered to go in her place, she'd reasoned that after what had happened to her back in Warsaw with the pogromists and Dieter, she was prepared for anything. She'd also hoped that the numbness she'd felt since losing Adela and Azriel would protect her. But lately that numbness was wearing off.

'That was so brave of you,' Bozena said, taking her hand and giving it a squeeze.

'Thank you,' Izabel replied, but as she rinsed the soap from her face, she couldn't help feeling deflated. Her act of bravery had come at such a high price, and now she was trapped, a doll in a house to be played with by monsters, and unable to do a thing.

Adela lay on her stomach with her head at the foot of her bunk, watching as the other women milled around in the central aisle of the hut, some of them talking, some trying to kill the lice in their clothes by hitting them with their shoes or tin cups. It was hard to imagine that, when she'd convinced the Germans she hadn't been working for the Resistance, she'd thought of herself as lucky. Looking at the women in the hut who'd been there for longer was like seeing the most sobering of premonitions. There was no doubt in her mind now that she'd reached the end. It was clear to her that they were all being worked and starved to death, but, unlike the ghetto, in Auschwitz there was absolutely nothing they could do about it.

She noticed Eta, from her section at the munitions factory, deep in conversation with a woman with large brown eyes and a warm smile. She watched as they made their way down the hut until they were standing level with her bunk. Not wanting to appear nosy, Adela closed her eyes, and pretended to be asleep.

'I'm sorry it's not much,' she heard Eta murmur. 'One of the other girls got nervous and threw hers away.'

'No!' the woman exclaimed.

Adela guessed they must be talking about food. Perhaps there was some kind of smuggling operation going on. It was incredible how enterprising people could be when they were starving.

'We need more,' the woman continued. 'The men are getting impatient.'

Adela half opened one eye, just in time to see Eta slipping a tiny rag bundle bound with string into the woman's hands. The woman glanced along the hut in the direction of the kapo, then quickly lifted the hem of her shabby striped dress and stuffed the tiny bundle inside her underwear.

'Thank you, comrade,' she whispered to Eta before heading up the hut to her bunk.

Comrade. The word made Adela's skin tingle.

As Eta got into the bunk beside her, she pretended to wake up.

'Sorry to wake you,' Eta said.

'It's OK,' Adela replied. 'I was having a bad dream.'

'And you woke to an even worse one,' Eta said with a wry smile.

'Yes. Being here makes me hark back for the days of the ghetto.' She propped herself up onto her elbow.

'Which ghetto were you in?' Eta asked.

'Warsaw.'

'Ah, I was in the ghetto at Będzin.'

Seeing the opportunity to prove her Resistance credentials, Adela leaned closer and lowered her voice. 'We once sent a comrade there with intelligence about the camp at Treblinka.'

Eta's face lit up. 'Are you in the ŻOB?' she whispered.

Adela shook her head. 'No, the Bund.'

Eta's smile grew. 'The Bund were great allies to us.'

'Likewise.' Adela shifted closer to her. 'I never thought I'd say this,' she whispered, 'but I really wish I was back in the ghetto. At least we could do something back then. At least we were able to fight back.'

Eta nodded, but she didn't say any more, and then the kapo yelled that it was time to sleep, and their bunk began to fill.

Despite her exhaustion, Adela found it impossible to sleep. Her stomach was hollow with hunger and her mind kept racing. What had been in the little package Eta had slipped to the other woman? Could it be there was some kind of Resistance here in Auschwitz?

She closed her eyes and clasped her hands together, thinking of Azriel and Izabel. She had no way of knowing where or how they were, but if there was even the slightest chance that she could do something to fight back in the camp, so that she might one day see them again, she was absolutely going to take it.

57

Azriel's heart sank as they approached the line of guards. They were on their way for their work duty, and he'd been hoping they wouldn't be stopped as Stanislaw's cough had grown even worse, and he looked weaker than ever.

'Stand behind me,' he said, hoping he could hide his friend from the guards' scrutiny. As they drew closer, he heard them mocking and laughing. Then one of them drew his whip and began beating a prisoner.

'Dance, Jew!' the guard yelled. 'Dance for your life.'

Azriel thought back to the time the guard had forced the old rabbi to dance in the ghetto, and anger bubbled inside him as the prisoner danced about, yelping with every crack of the whip.

'I wonder what charm school he attended,' Stanislaw said wryly before starting to cough again.

Azriel winced as he saw one of the guards look down the line to them. Stanislaw's cough grew louder, and the soldier began making his way towards them. Azriel wracked his brains trying to think of some way he could distract him, but he kept drawing a blank. He prayed instead that Stanislaw's throat would miraculously be soothed, but there was no such luck, and his coughing grew worse.

'Shut up!' the guard spat, level with them now.

Azriel clenched his fists, every sinew in his body wanting to wipe that mocking smile from his face.

Stanislaw coughed again. Azriel glanced at him and noticed a defiant glint in Stanislaw's eye.

'Stop coughing!' the guard yelled, looking furious.

Stanislaw stepped towards him, and there was a collective gasp from the surrounding prisoners as he spat in his face.

A deathly silence fell upon the group and Azriel looked on in panic.

'*You* are the disease,' Stanislaw said, squaring up to the guard before spitting at him again. 'Nazi scum!'

His hand trembling with fury, the guard raised his revolver.

'No!' Azriel yelped.

But the soldier coolly pressed the trigger and shot Stanislaw in the head.

Azriel stood frozen to the spot as his friend collapsed to the ground and the guard gave a satisfied smirk. As his shock began to fade, Azriel understood Stanislaw's motives. Even though he knew it would probably cost him his life, he'd taken his power back from the Germans. He thought of doing something similar. Smashing his fist into the guard's face. Turning his gun on him before his own inevitable death. But something stopped him. Was it cowardice, or was it the feeling that if his death was inevitable, he wanted to use it to greater effect, just as he'd planned to do in the ghetto, taking as many German soldiers with him as possible?

'Move!' another guard yelled, and the prisoners shuffled on, past Stanislaw's bloody body.

Azriel swallowed the growing lump in his throat. *Your death won't have been in vain*, he silently pledged to his friend.

. . .

Throughout the day, Azriel's grief over Stanislaw hardened into anger. Every time he brought his pick swinging down into the hard earth, his rage deepened. Their lives meant nothing to the Germans. They were no more than flies to be trodden on whenever the whim took them. Oh, how he longed to wipe the smug smirks from their faces. Oh, how he longed to give them a taste of their own medicine, just as the Resistance had done in the ghetto.

For once, on the long walk back to the barracks, he didn't feel pain or exhaustion. His anger and hatred felt like a furnace inside of him. As they walked through the camp, he saw the women returning from their shift in *Kanada* and he scoured their faces, looking for his Resistance contact. Normally, he felt nervous when he spotted her, but not this time. This time, when he saw her give an almost imperceptible nod, he felt a triumphant burst of defiance.

As she drew level, he dropped his gaze to her hand and saw something flutter to the ground. He stopped and fiddled with his shoe, scooping up the small fabric bundle with all the sleight of hand of a magician and slipping it inside. He continued walking with a small hard smile on his face.

Yes, the Germans were going to get a taste of their own medicine all right; he was going to see to it.

58

For the next couple of weeks, Adela watched Eta carefully. Although she didn't notice anything untoward going on in the munitions factory, most nights she would see Eta engaging in hushed conversation with the woman she'd given the tiny bundle to. She found out that the woman's name was Ryka and she worked in the depot where all the clothing belonging to the new arrivals was taken, known wryly amongst the prisoners as *Kanada*, due to it being the land of plenty. She didn't see the women exchange anything more and was about to give up hope, but then one day, when she was in the washroom in the factory, Eta came in behind her.

'I was wondering,' she whispered, joining Adela by the sink. 'What did you do for the Bund when you were in Warsaw?'

'I was a courier mainly,' she whispered back. 'They'd smuggle me out of the ghetto to pass messages to the Polish Resistance.' She paused. 'And sometimes I'd smuggle weapons or ammunition back in.'

'Is that so?' Eta met her gaze in the cracked mirror. 'How would you feel about smuggling again?'

Adela's skin erupted in goosebumps. 'I would love nothing

more.' She took a step closer. 'I'm being serious,' she whispered. 'I'd do anything to help.'

Eta nodded. 'But you do realise that being part of the Resistance in here is incredibly dangerous, far more so than in the ghetto. You've seen what the guards are like. If you were to get caught it would mean certain death.'

'I know. But it feels as if we're all facing certain death anyway. At least this way I'd be using my death for a cause.' Adela sighed. 'I know that sounds crazy.'

Eta shook her head. 'No, it doesn't. That's exactly how we all feel.' She placed her hand over Adela's on the edge of the sink and whispered in her ear. 'Some of us have been smuggling gunpowder to some male prisoners in the Resistance here. We've been doing it for months.'

Adela gasped. 'Are you serious?'

'Yes. Obviously, we can only smuggle it in tiny amounts – a teaspoon at a time, and we can't risk doing it every day. But, slowly but surely, the men are gathering enough to make detonators and grenades.'

'What are they planning to do with them?' Adela asked.

'I'm not entirely sure, but I think they're waiting for the Allies to arrive in Poland and then mount an escape bid.'

Excitement fizzed in Adela's veins.

Eta gave her a grateful smile. 'We need to get back to work now, but tonight in the hut I'll tell you more.'

Adela nodded. As she followed Eta back to their room, she felt hope for the first time in what felt like forever.

Her good mood lasted all day and even when the backs of her heels started to bleed on the long walk back to the barracks, she didn't feel down. It was later than usual and darkness was beginning to fall. They walked past a building with lights burning and she noticed a woman standing in the window. She was wearing a striped dress, but unlike the raggedy, ill-fitting dresses they were wearing, this one was clean and new, and figure-hugging.

'Bitches!' the woman next to her muttered.

'Who are they?' Adela wondered out loud.

'The camp whores,' the woman replied.

'They have prostitutes here?' Adela asked, horrified.

'Yes. To encourage the prisoners to work harder.'

Adela looked back at the window, but the woman had disappeared.

'They get special privileges for their work,' the woman continued. 'Extra food and soap and shampoo. But I don't care how hungry I was, I'd rather die than lie down for the Nazis.'

Adela nodded. She felt certain she'd rather choose death too, but rather than feeling angry about the woman in the window, the sight only made her feel achingly sad.

Izabel moved away from the window, not wanting the women returning from work to notice her. Seeing their painfully thin frames and shabby, ill-fitting clothes had sent a surge of guilt and shame right through her. She looked down at the food on her tray – a bowl of soup and bread. But unlike the watery soup the rest of the prisoners were given, hers was rich and full of flavour, containing chunks of sausage as well as vegetables. The bread here was much better too, fresher and softer. She couldn't help drooling as she looked at it. Part of her wanted to refuse the food, in an act of solidarity with the women outside, but her hunger was overwhelming, and if she wanted to get through the evening shift she needed her strength.

She sat down and took a mouthful of soup. 'Please help me, Saint Brigid, grant me one of your miracles!' she whispered. Just thinking of her beloved saint made her feel a little calmer and she finished her soup and prepared for her first visitor.

When the door opened and the soldier walked in, she felt a burst of relief, instantly tempered with caution. Just because he hadn't touched her during his previous visits, it didn't mean it would always be the case.

'Good evening,' she said, standing by the bed.

'Good evening.' This time, he made eye contact with her, before gesturing at her to sit. 'Please.'

She sat at the head of the bed, a knot of anxiety in her stomach as she waited to see what he'd do next. As before, he sat down at the foot of the bed, but this time, facing to the side so she could see his face in profile.

'Did you like my gift?' he said softly.

'Oh, yes, thank you. It smelled lovely.'

'Good.' His obvious relief both confused and annoyed her. Why did he care what she thought of the soap? And why had she been so gushing in her response? She didn't want to make him feel better about himself.

'My wife loves the smell of roses.'

Izabel fought to control her growing anger. She didn't want to hear about his wife, or his son for that matter. She didn't want to be this man's confidante. But then it was better than the alternative, and every minute he was in her room was keeping her free from being violated by some other brute, so she swallowed hard and forced herself to remain calm. 'It is a lovely scent.'

'Yes.' He shifted into his usual position with his back to her. 'We met at university.'

'Oh.' Again, Izabel had to suppress her annoyance. She really hoped he wasn't about to tell her how they fell in love – not when he and his fellow Nazis had so cruelly ended her own love story.

'We were both studying music.'

'Lovely,' she forced out through gritted teeth.

'It was,' he replied, thankfully not picking up on her bitterness. He was silent for a moment and Izabel prayed to Saint Brigid to keep her calm. 'She's a very good woman,' he whispered.

Izabel frowned at his back. How could a very good woman be married to a Nazi? It didn't make sense.

'I don't know how I...' He broke off.

'What?' Izabel asked, her curiosity getting the better of her.

'Never mind.' His head slumped forwards.

In the hall outside, Izabel heard the guard barking his orders to the prisoners who'd arrived. 'No more than fifteen minutes... Missionary position only...' and she shuddered. She thought of this soldier's 'very good woman' of a wife, safe at home in Germany, smelling the roses in her no doubt lovely garden, and she felt sick from a mixture of envy and rage.

'Do you believe in God?' the soldier said suddenly, his voice cracking slightly.

She was so taken aback by the question, she wasn't sure how to respond.

'I don't know,' she eventually replied. 'But I do pray to Saint Brigid,' she added, immediately cursing herself for mentioning her beloved saint in the presence of a Nazi.

'The patron saint of poets,' he said softly.

'Yes!' She sat up straight and stared at his back.

'Who once turned bathwater into beer.'

'Yes, which I always found just as impressive as turning water into wine.' Again, she cursed herself for being so effusive, but she couldn't help it. Saint Brigid was one of her favourite subjects.

'Personally, I found it more impressive,' he said, 'especially given that it was *dirty* bathwater.' He chuckled, then stood up, still with his back to her. He headed to the door and, as before, stopped by the dressing table and placed a small package upon it. Then, as he was about to leave, he stopped and turned, looking her straight in the eye. 'Thank you,' he said softly, before turning to go.

Izabel stared after him, confused. How did he know so much about Saint Brigid? And what was he thanking her for? She went over to the dressing table and opened the package.

'Oh!' she gasped as she saw a bar of chocolate inside. *You shouldn't accept it,* her inner voice scolded. But then she heard the guard outside the door instructing her next visitor on what he could and couldn't do to her body, and she shoved the chocolate inside her drawer.

∾

Later that night, once they'd eaten their putrid watery soup, Adela and Eta sat together on the edge of their bunk.

'Tomorrow, when you collect the rubbish from the others,' Eta whispered, 'one of the other women is going to put a little bundle in the bottom box. Bring the boxes back to your table and slip the bundle into the cuff of your dress. Then go to the washroom and I'll meet you there.'

Rubbish... bottom box... cuff... washroom, Adela mentally recited, trying to commit the instructions to memory. 'OK.'

'We'll share it out between us to bring back here,' Eta continued. 'Then I'll give it to someone who will take it to the men.'

Adela instantly thought of Ryka but didn't let on that she knew. 'OK.'

'Thank you!' Eta exclaimed, squeezing her hand.

Adela gave a nervous smile. She only hoped she didn't let them down. It had been bad enough when the Germans had caught her coming out of the tunnel from the ghetto, but if they caught her here, there was so much more, and so many lives, at stake.

59

The morning after Stanislaw's murder, there were more guards than usual at the roll call. Two SS men wearing long leather coats walked along the rows of prisoners, inspecting them carefully. Every so often, they'd beckon at one of them to fall out of the line, causing a ripple of anxiety in their wake. Usually when this happened the men who were chosen were the frailest, and never seen again.

Azriel stood a little taller. He didn't want to be picked. He wanted to avenge Stanislaw's death. He wanted to fight back against these monsters. But as one of the SS men drew level with him, he stopped dead.

'You,' he said, gesturing at Azriel to step out of the line.

Azriel's spirits plummeted. Surely this couldn't be how it was going to end for him. He glanced at the other men who'd been selected. None of them looked like the frailest but they all had yellow triangles on their uniforms. Maybe the Germans had decided that they hadn't killed enough Jews. Maybe this was all about meeting some kind of sick quota. His heart sank as he noticed that Abe, one of his Resistance comrades, had also been selected.

The SS soldiers ordered the chosen men to follow one of the kapos. Azriel's fear grew as the kapo led them past the huts towards one of the crematoriums. He looked at the three stone steps leading up to the crematorium door. Was he about to walk in there never to come out again? But, to his relief, the kapo led them right around the building to a courtyard at the back. Another kapo was waiting there to greet them, a mean-looking man with closely set eyes.

'Welcome to the *Sonderkommando*,' he said. 'You have all been selected to take over from the men who currently work here when they're transferred elsewhere.'

Azriel's chest tightened.

'Where are they being transferred to?' one of the prisoners asked. Azriel wondered if he'd also heard the rumour that every few months the *Sonderkommando* unit were transferred to their deaths.

'Elsewhere,' the kapo replied vaguely. 'Today, we need you to start by tidying up this place.' He gestured around the court-yard. 'Clear the weeds, rake the ground.' He nodded to some gardening tools by the wall. 'And you're not to go anywhere near the main building.'

Azriel instantly felt curious. If they were supposed to be working in the crematorium, what was he trying to hide? He and Abe exchanged pointed glances.

Grim-faced, the men went and fetched the tools. Azriel started raking a patch of ground, but he kept glancing at the windows of the crematorium. After a while, his curiosity got the better of him and he raked his way over to the nearest window and peered inside.

'No!' he gasped, dropping the rake in shock, prompting Abe to come hurrying over.

'What is it? What did you see?' he asked.

'Bodies,' Azriel whispered. 'So many bodies!' He blinked hard but it was impossible to erase the horrifying vision. The room was piled high with naked corpses of all ages. But how had they died and what were they doing there?

Abe went over to peer in the window and turned back to look at Azriel, ashen-faced. For the rest of the morning, they worked on in stunned silence.

After lunch, they were taken to a building next to the crematorium. The floor was covered in clothing of all kinds. Azriel looked at a little girl's red velvet dress and he felt an icy chill course right through him. First the bodies, and now the clothes. It was like fitting together the pieces of a terrible jigsaw puzzle.

A kapo showed them how to use the sleeves of jackets and shirts to roll the clothes into bundles. As Azriel worked, he felt dizzy from horror and disbelief. Every so often, he'd get a waft of perfume or sweat from the clothes, and he thought his heart would break for the people who had worn them. His fingers traced the pattern in a tiny woollen sweater, and he wondered who'd knitted it. The child's mother perhaps, or grandmother. He thought of Estera and how she'd knitted scarves and gloves for him and Adela when they were children. One year, when he was about thirteen, she'd knitted him a scarf in bright purple. He winced as he remembered how he'd moaned that he didn't like the colour. He'd give anything now to receive a knitted gift from his mother.

After a few hours, the kapo returned. 'Now you must pile the clothes outside,' he ordered.

Azriel numbly followed the other men, and they built a pile of bundles on the steps outside the door. *Please, let this horror be over*, he thought to himself, as the last of the clothes were taken outside. All he wanted was to go back to the barracks and get into his bunk and close his eyes and pray for sleep to help him escape. There had been moments in the ghetto where Azriel had thought that life couldn't get any worse. But he'd been wrong. Auschwitz, without a shadow of a doubt, was the worst place on earth.

60

Adela walked around the room holding the two metal boxes.

'Any rubbish?' she asked as nonchalantly as possible.

'Oh yes,' a woman named Asna replied. Adela passed her one of the boxes and watched as, quick as a trice, Asna slipped a little piece of bound-up rag inside, then put some rubbish on top.

'Thank you,' Adela said, and she took the boxes back to her table, heart pounding. Eta glanced up at her as she walked past.

Adela sat down and placed the bottom box on her lap, out of sight, under the table. Her fingers were shaking so much, she was worried she might send the box crashing to the floor, but, thankfully, she got it open and slipped the bundle under the cuff of her dress. Now to get it to the washroom.

She stood up, praying that their supervisor wouldn't ask for her help with anything. Fortunately, the supervisor was busy working, so Adela slipped into the corridor without being noticed. She hurried into the washroom, leaned on the sink and took a breath; her heart was pounding so loud, it felt as if it might burst right out of her chest.

After a few moments, Eta appeared.

'Did you get it?' she whispered.

Adela nodded.

They went into one of the cubicles and Adela produced the bundle from her sleeve. With the expertise of one who had clearly done it many times before, Eta produced another piece of rag and string, opened the bundle and divided the gunpowder inside into two. There were barely more than two teaspoons of the black powder – mere grains of sand compared to the vast amounts produced in the factory – but Adela completely understood their need for caution. If the Germans found any gunpowder on them, they could be shot on sight.

'Tuck it inside your underwear,' Eta said, handing her one of the bundles. 'And stay with me when we leave tonight. We need to make sure we're in the middle of the group, in case the guards stop us for an inspection. That way, we'll have some time to try to get rid of it before they get to us.'

'How do we get rid of it?' Adela asked.

'Drop it on the floor and tread it into the ground,' she replied, 'so there's no sign of it.'

Adela tucked the bundle into her underwear, her fear growing.

'Good luck.' Eta clutched her arms. 'And thank you!'

Adela's fear faded slightly. It felt so good to be a part of something again, to be organising against the Germans, just like she'd done in the Bund.

All the way back to the barracks that night, she jumped out of her skin at the slightest thing, so when they made it back safely, the joy she felt was overwhelming. As the kapo yelled at them to get into line for food, Adela had to stop herself from grinning. The Germans and their kapo minions might think they were all-powerful, but once again the Jewish people were fighting back, and this time, right under their noses.

~

Azriel hardly got a wink of sleep after his first day as a *Sonderkommando*. They'd been moved into the *Sonderkommando* barracks between the crematorium and the *Kanada* warehouse, but even though he was exhausted, all he could think about were the men who'd slept in the bunk before. Had they been executed to make way for the new shift? And if so, would that be his fate, in three months' time?

He followed the others to breakfast feeling numb with tiredness and shock. It turned out that the *Sonderkommando* were given more generous rations than the other prisoners, but as he looked at the chunk of bread on his tin plate, his stomach churned.

'Are you all right, comrade?' Abe whispered beside him.

Azriel nodded, not wanting to infect him with his growing fear, but in the light of what they'd seen, it was hard to stay strong.

After breakfast, a group of about ten of them were marched to the crematorium and down a flight of stone steps into the basement. Azriel shivered. It was eerie and cold, and the air was filled with a loud wheezing mechanical sound, as if a large machine somewhere was breathing in and out. A terrible acrid smell filled the air, a mixture of chemicals and human excrement. The wheezing sound fell silent, and they followed the kapo into an atrium and over to an open door. One of the men gasped as they looked inside and Azriel had to fight the urge to retch. The room was full of naked bodies. Some were clinging to each other in a frozen embrace, others piled on top of each other as if they'd been searching in vain for a way to escape. Just like the day before, there were the corpses of men, women and children.

'You need to take the bodies from the chamber,' the kapo instructed, 'and bring them through here.' He led them into an atrium where a row of *Sonderkommandos* were sitting waiting, holding scissors. 'Once they've had their hair cut off and any gold fillings removed, you need to load the bodies into this hoist.' He pointed to a hoist in the wall. 'It will take seven to ten bodies, which you then need to send up to the ovens.'

He said it all so matter-of-factly, as if he were giving a presentation on how to operate a piece of factory machinery.

Don't you care that these people have just been murdered? Azriel wanted to yell. *Don't you care that they were someone's son or daughter just like you?* He'd seen some horrors since the start of the war, but nothing could have prepared him for this.

Then he remembered something Izabel had once said, when she'd told him how she'd survived being attacked by the thugs during the pogrom. 'I went to a place in my mind where they couldn't reach me,' she'd said. 'A secret garden behind a big stone wall.'

As Azriel followed the kapo back to the gas chamber, he imagined holding hands with Izabel as they made their way into a secret garden together. Trying to escape further, he began adding details to the garden and pictured them walking past a rose bush. But when they stopped to smell the flowers, his nostrils were flooded with the scent of death.

That night, he returned to the barracks filled with a grim sense of determination. He could feel death pressing in on him from all sides, but he was not going to go down without a fight.

'We have to do something,' he whispered to Abe as they got into their bunk. 'We can't just wait for them to kill us in three months.'

'I agree,' Abe whispered back. 'But what?'

Azriel lay down and gazed up at the ceiling, his heart racing as the beginnings of a plot began forming in his mind. It was a plot so audacious, he half wondered if he had been driven mad by anguish and grief. But at least it gave him something positive to focus on and the alternative – to meekly become a part of the German killing machine – was too awful to contemplate. He turned to face Abe and gave a weak smile.

'I have an idea,' he whispered.

61

A couple of weeks passed and, just like the morning and evening roll calls, smuggling gunpowder back to the barracks became a part of Adela's routine. But then, one day when she'd taken the gunpowder from the rubbish box to the washroom, Eta hadn't shown up. Adela hadn't been sure what to do at first. Should she leave it in the bathroom or even flush it down the toilet? But then she thought of how painstakingly slow the whole process was, and that if they wanted to help the men with their plans, they couldn't afford to miss a day. She would have to risk hiding double the normal amount of gunpowder in her underwear.

As soon as they lined up outside that evening after work, Eta leaned close.

'I'm sorry,' she whispered. 'I got stopped by the supervisor when you went to the washroom. She needed me to run an errand.'

'It's OK, I have it,' Adela whispered back.

'What, all of it?' Eta looked at her, concerned.

Adela nodded. It hardly made a difference if she had one or

two teaspoons of gunpowder on her. If the Germans found it, she'd still be dead.

They started their long walk back to the camp. The pain of Adela's ill-fitting shoes no longer bothered her. All she could think about was the gunpowder hidden inside her underwear, and she kept silently praying they didn't get stopped. The further they walked, the more relieved she felt. She noticed a star shining above them and instantly thought of Jaski. She wondered what he'd have made of her gunpowder smuggling. She imagined him clapping his hands together with glee and cheering her on. 'It's proof that you're made of stardust,' she imagined him saying and she began to smile. But then she heard a sound that wiped the smile from her face. A piercing whistle cut through the gloom, and she saw that some guards had arrived at the head of the procession.

'It's a search!' Eta hissed.

Adela glanced around anxiously. A kapo was standing just a few feet in front of them. How on earth was she going to dispose of the gunpowder without him seeing?

You can be anyone or anything you put your mind to. Jaski's words to the orphans echoed back through time to her. *You don't need to be afraid.*

Then Izabel popped into her mind. Adela knew that her fearless friend would remain calm and collected in this situation. She'd probably even make some kind of dry quip, like it being an explosive turn of events.

Adela took a deep breath. The guards began making their way towards her, stopping periodically to make one of the women strip. She shot Eta a frantic glance.

'Is that someone trying to escape?' Eta called, pointing to the fence surrounding the camp.

'What? Where?' The kapo in front of them instantly sprang to attention, tapping his truncheon in the palm of his hand.

'Over there, in the shadows,' Eta said.

As the kapo hurried over to investigate, Adela slipped her hand through a hole in her dress and into the belt of her underwear. The bundle had moved down while she'd been walking and, for a horrible moment, she thought she wouldn't be able to reach it. But, finally, she felt the piece of string and pulled on it. As she tugged the bundle free, the guards moved ever closer. Keeping her gaze fixed firmly ahead, she thought of Izabel. *Stay calm,* moj skarbe, she imagined her saying. Weirdly, it had the desired effect, and she felt her pulse slow slightly. She undid the string, spilled the powder onto the ground, then stepped forward slightly and began grinding it into the soil. Her skin was clammy with cold sweat.

'There was no one there,' the kapo said crossly as he returned.

Adela tucked the piece of rag into her sleeve just as the guards drew level.

'You,' one of them said, pointing at Adela, causing her stomach to plummet.

Adela stepped towards them, praying she'd managed to hide the powder. Out of the corner of her eye, she saw Eta step to the side, no doubt to cover any residue with her foot, and she said a silent prayer of gratitude.

'Take off your dress,' the guard ordered.

Adela obeyed, feeling sick with fear as she tried to take it off without the rag falling from her sleeve. She dropped the dress to the floor, relieved that there was nothing in her underwear.

'Pick it up,' the guard barked, and sweat began to trickle down her temple.

She picked the dress up.

The guard pointed to the kapo and he took the dress and shook it out. Adela stopped breathing as the piece of rag fell to the floor.

'What is that?' the guard asked as the kapo picked it up.

'I've been using it as a handkerchief,' Adela blurted out. 'To blow my nose on,' she added.

The kapo grimaced and held the rag at arm's length.

The guard looked at her for a moment, then nodded. 'Get dressed,' she barked and continued on her way.

The kapo dropped the rag on the floor and, to Adela's horror, she saw the piece of string poking out from under it. Quick as a flash, she scooped it up, brought it to her face and blew her nose, whilst tucking the string back behind it.

The kapo hurried away, worried no doubt that she might be about to infect him with something.

She put on her dress and tucked the rag back in her sleeve. The guard blew her whistle, and they resumed walking. Adela looked up at the sky for the star, wanting to say thank you to Jaski, but it had disappeared behind a thick bank of cloud.

62

One day in early September, the *Sonderkommandos'* supervisor informed them that they'd be switching duties. Azriel and a man named Noah were told to report for work at the front of the crematorium.

'What do you think they'll want us to do?' Noah asked nervously as they set off.

'I don't know, but whatever it is, remember that we're not going to take it lying down,' Azriel replied. Ever since his seed of an idea for fighting back had planted itself in his mind, he'd quietly approached the other *Sonderkommandos* to see if they'd be willing to join him. Noah was one of the many men who'd made it clear that they'd do anything to thwart the Germans, should the opportunity arise, which filled Azriel with renewed hope and caused his seed of an idea to bloom into a rapidly developing plan.

But when they reached the crematorium, they saw a sight that made Azriel's breath catch in his throat. A seemingly endless queue of people snaked its way across the courtyard to the main door. The air was filled with nervous chatter, in Polish, Azriel noted, and the cries of young children. He froze. It was bad enough having to deal with the bodies after they'd been murdered in the gas chamber, but to be presented with people as they arrived, still alive, was beyond comprehension. How could he face them, knowing what fate was about to befall them?

An SS guard stood at the top of the crematorium steps and called something out in German. The crowd looked at him blankly, not understanding.

The guard noticed Azriel and Noah and beckoned them over. 'You Polish?' he asked.

The two men nodded.

'Tell them, they eat after disinfection.' He gave a dark grin. 'They eat very big meal.'

Azriel stared at him, horrified. This was clearly a lie to get the crowd to acquiesce.

'Go on.' The guard gestured at them to go.

'How can we lie to them?' Azriel muttered to Noah as they went down the steps. 'We should tell them the truth.'

But, to his surprise, Noah shook his head. 'If we do, we'll terrify them. They're going to be killed whatever happens. We shouldn't add to their agony.'

After a moment, Azriel nodded. Although it broke his heart to admit it, there was sense in what Noah said.

'We have to keep thinking of the plan,' Noah whispered. 'It's the only thing that will keep us sane.'

Azriel nodded numbly and followed him over to the queue of people.

'Don't worry, you're just being taken for a shower,' he found himself saying, his voice sounding weirdly disconnected and discordant. 'Then you'll have a meal.'

Some of the people he told still looked suspicious, but many looked relieved, especially the women with children, who started moving closer to the steps in their eagerness for food. Azriel's sorrow began curdling into a bitter hatred, both for the Germans and for himself at being a part of this evil scheme.

He and Noah began ushering the people down the steps and into the undressing room, which was lined with long wooden seats and numbered coat pegs.

'Tell them, leave belongings and remember number,' the guard instructed, once again with a smirk.

It took a moment for Azriel to realise the motives behind this. If the new arrivals were told to memorise the number of their coat pegs, they'd assume they were going to get their belongings back. His stomach churned as he thought of their clothes being bundled up and sent to *Kanada* instead.

'Tell them, tie their shoelaces together,' the guard barked, and again Azriel felt sick with rage and despair. Clearly this was to make things easier for the Germans once the owners of the shoes had been murdered. *Have you no humanity?* he wanted to yell. *How can you do this?*

He began numbly giving the orders as instructed and once the women and children had undressed and filed into what they thought was the shower room, the men began to arrive.

Azriel walked up and down, parroting the instructions over and over. 'Tie your shoes together. Hang your belongings on the peg. Make sure to remember your number.' *You're doing this to make it easier for them, not the Germans*, he had to keep reminding himself.

Then, just as he was about to walk over to address the people walking in, he felt someone grab his hand.

'Son?' a voice said softly. It was a voice he would recognise anywhere. His knees buckled as he turned to look down. There, sitting on the bench, with his shoes on his lap, was his father.

'Oh!' Azriel gasped. It felt as if all the air had been sucked from his lungs. 'Oh no!'

'Well, that's a fine way to greet your father,' Leopold joked. He put his shoes down and stood up. 'Oh son, I didn't think I'd ever see you again.' His face broke into a smile. 'I thought you'd been killed in the fighting.'

'I... I managed to escape.' Azriel's mouth went dry. 'What happened to you? How did you end up here?'

'I'd been living in hiding in Warsaw after leaving the ghetto. A member of the Polish Home Army let me stay in his attic. I was arrested last week when the Germans raided his property. Is there any news about Adela?' Leopold looked at him hopefully.

Azriel shook his head.

'Maybe she escaped when she went down the tunnel,' Leopold said.

'Yes,' Azriel replied, not wanting to dash his hopes. His mind began to race. How could he get his father out of there? He looked over at the door. Two German guards were standing there laughing and joking. The hatred inside him bubbled hot as lava.

'Oh son, this is the most wonderful thing!' Leopold exclaimed, clutching his arm.

Azriel stared at him, horrified. As far as Leopold was concerned, he was about to have a shower and a meal before joining the camp, before joining *him*. How could he lie to him? But how could he tell him the terrible truth: that he, his son, was going to watch as he walked, oblivious, to his death? How could he possibly be a part of this? The answer came to him in a flash. He couldn't. He would tell his father the truth, and then he would take off his wretched uniform, and he'd hang up his shoes, tying the laces together as instructed, and they would walk together to their deaths.

63

'Something is being planned,' Eta whispered to Adela as they split the gunpowder in two in the washroom. 'Ryka told me last night that the men are going to be doing something with all the explosives we've been smuggling to them.'

'Really? What?' Adela's pulse quickened.

'I'm not sure, but apparently it's going to be big.'

Adela wanted to cry for joy. The thought of the Auschwitz Resistance striking back against the Germans made all the stress and fear worth it.

'Just think,' Eta said, looking down at the gunpowder. 'One day soon, this might help some of our fellow prisoners escape.'

Adela felt a wistful pang as she looked down at the black powder. She would give anything to be able to escape this hell on earth, but it felt almost as good knowing that she might help another to freedom.

~

Azriel looked Leopold straight in the eyes.

'There's something I have to tell you, Papa,' he said softly, his voice cracking.

'It's all right, son, I know.'

Azriel's blood froze. 'What do you mean?'

'I know there's no warm shower on the other side of that door.' He glanced at the end of the room. 'I know there's no welcome meal. This is the end, isn't it?'

Azriel's eyes began swimming with tears as he nodded. 'But I'm coming with you,' he said, kicking off one of his shoes.

'No!' Leopold cried with a look of anguish. 'No, you can't.'

'I can't leave you.' Azriel stared at him, horrified.

'Yes, you can, and you must,' he said firmly.

'But why?'

'Because you still have a chance of surviving. I want you to survive!' Leopold sighed. 'I've always been a peace-loving man. It broke my heart to think of you fighting, and possibly killing, another human being. But those last days in the ghetto, I saw how brave you were. How brave you *are*. I'm so proud of you, Azriel. I want you to know that, and never forget.'

'Papa.' Azriel was unable to stop a sob from escaping. 'Please. I don't want you to die. I don't want you to die alone.'

Leopold gave him a gentle smile. 'I'm not alone. I'm never alone.'

Azriel looked at him blankly and Leopold pulled him close.

'I have God with me,' he whispered in his ear. 'And he's with you too. Never forget.'

Azriel nodded, although he found it hard to believe. How could any loving God allow a situation as cruel as this?

'And look at how God has given us the gift of meeting here,' Leopold continued, his eyes lighting up. 'Now I can go to my death with peace in my heart because I know you're alive. And you have to do all you can to stay alive. Please, I beg of you!'

'But why? What's the point?' Azriel looked at him helplessly.

'So you can tell people what happened here. You are a witness to their evil. You can let the world know so that this is never allowed to happen again. The Allies are advancing. This could all be over very soon. Please, son, promise me you'll do everything you can to survive. And if you do, and you find your mother and your sister, please tell them I love them.' His voice wavered.

Azriel swallowed hard, then nodded. 'I promise.'

Leopold gave him a grateful smile, then hung his shoes on his coat peg and began to undress.

As Azriel watched, he felt paralysed by grief and in awe of his father's strength. For so long, he'd thought of Leopold as a coward for joining the *Judenrat*, but now he could see that his father possessed a courage and dignity he could only dream of.

'I'm so sorry for those years we wasted not talking to each other,' he said. 'I'm so sorry I was too stubborn to try to make amends.'

Leopold gave a sad laugh. 'I was just as bad. But I'm so glad we got there in the end. And I never stopped loving you, all through that time.' Leopold's eyes became glassy with tears. 'Oh son, there's so much I want to say to you. I wish we had more time.'

Azriel felt a lump building in the back of his throat. 'I love you,' he gasped.

'And I love you,' Leopold replied in his usual calm tone, but his fingers trembled as he unbuttoned his shirt.

Azriel watched numbly as his father took off his trousers and folded them neatly before placing them on the bench. This couldn't be happening. It was the worst nightmare imaginable. And yet Leopold's calm and dignified demeanour was so powerful, he could feel it soaking into him, strengthening him for what was about to come.

'I'll walk with you,' he said, once Leopold was undressed.

Leopold nodded and they began walking up the room

towards the gas chamber, Azriel's heart breaking with every step.

64

This time, when the soldier walked into the room, Izabel could smell sour alcohol mingled in with his earthy cologne. It was a smell that reminded her of Dieter and instantly made her tense. She'd had one of her regular nightmares about Dieter the night before and the residue of fear lingered.

'Good day,' the soldier said, and she noticed that his jaw was dull with stubble.

'Good day.' She sat down at the head of the bed, but he remained standing at the foot.

'I couldn't sleep last night,' he said. 'Would it be all right if I had a glass of water?' He nodded at the jug and glasses on her dresser.

'Of course.' She watched as he poured himself a glass, then turned back to her. 'Would you like one?'

It was such a simple question, but there was something about the gentle way in which he asked it, and the fact that he had even asked it at all, that filled her with sorrow at all she had lost.

'Are you all right?' he asked and again she felt floored by his concern. How long had it been since someone had asked her that question? How long had it been since she'd felt the affection of another human being?

'Izabel?' He put the jug down and walked over to her.

'How... how did you know my name?' she stammered, wishing with all her might that she might regain her strength.

'I asked the guard,' he replied simply. 'Are you all right?'

'Yes... I-I didn't sleep well last night either. I'm feeling a little dizzy.'

He went back to the jug and poured her a glass of water. 'Here,' he said, handing it to her.

She took a sip and another. *Please, Saint Brigid, don't let me cry in front of him*, she silently prayed. *Please fill me with your strength.*

'Are you being treated all right in here?' he asked.

The question seemed so ludicrous, it instantly took away her tears, making her want to laugh with derision instead.

'If you aren't, you must tell me, OK?'

She nodded, fighting the urge to ask him exactly what he would do if she did.

He sat down on the bed next to her and gazed at the floor.

She took another sip of her water, hoping that this change in the normal routine didn't mean he was building up to becoming physical with her. She was still feeling too vulnerable.

Thankfully, he remained silent, and the minutes ticked by, punctuated only by them sipping on their glasses of water. And then he cleared his throat.

'I never thought...' he said softly, before breaking off.

'What?' she asked.

'I never thought I'd kill another human being,' he whispered. 'When I was younger, I mean.' He put his glass on the floor and slumped forward, head in hands.

Neither did I, she wanted to reply, thinking of the night she killed Dieter, driven mad by grief and despair. The night that kept coming back to her, each time more graphic, in her nightmares.

'I sometimes think that I'm going mad,' he murmured.

Me too, Izabel thought, instantly horrified that she should have something in common with an SS soldier.

'I used to think that there were winners in war,' he continued, 'but now...' He sighed and stood up and took something from his trouser pocket. 'I got this for you,' he said, placing it on the bed beside her. 'Thank you,' he muttered before walking to the door.

Izabel sat staring after him as he left, momentarily stunned. What had he meant by that comment about winners? Had he been about to show some remorse for what the Germans had done? She looked down and saw a small, oval cardboard pendant with a picture of a woman in a green robe and a glowing halo of gold.

'Saint Brigid,' she whispered, and it was as if something inside of her came undone. She clutched the cardboard pendant to her chest and let out a sob.

Once all the new arrivals had been ushered into the gas chamber, Azriel and Noah were ordered back outside. Away from Leopold's calming presence, Azriel felt a deadly mixture of panic and rage swirling inside of him. He'd never felt so utterly heartbroken, and so completely powerless.

'Are you all right?' Noah asked, clearly concerned.

'My... my father is in there,' Azriel stammered. 'They're about to murder my father.'

'No!' Noah gasped. 'I'm so sorry.'

A German guard went hurrying past, holding a gas canister.

'I have to stop him,' Azriel muttered, stepping forwards.

'No!' Noah grabbed hold of his arm.

'They're about to kill my father.' Azriel watched, horrified, as two *Sonderkommandos* began opening the heavy trap door over the gas chamber for the guard to pour in the gas. 'I can't let them do it!'

'You can't stop them,' Noah hissed. 'And you can't watch this.' He gripped Azriel's arm tighter and pulled him away. 'Remember the plan,' he whispered. 'We have a chance to do something about this.'

Leopold's last dying wish echoed around Azriel's mind – *'You are a witness to their evil. You can let the world know so that this is never allowed to happen again'* – and somehow he managed to make his legs walk away from the gas chamber. He thought of the gunpowder the women had been smuggling to the Resistance for months, and the grenades the men had made from it using old shoe polish and sardine tins, some of which were now hidden within the bricks of the crematorium walls. He thought of the weapons they'd been hiding all over the camp and the demolition charges they'd made to blow holes in the fence. Then his thoughts returned to Leopold.

I'm going to get out of here and I'm going to tell the whole world about the Nazis' evil, he silently vowed. *I'm going to make you proud.*

65

One morning in late September, there were extra guards at the women's morning roll call. When Adela saw them, she felt a burst of panic that they might have uncovered the gunpowder plot and exchanged anxious glances with Eta.

'We need more staff for the *Aufräumungskommando* today,' one of the guards yelled and Adela was flooded with relief. The *Aufräumungskommando* clothes warehouse, or *Kanada* as it was known, was seen amongst some as being a coveted role. Although, to Adela, the thought of going through the other prisoners' stolen belongings felt nothing short of gruesome.

Some of the prisoners began raising their hands, offering their services. The guard looked at them and smirked before walking right past. Of course she wouldn't be kind enough to give the job to someone who wanted it. Adela sighed. Then, to her horror, the guard stopped right in front of her.

'You'll do,' she said, perhaps detecting Adela's indifference.

'But...'

'Report to the *Aufräumungskommando* after breakfast,' she barked.

Adela nodded, then gave Eta a helpless stare. If she was no

longer employed at the munitions factory, it meant one less person to smuggle the gunpowder.

'It's all right,' Eta whispered as roll call ended and they walked back to their hut. 'You can still help us.'

Later, when Adela was finishing her breakfast of watery soup, Ryka came and sat down beside her. 'Put this in your shoe,' she whispered, before slipping a tiny rag bundle into her hand. 'On the walk to *Kanada*, I'll tell you what to do with it.'

Adela did as instructed, a shiver running up her spine. Rather than bringing an end to her Resistance activities, being moved to *Kanada* was taking her right into the heart of their operation.

As they set off for the warehouse, Ryka leaned in close.

'On our way into *Kanada*, we're going to pass a small storage hut,' she whispered. 'If I tell you that the coast is clear, I want you to go inside. A member of the *Sonderkommando* will be waiting there for you. You're to give him the package, then come straight back out.'

'OK.' Adela focused hard on looking calm, but as a couple of guards marched past, her heart skipped a beat. This felt even riskier than bringing the gunpowder back from the munitions plant.

They turned a corner and *Kanada* came into view, next to one of the dreaded crematoriums. Ryka gestured at a shed-like building in the shadow of the warehouses, then she glanced left and right before giving her a nod. 'Go!' she hissed.

Adela slipped off to the side and pushed open the door. It was pitch dark inside. 'Hello,' she whispered, praying it wasn't a trap. 'Is anyone there?'

There was a moment's silence, which seemed to stretch for an eternity, and then a man replied from the shadows. 'Little bookworm? Is that you?'

66

Azriel took a step forwards, hardly able to believe his ears. He was meant to be meeting his contact from *Kanada* to collect some more gunpowder. Never in his wildest dreams had he imagined Adela greeting him there. He had to be hallucinating. It had to be some kind of crazy wishful thinking.

'Azriel?' she whispered.

He took another step forward and there she was, right in front of him. He had to clamp his hand to his mouth to stop himself from crying out. Her hair had been cropped and her face was a lot thinner, but there was no doubting he was looking into the eyes of his sister.

'You're alive!' he gasped.

'So are you!' Her mouth gaped open in shock.

His knees almost buckling, he grabbed her arms and pulled her into a hug.

'Oh Azriel!'

'What are you doing here?' he whispered.

'I came to deliver something.'

'From Ryka?' he hissed.

'Yes. But what are you doing here?'

'I'm here to collect it. Are you...? Have you been helping smuggle it to us?' The thought of his sister being involved in the Resistance plot filled him with a joy he found hard to contain. If only he'd known before. If only he'd been able to tell Leopold. His joy became tinged with sorrow.

'Yes!' Adela replied. 'Are you one of the men who's planning to escape?'

'We're planning a lot more than that,' he replied.

Adela gasped. 'Oh, Azriel, this is a miracle. I thought I might never see you again.'

'I feel like I'm hallucinating,' he replied. 'When you didn't return to the ghetto, I was sure the Germans must have got you.'

'They did, but I didn't break under their questioning. I didn't tell them a thing.'

He filled with a fierce pride for his sister and hugged her again.

A woman cleared her throat outside and Adela slipped from his embrace and took a tiny bundle from her shoe. 'I can't stay; it isn't safe.' She pressed the bundle into his hand. 'Oh, Azriel, I don't want to leave you.' She hugged him again, then kissed his cheek.

'I don't either!' He grabbed her hand and held it tightly. 'I love you, little bookworm.'

'I love you too.' She gazed up at him. 'Good luck, and please stay safe!'

'You too.' He watched her turn to go, part of him still sure that he had to be dreaming. Then a memory jolted him to his senses. 'Adela,' he hissed.

She stopped and looked at him over her shoulder. 'Yes?'

'I saw Papa. He told me to tell you that he loves you.'

'Papa's still alive?' She looked so overjoyed, he didn't have the heart to tell her the truth.

'Yes, yes he is.'

'Oh, thank God. Oh Azriel, I'm so happy.'

'Me too,' he replied, but as she hurried outside and he tucked the gunpowder into his shoe, he couldn't stop a tear from spilling onto his face.

67

For the next few days, Adela was barely able to concentrate. All she could think about was Azriel appearing in front of her as if by magic. Just knowing he was there in Auschwitz, and working so close by, helped distract her from the horrors of her new job, sorting through the belongings of each new intake at the camp. And not only that, but their father was still alive and she'd received a message from him. *Magic really does exist*, she whispered to Jaski in her mind as she sorted through countless pairs of shoes, trying not to think of what had become of their owners.

The more she thought about the fact that Azriel was also involved in the Resistance plot, the happier she became. The notion that the gunpowder she'd smuggled could possibly help her brother escape made her ecstatic. She imagined Azriel racing through the fields and woods surrounding the camp and eventually making his way back to Warsaw, where Izabel would be waiting for him. If only they'd had more time together, she could have given him a message for her.

Adela felt a wistful pang as she pictured the two of them sitting at a kitchen table without her. But she could still join them, she reassured herself. According to the women in her hut who worked in the hospital where they had access to a radio, the Allies were making advances every day. Maybe she would survive this place and be reunited with Azriel and Izabel as soon as the camp was liberated. And Leopold could join them too. And if her father was still alive, then maybe, by some miracle, her mother had also survived. She smiled at the thought of them all together again.

She'd heard from other prisoners that the Warsaw ghetto had been razed to the ground, so it was highly unlikely that the family store was still standing, but that didn't matter. One thing the war had taught her over and over again was that when it all came down to it, the only thing that mattered, the only thing that couldn't be torn down or destroyed, was love. It didn't matter where she and her family and her beloved Izabel ended up; as long as they still had each other, they'd be home.

Izabel looked at her reflection in the dressing-table mirror, wincing as she applied a cold press to her swollen eye. She'd just had a visit from a German kapo named Kurt who seemed to have made it his life's work to terrorise her every time he set foot in the room. Normally, she was able to escape into the secret garden within her mind as he pulled and pushed her about, but this time, he'd been so violent, she was wrenched back into her body. And now she was in so much pain, there was little chance of forgetting him anytime soon.

She glanced at the clock. It had just gone nine, which meant she still had another hour of visitors to endure. As she stood up, she felt a searing pain between her legs. 'Don't cry!' she said to her reflection and she picked up the Saint Brigid pendant and clutched it tightly.

In the weeks since she'd been given the pendant, she'd held it so often and so tightly, poor Brigid's face had rubbed off. It didn't matter to Izabel though. The little pendant still symbol-ised strength and hope – things she needed now more than ever.

The door opened and she tucked the pendant into her pocket, mentally preparing for whatever fresh hell was about to befall her.

'Good evening.'

She looked up to see the soldier standing in the doorway and felt a surge of relief so strong it almost floored her. 'It's you,' she said, unable to contain her surprise. 'You don't normally come in the evening.'

'I know but...' He broke off, looking aghast at her face. 'What happened to you?'

'One of my visitors wanted to leave his mark,' she replied wryly.

'Who did this?' He came and stood right in front of her, so close she could feel his breath on her face.

'One of the kapos.'

'Which one?' His voice was low but tight with anger.

'His name is Kurt.'

'And when was he here?'

'About ten minutes ago.'

'Right.' He marched back out of the door and she heard him yelling something at the guard. When he returned, the tips of his cheeks were flushed pink. 'I'm very sorry,' he said tersely. 'He won't be bothering you again.'

'Oh. OK.' Once again, Izabel found herself in the slightly awkward position of being grateful to him.

'Please – sit.' He gestured at the bed.

As she sat down, another arrow of pain shot through her.

'I'm sorry,' the soldier said, as he watched her trying to get comfortable.

'You don't need to apologise. You weren't the one who did it,' she replied.

'No, but...' He tailed off and she wondered what he'd been

about to say. *No, but it's because of me that you're in this place.*
He sighed and shook his head. He looked paler than ever, apart
from the dark rings around his eyes. She wondered if he was
worried about the news from the front. She sometimes overheard the headlines on the guards' radio and knew that things
weren't looking good for the Germans, although she tried not to
think too much about the Allied advances. She didn't want to
have her hopes dashed yet again. 'Did you like my gift?' he
asked, looking at her expectantly.

'Saint Brigid?' She smiled and took the pendant from her
pocket. 'She's been my constant companion. Thank you.'

He shook his head. 'No need to thank me. I was happy to
do it.'

'Where did you get her from?'

'Someone I know, in the church. Like you, he has a
penchant for Saint Brigid.'

Izabel stared at him, confused. Auschwitz was such a hell
on earth, it seemed impossible to imagine that there could be a
church anywhere near, much less a church that this SS soldier
visited.

He began pacing back and forth in front of the dressing
table. Finally, he stopped and looked down at the floor. 'I was
wondering if I could ask something of you – a small favour.'

'Yes?' she asked, instantly on her guard. The thought of
doing anything for a Nazi – even one who had actually shown
her some kindness – filled her with dread.

'Could I tell you something, and would you listen?'

As if I have a choice, she felt like responding, but bit her lip.
'I always listen,' she said instead.

'Yes, but this is different,' he said, still not making eye
contact with her. 'This would be more like a confession, of
sorts.'

'I have to say, I make quite an unlikely priest,' she couldn't
help quipping, but he didn't smile.

'Please?' he asked, and there was a plaintive tone to his voice that caught her by surprise.

'Of course,' she replied, and he took his old position, sitting with his back to her at the foot of the bed.

A silence fell on the room, broken only by the sound of men's voices outside.

'I-I killed someone,' he eventually stammered.

Only one? she thought but remained silent.

'And I can't stop thinking about it,' he continued. 'Even when I'm asleep, I dream about it.'

Izabel thought of her nightmares about Dieter. Was she really in any position to judge the soldier when she too had taken a life and been plagued by feelings of guilt? She wanted to ask who he'd killed to have made him so upset but remembered that she was supposed to be the priest in this confessional and remained quiet.

'I don't know how I'm ever going to forget.' His voice rose a little. 'Maybe I'm not supposed to. Maybe this is my punishment, to be tormented by the memory forevermore. But then, how will I face my wife, my family?' He shifted slightly so that she could see his face in profile. 'Do you think there's any way I can atone for what I did?'

Izabel looked down at her pendant. *Please, Saint Brigid*, she silently prayed, *what should I tell him? What should I tell myself?* She closed her eyes and waited and then a voice rang through her mind, clear and sweet as a bell. *You must forgive yourself so you're free to love.*

'You must forgive yourself,' she echoed softly, and the words felt like a balm to her soul. For the first time in her life, she realised that forgiveness wasn't about excusing or condoning, it was about ridding yourself of the toxins of anger and guilt so that you could return to love.

'How can I forgive myself?' He turned to look at her and his eyes were shiny with tears. 'I killed a child!' he cried, and his body began heaving with sobs.

An image of Kasper's limp and battered body the day he'd been caught smuggling sprang into Izabel's mind. If the soldier had killed a child, then he was no better than the police officer who'd left her brother for dead. She looked at him, bent over double and crying in front of her and she filled with contempt. So what if he'd brought her gifts and protected her from that brute, Kurt. He'd killed a child.

She looked back at Saint Brigid, expecting her to convey some kind of message of righteous anger in solidarity, but as soon as her gaze fell upon Brigid's glowing halo, her anger faded. *You must forgive*, she heard the saint whisper, *or you'll never be free to love.*

'Please forgive me,' the soldier gasped between sobs. 'Please, please forgive me.'

Izabel wasn't sure if he was talking to the child he'd killed or to God himself. All she knew was that she suddenly felt utterly exhausted from the years of pain, anger and sorrow. She leaned forward and pressed the cardboard pendant into his hand.

'I forgive you,' she said softly, and her body softened and filled with peace.

68

October arrived, bringing chill winds and darkening skies. Although the Soviet Army had arrived in Poland, they were still nowhere near Auschwitz. But the twelfth *Sonderkommando* unit was growing closer to the end of their three months in the crematoria and Azriel felt as if they had a giant clock ticking over their heads, marking down the seconds until their inevitable deaths.

'We can't afford to wait for the Russians to get here to stage our revolt,' he whispered to Abe one morning over breakfast. 'The Germans will do for us long before they arrive.'

To his relief, Abe nodded. 'The plan is in place,' he whispered back. 'The men are all ready. We just have to give the word.'

Azriel pushed his soup away, fear causing his throat to tighten. *What if it doesn't work?* his inner voice warned. *What if you're all killed?* But they were all going to be killed anyway. They literally had nothing to lose. Remembering this felt strangely fortifying and his fear was replaced by a surge of adrenaline. 'We'll do it tomorrow at morning roll call,' he said. 'Let's spread the word.'

. . .

That night, Azriel didn't get a wink of sleep. The other *Sonderkommandos* had all been in ready agreement that they needed to bring the revolt forward, but would they just be hastening their deaths? He could only hope that some of them would live to tell the tale, and now that he'd seen Adela and knew she was alive he really hoped he was one of them. But even if they didn't survive, at least they would die fighting, and after months of being made to watch, helpless, as the Germans massacred thousands, this would be some solace at least. And hopefully he would make his sister proud.

The next morning as they got up from their bunks and filed out for roll call, the air crackled with nervous energy. Azriel took his place in line, palms sweating and heart pounding. The previous day, they'd retrieved many of their weapons from their hiding places and he had a home-made knife and a hammer in his pockets. He watched as a German guard strutted along the line, full of his own self-importance. Oh, how Azriel longed to see that smug smirk wiped from his face.

As the guard began addressing the men, Abe gave Azriel a nervous smile, then stepped forwards.

'Get back in line!' the guard yelled.

Azriel's pulse raced as Abe advanced on the guard, taking a hammer from his pocket.

'What are you—' the guard spluttered before Abe cracked him on the side of the head.

'Hurrah!' Abe cried at the top of his voice, the signal to begin the revolt, and then all hell broke loose. As the kapos tried to apprehend Abe, Azriel and some of the other *Sonderkommandos* swarmed around them, kicking and punching.

Hearing the uproar, a couple of guards came running over, but a swarm of *Sonderkommandos* descended upon them before they could draw their weapons.

Adrenaline coursed through Azriel's veins as he punched and kicked and screamed at the Germans. All of the rage and impotence he'd felt over the past few months, all of the hatred caused by the murder of his father, all of the pain at being separated from Estera, Adela and Izabel, finally had an outlet.

He heard a whistle being blown somewhere and saw Noah running towards him.

'Come on!' Noah yelled. It was time for the second part of their plan.

The two men raced to the back of the crematorium, where they'd hidden the demolition charges amongst a pile of bricks. As they returned to the front of the building, Azriel heard a scream and saw three *Sonderkommandos* dragging one of the most brutal SS guards in through the entrance to the ovens. The guard screamed again, and then fell silent. Azriel shuddered as he thought of what must have happened. But it was no worse than what the guard had done to so many innocent people, including his father. An image of Leopold walking into the gas chamber entered his mind and his resolve hardened.

'Go, go, go!' he yelled to a group of *Sonderkommandos* who were now brandishing the handful of rifles they'd managed to smuggle into the camp, as well as the guns of the guards they'd just apprehended. 'Get to the second floor.'

The armed group raced into the crematorium, as planned. Just as they'd done in the Warsaw ghetto, the Resistance were hoping to use an elevated position to their advantage.

Sure enough, as more German guards swarmed in, the rattle of gunfire filled the air and they began dropping to the ground like flies.

'Yes!' Noah cried.

'Come on,' Azriel said, 'let's get to the fence while the guards are distracted.'

They ran past the crematorium and Azriel spotted Abe and a couple of others huddled in a corner. He knew from their planning that they would be inserting explosives into the wall – the most ambitious part of the entire revolt.

'Good luck, comrade,' he whispered as he raced past.

The smell of gunpowder was now heavy in the air, reminding him of the ghetto uprising and his excitement grew. They were doing it! They were fighting back! Now he just had to make sure that some, if not all, of them could escape.

They reached the fence and began setting the demolition charges. As Azriel did so, he thought of Adela, and how she had helped provide the gunpowder he was using. *I love you, little bookworm*, he thought as he attached a charge to the fence, his fingers trembling.

Behind them, more gunfire filled the air, along with the sound of men yelling and grenades going off.

'Ready?' Azriel said to Noah.

Noah nodded and, using matches that had been smuggled from the pockets of clothing in *Kanada*, they lit the fuses and ran to take cover. There was a loud boom and the air filled with a cloud of smoke.

'Yes!' Azriel exclaimed as the smoke cleared, to reveal a gaping hole in the perimeter fence.

69

Adela sat on her bunk exchanging anxious glances with Eta and Ryka. They'd just been finishing their breakfast when they'd heard gunfire echoing across the camp, causing a commotion amongst the guards, who'd ordered their kapo to lock them in the hut.

'Do you think it's begun?' Adela whispered to Eta, and she nodded.

They'd heard from Ryka the night before that the men were planning their uprising today, and Adela had been riddled with fear ever since. The guards in the camp were so powerful and so brutal, it was hard to imagine the malnourished prisoners standing a chance. Adela thought of Azriel and prayed with all of her might that he was OK.

Eta and Ryka looked as anxious as she felt. Whatever the outcome of the uprising, the Germans were bound to want to know where the men had got the gunpowder from, and even though there were several munitions plants in the area, they were sure to be among the suspects. As long as nobody broke under interrogation, Adela reassured herself, they would be all right. But would Azriel?

She closed her eyes and prayed and prayed and prayed for her brother's safety.

Azriel watched as some of the *Sonderkommandos*, who had been waiting for the fence to be breached, started appearing from the nearby buildings.

'Quick!' he and Noah yelled to them. They tore at the fence to make the hole bigger and the men began scrambling through.

'Go on, go!' Noah called to Azriel.

'Aren't you coming too?' Azriel replied.

'Not yet. I'm going to stay and help with the fighting, but I'll see you soon.'

Azriel frowned. Surely if Noah stayed, the Germans would kill him.

'Go!' Noah yelled. 'You have to tell people what's happening here.'

Azriel thought of Leopold's last wish for him, and he placed his hands on Noah's shoulders and stared him in the eyes. 'Good luck, comrade.'

'And you.'

An almighty noise echoed through the air.

'They've done it, they've blown up the crematorium!' Azriel exclaimed.

'Yes!' Noah cried, with a beaming smile. 'Now go, please!'

Azriel ducked through the hole in the wire and he began to run.

Izabel stared at Bozena's reflection in the mirror.

'What was that noise?' she exclaimed. 'It sounded like a bomb!'

Bozena, who'd been cutting Izabel's hair, put down her scissors and hurried over to the window.

'Do you think it's the Allies?' Izabel whispered. 'Do you think they're attacking?' A shiver of excitement ran up her spine. The thought of the Allies destroying this hell on earth was so appealing, she didn't care if she was blown to smithereens in the process.

'I don't know,' Bozena replied. 'But all hell is breaking loose outside.'

Izabel dashed over to the window to join her. Scores of German soldiers were racing past, guns drawn.

The door crashed open and the guard stormed in. 'Get away from the window!' he yelled.

'What's happening?' Bozena asked.

Izabel felt for the Saint Brigid pendant in her pocket. *Please, please, let it be the Allies*, she silently prayed.

'Some of the prisoners are causing a disturbance,' he replied. 'Go back to your rooms and stay there until I tell you it's all right to come out.'

Izabel made her way down the narrow hallway, trying to process this turn of events. While she was bitterly disappointed that the commotion hadn't been caused by the Allies, she was thrilled that some of the prisoners were fighting back. But how on earth were they doing it? she wondered to herself as she went into her room and sat down on the bed. The Germans ruled this place with a rod of iron, with most of the prisoners starved half to death. The thought that some of them had found the strength and the grit to fight back was inspiring and thrilling.

She took out her Saint Brigid pendant and clutched it tightly.

'Please protect them, Saint Brigid,' she whispered. 'Watch over their brave souls.'

Azriel's lungs burned as his feet pounded the hard ground. It felt so surreal to be on the other side of the fence. To feel free for the first time in years. A memory from his childhood suddenly came back to him. It was of him and Adela playing in the fields by their aunt and uncle's house. Adela had suggested that they pretend to be airplanes, taking off from the top of the hill. He'd thought it a little childish at first, but then he'd started to run down the hill with arms outstretched, and it was as if his legs had taken on a momentum of their own. Faster and faster, they'd both run down that hill, and he'd let out a scream, pretending to be a fighter plane.

He thought of Adela now and imagined she was running alongside him. Izabel too. The three of them reunited again. Tears filled his eyes and blurred his vision, and he stretched out his arms. It was as if he could feel them either side of him holding his hands. And now all three of them were taking off from the ground.

Somewhere behind him, he heard shouting and then the crack of a gunshot. A man running in front of him collapsed onto his knees, screaming out in pain.

Azriel pictured gripping Adela and Izabel's hands even tighter as they flew ever higher. Another gunshot rang out and he felt something slam into the back of his head. He looked up at the sun. The light was dazzling, brighter than he'd ever seen. He was flying higher and higher towards it. Free at last.

70

As the hours ticked by in the women's hut, Adela's apprehension grew. It was clear from the long-running gun battle raging outside that the Resistance had pulled off something quite spectacular, but would it be enough for Azriel to make it to safety, or would he... She couldn't even bear to think of the other option. A sudden shiver ran up her spine, so strong it made her tremble.

'Are you all right?' Eta asked from beside her.

'Yes. I'm not sure what happened,' she replied, feeling confused. 'I felt so cold all of a sudden, it was as if...' She broke off as the hut supervisor walked in.

All the women watched in silence as she talked in hushed tones to the kapo. The women in the bunks closest to the door and able to overhear the conversation began whispering what they'd heard to the next bunk, who passed it to the next bunk and so on. Finally, the news reached Adela.

'The *Sonderkommandos* blew up Crematorium Four and some of them managed to escape through a hole in the fence,' a woman in the next bunk whispered over to them, eyed wide in disbelief.

Adela and Eta feigned surprise, while squeezing each other's hands tightly beneath their fraying blanket.

'But the Germans instantly struck back,' the woman continued, grim-faced. 'Apparently they executed two hundred *Sonderkommandos* on the spot.'

'No!' Eta gasped.

Adela thought of Azriel and fought the urge to retch. *Please, please be one of the men who escaped*, she silently willed.

'They sent dogs after the men who escaped, and they've all been shot too,' the woman added.

As the other women in the bunk started discussing the news, Adela collapsed back, feeling winded, and completely overwhelmed with sorrow.

'At least they died fighting,' Eta whispered in her ear. 'And hopefully they killed some Germans too.'

Adela tried to blink away her tears but more kept coming. Could Azriel be dead? She thought of the terrible chill that had passed through her earlier. Had it been some kind of ominous knowing? Had her body sensed his passing? She wanted to dismiss the thought as crazy but was unable to. She had a terrible feeling deep in her gut that he'd gone.

'Adela, what is it? What's wrong?' Eta whispered, shifting closer, and gently wiping away her tears. But more kept coming.

'My brother...' Adela gasped. 'He was one of them.'

Eta's eyes widened. 'The *Sonderkommandos*?'

'Yes. I only found out recently,' Adela whispered. 'I didn't even know he was in Auschwitz, but then I saw him when I was with Ryka, delivering the...' She broke off and Eta nodded. 'He was the one who collected it. Oh, Eta, it was so incredible to see him again, to know that he was alive, but now...' She began sobbing again.

'Oh Adela.' Eta put her thin arm around her and hugged her tight. 'I'm so sorry.'

Adela's pain became so overwhelming, she could barely breathe. 'I feel as if I'm partly to blame.'

'Why on earth would you say that?' Eta hissed.

'Because I helped get them the—'

'Shh!' Eta interrupted, jolting Adela back to her senses.

'I'm sorry, it just all seems like such a terrible waste.'

Eta frowned and shook her head. 'The Germans have tried everything they can to destroy us. They've kept us in the worst conditions imaginable. And yet somehow those men managed to blow up one of the crematoriums. They managed to escape. And even though they were killed, it wasn't in vain because they've shown us that the human spirit is able to triumph over everything.' She clutched Adela's hands tightly and gazed into her eyes. 'They're going to go down as some of the bravest men in history.'

Adela nodded. Eta's words were filled with such conviction, it was impossible to not be moved by what she was saying. She'd always known how brave Azriel was, but now everyone else would too.

'So wipe away those tears and feel proud of your brother,' Eta continued, 'the way I feel proud of you.'

'Oh, Eta, thank you!' Adela put her arm round her and hugged her tightly.

'We've done an incredible thing,' Eta whispered in her ear. 'We've shown that we're stronger and more enterprising than the Germans ever could have imagined.'

Adela nodded and closed her eyes, finally feeling a comfort of sorts. *You've shown that you're made of stardust*, she imagined Jaski whispering in her other ear and her feeling of comfort grew. *You're proof that magic exists.*

71

Over the next couple of days, more information about the *Sonderkommandos'* revolt started filtering through the camp. The men had destroyed one of the crematoriums, killed several guards, and blown a hole in the fence, but the German reprisals had been swift and brutal, and it was confirmed that none of those who'd escaped or planned the rebellion had survived. Hearing this had felled Adela anew and on the third day after the uprising, she and Ryka returned to the barracks from their shift in *Kanada* to some more terrible news.

'Some of the women who work in the munitions factory have been arrested,' one of Adela's bunkmates whispered to her as they lined up for the evening roll call.

Adela searched the lines frantically, but there was no sign of Eta. She returned to the hut after roll call feeling sick to her stomach.

'What happened?' she asked one of the other women who worked in the factory as they lined up for their soup.

'Some guards marched into the gunpowder room and called out the names of three women and took them away,' she whispered.

'But why?' Adela asked, feigning ignorance.

The woman leaned closer. 'They think they might have provided the *Sonderkommandos* with the gunpowder they used in their revolt. I can't see how though,' she added. 'It would be impossible to smuggle anything out of there.'

'Absolutely.' Adela tried to look calm, but inside she was a bundle of nerves. How had the guards got the women's names?

She glanced over her shoulder and saw Ryka halfway down the queue behind her, looking grim-faced. No doubt she was experiencing the same thoughts and fears. Had someone informed on the women? Maybe one of the *Sonderkommandos* had cracked under torture. What if they gave up her and Ryka next? And what was going to happen to poor Eta?

The hut supervisor came marching down the line and Adela's heart leapt into her throat as she stopped beside her.

'You,' she barked, prodding her stocky finger into Adela's chest.

'Yes?' she squeaked, her mouth dry.

'You're to return to the munitions factory tomorrow. They need the staff.'

'OK.'

As the supervisor stalked away, Adela's legs almost buckled from a mixture of relief and horror. Clearly they didn't know about her involvement in the plot, but if she was being sent back to the factory to replace Eta did it mean that her beloved friend wouldn't be coming back?

Izabel gave a sigh of relief as the door opened and the soldier walked in. After his tearful confession, he'd hurried from the room without saying a word, leaving her wondering if she'd ever see him again.

'Good day,' he said softly, with a slight smile.

'Good day,' she replied, sitting down at the head of the bed.

'How are you?' It was the first time he'd ever asked her that and the question took her slightly off guard.

'Oh, I'm OK, I suppose.'

'You haven't had any more problems with that kapo?' He stared at her face and she realised he must be looking for fresh bruises.

'No. I haven't seen him at all.'

'Good.' He nodded and his smile grew.

'How are you?' she asked as he sat down at the foot of the bed. 'I hear there was a bit of a commotion the other day.' She held her breath as she waited for his response. She was desperate to find out more about the prisoners' revolt, having only caught snatches of conversation about it from the doll's house guards.

'Yes, some of the *Sonderkommandos* blew up one of the crematoriums.' He shook his head in disbelief.

'How on earth did they manage that?' Izabel replied coolly, although inside she was cheering.

'I have no idea, but I'm sure we'll find out.' There was an air of resignation in his voice that took her by surprise. Whenever Dieter had talked about German reprisals, he'd done so in a crowing, bloodthirsty way, but the soldier looked anything but triumphant. He sighed and leaned towards her. 'I want to thank you,' he said softly, 'for listening to me the other day. It really helped.'

Izabel felt discomfort stirring inside of her. Helping a German soldier feel better about killing a child was not something she would ever want to do. But then she remembered how she'd felt when she'd heard Saint Brigid's words and she decided that it was best to not think about it.

'And one day I'm going to repay you,' he continued, meeting her gaze. He seemed different somehow, less guarded, but she still felt wary.

'Oh well, I—'

'I mean it,' he interrupted. 'I'm going to help you the way you helped me.'

He stood up and adjusted his jacket. Izabel wondered what he looked like out of that sinister black uniform. If she saw him on the street or in a bar, dressed in a normal shirt and trousers, she'd probably think of him as just a regular Joe, as they said in America. How strange war was, that it gave uniforms and flags such power.

'Thank you,' he murmured before turning to leave.

Izabel gazed after him, wondering what he'd meant. But before she could think any further, the guard burst in.

'I need you to go to the infirmary to get some more ointment for the prisoners,' he said curtly, and she nodded and stood up from the bed.

All the way back to the camp that night, Adela's feeling of dread grew. Returning to the gunpowder room had been horrendous; the absence of the three women who'd been arrested was a constant reminder of the fate that could be about to befall her too, and she was wracked with worry for their safety.

As they marched towards the camp brothel, she saw one of the women coming out in her nice clean dress and she felt a stab of indignation. It felt so unfair that while Eta and the other women were enduring who knew what horrors during their interrogations, the women in this doll's house, as it was known, were living in relative luxury.

The woman came closer and Adela frowned. There was something about her purposeful walk and the sway of her hips that seemed strangely familiar. As they drew level with each other, she glanced at the woman's face and then everything seemed to slow down as the woman briefly met her gaze.

Adela stopped dead still, causing the prisoner behind to almost crash into her.

'Keep moving!' one of the kapos yelled.

But Adela couldn't move. She couldn't tear her gaze from the woman, who had also come to a halt. Slowly, she turned back to look at Adela, her mouth gaping open.

'I said keep moving!' Adela felt the sting of the kapo's baton as he whacked her across the legs.

But still, Adela remained motionless. She looked at the woman's dress and the fitted waist. Surely she was mistaken. Surely it couldn't be...

'*Moj skarbe!*' the woman whispered. 'Is it you?'

'Izabel!' Adela gasped.

'Move!' the kapo screamed, pushing her forwards, and she was swallowed back into the crowd.

Adela's mind raced as she stumbled onwards. Izabel, her beloved friend, was there in Auschwitz. Izabel was one of the women in the doll's house!

'I have a reason to live again,' Izabel whispered to her reflection as she applied some rouge to her cheeks. Ever since she'd seen Adela, she'd added this mantra to her routine as she prepared for her evening shift. 'I have a reason to live again!' Adela was alive. She was in Auschwitz.

Izabel picked up her Saint Brigid pendant and gave it a kiss. 'Thank you, thank you!' she exclaimed, holding it to her chest. Izabel had been so certain Adela had perished in the ghetto. Discovering she was alive, and not only that but so close by, felt like another miracle bestowed upon her by her beloved saint. And if Adela was still alive, could Azriel be too? She hardly dared imagine, the excitement was too overwhelming.

Now, when the men came to visit Izabel and she retreated into the secret garden inside her mind, she dreamed of a future beyond the camp and beyond the war. A future in which she and Azriel and Adela all lived together. Night after night, she added brushstrokes to her dream, picturing the lives they would live. She imagined Azriel resuming his studies in medicine and Adela training to become a teacher. And for the first time in what felt like forever, she allowed herself to dream of becoming an actress. For, in this new dream life, she'd be free from her father and his ridiculous dictates. Yes, she would have a thriving career on the Warsaw stage and maybe one day even travel to Hollywood.

She heard men's voices in the corridor outside and blotted her lipstick on a piece of tissue. 'I have a reason to live again,' she whispered, smiling into the mirror. And for the first time since she'd been sent to that godforsaken place, hope shone in the eyes of the woman smiling back.

The weeks following the arrests felt like a long dark tunnel for Adela as she went through the motions of daily life in the camp, all the while terrified for Eta and the other two women who'd been taken by the Germans. The only thing she was able to console herself with was the fact that Izabel was at Auschwitz too. Although any feelings of consolation were tempered with concern when she thought of what life in the doll's house must be like for her friend. She'd seen the haunted expression on her face and now it was impossible to forget. 'Stay strong,' she'd whisper over and over in her mind all day long, as she thought of Eta and Izabel. 'Please stay strong.'

Then, one night, about a month after the uprising, Adela returned to the barracks to see a sight so sweet, she thought she must be imagining it. But no, Eta was sitting at the end of their bunk.

'Eta! Please tell me I'm not seeing things!' she cried, racing to embrace her. As she drew closer, she saw that she was thinner than ever and her face was covered in bruises. 'Oh, what have they done to you!' she exclaimed.

'Not enough to get me to break,' Eta whispered defiantly. 'None of us did, so they had to let us go.'

Adela's heart filled with pride for her courageous friend.

'Thank you,' she whispered in her ear as she hugged her tight. And then, remembering what Eta had said to her when she'd consoled her over Azriel, she added, 'Thank you for being one of the bravest women in history.'

Eta leaned into her embrace and Adela felt her begin to silently sob.

'I love you,' she whispered, stroking her hair.

The next day when the women arrived at the munitions factory, a new supervisor wearing a yellow star was there to greet them.

'My name's Eugen,' she said with a warm smile. 'I'm from Czechoslovakia.'

Adela sat down at her table and gave Eta a relieved smile. Hopefully, now things could return to some kind of normality. And at least they wouldn't be smuggling gunpowder anymore. They just had to hold on to the hope that the camp would be liberated soon. Every night now, prisoners who had access to radios were bringing news of the Allied advances. And if, and when, the camp was liberated, the first thing she'd do would be to hotfoot it to the doll's house to try to find Izabel.

Another week passed and every time Adela walked past the brothel on the way to and from work, she would glance at the windows, hoping for a glimpse of her friend. *Please stay safe*, she said silently, over and over as she walked past. *Please stay safe*.

Then, one sunny day in November, as they were working, the door to the gunpowder room burst open and a group of guards stormed in. They marched straight over to Eta, Asna and Jemima and dragged them off by the scruffs of their necks. The other women watched in stunned silence, apart from their new supervisor, Eugen, who carried on working as if nothing had happened.

Adela sat, paralysed by terror, as fearful questions flooded her mind. Why had the guards come back for the women? Had they uncovered new evidence of their involvement in the revolt? Had somebody else informed on them? Was it someone right there in the gunpowder room? She glanced around furtively, her gaze returning to Eugen, who was humming away as she worked. Why did she look so calm and collected? Had she known that the guards were coming? Was she the new informant?

Adela forced herself to return to her work, but as her body went through the motions, her mind whirred with paranoid thoughts.

Back at the barracks that evening, there was more bad news. Ryka had also been taken by the guards and all four women were being held prisoner in the infamous Block 11, notorious for its torture and executions. Adela lay in her bunk that night, beside herself with worry. How would the women survive the brutal torture of the Nazis? What if they cracked under the pressure and gave away the other women's names?

Weeks passed, and with each day, the fear inside Adela grew. She knew from the camp grapevine that the women were still alive, but she had no idea how they were surviving such prolonged torture. She was filled with awe at their bravery and strength. Then, one Sunday, on the way back from their weekly disinfectant bath, she decided to pay the kapo guarding the women a visit. She'd heard on the grapevine that he was sympathetic to their plight, so she'd written Eta a letter, in the hope that he might pass it to her. She approached him with a knot in her stomach.

'I was wondering if you would give this letter to one of your prisoners,' she said, hardly daring to make eye contact.

'Of course,' he replied, 'which one?'

'Eta. Eta Begin,' she mumbled.

He took the letter from her, and she plucked up the courage to meet his gaze. To her surprise, he looked sad. 'It's a terrible business,' he said softly.

She wasn't sure if he was referring to the gunpowder plot, so she simply nodded.

'It's incredible what those women are able to endure.' He shook his head. 'I've never seen such strength before.'

Still slightly unsure if he could be trusted, she simply nodded again. 'Thank you,' she muttered and hurried on her way.

A couple of days later when Adela was leaving for work in the morning, she found the guard waiting outside their hut.

'Adela?' he asked, and her stomach dropped.

'Yes.'

'I have something for you.' He handed her a folded piece of paper and turned and walked off.

She tucked the paper into her pocket, praying they wouldn't be stopped and searched on the way to work.

Thankfully, they made it to the munitions plant without incident and Adela asked the new supervisor if she could go to the bathroom. She still hadn't forgotten Eugen's strange behaviour the day the women were taken, and she didn't want to risk reading it in front of her.

Once inside a cubicle, she took the paper from her pocket and unfolded it with trembling hands. The moment she saw Eta's handwriting, she wanted to sob with gratitude and sorrow.

My dear Adela,

Thank you so much for your letter. What an unexpected gift it was. As you can imagine, life is tough in here. But I'm tougher! And, thankfully, Jakub, our guard, is very supportive.

It's the funniest thing being stuck in here – it makes me long to be back in the hut again, lying next to you in that bunk. Those wooden slats seem so comfortable now. That scratchy blanket positively luxurious! The other morning, I was even thinking wistfully of the so-called soup. Can you imagine? Oh, how I crave the freedom of being an ordinary prisoner here!

I hope you are all right, my dear friend, and please do not worry about me, or anything. I feel so grateful to have been bunkmates with you and to have got to know you. Please make the most of your freedom. For my sake, I beg you.

Your loving friend,

Eta

As the subtext of the letter sank in, Adela's eyes filled with tears. Even in her darkest hour, Eta was thinking of her, letting her know that she didn't need to worry, and urging her to live her life to the fullest. There was also a terrible sense of foreboding in her words, a knowing that they'd never see each other again.

Adela wiped her tears away and clenched her fists. The women had held on for this long. The Allies were getting closer every day. Surely if they could just survive another few weeks, the camp would be liberated and Eta would be free again. Truly free.

She tucked the letter back in her pocket and returned to her work determined to hold on to that hope with everything she'd got.

The new year arrived, Izabel's second in Auschwitz.

'But surely it has to be my last,' she said to her Saint Brigid pendant imploringly a few days into January. 'Surely the Allies will be here to save us soon!' As she started brushing her hair, there was a loud pounding on the door. She opened it to find the guard standing in the corridor, grim-faced.

'You all need to get outside,' he called as the women emerged from their rooms.

'Why, what's happening?' Bozena asked from her doorway.

'There's going to be an execution,' he replied.

Izabel and Bozena exchanged horrified glances. Normally, they never had to witness the executions, another so-called perk of working in the doll's house.

'Whose is it?' Bozena asked.

'The women who stole the gunpowder for the *Sonderkom-mandos*,' the guard replied. 'Now hurry!'

Once outside, Izabel's feeling of dread grew. She'd tried so hard to remain positive since seeing Adela, but it seemed that Auschwitz existed solely to crush all hope. Ever since she'd learned of the *Sonderkommandos*' revolt, she'd wondered how they'd got the explosives to blow up the crematorium. The thought that some women had been brave enough to help them filled her with awe. She couldn't bear to think of what they must be going through now as they prepared for their execution.

As they neared Block 11, she realised that the entire women's camp must have been made to come and watch; the place was lined with row after row of prisoners, their faces etched with horror. Izabel searched the crowd for Adela, but there was no sign of her, and all she got back were cold stares. She grimaced as she looked down at her clean and well-fitted dress. It was sickening to think that, just like the German soldiers, her own uniform inspired feelings of hatred and dread. *I'm on your side*, she wanted to cry. *I hate this place too!*

As they took their place in the crowd, the German guards brought two women out of the block and over to a pair of gallows. A terrible silence fell, broken only by a distant cawing of crows.

Oh Saint Brigid, please protect them, Izabel silently prayed, clutching the little pendant in her pocket.

The silence deepened as the women were led onto the gallows and made to stand on stools as nooses were slung around their necks. Izabel swallowed hard and looked down at the ground. Then came the sound of the stools being kicked away and a collective gasp filled the air. Izabel looked up to see the women dangling from the ropes and she looked away again in despair.

'Oh, *moj skarbe*, I hope you're all right,' she whispered, thinking of Adela somewhere in the sea of women, witnessing this same horror.

∼

Adela trudged past the camp on her way to the munitions factory feeling hollow with sorrow and despair. Along with seeing Jaski and the orphans and her mother being deported, witnessing Asna and Jemima being executed at morning roll call had been one of the worst experiences of her life without a doubt. The only thing keeping her from collapsing to the ground and wailing was the fact that Eta and Ryka hadn't been killed. Could it be that the Germans had decided to spare them? Perhaps they were still hoping to make them crack under torture. It was a measure of how bad things were that she found the prospect of her friends facing more torture to be the preferable option.

The day passed painfully slowly and when it was finally time to return to the barracks, Adela couldn't even bring herself to look at the sky for the stars. If she thought of Jaski now, she'd only be reminded of more loss.

When they reached the camp, her heart sank even lower. The German guards were out in force, and they were ushering the women back to the scene of the morning's executions. Adela wondered if it was possible to die from a broken heart. The horror of what was unfolding was too awful to comprehend.

As they all lined up again in front of the gallows, she wondered how it was possible that such evil could be allowed to exist. Even if some of them did live to tell the tale, would other people even believe them? It was a horrible thought and it left her feeling utterly desolate.

As before, the guards appeared from Block 11 with two women. Even from a distance, Adela recognised Eta and Ryka immediately. She bit down on her lip, barely able to breathe. Another stunned silence fell over the crowd. But then, as the women were led onto the gallows, the silence was broken as Ryka stood, defiant, yelling something at the top of her lungs.

'What's she saying?' a woman behind Adela asked.

Adela strained her ears to listen as Ryka shouted again.

'*Nekemah!*' Adela echoed, a shiver running up her spine. 'She's shouting "vengeance".'

And then Eta shouted something, and Ryka joined in.

'*Chazak v'amatz!*' they both cried, and Adela didn't know whether to cry or punch the air with delight. '*Chazak v'amatz,*' they yelled again, the words blazing like shooting stars right to the core of Adela's being. It was the Biblical phrase that God used to encourage Joshua after the death of Joseph, meaning, 'Be strong and have courage'. The women continued shouting it as they were jostled onto the stools and the nooses slung around their necks. 'Be strong and have courage!'

Tears poured down Adela's face as she kept her gaze fixed upon them. That morning she'd had to look away as Asna and Jemima were murdered, but not this time. This time, she wanted to bear witness. Not to the horrors being inflicted upon Eta and Ryka, but to the incredible courage of two women whose spirits couldn't be broken.

'Be strong and have courage,' Adela whispered under her breath as the guards kicked the stools away. And then she looked up at the sky. There, glimmering in the dark, was the most incredible array of stars, also bearing witness to the breathtaking resilience of the human spirit.

74

In the days following the women's executions, Izabel tried with all her might to stay hopeful. She no longer needed to listen to the radio to learn of the Allied advances – she could hear the distant thud of the artillery fire as the Russians drew closer – and every day now the air-raid sirens wailed, causing the German guards to scuttle like grey mice to their shelters. Oh, how she loved the sound of that siren when it went off during the evening shift. It was sweeter than any birdsong. The only men who came to the doll's house now were the kapos and German guards, who were becoming increasingly brutish, as if they knew that their days of power were numbered so they wanted to have a macabre last hurrah.

One evening in mid-January, Izabel was sitting at her dressing table listening to the siren when the door burst open and the soldier strode in.

'Why aren't you taking shelter?' she asked, surprised.

He closed the door and came and crouched beside her. The whites of his eyes were streaked red and his chin shadowed with stubble. 'I need you to listen to me,' he whispered, 'I have something very important to tell you.'

She nodded, heart pounding. Could he be about to tell her that the Germans were going to flee? *Please, Saint Brigid,* she silently implored, *grant me one more miracle.*

'Tomorrow we are going to begin evacuating the camp.'

'Evacuating? But where to?' An icy disappointment began seeping into her. For months now, she'd dreamed of the Allies liberating the camp. She should have known that the Germans wouldn't allow the prisoners to be saved. She should have known they'd have yet another malicious card up their sleeves.

'To a different camp, in Germany,' he replied.

She slumped forwards, unable to hide her dismay.

'You mustn't despair,' he whispered. 'Do you remember me telling you that I was going to help you, the last time I came to see you?'

She nodded.

'I wasn't lying.'

She looked up and met his gaze in the dressing-table mirror, her skin prickling with goosebumps. 'What do you mean?'

Outside, the siren stopped wailing. The soldier stood up, still holding her gaze.

'I'm going to help you escape.'

Adela lay in her bunk gazing blankly at the ceiling. When the air-raid siren had gone off earlier, she'd willed the Allies to drop their bombs and wipe Auschwitz from the face of the earth. She didn't care if they killed her too; she was so exhausted, even her mind felt as if it was running out of power, like a clockwork toy getting slower and slower.

Just as she was finally drifting into an uneasy sleep, the door of the hut burst open and she heard the sharp clip of boots on the floor. Rolling onto her side, she saw the night watch lift her lamp, and the tall figure of an SS soldier appeared, silhouetted in the doorway. It was a sight that instantly filled Adela with terror. They'd all heard the rumours about drunken soldiers coming to the barracks in the middle of the night and spiriting women away to use as their playthings. They'd all prayed that it wouldn't happen to them.

The soldier muttered something to the night watch and she led him down the hut, her lamp causing eerie shadows to dance upon the walls. Adela closed her eyes tightly. Maybe she was having a bad dream and soon she'd wake and he'd be gone. But the footsteps grew louder, finally coming to a halt at the foot of her bunk.

'Adela Rubinstein.'

The sound of her name coming from the soldier's lips filled her with a sickening dread. Someone must have told the Germans about her involvement in the gunpowder plot.

'Adela Rubinstein,' he said again.

She hoisted herself up and blinked in the lamplight.

'Yes,' she croaked, her mouth dry as parchment.

'You need to come with me. Now!' he barked.

The woman lying beside Adela gave her hand a comforting squeeze.

She wriggled from the bunk, her legs quivering like a newborn foal's. The soldier clamped his hand on her shoulder and her previously sluggish mind now whirred with panicked thoughts. He was going to take her to Block 11. They were going to torture her. And then, just as they did with Eta and the others, they'd kill her in front of everyone. She swallowed hard, trying to rein in her fear. She'd show them that she was just as strong as Eta. She'd stand there on those gallows and she'd yell at the top of her voice to her fellow prisoners that they were made of stardust and proof of the existence of magic. She would keep fighting until her very last breath.

The soldier bustled her outside and a bitter wind whipped around them, stinging her face. 'This way,' he ordered, marching her past the rows of huts. She felt a small burst of relief as they walked past Block 11, but her heart sank again as he steered her towards a small outhouse. Why was he taking her there? Had he found out about her involvement in the revolt and decided to mete out his own personal punishment?

He opened the door and gestured at her to go inside. She looked at the gun on his belt, wondering if she'd be able to grab it and use it against him. One thing was certain, she'd rather die than let him touch her. Clenching her hands into tight fists, she stepped into the darkness, preparing for the worst.

The door slammed shut behind her and she heard the key turning in the lock. *You are made of water and stardust*, she told herself, *you are proof that magic exists*. Then, slowly, she turned to face him. But the soldier wasn't there. She strained her eyes to make sure and heard his footsteps fading into the distance. Perhaps he was leaving her there until the morning when her interrogation would begin.

She heard something move in the pitch-dark corner and let out a yelp. Being trapped in this outhouse with a rat was hardly going to ease her fear. But maybe that was the point. Maybe the Germans were leaving her there to weaken her before their interrogation.

'I am made of water and stardust,' she muttered, her voice wavering. 'I am proof that magic exists.'

She heard another rustle from the corner.

'*Moj skarbe*,' a voice whispered in the darkness. 'Is that you?'

75

Izabel flung her arms around Adela and squeezed her tight.

'Oh, you're so thin. Here...' She fumbled in her pocket for the bar of chocolate she'd stuffed there when the soldier had told her she had to leave.

'Is this a dream?' Adela murmured. 'Is this really happening? Is it really you?'

'Of course it is. Now eat this.' She felt for Adela's hand and pressed a piece of chocolate into it.

'Now I know I'm dreaming!' Adela gasped. 'I can't be eating chocolate!'

'Oh, *moj skarbe*, it isn't a dream, but it is a miracle!' Izabel whispered. 'I didn't think he'd be able to find you. I wasn't even sure he'd try.'

'Who?' Adela asked.

'The soldier.'

'You asked him to come and get me?'

'Yes.'

'So he doesn't know about...' She broke off. 'I'm not about to be interrogated or killed?'

'No!' Izabel moved closer so she could whisper in her ear. 'Hopefully you're going to be saved.'

'Saved!' Adela exclaimed.

'Shh! Let's sit.' Izabel helped Adela down to the ground and wrapped a blanket she'd brought from the doll's house around them. Adela was so thin, her shoulder bone jutted into Izabel like a stick. 'Have some more,' she said, breaking off another piece of chocolate.

'How did you get this?' Adela whispered.

'Somebody gave it to me.' As soon as she said it, Izabel felt worried. Would Adela judge her for being a part of the doll's house? Would she resent her for receiving such gifts?

'I'm so sorry,' Adela whispered.

'What for?'

'That you ended up here – and... and in that place. I can't bear to think of what you must have been through.'

Izabel felt a rush of relief so intense, it caused her eyes to sting with tears. Ever since Adela had seen her in her telltale uniform she'd been wracked with worry that she might think badly of her, as so many of the other women in the camp clearly did. 'You don't mind,' she whispered.

'Of course I don't!' Adela exclaimed. 'But how did it happen? How did you end up there? And how did *we* end up *here*?' She let out a laugh. 'I have so many questions!'

Izabel hugged her close and kissed her cropped hair. 'Boy, oh boy, do I have a tale to tell you!'

Delight at being reunited with Izabel, combined with the creamy sweetness of the chocolate, brought new life surging into Adela's veins. As she listened to Izabel recount her experiences in Auschwitz, she felt overcome with a mixture of horror and awe, and when Izabel explained how the soldier had promised to help her escape and she'd demanded that he find Adela and help her too, her mouth fell open in shock.

'But why would he want to help us?' she asked.

'Because I helped him once,' Izabel replied.

Adela felt a stab of concern. 'In the doll's house?' she asked, trying not to think of what this meant.

'Yes, but not like that.' Izabel sighed. 'He's the only one who's never touched me. He comes to my room just to talk.'

Adela wasn't sure what to make of this.

'I think he feels guilty about what he's done here,' Izabel continued. 'I think that saving us is his way of trying to atone.'

The notion of a German soldier feeling guilty about anything or wanting to atone for his sins was so alien to Adela, she immediately felt suspicious. 'Are you sure he can be trusted?' she whispered.

'Well, he went and found you for me,' Izabel replied, 'which feels like the best gift I've ever been given.' She took Adela's hand and gave it a squeeze. 'And he says he has a plan to help us escape. But before I tell you about that, I have to ask you something...'

Panic began fluttering inside Adela. Was she going to ask about Azriel?

'Do you know what happened to Azriel?' Izabel asked. 'I'd been so certain you both perished in the ghetto. Did he survive too?' She gripped Adela's arm. 'Oh, please tell me he did.'

Adela remained silent for a moment. If she told Izabel the truth, it was bound to break her heart, but how could she lie to her about something so important?

'He did survive the ghetto,' she began.

'Thank you, Saint Brigid!' Izabel exclaimed.

'But...' Adela broke off.

'Oh no, please don't let there be a but!' Izabel cried.

'He ended up in Auschwitz too.' Adela gazed into her lap, unable to look at her. 'And he... he was one of the *Sonderkommandos* involved in the revolt.'

'The men who blew up the crematorium?' Izabel gasped.

'Yes. But... but none of them survived.'

'Are you sure?' Izabel gripped Adela's arm tighter.

Adela nodded. 'At least he died a hero. He's going to go down as one of the bravest men in history,' she said, parroting the words Eta had used to try to comfort her in the aftermath of Azriel's death.

'Oh, Adela.' Izabel began to cry. 'I'm so sorry.'

They huddled together and Adela stroked her hair.

'Ever since I saw you that day and realised you were still alive, I dared to dream that he might be alive too,' Izabel sobbed, 'and that one day we might all be reunited.'

Adela wracked her brains trying to think of something positive to say. 'But *we're* still alive and we still have a chance of getting out of here. And I know that Azriel and Jaski would want us to take it.'

Izabel sniffed and sat up straight. 'You're right. They'd want us to be strong... it's just so unfair.'

'I know.' Adela leaned her head against Izabel's. 'But at least we're together. I can't believe we're together!' she exclaimed. 'It still feels like a dream.' She felt Izabel nodding beside her.

'I always used to dream about the man I'd spend my life with, my one true love, my kindred spirit, and the children we'd have together.'

'I remember.' Adela smiled. 'You even chose their names.'

'I did. And I was so sure that man was Azriel.' She shifted slightly and cleared her throat. 'This will probably come as a surprise to you, Adela, but I always loved him, ever since the very first moment I laid eyes on him. I just didn't want you to know when we were younger because I didn't want it to affect our friendship. Thankfully, I was able to fool you with my acting skills.'

Adela giggled. 'I'm sorry, *moj skarbe*, but you didn't fool me at all!'

Izabel frowned. 'What do you mean?'

'It was always written all over your face.'

'But I tried so hard not to let you know!'

'Let's just say that for once your formidable acting skills failed you.'

They both laughed.

'But I was wrong,' Izabel continued after a few moments of silence.

'About Azriel?' Adela stared at her, shocked.

'Not about him being my one true love, but about him being the kindred spirit I was destined to know my whole life.' Izabel took her hand. Her fingers were icy cold. 'I think that person is you. Don't you think that friends can be kindred spirits too?'

'Of course.' Adela gave her hand a squeeze. 'You always said we were destined to meet. Remember that day we first saw each other in the store? You said you thought we'd been twin sisters in a previous life who'd tragically perished in a fire and vowed on our last dying breaths to find each other again.'

'Goodness, what a melodramatic child I was!'

'I wouldn't say you've changed all that much.' Adela gave her a playful nudge and despite the bitter cold, she felt a warm glow radiate from her heart. 'You were the most interesting person I'd ever met. More interesting than any book. I knew straight away that I wanted to be your friend.'

'Oh, *moj skarbe*, I love you.' Izabel leaned into her.

'I love you too.' The warmth inside Adela bloomed.

'I was right though, wasn't I?' Izabel said. 'About us being destined to find each other. What's happened tonight is proof. We've found each other again.'

'Yes.' Adela smiled and once again Jaski's words came back to her. 'We're proof that magic exists,' she whispered, and she imagined two stars – Jaski and Azriel – glimmering in the sky above the outhouse, shining down love and hope.

76

For the next couple of hours, Izabel listened, rapt, as Adela told her how she'd ended up in Auschwitz and about her life in the camp. When she reached the part about smuggling the gunpowder for the *Sonderkommandos'* revolt, Izabel was barely able to breathe.

'Oh, *moj skarbe*, you're so brave!' she gasped. 'You and Azriel are my heroes.' Once again, she felt a hot flush of shame for her life in the doll's house and she fell silent.

'Are you all right?' Adela asked.

'Yes, I just wish...'

'What?'

'I wish I could have done more to help, instead of being stuck inside that wretched doll's house.'

'But you were stuck there because you saved another woman from being sent there,' Adela replied. 'Think of what you saved her from. If that isn't heroic, I don't know what is.'

Izabel felt her spirits lift a little.

'And it's thanks to you that I'm here now,' Adela continued. 'If we make it out of here, you'll be able to say that you saved my life.'

Izabel gave her a grateful smile.

'How exactly does the soldier plan to save us?' Adela asked.

'I don't know the exact details, just that he's going to help us escape on the march.'

'The march?' Adela stared at her. 'You mean they're going to make us walk all the way to Germany.'

'I think so.'

'But it's so cold. The prisoners are so weak. They'll never survive.'

They sat in silence for a moment. Then from outside came the sound of the guards shouting.

'It's roll call,' Adela hissed.

Izabel felt her stomach flip. What if the soldier didn't come back and they were left locked in the outhouse? At least she was now with Adela, she consoled herself.

She felt a stabbing pain as she thought of Azriel. Discovering that he'd actually survived the ghetto only to perish at Auschwitz felt like losing him twice over. She pushed the thoughts away. If she and Adela were going to survive what was to come next, she needed to be strong and have her wits about her. And Adela was right – Azriel would want them to survive – he would want them to *thrive* – and she wanted to make him proud of her.

The noise from outside grew louder.

'They're announcing the evacuation,' Adela whispered.

Izabel's heart thudded harder and faster and she felt for the cardboard pendant in her pocket. *Please, please, Saint Brigid, don't let him forget about us*, she silently implored. *Please help us survive this.*

After what felt like an eternity, they heard the sound of a key in the lock and the door creaked open.

'Quick!' she heard the soldier whisper. 'You need to come now.'

They staggered to their feet and stumbled over to the door. The soldier looked at Izabel, his gaze deadly serious.

'You need to stay with me and do as I say.' He glanced over his shoulder to check no one was coming, then leaned closer. 'When we reach some woods I'm going to pretend to be taken ill to distract the other guards and that will be your cue to escape. You need to cut through the woods to the village, and when you get there, you're to go straight to the church. Tell the priest that Johann sent you.'

'Your name is Johann?'

He nodded.

For so long, Izabel hadn't wanted to be on first-name terms with the soldier, but learning his name now seemed oddly poignant. 'Thank you, Johann,' she whispered.

He gave her a brief smile, then looked past her to Adela, who was staring at him suspiciously from the shadows.

'Are you all right?' he asked.

She nodded.

He took a silver hip flask from his pocket. 'Both of you take some of this,' he said, passing it to Izabel. 'It will help against the cold.'

Izabel took a sip and her mouth filled with the warm, aromatic taste of brandy. She passed the flask to Adela, who still looked suspicious. 'Take some,' she whispered. 'It will warm you.'

Adela took a sip, then they followed Johann along the side of the outhouse. Lines of prisoners were shuffling past the end of the passageway, looking dazed and confused.

'Come,' Johann said, and they slipped into the crowd.

Izabel felt for Adela's hand and gripped it tightly. *Please, please, Saint Brigid, help us survive this*, she silently begged again as they walked towards the camp gates.

~

Adela's feet were so cold, she could no longer feel them and her face had been whipped raw by the icy wind. Somehow, she managed to stay upright, arm in arm with Izabel, and somehow she kept moving forwards.

They'd been marching for hours now, and she'd realised that if she was to have any hope of surviving, she had to shrink her focus right down, like a horse wearing blinders, so that all she could see was her and Izabel. If she thought about what was happening around them, her spirit might break.

From somewhere behind her, she heard the crack of a gunshot. It had become an all too familiar sound and no longer caused her to jump. Any time a prisoner succumbed to the cold or exhaustion and broke away from the march or collapsed to the floor, one of the SS guards would shoot them right there on the spot.

Izabel's soldier seemed to have disappeared and they still they hadn't arrived at the place he'd told them about. Perhaps they never would. It was like a nightmare they were never going to wake from, and she was starting to feel delirious from a mixture of hatred, fear and cold.

Then, just as the sun was dipping down in the sky and the air becoming so cold, it hurt her lungs, they reached the edge of some woods. The soldier reappeared beside them and gave them a knowing look. Then he marched ahead of them for a few yards and doubled over as if in pain, shouting something in German. The other guards in the vicinity all raced towards him.

'This is it, we have to go,' Izabel whispered in her ear. But before they could do anything, some of the prisoners behind them began running into the woods.

'Halt!' one of the soldiers yelled before opening fire.

Adela looked on in horror as the prisoners dropped to the ground. All around them, people began to scream and cry.

Adela looked at Izabel, terrified. 'What do we do?'

Before Izabel could answer, the soldier was back at their side.

'You need to run in that direction,' he muttered, nodding to a trail between the trees. 'And when I shoot at you fall down and pretend to be dead.'

'But...' Izabel said.

'Run!' he snapped.

Izabel gave Adela a questioning look and she nodded. The truth was, she no longer cared if the soldier couldn't be trusted. She didn't care if she was shot; all she wanted was to be free from this hell.

'I love you, *moj skarbe!*' Izabel cried, grabbing her hand, and they stumbled off between the trees.

A shot rang out and Adela felt something whistle past her ear. Izabel collapsed to the ground and for a terrible moment she thought she'd been hit, until she felt her tug on her hand.

'Get down!' Izabel screamed and Adela collapsed down beside her.

Another shot rang out, and another. Adela closed her eyes and held her breath as she waited to feel one of the bullets hit her. More pandemonium broke out and the guards started yelling at people to move. High above, a crow starting cawing, and she heard the shuffling sound of the prisoners resuming their march. On and on and on it went as Adela lay there, still as stone. Her body was becoming so numb from the cold, it no longer hurt and felt strangely soothing.

How funny it would be, she thought, *if I were to die from pretending to be dead.* She pictured Azriel looking down on her and chuckling. *What a way to go, little bookworm,* she imagined him joking.

But she didn't want to die, she suddenly realised, and the thought roused her from her stupor. Now that the march had passed and the soldiers were gone, she wanted to live. She wanted to survive this with Izabel.

Izabel. Adela opened one eye and then the other. Her eyelashes were frigid with frost. She blinked and moved her head slightly. Izabel was lying right beside her, her face as white as snow.

'*Moj skarbe,*' Adela whispered, but there was no response. 'Izabel!' she hissed. She slowly moved her numb hand and prodded her. Izabel remained motionless.

Adela shifted up onto her elbow. All around her, the frozen ground was littered with corpses. She felt overwhelmed with horror as the reality of what had happened hit her. The soldier must have killed Izabel by accident. Or maybe he'd lied and he'd meant to kill them all along. She sank back down, a tear spilling onto her face, bringing a trail of warmth to her frozen skin. She closed her eyes. She would wait for death to take her. There was no point in living without her beloved friend. She felt her body sinking deeper and deeper into the ground and her mind fading like a dying ember.

'*Moj skarbe.*'

The sound of Izabel's voice caused her consciousness to spark back to life. Perhaps she was dying and Izabel's soul had come to greet her. Maybe Jaski and Azriel would be there too.

'Why are you just lying there?' Izabel said.

Adela forced her eyes open to see her gazing down at her. 'Are you alive?' she whispered.

'Of course I am!'

Adela forced herself up onto her elbow. Her body felt heavy as lead. 'But... you... you looked like you were dead.'

'I was acting! I didn't want any Germans to see that I'd survived.'

Adela sat up and blinked hard. Sure enough, Izabel was grinning at her, looking very much alive.

'It would appear that I still have all of my acting skills,' she said with a giggle and Adela began to laugh.

'I thought you were dead,' she gasped, her laughter turning to tears. 'I thought your soul had come to greet me.'

'Hmm, and you call me melodramatic!' Izabel held out her hand. 'Come on, we need to get out of here.'

Adela scrambled to her feet and, trying not to look at the bodies all around them, they followed the pathway into the woods.

Finally, the trees began to thin, and they saw the lights from the village glowing in the dark ahead of them. The air was sweet from the scent of the woodsmoke coiling from the cottage chimneys. Adela inhaled deeply. After the endless stench of death in the camp, it was like breathing new life into her body.

'There's the church,' Izabel whispered, pointing to a spire silhouetted above the rooftops. A beautiful crescent moon shone above it, like a silvery arrow pointing the way.

Don't get too excited, Adela cautioned herself. *Things could still go wrong.*

Holding hands, they stealthily made their way around the edge of the village until the rest of the church came into view.

'Well, this is it,' Izabel whispered as they crept up to the old wooden door. Thankfully, it was unlocked, and they slipped inside. Compared to outside, the air was instantly and blissfully warm. The only light came from a row of thick white candles flickering away on the altar, their flames glowing gold.

'What if it's a trap?' Adela whispered as they tiptoed along the stone floor of the aisle.

Izabel took a small cardboard pendant from her pocket and pressed it to her chest. 'Saint Brigid won't let us down,' she whispered.

They reached the altar and Adela raised her frozen hands to the flame of one of the candles. 'I thought I'd never feel warm again,' she said with a sigh.

Something creaked behind them and Izabel let out a yelp.

'Please protect us, Saint Brigid!' she cried before grabbing Adela's hand and they both turned.

A priest was standing there staring at them, holding a string of rosary beads and dressed in his robes.

Adela held her breath and time seemed to slow to a stop.

'Johann sent us,' Izabel said, her voice quivering as she gripped Adela's hand tighter.

'Do you think we should run?' Adela whispered as the priest began walking towards them.

'Johann sent us,' Izabel said again, the fear in her voice palpable.

'What did they do to you?' The priest stared at Adela, his eyes wide with shock.

'Do you know Johann?' Izabel said, more forcefully this time.

He looked at her and nodded. 'Yes, yes. Please, follow me.'

'What if it's a trap?' Adela hissed to Izabel as they followed him through to the back of the church.

Izabel came to a halt, staring at the picture of a woman on the wall. She was wearing a green robe and her head shone with a halo of gold. 'He has a penchant for Saint Brigid,' she murmured, before looking at Adela, her eyes sparking with excitement. 'It isn't a trap,' she whispered. 'He can be trusted.'

They followed the priest out of the church and into a house right behind it. It was even warmer than the church and Adela's stomach let out a plaintive gurgle as she smelled onions and some kind of meat cooking. The priest led them up two flights of narrow stone stairs and into a room in the eaves of the house. A fire crackled away in the small hearth, sending ruby red sparks spiralling up the chimney. An oval mirror hung above the fireplace and two small beds made up with thick woollen blankets and fat downy pillows lined the walls either side. It was a sight so inviting, it felt as if every cell in Adela's body gave a sigh of pleasure.

'Please, make yourselves comfortable,' the priest said. His voice was soft and gentle. 'I promise you'll be safe now.' He looked at Adela and she saw that his eyes were filled with sorrow. 'You must be very hungry. I'll go and get you some soup.'

'Thank you,' she whispered, suddenly feeling tearful.

As he went back downstairs, they stood in front of the fire.

'We made it,' Izabel murmured. 'We escaped!'

Adela looked at their reflection in the mirror over the mantelpiece and couldn't help gasping. No wonder the priest had stared at her in horror. She looked like a skeleton, with her hollow eyes and sunken cheeks.

'We made it,' Izabel said again, linking her arm and pulling her close.

Adela met her gaze in the mirror and her eyes filled with tears. 'You saved my life,' she whispered.

'No, *moj skarbe*,' Izabel replied firmly. 'We saved each other.'

Adela thought of Azriel and Jaski and her parents and Eta. There had been so much pain, so much loss, and yet somehow, she and Izabel were still standing. Somehow, they had been saved.

'We are proof that magic exists,' Adela whispered.

'Magic *and* miracles,' Izabel said, turning and kissing Adela on the cheek.

EPILOGUE
NEW YORK CITY, 1954

Izabel looked down at the three place settings and frowned. An occasion this momentous required more than just a plain white tablecloth and some dull green napkins. She went over to the windowsill and picked up her porcelain figurine of Saint Brigid. On the other side of the glass, the lights of New York glimmered in the dark. She'd lived in the twentieth-floor apartment for eight months now, but the view still took her breath away. All of those lights, all of those lives being played out down below were like a fuel for her soul.

'Thank you,' she whispered, clutching Saint Brigid tightly.

Noticing her reflection overlaying the view through the window, she reached up and touched her short blonde hair. She'd had it cut for her current role as a feisty spitfire of a singer in an off-Broadway play. When the hairdresser had set about her, snip-snip-snipping with her scissors, Izabel had instantly been cast back to her arrival at Auschwitz and she'd had to close her eyes until it was over. But as soon as she'd seen the finished result, she fell in love with it. The gamine style didn't just suit the character she was playing; it suited Izabel and the new life she'd created for herself.

She took Saint Brigid over to the table and placed her in the centre. A loud knock on the door caused her to shiver with excitement. 'She's here!' she exclaimed.

She hurried into the hallway and opened the door to see Adela grinning at her. A brown leather suitcase sat by her feet.

'*Moj skarbe!*' they cried in unison and Izabel flung her arms around her. Adela felt stronger than ever and her skin glowed with health. It was a sight that filled Izabel with joy and relief.

'It's so good to see you! I love the hair!' Adela exclaimed.

'Thank you, and ditto.' Izabel took a step back and took a good look at her. Adela's hair now reached past her shoulders and gleamed chestnut brown in the lamplight.

'Oh, Izabel, I've missed you so much,' she said with a sigh.

'Not as much as I've missed you! You need to come and work at a university here. I'm sure they need English professors just as much as they do in Krakow.' She picked up Adela's case and ushered her inside.

'It's funny you should mention that...' Adela said.

Izabel stopped dead and stared at her. 'Are you saying what I think you're saying?'

'I might just have an interview lined up with the Dean of English Literature at Cornell tomorrow.' She laughed. 'I didn't want to tell you in case I don't get the job but—'

'Oh, *moj skarbe*, this is the best news ever!' Izabel cried.

'I might not get it,' Adela cautioned.

'You will! We are proof of magic and miracles, remember?'

Adela nodded. 'This is true.'

Fizzing with excitement, Izabel took Adela's coat and hung it on the stand in the hall before leading her through to the living room. Moving to New York to pursue her career as an actress had changed everything for the better, but if Adela were to move there too, it would be beyond her wildest dreams.

'Something smells good,' Adela said, sniffing the air. 'Don't tell me you've finally learned how to cook.'

Izabel laughed. 'Hardly! But I did get some pierogi and hunter's stew from a Polish store in Brooklyn. It's warming in the stove as we speak. Please, take a seat.'

'What a view!' Adela exclaimed as she sat down at the table and Izabel opened a bottle of wine.

'Isn't it wonderful? Hopefully, you'll be seeing a lot more of it, once you've got the job at Cornell. You could move in here!' Izabel added, barely able to contain her excitement. 'We could be roommates, as they say in America. Wouldn't it be great?'

Adela laughed and shook her head. 'I still have to pass the interview!'

'Of course you'll pass the interview.' Izabel smiled at the figurine standing serenely at the centre of the table. 'I'll be praying to Saint Brigid for it constantly.'

'Thank you.' Adela glanced at the third place setting. 'Is he still coming?'

'Yes, he should be here any minute.' Izabel poured them both a glass of wine. 'I can't believe it's been ten years.'

'I know. Sometimes it feels like another lifetime ago.'

'I still can't believe that you were a part of it!' Izabel exclaimed. 'My best friend the gunpowder smuggler.'

Adela nodded. 'It still feels like a miracle that I didn't get caught – and that the other women didn't crack under torture and give away my name.'

'They were such heroes,' Izabel said gravely.

'Yes.'

'And so was Azriel.' Izabel felt a lump building in the back of her throat. She and Adela marked the anniversary of the *Sonderkommandos*' revolt every year, but it still hadn't got any easier.

They both looked at the empty place setting and sat in silence for a moment. Then they heard the front door opening.

'He's here,' Izabel said cheerily, trying to mask her growing sorrow.

'Sorry I'm late,' Kasper said, striding into the room. There was a box of fruit tucked under his arm and a mass of blonde curls sprang from beneath his flat cap.

'It's so good to see you!' Adela exclaimed, springing to her feet and giving him a hug.

Izabel couldn't help smiling at the way Kasper towered over her friend. It seemed like only yesterday that he was her little pipsqueak brother; now he was a fully grown man. Being reunited with him in Warsaw after they'd made it back from the camp was one of the happiest moments of her life, and when he'd asked to move into the apartment she and Adela had found she'd readily agreed. Neither of them could stomach being around their father after what had happened, and when Lech and Krysia slunk off to the country to escape the shame of being Nazi collaborators, the fissure in their family was complete.

'I might be late, but I come bearing gifts.' He set the fruit down on the table beside Izabel.

'Excellent, thank you.' She chuckled. 'Do you remember when you used to charge me two zlotys for an orange?'

He grinned and sat down, taking off his cap. 'Yeah, well, I had to make a living somehow.'

'You were eight years old!'

They all laughed.

'How's your new life in America?' Adela asked as Izabel poured Kasper a drink.

'Great thanks. I have a job in a greengrocer's in the Bronx. The boss is really pleased with me. He says he wants to train me to take over one of his smaller stores.'

'That's fantastic!' Adela exclaimed.

'Just as long as you remember your very first customer.' Izabel grinned.

'Of course!' Kasper leaned over and slung his arm around her shoulder. 'I love you, sister. Thank you for inviting me to join you here.'

'You're so welcome, and I love you too. Both of you. Let's make a toast.' Izabel raised her drink. 'To absent loved ones.'

'To absent loved ones,' the others echoed, chinking their glasses to hers.

'And to new beginnings,' Adela added.

'To new beginnings,' Izabel murmured. She thought of Adela joining her and Kasper in America, all three of them pursuing their dreams in the city of bright lights and liberty, and for the first time on the anniversary of Azriel's death, she felt hope dilute her sorrow. She looked at the empty seat beside Adela. Oh, how she wished their vow to each other had come true and they'd all been able to sit around a table together again. Oh, how she wished she could spend just another few hours in Azriel's presence.

She felt a hand take hers and give it a squeeze, and even though she knew it was Kasper, for the sweetest moment it felt as if it was Azriel, reaching to her from beyond, as if to tell her that he was right there beside her, and always would be.

Later that night, when Izabel and Kasper were in bed, Adela snuck out onto the apartment balcony. Down below cars honked and sirens wailed, but Adela found it strangely soothing. She liked being somewhere so full of noise. New York, with its towering skyscrapers and relentless energy, was a moving reminder of just how irrepressible the human spirit could be. She could see why Izabel loved it, and the thought of joining her and Kasper filled her with excitement. In all the years they'd been meeting on this date, this was the first time she felt happy as well as sad.

'Oh, Azriel, if only you were here too,' she whispered into the cool night air. She noticed the gliding light of a plane overhead and a memory came back to her. It was of her and Azriel one summer holiday at their aunt and uncle's. She couldn't remember exactly how old they were, only that she was at an age where she was constantly trying to impress her big brother.

'Let's pretend we're airplanes and run down the hill,' she'd suggested.

At first Azriel had looked distinctly unimpressed but as they'd run faster and faster with their arms outstretched and the wind in their hair he'd started whooping with glee.

'That was epic!' he'd exclaimed, his eyes shining, when they reached the bottom, and his praise felt like sunshine warming her skin.

Leaning against the balcony wall, Adela closed her eyes and imagined him holding her hand and for a moment it felt so real she was certain she could feel his fingers laced between hers.

'I love you,' she whispered.

'I love you too, little bookworm,' she imagined him replying.

She opened her eyes and blinked away her tears. She'd always craved Azriel's love and respect, but it was only now that she realised how the war had made that happen and brought them so much closer. It had been the same with her parents. Those last few months they'd spent together in their hideout behind the baker's oven had reminded Adela of one of her favourite childhood books about a family of mice who lived in a snug little burrow in the roots of an oak tree. As a kid she'd loved looking at the illustrations that accompanied the story, and how cosy the mice looked, all snuggled together. In those last months with her parents they'd shared moments of closeness she'd treasure forever. It was hugely ironic really. The Germans had tried so hard to destroy and divide them but in doing so they had only intensified their love.

She took a gulp of the crisp air. This was the first time she'd been able to see any kind of silver lining to what had happened at the end of the war and it was like having a pair of heavy blinders removed. When the Allied soldiers had arrived in the village where she and Izabel were hiding, the priest had come to them and told them it was all over. 'You can go back home!' he'd said excitedly. But returning to Warsaw and eventually receiving official confirmation that Azriel and both her parents and Jaski had all perished had almost been the undoing of her. How could she possibly have a home when the people who'd made her feel at home were gone? If it hadn't been for Izabel encouraging her to return to her studies and dreams of being a teacher she wasn't sure she would have survived.

She looked up into the dark night sky. Jaski had once told her that some of the stars twinkling there had died a long time ago, but their light had to travel so far to reach earth it was as if they'd continued shining for years after their death. As she contemplated this now, she realised it was the perfect analogy for what she was feeling. The love she'd shared with Azriel, Leopold, Estera and Jaski was so strong it had continued shining long after their deaths, and would continue to do so. It was harder to spot stars in the New York sky due to the light pollution but slowly she counted one, two, three, four.

'I love you,' she whispered to them and, just for a moment, she could have sworn that they each glowed a little brighter.

A LETTER FROM SIOBHAN

Dear reader,

Thank you so much for choosing to read *The Stars Are Our Witness*, I hope you found it an interesting read. If you want to be kept up to date with all my latest releases, just sign up at the following link. Your email address will never be shared, and you can unsubscribe at any time.

www.bookouture.com/siobhan-curham

When I was researching for one of my earlier World War Two novels, *The Storyteller of Auschwitz*, I came across a reference to a prisoner uprising in the camp which immediately caught my attention and made me eager to learn more. What I discovered both fascinated and inspired me – in 1944, a group of *Sonderkommandos* (the Jewish prisoners assigned to work in the crematorium) hatched a plan to blow up Crematorium Four and escape through the perimeter fence, using gunpowder smuggled to them by a group of women prisoners who worked in one of the munitions factories. These women risked everything to smuggle tiny amounts of gunpowder to the men over a period of months. The revolt took place on 7 October 1944, when the men succeeded in destroying the crematorium, killing three guards and launching an escape bid through holes they'd blown in the fence. Hundreds of men escaped, but tragically none of them survived as the Germans mounted a swift and brutal response, shooting them all. Four of the women who'd smuggled gunpowder to the *Sonderkommandos* – Ester Wajcblum, Ella Gärtner, Regina Safirsztain and Róza Robota – were later captured and although they were subjected to brutal torture, they failed to break and give up the names of anyone else involved in the plot. The women were executed on 6 January 1945, weeks before the camp was liberated, and they remained defiant until the very end, reportedly shouting, 'Be strong and have courage,' before dying, to the prisoners who'd been forced to watch their executions. I was so moved by the bravery of these women and men, I knew I had to write a novel inspired by them, and as I fleshed out my story and deepened my research into the Resistance movement in Poland, I uncovered similar stories of incredible courage. And so, *The Stars Are Our Witness* was born.

Although the characters in the novel are fictional, all the major events covered in the book happened. The Bund saved the books from the Bronislaw Grosser Library and mounted a successful fightback against the pogrom that took place in Warsaw before the formation of the ghetto. Likewise, the Jewish Resistance movement staged a successful revolt against the deportations in January 1943, prior to the ghetto uprising. When I was writing these scenes, I relied heavily on eyewitness accounts to try to make the details of the fighting as realistic and close to the actual events as possible. Ditto the key scenes in Auschwitz, where I drew upon first-hand accounts of life as a *Sonderkommando* and read everything I could about the gunpowder plot. I couldn't find any first-hand accounts of life in the 'doll's house' as, understandably, the women who were forced to work there didn't want to talk about their experiences after the camp was liberated. However, I did find details about the rules and regulations of the brothel, and how the women ended up there, which I wove into the story. Although many people perished on the death marches from the camp I uncovered a couple of personal accounts from prisoners who were helped by German soldiers in some way and the scene where Adela and Izabel pretend to be dead was based on a real-life story.

On a more personal note, while I was writing this novel, my son moved to Ukraine to work for an aid organisation, helping victims of the war there. Seeing someone I love being directly impacted by a war going on in Europe today while I was writing about World War Two made me feel quite down at times, wondering if humans will ever learn the lessons from history. But, ultimately, writing *The Stars Are Our Witness* restored my faith in humanity because the true stories woven into this book provided me with a much-needed reminder of the incredible strength of the human spirit. Perhaps none more so than the true story of orphanage owner Janusz Korczak, who was the inspiration for the character of Jaski. Korczak was a Jewish paediatrician and children's author who owned an orphanage in Warsaw. During the German occupation, he turned down multiple opportunities to escape the ghetto, and he refused to leave the children when the Germans came to deport them to the death camp in Treblinka. If you want a reminder of how kind, creative and brave humans can be, I highly recommend you do an internet search for Janusz Korczak. I hope it leaves you as inspired as it did me.

Above all, I hope that reading *The Stars Are Our Witness* reminds you that – to quote Jaski – you too are made of water and stardust and proof that magic exists.

Siobhan

KEEP IN TOUCH WITH SIOBHAN

siobhancurham.com

facebook.com/Siobhan-Curham-Author

x.com/SiobhanCurham

instagram.com/siobhancurhamauthor

ACKNOWLEDGMENTS

MASSIVE thanks to Kelsie Marsden, my wonderful editor, for your expert eagle editorial eye, and for always pushing me to keep raising the bar with my writing. I appreciated your insights more than ever with this book. Thank you for helping me find the plot – and stopping me from losing it! And while we're on the subject of genius editors, I'm also so grateful to Jade Craddock, the most talented copy editor I've ever worked with. Thank you for the enthusiasm and focus you bring to my books – receiving your notes always feels like the editorial icing on the cake! Huge thanks to Richard King, Foreign Rights Director at Bookouture, and all the foreign publishers who have now bought the rights to my World War Two novels. It's been so exciting to see them coming out around the world. And none of this would have happened without the incredible support of the whole team at Bookouture. I'm so thankful to be with such a supportive and dynamic publisher. Much gratitude to Sarah Hardy, Kim Nash, Noelle Holten, Ruth Tross, Alex Crow, Alba Proko, Hannah Snetsinger and Sinead O'Connor, to name but a few. Much love and thanks to Jane Willis at United Agents for all your support. And special thanks to Andrea Alves Silva at Porto Editora, and BookTuber extraordinaire Dora Santos Marques for bringing so much Portuguese love to my books.

I wrote part of this novel while staying at the Writers' Colony in Eureka Springs, Arkansas, and what a treat that was! HUGE thanks to Jessi Barfield and all the staff for making it such a great experience, and to Jana for feeding us so well!

I've been blown away by the number of lovely people who take the time to review my historical novels on their social media, blogs, Goodreads, NetGalley and Amazon. There are so many, it's impossible to mention you all here, but please know that I read and deeply appreciate every review. I also really appreciate all the messages I receive from readers; it's so encouraging to receive your feedback about my books.

Last but never least, much, much love and gratitude to my friends and family. Writing can be a lonely business, but I never feel alone thanks to your love and support. Massive thanks to my family: Jack Curham, Zoreslava Plakhtyna, Michael Curham, Anne Cumming, Alice Curham, Bea Curham, Luke Curham, Katie Bird, Dan Arthur, John Arthur, Lacey Jennen, Gina Ervin, David Ervin, Sam Delaney, Carolyn Miller, Amy Fawcett, Rachel Kelley, Charles Delaney. And to my friends who feel like family: Tina McKenzie, Steve O'Toole, Sammie and Edi Venn, Linda Lloyd, Sara Starbuck, Pearl Bates and Caz McDonagh.

And huge thanks to my friends who have been so supportive of my books: Sass Pankhurst, Linda Newman, Lesley Strick, Lara Kingsman, Diane Sack Pulsone, Thea Bennett, Jan Silverman, Marie Hermet, Jan Silverman, Patricia Jacobs, Mavis Pachter, Suzanne Burgess, Liz Brooks, Fil Carson, Jackie Stanbridge, Gillian Holland, Doug Cushman, Glenn Bryant, Linda Joy Myers, Ruth Mitchell and Wendy Taylor Carlisle. Your friendship and encouragement mean the world to me.

PUBLISHING TEAM

Turning a manuscript into a book requires the efforts of many people. The publishing team at Bookouture would like to acknowledge everyone who contributed to this publication.

Audio
Alba Proko
Sinead O'Connor
Melissa Tran

Commercial
Lauren Morrissette
Hannah Richmond
Imogen Allport

Cover design
Eileen Carey

Data and analysis
Mark Alder
Mohamed Bussuri

Editorial
Kelsie Marsden
Sinead O'Connor